BEYOND
HIS
MERCY

BEYOND HIS MERCY

A Novel

Johnny Neil Smith
and
Susan Cruce Smith

SUNSTONE
PRESS

SANTA FE

Cover and horse and rider illustration by Jill Dyer.
Other illustrations by Norma Jeanne Trammell.

Sunstone books may be purchased for educational, business, or sales promotional use.
For information please write: Special Markets Department, Sunstone Press,
P.O. Box 2321, Santa Fe, New Mexico 87504-2321.
Body typeface › Minion Pro
Printed on acid-free paper
∞
eBook 978-1-61139-523-5

Library of Congress Cataloging-in-Publication Data

Names: Smith, Johnny Neil, 1939- author. | Smith, Susan Cruce, author.
Title: Beyond his mercy : a novel based on a true story / by Johnny Neil
   Smith and Susan Smith.
Description: Santa Fe : Sunstone Press, 2017.
Identifiers: LCCN 2017021614 (print) | LCCN 2017030391 (ebook) | ISBN
   9781611395235 | ISBN 9781632931870 (softcover : acid-free paper)
Subjects: LCSH: United States--History--Civil War,
   1861-1865--Veterans--Fiction. | War--Psychological aspects--Fiction. |
   Veterans--Mental health--Fiction. | Psychic trauma--Fiction | GSAFD:
   Historical fiction.
Classification: LCC PS3569.M5375514 (ebook) | LCC PS3569.M5375514 B49 2017
   (print) | DDC 813/.54--dc23
LC record available at https://lccn.loc.gov/2017021614

SUNSTONE PRESS IS COMMITTED TO MINIMIZING OUR ENVIRONMENTAL IMPACT ON THE PLANET. THE PAPER USED IN THIS BOOK IS FROM
RESPONSIBLY MANAGED FORESTS. OUR PRINTER HAS RECEIVED CHAIN OF CUSTODY (COC) CERTIFICATION FROM: THE FOREST STEWARDSHIP
COUNCIL™ (FSC®), PROGRAMME FOR THE ENDORSEMENT OF FOREST CERTIFICATION™ (PEFC™), AND THE SUSTAINABLE FORESTRY INITIATIVE® (SFI®).
THE FSC® COUNCIL IS A NON-PROFIT ORGANIZATION, PROMOTING THE ENVIRONMENTALLY APPROPRIATE, SOCIALLY BENEFICIAL AND
ECONOMICALLY VIABLE MANAGEMENT OF THE WORLD'S FORESTS. FSC® CERTIFICATION IS RECOGNIZED INTERNATIONALLY AS A
RIGOROUS ENVIRONMENTAL AND SOCIAL STANDARD FOR RESPONSIBLE FOREST MANAGEMENT.

WWW.SUNSTONEPRESS.COM
SUNSTONE PRESS / POST OFFICE BOX 2321 / SANTA FE, NM 87504-2321 /USA
(505) 988-4418 / ORDERS ONLY (800) 243-5644 / FAX (505) 988-1025

Dedicated to Jesse Davis Cruce, a marine who fought in the battle of Iwo Jima and suffered for years following the war with Post Traumatic Stress Disorder, and to all other veterans, past and present, who gave their all, both physically and emotionally, to preserve freedom.

Preface

With the surrender of General Lee's Army of the Northern Virginia on April 9, 1865, the remaining Confederacy collapsed, closing a tragic era in American history. Earlier historians claimed our country lost approximately 620,000 lives but today the calculation exceeds 700,000. More died from disease than battle, but most were buried in faraway graves, often mass graves. Twenty-five percent of the South's men lost their lives and many others lost arms and legs along with the ability to farm and provide for family. Many returning soldiers found that all they loved was gone and ventured westward never to return to their beloved South. Most tragic were the women left destitute after losing sons and husbands. The South was broken—property, land and livestock destroyed. The South sadly embraced extreme hardship and long term poverty.

After the death of President Lincoln, the hope of a reasonable re-admission for the rebelled Southern States was lost. The republican-led Congress swayed by the anguish of war felt no passion for the South and imposed severe punishment as reward for rebellion. Local elected public officials were stripped from office and replaced with men supportive of the Union regardless of qualifications. Northerners called carpet baggers came south to seek gain by taking advantage of poor struggling southerners and newly freed Negroes placed in positions of authority. The South lay conquered, ravished and in total chaos. The greatest fear was the fear of the unknown and the anticipated hardships from a government that no longer cared about their needs.

Soldiers who did survive the perils of four years of war lived with the horrors of battle and death. Their terrifying experiences returned each night, as dreams became demons which lingered through the day. Some exhausted from the personal struggle sought relief in death and others refused to even speak of the gruesome destruction they witnessed. This is the story of Thomas Wilson who enlisted in the summer of 1861 in a Mississippi Infantry Regiment and returned to face this journey through hell. Only an act of God could bring peace and fit the fragments of his life together again.

1

Trials and Tribulations

*We glory in our tribulations knowing tribulation brings about
perseverance; and perseverance, character; and character, hope; and
hope does not disappoint because the love of God has been poured out
within our hearts through the Holy Spirit who was given to us.*

—Romans 5:3-5 NASB

Off in the distance a yip of a coyote broke the silence of the night, and instantly a dog across the camp answered the lonely cry. A slight breeze crossed the man's face, and as he squinted upward, he faintly saw clouds brush across a full moon. Smoke from numerous campfires burned his nostrils stealing his breath. Intense pain and numbness gripped his taut body bound with hands to a hitching post and feet staked to the ground. With one eye completely battered shut and the other slightly open, the captive could taste his own blood, thick and clouting in his mouth. The pain was excruciating, but the knowledge of his impending death would actually be a relief from the guilt that consumed him. He didn't deserve to live because he felt beyond God's mercy.

Little Rock, Mississippi; February, 1866

Lot glanced at his old and wrinkled hands, but knew that even with age, he was still strong. He stood a little under six feet tall, had sturdy broad shoulders holding up about two hundred pounds, a head full of snowy course hair, and a short cropped beard on his chin.

Suddenly aware of the conversations around him, he glanced over the room, thankful for the large log cabin he and his brother Jake had built back in the thirties. Taking a moment to admire his family, he then cleared his throat and said, "Folks I think we need to talk about the circumstance we're facing and what we plan to do about it."

Lott Wilson, an early settler of Mississippi, had struggled when his eldest sons, James Earl and Thomas, decided to enlist in the war and was devastated when two years later his youngest son John joined his brothers. In late 1862 Lott lost his eldest son James Earl to death in a Virginia military hospital and his youngest son John was reported killed in battle. Because Thomas could not locate John after the conflict in Gettysburg and knew he had broken his promise to take care of his younger brother, he deserted the army and fled to the Arizona Territory out of the hands of regulators. Lott remembered the day his emptiness became joy when two of his sons returned home. In answer to a mother's fervent prayers, John who had only been wounded, captured and transferred to a prison camp at Camp Douglas, Illinois, managed to survive the harsh conditions and returned home to spend Christmas with his family. Thomas arrived at the Little Rock Church on Christmas day surprised that the service was actually John's wedding to Rebecca. Although the war had ended and his sons were home, Lott knew that struggles for his family were just beginning.

The fire in the old open fireplace popped and sizzled and spread its flames upward warming the room where Lott and his family gathered. Even with the loss of his eldest son, Lott knew he had more blessings than he deserved. His family had a productive farm where they grew vegetables and raised hogs, chickens and cattle. During the war years, they had never gone hungry or without a warm shelter. Although General Sherman's troops, after a raid on Meridian, camped near his place and took his rail fencing for firewood, killed his cattle, hogs and chickens for food and even cleaned out his smokehouse and kitchen, his family had managed to survive. When Lott realized Sherman might try to take his prized and valuable saddle horses and mules, Toby, his friend and farmhand, corralled and led the beasts to a secluded area in the nearby swamp and hid them until it was safe to return. The Yankees had not burned his house or barn, and Lott and Toby had slowly been able to replenish the farm with animals.

His wife, Sarah, a petite woman with graying hair rolled in a bun, stopped her knitting and glanced at the dark curly hair of John, their youngest son. John, who was about the same height as his father, quickly clasped the hand of his beautiful wife, Rebecca, and they both faced Lott.

"You too, Sister. You can straighten the kitchen later," called Lott.

Sister, actually named Lucretia, pushed the door open and brushed the flour from her apron as she swept into the room. Sister, much like her mother, was several inches over five feet and had long blond hair and clear blue eyes. She was becoming the challenge for all the young men in the Little Rock community.

All became quiet as the cold winter's wind twisted the bare limbs of the ancient oak trees outside. Thomas stood by the window and watched the brown leaves skirting across the bare yard. Cold air crept inside brushing his face as his thoughts kept him at distance with the world. Thomas was over six feet tall, muscular and with long straight brown hair hanging down his back.

"Son, did you hear me?" muttered Lott troubled by his son's detachment.

Lott reached for Thomas's shoulder and immediately Thomas jerked around, pushed his father's hand away and tried to re-focus his eyes at those in the room. His family watched his bizarre behavior with concern. In seconds, Thomas took a deep breath, shut his eyes and opening them again said, "Did you say something to me, Papa?"

"Son, are you all right?" Lott was troubled but knew the discussion ahead was necessary so he pushed back his worries for now. "We need to talk about how we're gonna handle the situation we're in."

Thomas eased down on the edge of the hearth next to the fireplace, resting his back on the warm stones.

"Son, is that comfortable?"

Thomas shook his head. "Papa, I'm fine. You have no idea how many times I've wished that I could be sitting just where I am now. What's on your mind?"

John got up and took a seat on the floor next to Thomas and whispered, "I know what you mean. You all right?"

Lott reached toward the open fire, knocked the spent tobacco from his pipe, laid it on the mantel and continued, "The way I see it, is that we still have land, a mule and thank goodness the Yankees didn't take all our seed, so there's no reason we can't work the fields this spring."

"What you plan on planting, Papa?" asked John with a frown.

Scratching his beard in thought, Lott replied, "Well, cotton will bring a good price and corn always is needed."

Tired from sitting on the floor, John stood up and stretched. "Papa, I don't know about cotton. From what I hear, the Yankees are confiscating farmers' cotton claiming it is to help cover the expense of the war. Word is that some of them Yankees are stealing it in the name of the government and pocketing it for themselves."

"They ain't nothing but a bunch of thieves, and if we do grow a crop, those devils will surely try to take it," scowled Thomas.

"Thomas, you've always enjoyed farming. What's your idea?" asked Lott.

Thomas stood and backed up to the fire for warmth. "Well, the way I see it, cotton is out for the present time. We've got our hogs feeding in the swamp and some chickens, so we'll start the garden come spring and plant as much corn as possible which will put food on the table and give grain for the livestock, but then we got to figure where we can make good money. After four years of war, the horse population in the South took a big hit. I think our future should be focused on what we know best and that is raising and training horses. Now the railroad is making a difference in the way folks travel, but most traveling is still on horseback. Toby saved three of our mares and two stallions, and with the two mustangs I brought back from Texas, we can make a strong start. We got a reputation for raising the best. Many a time around town I've heard, 'Ain't that a Wilson horse?' Our name alone will sell horses."

"You don't want to breed our thoroughbreds with those mustangs you got, do you?" Becca asked.

"Yep I do, but we'll still breed our thoroughbreds too."

Brushing some loose hair from across her face, Becca asked, "Why?"

"Let me tell you about the mustang. The Spanish brought the horses in years ago and these horses roamed the plains for over two centuries. Those that survived are tough, hardy and can last a lot longer on the ride than thoroughbreds. For the first quarter mile I'm not sure that our long legged horses could catch one. So my idea is we market them separately. As far as training them, there ain't a man in this state that can handle horses like John and me. First thing we're gonna have to do is get them fences up and clear our pastures."

The family readily agreed with Thomas's plan, and Lott took the Bible from a table nearby and said, "This book says there will be trials and tribulation, but if we keep the faith and place our trust in the Lord, we will persevere and that's what we are going to do." Then the family joined hands and thanked the Lord for his blessings and asked for his guidance for the future.

The women headed to the kitchen to prepare for the evening meal while the men met Toby and walked Big Woods to confirm their plans. Big Woods was 640 acres that had never seen the touch of an ax and contained a large swamp bordering the Little Rock Creek. The massive oaks, hickory, and occasional pines stood as sentinels guarding a fortress, keeping all serene and safe in the forest. Here they located their herd of pigs and to their delight discovered two new litters of piglets. The men sat down on a mossy mound overlooking the creek to enjoy the late afternoon and turned their talk toward politics. John was the first to give his account on the condition of the state. "Well, the federal troops, are in total control and only Northerners, Negroes and those sympathetic to the Union are placed in positions. The upper courts are run by a federal officer, usually with a captain or colonel. It looks like we better get ready for higher state and county taxes because we Southerners are going to be covering the expenses of this war. High taxes mean a lot of Mississippians are going to be in debt and lose their land to rich Northerners."

Toby, a short and heavy set Negro with a continuous smile, laughed, "I'm shore glad they didn't send me to Jackson to do no governing. Don't know a thing 'bout it." Then with a serious frown he continued, "I'm glad you folks give me them forty acres for my own but I ain't even got a dollar to pay taxes. I guess them Yankees gonna just have to take my land."

Placing his hand on Toby's shoulder, Lott said, "There is no way that I will ever allow anyone to take your place from you."

Glancing to his father, John cantered, "Watch what you promise, Papa. This government is going to do its best to bring the South to its knees and that means us."

That night Lott and Sarah retired to their bedroom while John and Becca took the room across the open hallway which contained a fireplace. Sister occupied a small room located between her parents and the kitchen. Since she was teaching at the Little Rock school, she used these late hours to prepare for the next day's lessons. Even though there was an empty room next to John's, Thomas, because he needed privacy, chose the room in the barn that had been Toby's. At one time the room was a ten by ten foot corn crib with walls tightly sealed to keep the grain safe from rats. Lott had added a fireplace for warmth and cooking and an outside window that would give Toby light. It was perfect for Thomas except for the smells of cow and horse manure drifting in the door which opened to the inner barn. This room was cool in the summer and warm in winter, but most importantly, it gave Thomas a safe, private place to fight his war demons and pray that his visions of death would disappear. It was also a refuge from his family's watchful eyes as he sank deeper into an empty and infinite abyss.

Lott and Sarah cuddled in the feather bed deep with quilts and watched the fire slowly turn to embers. Tonight they lay silent in thought. Sarah recalled the happy, cheerful, and rambunctious young man her son had been; his life brimmed with friends and frivolous talk. Oh how he loved church, and Thomas seemed to absorb every word the pastor shared. She had prayed diligently that God would send her son home and she praised the Lord for that, but the son that came home was a different man.

While Sarah pondered these thoughts, Lott silently worried about the wild expression on Thomas's face when he had touched him that evening. Where was the son who loved to work shoulder to shoulder with him and his brothers? Well, maybe his love for training and riding horses would bring Thomas back to his joy. Lot remembered the amazed faces of those present when Thomas, on a bet, paced thirty steps from a tree with his musket in hand, turned, aimed and fired a bullet that drove a nail solidly into the tree. Thomas loved to hunt and never seemed to miss his target. Lott was hopeful that home would help Thomas find himself again.

Sarah finally murmured, "Lott, you asleep?"

"No, and I see you ain't either. You thinking about Thomas too?"

Cuddling closer she whispered, "When he first came home, he seemed much like his old self, but now I'm noticing things that seem unnatural for the boy. Seems like every day he is withdrawing into a shell. I'm worried, Lott."

A light tap was heard on the door. "Mother, are you and Papa awake?"

"We are. What do you need?"

"It's me and Becca. May we come in?"

John and Becca wrapped in heavy quilts eased into the room and settled at the foot of the bed. John looked at Becca and said, "We couldn't sleep."

"Looks like we all have the same concerns," Sarah replied.

John took a deep breath and sighed, "I love him with all my heart, but he just isn't himself. What can I do? No, what can we do to help him?"

Lott trying to control the tears beginning to puddle in his eyes replied, "First we got to do a lot of praying, and John, if you can, sit down and talk with him. He might open up to you."

"How about speaking with Doc McMahan? He's been around for a long time; maybe he can give us some answers," whispered Becca.

"Might can," replied Lott. "Now you young'uns get on to bed and let the Lord do His work."

2

Unanswered Prayer

"For I know the plans I have for you," says the Lord. "They are plans for good and not for disaster, to give you a future and a hope."
—Jeremiah 29:11 NLT

*C*louds of smoke driven by an easterly wind drifted across the field as the intensity of musket fire increased. Out front came the loud belching roar of cannon fire. With a scoped musket strapped over his shoulder, the confederate sharpshooter carefully pulled himself limb by limb up a large oak tree seeking the Union line. A Southern band played a feisty tune, but his mind was consumed with killing. A bugle blared out a call and the Southern troops stepped forward, officers shouting orders and drums rolling.

"What you see up there, Wilson?" shouted a man below.

"Nothing yet," came the reply.

Dirt, limbs and pieces of the man below showered the sniper clinging to the tree as a shell burst forth. Regaining his senses, the sniper climbed higher to view the Union line to his front.

Carefully he raised his musket, peered through the scope and began searching the Union line. "Let's see," he mumbled to himself. "It's either an officer or those manning the cannons. They certainly want me to take them out."

Spotting nothing, he scoped over to the Yankees advancing in line. Once again, he looked for an officer and the flag bearer identifying the unit. Moments passed. "Maybe I should look more to the rear."

On the hillside across the field rode a soldier on horseback. "Man on horseback just might be an officer," he muttered. "I think I'll take a chance." He carefully leaned the barrel of his Whitworth across a limb, adjusted his sights and zeroed in on the horseman.

"Squeeze slow, squeeze slow," he mumbled as he peered through the scope. After setting his trigger, he squeezed off the round.

"General, you need to get down from that horse or go to the rear!" shouted a Union soldier taking hold of the horse's reins. "They'll kill you for sure."

The general could see that the Southern troops were more than six hundred *yards to his front, so he pulled the horse's reins from the soldier's hand and laughed, "At that distance, they couldn't hit an elephant."*

A puff of smoke was seen across the way, and a loud thud caught the attention of the soldier below. The general reeled in the saddle and crumpled to the ground. The soldier kneeled to help but realized the shot had hit its mark.

Looking back to locate its origin, the soldier yelled to those posted with cannons, "Hey, see them woods to our southwest, fill it with shot. They just killed our general!"

Cannon shells tore through the trees leveling the hilltop. Smothering in smoke and beaten by flying limbs, the sniper began to lose his grip. He continued to fall, never reaching the ground. A large spinning hole emerged sucking him downward and a loud voice shattered his hearing, "Welcome to hell you murderer!"

Thomas opened his eyes and jerked himself up from his bed. Wet with perspiration, he slowly lowered himself on his bed and made himself realize he was safe at home.

"Thomas, open the door. You all right?" John called as he gently opened the door. John entered quietly and touched Thomas on his shoulder. "It's me, John."

Thomas turned away from him and muttered, "You best leave me be."

"It was just a bad dream. That's all it was. I've had 'em too," John added.

"Not like mine, little Brother. It seems like I'm gonna have to live with them, if I can."

"Thomas, you need to place your problem with the Lord. He can carry this load for you."

Thomas shook his head. "The Lord don't want any part of me."

"And why not?"

With tasseled hair and bloodshot eyes, Thomas turned to John. "Just leave me be and keep this between us. Our parents have enough on them without worrying over me."

John left the barn knowing Thomas needed help and whispering a prayer for the Lord to provide peace and mercy for his brother.

Spring finally arrived with the native dogwoods and redbuds flowering the landscape. Even though this beauty brought life and hope to the Wilsons, it also brought hard labor. Lott, Thomas, Toby, and John were in the fields from daylight to dark in hopes that one hundred acres of land would soon be tilled and ready for planting corn. The men also began splitting logs and creating fences to hold the horses.

During this time Sarah and Sister not only handled the housekeeping and cooking, but spent hours tending a large garden behind the house. The women had both the responsibility of keeping food on the table and preparing for the winter needs. What little time left was spent in church or in Little Rock, a small village one-half mile south of their place where they collected their mail, purchased supplies, and had corn ground into meal.

Mister Sam Everett, an attorney in Meridian, had inquired around Newton County for an educated and personable young man who could work under his supervision to research cases occurring in the county. Professor Hendon, a noted educator in Little Rock, immediately recommended his former student, John Wilson. While John was excited, he was also worried about the needed farm work, but Lott both gave his approval and encouragement. They soon worked out a schedule so John could help in Meridian two days each month. To John's pleasure, Mister Everett also offered him an apprenticeship.

Each morning Thomas would get up at daybreak to take a horse for a run. By experience, he knew that constant training was necessary to keep horses in shape and disciplined, and early morning was the best time to begin their workouts.

Down in the swamp, the shrill call of a whippoorwill and the flutter as chickens flew from their roost in the chinaberry tree awakened Thomas. Running his fingers through his long hair, Thomas eased out of bed, slipped on trousers and a heavy cotton shirt. He reached for his western boots and grabbed a woolen coat and slouch hat for the crisp morning. The familiar smell of manure and hay welcomed him to another day. He stretched, then headed to one of the mustangs. Dusty, a light tan stallion, had a mind of its own, but had the potential of becoming a fine saddle horse. Saddling the stallion was difficult due to the certain nip directed at the interloper of its freedom. While throwing the blanket over its back, Thomas put a quick fist to its head to counter the biting behavior. Thomas slowly eased up on the saddle as Dusty balked, shook the bits in its mouth and refused to move. A quick kick to its side sent Dusty bucking while Thomas firmly hung on.

Finally realizing defeat, Dusty calmed down and trotted out from the barn. Thomas reached down and patted the horse on his neck. "It's been a while since you and I have enjoyed each other and you had better behave yourself. We're gonna have some fun today." At that he squeezed the horse on its flank and commanded the horse to a gallop.

Slowing the horse to a canter, Thomas edged past the newly plowed field and reined Dusty down a path that led to Big Woods. Thomas took in a big breath of crisp, invigorating air and glanced to the eastern horizon. An orange glow was now visible, revealing a trace of purplish clouds scooting across the heavens, pushed by an early March wind. "What a beautiful morning. Come on boy, let's head for the woods," Thomas whispered.

He slowed the pace as they wandered under the massive century old oaks and hickories. With a shadowy canopy, the leafed trees left little sunlight filtering to the ground. Underneath was a plush carpet of grass, ferns and an occasional canebrake in low areas. The smell of decaying leaves and fresh earth filled his lungs. *This must have been God's Eden* thought Thomas, slowly scanning its beauty.

As Dusty shook his head, rattling his bits, an unseen deer gave a snort, raised his tail and bounded into a thicket near the creek. Thomas entered a clearing and saw a flock of turkeys pecking at insects and couldn't help but notice the beauty of the untouched land. Thomas pushed Dusty up a steep bank to approach the road that led to Decatur, the county seat. This road in the early morning was used by Thomas to race his horses to their limits. It was two miles to Moore's Mill, and a good horse would reach it only slightly winded. After a short rest, he would push the horse even harder on the return run. Pulling his hat down tight on his head, he pressed the horse in the flanks, and screamed, "Heah!"

Leaning low in the saddle, clods of dirt kicked up as they sped down the dirt road. It was times like this that Thomas lost the war demons that were chasing him and embraced peace. The sound of thundering hooves filled his ears as the wind swept past him in a fury. In the curve Thomas leaned down to straighten his right foot which had slipped out of the stirrup, and a massive black object struck him, spooking his horse and sending him tumbling down the embankment.

Once again he was free falling through space and far below he could see the dark tunnel clutching to consume him. *This time Satan will take my soul.* Then a clear voice called through the darkness, "You all right? Oh my, have I killed you? Please Lord, let him be alive."

Thomas could feel soft hands on his face, and he slowly lifted his eyelids. As his vision cleared, a woman with dark complexion, soot black hair braided down her back and sparkling eyes stood over him.

18

"Are you an angel?" Thomas answered gazing up at the most beautiful woman he had ever seen.

"Hardly an angel."

Thomas slowly tried to move his neck. "Well, I guess you didn't kill me, so the Lord must have answered your prayer."

"If you can sit up, I'll see if I can stop the bleeding and check on anything that might be broken," she said reaching for his arm.

With her help, Thomas struggled up and moved over to lean his back against the trunk of an old pine. Even though he ached all over, it seemed as nothing was broken. The woman took a handkerchief from her black riding jacket and carefully wiped the blood from his head. "It's not that bad, but you're going to have a pretty good goose egg up there," she said settling down beside him.

Now that she felt assured that his life wasn't in danger, she looked intently at the man who sat beside her. He was a large man with long hair, brown eyes hinted with green, and a squared dimpled chin. While studying his features more carefully, she realized that he seemed familiar to her.

Thomas gave her a slight smile, "You know, in three years of war, I never got a scratch and I come home and a woman almost kills me."

As she assisted him to his feet, she asked, "Do I know you? Should I know you?"

Thomas didn't answer as he moved around testing his leg. Standing at full height, he was taller than the woman realized.

"Where's my horse?" Thomas said twisting his back. The woman pointed down to the creek. Thomas and the woman walked to get the horse that had now found some good grass to munch and was completely contented. Thomas carefully ran his hands over the horse's legs and flanks and realized the horse had fared better than he had.

With his fingers, he straightened his tangled hair. "I'm Thomas, Thomas Wilson."

A slight smile formed on her face. "You know, I thought I recognized you, but it's been a long time. You've changed."

Thomas walked over to retrieve his hat and then taking Dusty by the reins, led him back to the road.

"Your horse all right?" Thomas asked looking back to the woman following him.

Frowning she placed her hands on her hips. "You could have asked if I am hurt or maybe, who I am?"

Thomas began to mount the horse, then turned back to the woman. "Sorry ma'am, but by your looks, you seem fine."

"You really don't remember me, do you?"

"No ma'am."

"I'm Suzanne Olliver."

"Oh yeah, the skinny little girl with knotty knees."

"Is that all you have to say?" Suzanne shot back as she mounted her horse.

"Well, that's all you asked."

Suzanne clicked to her horse. "Are you always this rude? Here I've tried to help the man who charged into me, and this is how you repay me."

"That's a joke. You almost killed me."

As Thomas rode off, Suzanne called out, "I guess I'm coming with you in case you get a dizzy spell, but you sure don't deserve my attention."

Without looking back, Thomas called, "Suit yourself. It's a free country."

Suzanne sped after him. She was amazed at the speed of the smaller horse and realized that no matter how hard she pushed her Kentucky thoroughbred, it would not be able to catch up with Thomas. Reluctantly, she slowed to a canter and was about to turn for home when she saw Thomas up the way sitting calmly watching her.

As Suzanne approached him, she called out, "What kind of horse you got?"

Thomas smiled and patted Dusty on the neck. "It's a mustang."

"Never heard of it."

"You might not have heard of a mustang, but you will. The Spaniards left them out west hundreds of years ago, and in the wild, they prospered. They're a tough lot."

After gazing at her glistening black hair, Thomas paused and then asked, "You still want to ride with me?"

"I'm still here," Suzanne said.

Leaving the road, he led her into a meadow covered with the morning dew that sparkled with the rising sun. Suzanne glanced at Thomas as he made a path through the woods for them. She remembered how comfortable and protected as a little girl she had felt in his presence. She also realized that she knew nothing about this quiet man. Silence filled the air as they winded their way through the forest. She decided there was really no need to try to talk to this man who seemed to prefer solitude to friendship.

As they approached Little Rock Creek, Thomas reined in his horse and dismounted. "You might want to give your horse a drink."

Kneeling down on the creek bank, Thomas cupped his hands and drank his full, then lowered his whole head into the water, washing the dirt and blood from his face and hair.

Suzanne quickly dismounted and quipped, "A gentleman would help me down to the water, but I already see that you are no gentleman."

Thomas rubbed his chin and shaking his head said, "You look like you're healthy enough to take care of yourself; I wouldn't want to insult your independence."

Suzanne dismounted then countered, "I do treasure my independence, but it is also nice to have a gentleman help a lady when needed."

Thomas led his horse from the creek to give Suzanne's mount room. "Never said I was a gentleman. Can't say I want to be one either."

Suzanne pointed to the large sheath and knife attached to his leather belt and bantered, "Mighty big knife you carry."

Like a flash, Thomas reached down, grabbed the knife by the handle and hurled it toward a tree a good thirty feet out front, sinking it dead center. Walking over to retrieve the weapon, he turned to her. "I've always carried a knife. It's good for killing rattle snakes and a good bit more, if you know what I mean."

Susanne shook her head, "I understand exactly what you mean, Mister Wilson. But civilized folks don't keep a weapon at all times."

"It's not the civilized folks you have to worry about, Miss Olliver." Thomas paused to observe her reaction. "You still think you want to ride with the likes of me."

Her first impulse was to ride away from this rude, uncaring ruffian and head for home, but his slight smile and the tender way he treated his horse made her rethink her decision. "I always love a good ride."

Silence again filled the air as they headed from the creek until Suzanne asked, "You said you were in the war. Tell me about it. What was your unit?"

Thomas abruptly brought his horse to a stop and hatred filled his face. "Don't ever ask me about the war! I have no desire to talk about it with you or anyone else. That subject is best left closed."

Surprised by his strong reaction, she compassionately whispered, "I'm so sorry. I had no right to ask."

Seeing the tenderness in her face and the sincerity of her voice, Thomas replied, "It's not your fault. Just something I choose to forget."

Suzanne, knowing it was time for her to head home, cleared her throat and asked, "Do you ride every morning? If you do, I might join you, if it's okay."

Thomas took his hat off, brushed his hair back and eyed Suzanne. "Yes, I ride every morning, and I've told you this is a free country."

"With time, I think I can learn to tolerate your rude behavior, Mister Thomas Wilson."

Thomas sat there studying the beautiful and strong woman who faced him waiting for an answer. "Daybreak at Moore's Mill, but I won't wait for you." Squeezing Dusty in the flanks, he turned and rode away. "By the way, I don't ride on Sundays," he called back.

On the short ride to her home, Suzanne contemplated the morning's events and conversations. *Thomas is certainly not like the men in my life, and his being a Wilson will not sit well with my family. The men of Louisiana cater to my every whim, but this man doesn't seem concerned at all. No, Mister Wilson is not the one for me, and riding with him could bring me more trouble than he is worth.*

Reining Dusty into the corral, Thomas took off his hat and reaching for his handkerchief, wiped the perspiration from his face. "What a heck of a morning," he said to himself. "She won't show up again."

"What you say, Mister Thomas?" asked Toby coming out of one of the stalls with pitchfork in hand. "You talking to me?"

Thomas shook his head and smiled down to the old gent. "Naw, I'm just talking to an ole fool and that'd be Thomas Wilson."

Toby began to laugh. "Well, that bein' so, you can just join the human race."

That night while lying on his bed watching the fire slowly die away, Thomas could see those dark brown eyes and feel the tender touch of her hand even after his severe words. *No, he reasoned, she won't be seeing me again. I wouldn't if I were her. Probably best.*

On Sunday morning the family brought out their best clothes and headed to church to hear the circuit riding preacher. To Sarah's surprise, Thomas, who usually refused to attend church since returning home, came strolling out of the barn dressed in his very best. He climbed up onto the back bench with his sister and announced, "We can go now."

As they headed to the church in Little Rock, the sky burst forth in sunlight promising a clear and beautiful day. Buggies, wagons, saddle horses and playing children covered the church grounds. The pump organ gave a strong welcome as people entered with family members. Thomas noted Suzanne on her family bench two rows up, and she caught his glance and gave a small wave. Sister saw Suzanne and thinking the wave for her, she smiled and waved back. Thomas just turned his head and gave a nervous cough as he sat on his family bench.

As soon as the service ended, Thomas decided it best to leave as soon as possible to avoid talking to anyone, especially to Suzanne, but found he was hemmed in by his parents who were socializing with some of their friends. Out of the corner of his eye, he saw Suzanne making her way through the crowd toward him. She was beautiful in her light green dress and dark hair flowing down her back and across her shoulders.

Suzanne brushed up to him with a teasing smile and reached to his cut. "Well, Mister Wilson, I see you are recovering from the accident that almost killed you." She spent a moment admiring his light grey suit and clean shaven face.

Sister taking in the exchange smiled and added to Thomas's discomfort. "Now doesn't he look like a Southern gentleman, Suzanne?"

Suzanne chuckled enjoying the redness of his face. "You know, he might just become one at that."

Suzanne deliberately turned her back to Thomas. "Lucretia, you look amazing in that dress. I bet all the young men are taking notice."

Sister enjoyed the compliment. "Oh I've met some who are interesting, but I really don't have time to give."

"Why is that?"

"Between my tasks at home and my teaching job, there's little time left for fun."

"Teaching is a very noble profession, and I know you will do well with the children, but you need to make some time for enjoyment too." Turning to go, Suzanne added, "I hope you have a great day today, and let's get together some time to talk." She nodded to Thomas as she headed down the aisle and out of the church.

Sister quickly walked to catch up with Suzanne on the church stairs. "How is Frankie doing?"

As a breeze swept across the church yard, Suzanne pushed her hair out of her face and smiled at Sister. "Oh, I guess he is fine. He's down at Papa's plantation in Louisiana, and as hard as he tries to be a planter, his heart is not in it. He does like being close to New Orleans, and he is certainly catching the eyes of those Cajun girls down there."

Sister laughed, "That sounds like him." Then remembering how Frankie had courted Rebecca, while John was thought to be dead, and how Frankie had almost married her, but on their wedding day, John had arrived at the church not realizing he was about to witness a marriage. She remembered how the minute Rebecca saw John, Frankie was devastated and left the church quietly knowing Rebecca would never be his. Sister blushed and said, "I'm sorry I should not have made that remark."

Suzanne pleasantly replied, "Don't apologize for that. You told the truth." Smiling down, Suzanne concluded, "You need to be careful if my brother ever visits up here. You might just catch his eye."

Sister remembered how good looking Frankie was and how much she had enjoyed dancing with him at the party given in honor of Suzanne's return from Louisiana. Sister blushed at her thoughts and replied, "You don't have to worry about that. I really don't think I'm the type of girl he would want."

"Well, you are probably right because you are definitely too good for Frankie."

As Suzanne walked away, Sister began to wonder about Suzanne and Thomas. She certainly was planning on finding out exactly what had happened between them, one way or another.

Lott carefully coaxed the old mule past numerous muddy potholes as he and Sarah discussed the day's sermon and the conversations with their friends. Sister, determined to discover the mystery surrounding her brother, reached over, pushed his hair to the side revealing the cut, and exclaimed loud enough for her parents to hear, "I didn't know you were almost killed."

Catching the word killed, Sarah turned. "Are you hurt, Son? It's not that serious, was it?"

Giving his sister an ugly look, Thomas replied, "No ma'am, I'm fine."

Sister reached up and pulled on her mother's coat collar gaining her attention. "That's not so Mother. Suzanne said he almost got killed yesterday."

"Thomas, what is this about?" asked Lott slapping the reins against the mule's back to coax him on.

Angered, Thomas shook his head at Sister. "I'm doing fine. Let's just drop it."

All was quiet for a few moments, but Sister was determined to get to the truth. She leaned in and whispered to her mother. "I think he's hiding something, don't you?"

Seeing the anguish and frustration on Thomas's face, Sarah admonished, "Leave it be, Daughter. If Thomas wants to share something with us, he will."

Relieved, Thomas reached over and grabbing his sister, began tickling her. Laughing and squirming around she squealed, "You better stop or I might wet myself."

"Serve you right little sister. You're nothing but a gossip and pest."

"All right children, none of that. We behave on the Lord's day," Sarah reprimanded.

When they arrived home, Thomas and Lott unhitched the wagon at the barn and let the mule out to the field while the women went inside to prepare dinner. As they walked toward the house, Lott placed his arm on Thomas's shoulder. "Now Son, you need to tell me what happened to you yesterday."

Thomas was reluctant, but knew he had no choice. "I was running the horse at full speed when approaching the curve in the road near Moore's Mill where I met Miss Olliver pushing her horse as well. Hers ran into mine, spooking it, and I ended up thrown to the ground. Really, that's all there is to it."

"Well, that don't seem like a momentous event. Why didn't you just tell Sister what happened?"

"Papa, she can be such a pest at times and as much as I love her, she seems to find ways to irritate me."

"Son, that's just what sisters do. Come on, I'm hungry."

Early the next morning, Thomas saddled up Champ, the prize stud thoroughbred, for his weekly workout. At seventeen hands tall, black as night, he was truly a beautiful animal. Thomas knew, because of Champ's training, it would be an easy ride. The day was cloudy, so Thomas decided not to venture far. A ghostly silence engulfed him. Even the wildlife had disappeared taking cover from the impending rain and the breeze had ceased to welcome him. As he reached the road, he considered turning for home, but as he reined to turn Champ, he thought about Suzanne. He headed southward to the mill, just in case she had decided to join him. Although his expectation was dampened by the dreary weather, as he approached the old mill, he spotted a horseman silently waiting.

"You're late," Suzanne called out. "What kept you?"

By habit, Thomas rubbed his beard. "You know you're a fool to be out on a day like this."

"I guess that makes two of us, Mister Wilson. Now, do we ride or talk?"

As the days and weeks passed, Thomas and Suzanne never missed a morning ride, and with time, Thomas began to feel comfortable in her presence. The thoughts that once plagued him during the day had begun to leave him, but the dreams at night were still terrifying. Thomas began praying that the dreams would disappear, but God seemed to be very far away.

3

Tested by Fire

So then neither the one who plants nor the one who waters is anything, but God who causes the growth. For no man can lay a foundation other than the one which is laid, which is Jesus Christ. Each man's work will become evident; for the day will show it because it is to be revealed with fire and the fire itself will test the quality of each man's work.

—1st Corinthians 3:7, 11, 13 NASB

Spring quickly turned to summer with its intense heat, humidity and occasional thunder storms. With steady rains, the corn was now knee high and the garden was flourishing. This season brought relentless work and little time for relaxation or recreation. It was daylight to dark six days a week.

Lott faced another demanding day and began by sharpening a plow share, but he was abruptly interrupted by a voice waking him from his world of work. "Anybody at home?"

Lott stopped what he was doing and walked outside the barn to see Mister Everett, a slim, tall man with gray hair who was dressed meticulously. "Sorry to bother you."

Lott reached over and extended his hand. "It's been a while since I've seen you. How can I help you?"

"Has John spoken with you lately?" asked Everett.

"I see him every day," Lott replied. "What's going on?"

Everett took off his glasses and wiped them with a handkerchief and then turned his attention back to Lott. "Mister Wilson, your son has a lot of potential in the law field, and it pains me that he has apparently lost interest."

"What do you mean?"

Tightening his lips, he eyed Lott. "I haven't seen John in over two months nor heard anything from him. I'd like to know why he has neglected his work with me."

Lott scratched his head in thought. "Well, he still talks about it, and he seems to have his head in those books you gave him. Mister Everett, I just don't know."

"Can you tell me where I can find him? I think we need to talk."

"I sent him to Decatur on a legal matter, and he won't be home until late this afternoon."

"Well, I've got to be on my way. Please talk to John and let him know that I think he has a future with our firm and we don't want to lose him, but he must decide quickly about his job or I'll have to look for a replacement."

That afternoon after dinner, Lott quickly directed John away from the family and to the front porch. "John, Mister Everett came by today and was pretty upset that you have not been to the office in two months."

"Papa, I really love the work at the law firm, but I think I'm needed here a lot more than with Mister Everett."

Both men sat quietly in thought as the darkness began settling over the land.

"Son, I'm proud of you and the work you do here, but you've got to follow your own dreams. More than ever before, this country is gonna need good men in the law field. I want you to go back to work with Mister Everett, and when time permits, you can help us here. I prayed about this earlier and feel that God has a plan for you, and it just ain't on this farm."

John got up and hugged his father. "You know, Papa, I appreciate and love you more than you can ever know"

Summer approached and the school year ended, and Sister smiled as the children scampered away. She sat at her desk and contemplated her first year of teaching. It had been a good year, and she loved the children and knew that she was exactly in God's will for her life.

Sister headed to Walker's store to get the mail before leaving for home. Mister Walker, Rebecca's father, handed her a letter postmarked from Texas. She turned the letter over and held it to the light but could not think of anyone her father knew from Texas. Her curiosity made her rush as quickly as her small stride would carry her. Breathless, she ran up the steps waving the letter over her head beckoning, "Mama! Papa got a letter from someone in Texas! We don't know anyone from there, do we?"

Sarah took the letter, and a bright smile filled her face. "Sure we do. Papa's sister, your aunt lives out there. We haven't heard from them in years."

Still excited, Sister asked, "Can we open it?"

Sarah shook her head. "No darling, this letter is addressed to your father.

We'll give it to him when he gets home this evening."

As dusk approached, Sarah saw her husband slowly leave the barn and head for the outside wash basin to clean up. Next coming inside to change his clothes, Lott sought comfort in his padded chair. Sarah met him with a cup of steaming coffee, and Sister rushed into the kitchen. "Have you given him his letter yet?"

Sarah turned, reached up to a shelf next to the stove and retrieving the letter, handed it to her husband.

Lott gingerly took the letter, studied it for a moment, then opened it. His expression hardened and he dropped the letter to the floor, then walked to the window nearby, braced his hands on the seals, and stared out into the darkness.

Sister motioned to her mother and whispered, "Mama, something must be wrong."

Sarah reached to retrieve the letter and read it silently then placed it on the table before walking to Lott and holding him closely. "I'm so sorry, darling."

Sister watched and wondered what could upset her papa so badly. She reached for the note which read. *Dear Brother, It is with a sad heart that I must inform you my husband has been murdered.* There was more but Sister knew she should wait for her papa to tell the whole family about Jonathan Lewis, the man married to her papa's sister.

Later that night Lott began discussing the death of his brother-in-law and the plight of his sister. "Sara Ann, my sister is going to need some family close to her. She is going to have a hard time providing for herself and her children. I'm going to have to go and make sure she is okay. What would you think about me bringing her and her children here to live?"

"Lott, maybe we need to first send one of the boys to check on her and see what she wants to do. I know one of her sons is approaching manhood, and he may want to take care of his mother and might not want us interfering, but if they do want to live here with us, it would just add more joy to our family."

After the family grabbed hands and prayed, Lott found some paper and began a letter asking Sara Ann what he could do to help and letting her know that she and her family would be welcome to live with them. Lott was determined to do whatever his sister needed.

Early the next morning Lott dressed and later found Thomas throwing a saddle over Dusty, the mustang. Lott quietly reached for the mustang to stroke him as Thomas finished the saddling. "What you know about east Texas, Thomas?"

"You mean Cass County?"

Lott nodded and watched a solemn expression form on Thomas's face. "Papa, me and a few of my war friends went by there on the way home, and the only way I can explain it, is it is a hell on earth. The place where Aunt Sara Ann lives is near the Sulfur River. Papa, you won't believe the swamps and thickets, just thousands and thousands of acres. A man can go in there, if'n he knows the place, and an army could never find him. And Papa, you ain't seen such violence as is in that county. There are gangs of renegades killing, stealing and doing whatever evil their mind desires."

"What about the law, Son?"

Thomas scratched his beard. "Papa, they have some law out there, but they can't handle all the evil. If they crack down too hard, they'll end up dead."

Thomas paused for a moment. "But I did hear that they're sending Yankee troops to help, but if those poltroons hit the swamp, they won't be able to flush 'em out."

"It's hard to believe such a place exists and people can be so evil."

"Papa, I hate what happened to Uncle Jonathan, but I ain't surprised. If he had something someone wanted or had a cross word, it probably got him killed. I don't know what you got on your mind, but those folks of ours don't need to be there."

By late July the corn was head high and tasseling, leaving no more work for the men until harvest, and the women's work was coming to an end. The garden was producing, and preserving the vegetables in glass jars began. Now, Saturday brought rest and play instead of work. Sarah, Sister, and Rebecca decided to visit the Rogers family up the road and take some gifts for their newborn child while Thomas headed to the creek for a day of fishing. John chose to stay in his bedroom nestled in Blackstone's Dictionary of Legal Terms, and Lott sat on the front porch, relaxing and whittling. Old Red, John's favorite coon hound, curled up next to Lott. Lott began to smile, realizing that Thomas was improving and God had been mighty good to his family.

A little after noon, Lott noticed the hound perk his ears, and soon it began barking and then raced out from the porch and into the yard. Lott heard the thunder of horses' hooves and saw dust rising down the road as two horsemen turned from the Little Rock road and quickly cantered up to his house. One was a plump little man, with thick glasses, dressed in a gray suit and a funny looking short brimmed hat while the other was a federal soldier. Lott let the dust clear, then laid his knife and stick down, and walked over to the edge of his steps. "Hello gents, how can I help you?"

The quaint little man adjusted his glasses as he slowly scrutinized the house and fields beyond, then said, "You Lott Wilson?"

Lott walked down the steps to extend his hand, but the man ignored the gesture. "Yes, I'm Lott Wilson. What do you want?"

The federal soldier, a sergeant, unconcerned, took out a slip of paper, poured some tobacco in it, made a nice roll and lit up a smoke.

Wiping the dust from his face, the man with a northern accent said, "I'm Travis Davis and I'm one of the tax assessors here in the county. I'm here to look your place over."

"Won't you two come on up on the porch out of the heat?"

"Mister Wilson, this isn't a social call. This is strictly business."

"Well, have your say then." Lott pulled his chair near the steps and eased down while Davis reached into his saddle bags, retrieved a notebook and began turning pages. Momentarily, he frowned, adjusted his glasses and glared directed at Lott.

"It says here you have three sections of land. That's six hundred and forty acres times three and that equals one thousand nine hundred and twenty acres. That is a lot of property, Mister Wilson."

"Well, Mister Davis, it ain't exactly all mine."

"The book says that you have been paying taxes on it. Am I mistaken?"

"This section and house is in my name, and the one to the south was my brother Jake's land."

Davis squirmed in his saddle. "Maybe, I need to talk with him. Where can he be located?"

Lott shook his head. "You can visit the cemetery if you want, but it won't do you any good. He was killed years ago. I'm keeping the land for his son, Homer."

"All right then, how can I get in contact with this Mister Homer?"

"He's out in the Oklahoma Indian Territory. Being half Choctaw, he left with his mother and before you say anything else, I've been paying those taxes for him."

"A little confusing Mister Wilson, but now about the third section to our west?"

"Mister Davis, can't we hurry this up?" asked the sergeant who was becoming impatient.

Quickly turning, Davis said, "Keep your mouth shut. This is state business."

Angered, the soldier dismounted and walked away from the two to stretch his legs.

"The other section is listed under Minsa," Lott waited for the next obvious question.

"Minsa, that's a funny name. I guess he is also a Choctaw and can be found in the Territory."

Lott gave Davis a deliberate and impatient smile. "Mister Davis, for once, you are exactly correct, and yes, I am paying his taxes as well. I don't know exactly what you're up to, but I can assure you everything I do is legal, and I'm getting mighty tired of your rude behavior."

John could hear the voices increasing in volume and headed out to check on his father. "What's going on out here?"

Davis cocked his head and smirked at John. "We're just talking about this Minsa fellow and how the idea that a Choctaw could hold land is ridiculous. And who might you be young man? Perhaps Minsa himself?"

John smiled at his father and then back to Davis. "I'm John Wilson. Lott is my father, and I can see you know little about Mississippi law."

Davis squirmed uneasily in his saddle and studied John for a moment. "Are you some kind of lawyer, or is this talk all foolishness?" he queried thinking the boy was just another dumb Southerner.

John straightened himself and confidently replied. "I'm an apprentice with the law firm of Mister Sam Everett in Meridian. I hope to become a lawyer one day. Just excuse me a minute."

John walked down the hall, entered his father's bedroom and momentarily returned with a slip of paper. Handing the form to Davis, John continued. "In 1834 when the Choctaws were being removed, Mississippi issued a law stating that if the head of a Choctaw family relinquished their tribal alliance and followed the laws of Mississippi, they in turn could obtain a section of land. Many wanted to apply, but for one reason or another, few followed through, but some grants were issued. In your hand is proof that the land to our west is legally listed as Minsa's property. By paying his taxes, we are preserving his grant."

Davis's face flushed with anger and resentment. Slowly he turned his head toward the corral full of fine horses, the flourishing field of corn and then back to Lott. "Mister Wilson, you have three prime sections of land, horses, what appears to be a bumper crop of corn and a somewhat unique house, but grand. As you probably know, with the ending of the rebellion last year, tax notices did not go out, so this year you will owe the taxes from last year as well as this year. In addition, to get our government back and operating, this year's taxes have been increased."

"Is that all you have to say, Mister Davis?"

Davis closed his tablet, and placed it back in his saddle bag. "Well, Mister Wilson, the way I see it, is that you just might be a little surprised at the statement you will be receiving. Unless you can provide more proof of income than I can see, you may just have a problem covering your state debt."

Stepping out from his father, John stared keenly at Davis. "Is that some kind of a threat? If so, you may have underestimated us."

Another smile. "Not at all. I'm just giving you the facts. You people should have thought about what could occur when you rebelled."

Taking his hat off and nodding, he continued, "I must take my leave now, and the top of the day to you."

Glancing over to the sergeant who was rolling another smoke, he quipped, "Now it's time to go, shall we?"

Davis turned to his escort as they were leaving and spoke under his breath. "Fine place we have here. Yes, quite a farm. You know, I have a friend up in Ohio who's coming down soon and I think the Wilson farm will suit him well."

A dark cloud descended upon Lott sapping the strength from his body. Clutching the porch beam for support, Lott sank down on the step below and dropped his head. *Lord, I thought my trials had ended, but it looks like I'm facing yet another.*

John eased down and placed his arm on his father. As dusk approached, the two sat together in thought and silent prayer. Finally John broke the silence. "Papa, all is going to be just fine. You've always said that God will take care of those who love Him."

"But the Good Book also says that the Lord giveth and the Lord taketh away, Son. Blessed be the name of the Lord. I just pray that we get to keep this land for us and Homer and Minsa, as well as Toby."

Lott took his handkerchief, wiped his face to hide the impending tears and softly said, "John, you might have thought Davis was just threatening us, and he was, but a lot of what he said was true. We do own a lot of land and God knows we have little money. If I can't come up with the sum he names, this place will go to the courthouse steps for auction. We could lose everything."

John took a deep breath and squeezed his father's shoulder. "Papa, you said 'if I can't raise the sum,' but you're forgetting that it is we. It's not just you, but Thomas, me, and even Toby as well as mother, Sister, and Rebecca. We are a family and with God's help we can weather this storm, if it comes."

Pulling himself up, Lott replied, "Son, it's coming. I can feel it. It's coming. We best get prepared."

Later that night as John snuggled in bed with Rebecca, he shared the afternoon's problems. Rebecca quietly contemplated all and then whispered, "Can we really lose this place?"

John pulled her close. "That we can. It's a law that if you don't cover your taxes, your property goes to the state for auction."

Silence filled the room except for a lonesome cry from a whippoorwill down in the swamp. "You know Rebecca, with our land, horses and crop, we have more sources of income than most folks around here. As well off as we are and we aren't able to manage the taxes, then just think about all the other farmers around us. Darling, they have even less."

Leaning over and placing her head on John's shoulder, she asked, "Who would dare take all these folks' farms, take our farm?"

"From what I've heard, Northerners with means are coming down here to speculate."

"What do you mean by speculate?"

"Becca, these men have money and with deflated land values, they can easily purchase any and every piece of land available. They'll either try to work the land, or wait until our economy improves and sell it for a huge profit."

Rebecca shuddered, "That means all of us Mississippians could lose everything we have worked so hard for. It just doesn't seem fair."

"You're right, darling, we could lose it all." Pushing her hair from her face, John tenderly kissed her forehead and lovingly said, "But we are not going to lose it without doing everything possible to keep it. After all, I plan to spend many a night here with my beautiful and sweet wife."

There were no celebrations in the South on the fourth of July, the birthday of the nation. Southern farmers were facing a greater crisis than even the war had caused—the loss of all they held dear. Mississippians were not in a festive spirit.

As July sneaked into August, the Wilsons were faring quite well. Their crops were beautiful and bountiful, the women were finishing their garden work and had much stored for the coming months, and one of their mustang mares foaled. A feeling of security crept in and Lott refused to share his impending dark shadow with the rest of the family. On August thirteenth, the shadow became a storm which broke loose.

John returned from a trip to Hickory, a small town in the southern end of the county, where he had sought information about a shooting. He had stopped at Walker's Store to purchase paper for a report, and as he left the store, Mister Walker, his father in law, informed him that Lott had received two letters. John quickly noticed that one was the much anticipated letter from his aunt in Texas and the other appeared to be an official letter. John hurried home knowing his family eagerly awaited the news.

When John reached home, he saw his father returning from the barn and held up the letter from his aunt. "Got something for you."

Lott hurried his pace and motioned John to the porch where he eagerly sat down and eyed the letters in his hand. He quickly tore into his sister's letter and after reading it, sat silently in thought.

"What did it say, Papa?" John probed straining to look over his father's shoulder.

Lott cleared his throat and replied with a smile, "Not much, really. She said they were still trying to run the ferry and she had been a little ill for the past few days. She also said that they all were doing fairly well under the circumstances."

"That's all she said?"

"She said that if she needed us, she would let us know. Wanted us to keep them in our prayers."

Remembering he had another letter, he laid down his sister's and opened the other. Seconds later, Lott's face sank and his breath shortened as he placed his hand on the railing for support. Without looking at John, he stammered almost inaudibly, "Go get your brother."

Thomas straddled the top railing of the corral and was mesmerized as the young colt danced on his long, wobbling legs. Gazing upward, he noticed a lone eagle soaring high above the sky. Moments like this brought respite from the nightmares which returned with each clap of thunder or gunshot from a hunter in the swamp. Thomas felt the sun warm on his face and also felt a peaceful presence with him. Shutting his eyes, his mind could see images of his rides with Suzanne, and he wondered why she chose to ride with him. He loved spending time with such a beautiful woman, but there was really no future in the relationship. It was time for him to be fair and let her know that he couldn't make a commitment to anyone. His nightmares were the only commitment he had, and no one should be invited into his dark world.

"Hey Thomas, you out here?" called John walking through the open hallway of the barn.

Thomas opened his eyes and turned, "Yeah, I'm at the corral! What you want?"

"Papa wants to see us up at the house."

As Thomas approached and saw the expression on his father's face, he knew they were facing a pretty severe problem.

"Boys, you might want to take a seat." Lott motioned to them, and John and Thomas sat on the top step next to each other as Lott handed them the letter to read.

John stood up quickly. "This just don't make any sense. It can't be right. It's nothing but thievery."

Thomas took the letter, crinkled it up in his hand and threw it as far as he could. "I'll kill 'em all! I've done it before, and I'll sure enough do it again. Those Yankees will not take our land."

Lott grabbed his arm. "Son, you can't think like that. You can't just go out killing folks."

Thomas jerked his arm away, "You just watch me. I'll make sure they get what they deserve." Thomas stormed off the porch and headed to the barn and in a few moments returned mounted bareback.

Speechless, John and Lott watched as Thomas, leaning low and hair flowing, headed toward Big Woods.

"What should we do?" Lott asked disturbed by the fierce anger he had seen on his son's face.

"He's angry. Let him cool off, and I'll go check on him in a while. He'll be all right."

Walking to retrieve the letter, John replied, "It's the war, Papa. It has ways of destroying men."

John smoothed out the letter which read, "Taxes for the Lott Wilson's property: $100.00 per section and $50.00 additional for house, barn, livestock and crop. Total: $350.00 payable by December 31, 1866."

John knew his family had no way to raise that kind of money. Then looking upward, he prayed, "*God we certainly need a miracle, one like I read in Your Word.*

It seems like our struggles never end on this earth. Test our work, Lord, and see that our foundation is You. And Lord if it is Your will, please provide a way for us to keep this land."

4

The Plan

Be strong and let your heart take courage, all you who hope in the Lord.

—Psalm 31:24 NASB

The days following the tax notice were ones of solemn existence with little laughter and many fears. The Wilsons conversed with other families in the community who were experiencing the same horror, but most tax notices had not been as excessive as the one the Wilsons received. An anger toward a government that was bent on punishing every Southerner and a realization that their destination was in the hands of the fire-eating republicans in Washington initiated hopelessness in the town of Little Rock.

Thomas brushed down the horse he had been training, walked up to the house and called to his mother who was hanging clothes on a line, "Mama, I want you to round up the family and meet me on the porch. It's cooler out there."

"What do you want, Son?"

"Got an idea. Just round them up."

Sarah saw the determination on her son's face and decided to stop her work and comply with his wishes. Family members began to assemble on the porch, each trying to find a comfortable place to listen as Thomas waited impatiently for them to settle.

To get everyone's attention, Thomas got up from where he was seated, moved down, and faced his family. "Folks, I want you to hear me out and ask no questions until I'm finished. An idea came to me the other day when I rode ole Dusty down by the track next to the Little Rock Creek. As a little boy, I remember the races we had there with all its excitement, and Papa, I can still see you up there on that platform barking orders and firing that pistol to get 'em started."

Lott began to smile at Sarah remembering his brother Jake and his love for racing horses.

John squeezed Rebecca's hand. "I remember too, Thomas."

Thomas held his hand up to get back to his speaking. "The way I figure it, folks around here need some uplifting and entertainment."

Taking his hat off to push some gnats away, Thomas ran his fingers through his hair and then slid his hat back on. "What I got in mind, if you folks think we can pull it off, might give us the money we need for the taxes and maybe even a little more."

Sister caught up in the excitement called out. "Tell us more. Tell us more." Then realizing she had interrupted Thomas, she lowered her head. "Sorry. Just got a little excited."

Everyone couldn't help but laugh, including Thomas.

"Now, first we need to clean up the old race track, rebuild the starting platform and be sure the grounds are suitable for camping. Then we get the word out that we are sponsoring a horse race with cash prizes."

"Cash prizes! How are we going to get cash prizes?" interrupted Lott.

"Just wait and listen, Papa. Remember, no interruptions until I share my whole idea."

"Now we personally don't put up a copper cent. Most folks around here don't have much money, but state wide, folks do, and when it comes to horse racing, they will shell it out. This is my plan. It will cost a rider ten dollars to enter his horse. We'll run five of 'em at a time, and the winner in each race will get twenty dollars per race. Yep, we'll clear thirty and we'll run these races until all that want to race have competed. I figure there'll be a lot of qualifying races. Now this is where it gets more interesting. Next, we'll have the race of champions. We'll take only the winners of each race and for a registration fee of twenty dollars, we'll start them all over again. The winner of each of these races will win fifty dollars, and we could bank up to fifty dollars a race. Finally, for those who have the funds and the fever, we'll sponsor a grand champion race. For a low fee of twenty dollars, those who have qualified and desire can list their horses, and the winner of this final race will receive one hundred dollars. Now their horse will be known throughout our state as the best and fastest."

"Son, that is a good plan, but it seems we won't make anything on the last race," interrupted Lot.

Thomas smiled at his father. "You're exactly right, Papa, but you see, we've already made our profit, and that final race is what will draw everyone who wants to prove his horse is best. What do you folks think?"

The family sat in silence a moment letting this plan permeate their brains, and finally Sister said, "I think it's ingenious. How did you think all this up?"

"Well, Sister, when a man has trouble sleeping, it gives him time to think."

"How do we organize these races?" asked Sarah.

"Well, me, Toby, and his son will clear the track and rebuild the starting platform. Sister, you get some of your friends and make a lot of posters advertising the races, and John, your task is to get them circulated, and I do mean state wide."

"I can do that. I'll get it to the paper in Meridian, and since I have to go to Jackson on business Wednesday, I'll drop them off on the way at Lake, Forest, Morton, Brandon and at every town and village I see, as well as at the state capital. I'll also list it with the paper there in Jackson."

"Now to start the festivities, I thought we'd throw a big hog barbecue. Toby, Andy and I can kill and dress the hogs, and Toby will want to do the roasting. All you women can prepare beans, potatoes, rolls, and dessert. We'll purchase flour and all you need to prove you are the best cooks in town. We'll plan enough for a host of folks. And Sister, make sure you put that in your posters."

With raised eyebrows, Sister sighed, "Well, I hope that is all."

"Not quite. You know the string band that played after church the other Sunday? I want you to tell them we'll pay 'em ten dollars each if they will play for us on the evening of the races."

"Son, there may be one problem. Folks know we have the fastest horse in the country. They'll think we brought them down here to take their money."

"Once again, you're exactly right, but we'll let them know we are not racing Champ. We don't need him to raise our funds, but we'll also sponsor a different type of race. On the west side of our tracks there is a clear flat area so we can extend the track northward and create a quarter mile straight away."

A wide knowing smile spread across John's face.

"We'll register and run this race like the others except John, since you are our best horseman, you'll ride Dusty. If you and Dusty win that race, we'll not only have the profit, but we'll get the purse also. Plus it will be great advertisement for our new breed, the mustang."

Lott wiped the perspiration from his face with his shirt sleeve. "Thomas, this all sounds good, but you know folks around here don't have much money to throw about and how do you know they'll come?"

"We'll advertise statewide and we'll get the word out to people who have money, and Papa, we Mississippians are hungry for some entertainment. Lot of folks will just come down here to view the races, fellowship with one another and believe it or not, just to have some fun. Others will come to show their horses and hope to win a purse. Believe me, they'll come."

Rebecca asked, "When do you plan to have this extravaganza?"

"We've got to decide that. It's gonna take time to get the word out and make preparations. What if we wait until the first weekend in October, when the weather cools?"

The family was excited about the plans, and all felt for the first time that they might be able to keep their land. Later that night Thomas invited Toby and Andy up to the house, and all the men began laying out plans for the racetrack and barbecue. They felt Lott would work the platform as starter while John and his father in law, Mister Walker, would register the riders, collect the fees and award the winners. Thomas in turn, would collect a group of men he trusted who would maintain and keep order in case gamblers, tempers, and liquor became a problem. With the plans made, the Little Rock races were becoming a reality.

News of the race spread like a wildfire pushed by a sturdy wind. It became the talk of the town, and everyone around Little Rock had an opinion. Some thought it was a brilliant idea while others were convinced it could never happen. It was definitely stirring up attention.

Thomas, Toby and Andy started clearing the area down by the creek where people would camp, and since the massive oaks allowed little sunlight to reach the ground, there was relatively little underbrush to remove.

The August sun was sweltering so the men decided to take a break on the edge of the creek bank where they could catch a soft cool breeze. Toby found a comfortable spot and wiped the perspiration from his face. "Mister Thomas, we done cleared about twenty acres, you think that many folks is going to show?"

Thomas cupped his hands to grab some cold creek water and splashed it over his parched head. "My gut feeling is they'll be here. I do think we've cleared enough so now we need to concentrate on the track. That's what's gonna be really important." Shaking the water from his hair, he continued, "Men, let's head to the track. We still got some days of work ahead of us."

By the middle of September, the grounds were in good shape, the track was immaculate and the starting platform and bandstand were finished. Now all the Wilsons had to do was wait. And to their delight, from what they could tell, the word was spreading statewide.

As Champ lazily waded down the creek, watering, Thomas lay on his back resting on a soft bed of creek moss gazing up at the clouds dancing high in the sky and hearing only the twittering of some birds with an occasional barking squirrel joining the chorus. In this moment of peace, Thomas's mind drifted to another beauty. He had planned to tell her their relationship would not work, but he did enjoy his time with her. Even in their silence, there was a comfort in her company. She had not asked again about the war and he purposely chose to forget as much as he could. But he couldn't forget her and he couldn't bring himself to tell her that there was no future for them. He whispered to himself that neither of them would get hurt, but he knew in his heart that hurt was inevitable if he didn't speak soon about his feelings.

Clicking to Champ, Thomas rose to meet the stallion as it sloshed back up stream. He headed to the spot where he and Suzanne would meet and waited to talk truthfully to her. He mounted Champ as Suzanne rode up beside him.

"Beautiful day, don't you think?" Suzanne looked at Thomas and wondered why he was so slow in answering. "What you thinking so hard about? You still have your mind on the upcoming race?"

As they reached the upper road where they usually separated, she reined her horse to a stop. Pushing loose hair from her face, she looking directly at him and said, "Is there something that I've done to upset you?"

Thomas took off his hat and placed it on his lap and just gazed at the beautiful woman in front of him. "Why do you spend time with me?"

Suzanne twisted in her saddle and flushing, answered, "I enjoy riding with you. I feel safe and I enjoy your company."

"Then I'm kinda like a bodyguard? Is that it?"

"No! That's not it at all," Suzanne replied.

"Then what in tarnations do you mean?"

Suzanne lifted her face to feel the warm rays of sunlight and shook her dark hair then smiled. "You don't have the vaguest idea do you? Men can be so dumb at times. Well, tell me then. Why do you spend time with me?"

Thomas felt his face flush and rubbing his hand across his beard he replied. "I feel comfortable with you."

"Sort of like an old worn-out shoe?"

Thomas cocked his head and slowly answered as if facing the death squad, "No, that's not what I mean. I enjoy your company, and let's face it, you are the most beautiful woman in the county."

"Well, I can tell that was really easy for you to say." Suzanne teased. "But to be honest, I've grown to like you, and I really do enjoy our time together. So why the long face?"

"Truth is, there just ain't no future in us spending time together. You are kind and thoughtful and everything I would want in a woman and I have deep feelings for you, but it just isn't meant to be."

Suzanne nuzzled her horse next to him and leaning closely, she lifted her lips to him in a way that Thomas couldn't refuse. When the kiss ended, she pulled her horse around and bantered, "As for our future, Mister Wilson, I strongly disagree with you." Then heading out, she yelled, "Bet you can't catch me."

Thomas could never turn down a challenge and quickly urged Champ to catch the woman he knew he would have to let go.

The sun slowly sunk below the treetops releasing flickers of light on the beautifully manicured rose garden where Frank Olliver Sr. sat with his wife and daughter. The rose garden with its tiled walkway and luxurious terrace was magnificent—a work of perfection. Relaxing in his favorite chair and nursing a glass of Kentucky bourbon, Frank laid his glass down to speak. "Suzanne darling, I've been gone a spell, but I do keep up with you. Don't you have something to share with me?" Frank already had begun to slur his words, and Suzanne frowned as she realized that he would soon be in a state of drunkenness.

"What is he up to now?" she whispered to her mother. "Papa, I don't know what you're talking about."

Frank slowly poured himself another glass of liquor and glowered, "Darling, I know about your morning adventures."

Suzanne could feel the severe disapproval of his words and knew that she had better find a way to pacify him. "Papa, I'm a grown woman and I can take care of myself."

Frank took a deep draw from his glass and laughed sarcastically, "Don't be so defensive. A beautiful woman needs an escort, or should I say bodyguard. Just make sure you keep it that way."

Suzanne hated his insinuation especially since Thomas had questioned her using the same exact word.

Frank jerked a chair next to Suzanne and came so close she could smell the effluvia of alcohol. He took her hand and clearly voiced his proscription, "Darling, this escorting is over. You won't see that man again. You understand?"

Judith, his wife, cleared her throat and spoke determinedly. "Frank, you're drunk. This can wait."

Frank got up and hurled his glass to the tiled surface sending shattered pieces in all directions. "We don't associate with the Wilsons! None of them!"

Suddenly Frank's demeanor shifted and with a malevolent smile, he continued, "They are the scum of the earth, and I will have no daughter of mine associating with them."

At those words Judith stood in defiance and faced her husband. "You have no right to say those dreadful things. Thomas seems to be a fine young man. Your problem is not with the Wilson family; your problem is with Lott." And then she whispered, "No, that's not right, the problem is you."

"You don't know what you're saying, and you better respect your place in this family, Wife."

Judith dropped her head knowing that it was useless to talk with him in his state.

Frank then took a step toward his daughter. "You heard your mother. What do you have to say about all of this?"

Suzanne struggled with her tears, but formidably faced her father. "I want the truth, Papa. I've heard you had his brother, Jake, murdered to gain some poor Choctaw's property. I hear that you steal and cheat to get what you want. I also hear you are a womanizer. Is all of this truth? I don't want to believe what I hear, but I don't know what to believe when I see such anger. Tell me, Papa. Tell me none of this is true."

"Well, darling, you will just have to make your own choice, won't you." Frank poured himself another glass of bourbon then he staggered toward the house but stopped and raised his glass to his wife and daughter. "I will say that you both have made this an interesting homecoming. Just remember Daughter, be careful of the choice you make. If you need an escort, my foreman can do the job, and if you choose to disobey me, I just may take care of the problem in another way. My foreman might just ride up one day on Thomas taking advantage of you which means he would have to be shot on the spot. Wouldn't want a Wilson hurting another one of my children, would I? And darling, that's not a threat; it's a fact. So be careful about the choice you make."

Suzanne began sobbing as her mother took her into her arms. "Mother, why is he like this? He wouldn't really hurt Thomas, would he? How can you stay with someone who has such hate in his heart? Why don't we just pack up and move to the Low Country? You know your heart is there."

"Hush my sweet baby girl, I was raised Catholic, and we don't believe in divorce. He's drunk, and his heart is filled with hate for so many reasons. The worse is the way Rebecca left Frankie at the altar because of her love for John Wilson. We just have to make the best we can of each situation."

"Will he do what he says?" sniffled Suzanne.

Judith hugged her daughter closer. "I'm sorry to say, but I'm afraid he will. You best get word to Thomas to stay away."

Suzanne's heart was broken, and she knew how much she would miss her time with Thomas. "Mama, I may be in love with him. I don't know if I can bear not seeing him again."

"Sometimes you have to protect the ones you love. I know that too well. If you care for Thomas, you won't see him again and you will try to forget the feelings you have for him."

As dusk approached, the flapping of wings let Lott know the chickens were roosting for the night. He could hear the soft sound of distant thunder and see a dark cloud on the western horizon. Slowly dusk became darkness and the songs of the tree frogs and locust reverberated through the woods. Lott loved this time that allowed him to rest after a good meal and reflect on the day's work and make plans for the future.

Tonight John heard the squeak of the rocking chair and detected the soft scent of his father's pipe. He walked out on the porch to spend some quality time with the man he held in both respect and admiration. For a while they enjoyed the comfortable silence until John noticed a stir down the road. "You hear that, Papa? Sounds like a rider."

"Mighty late to be out and about, Son." Lott replied, taking another draw from his smoke.

Through the darkness, the two saw a Negro man straddled on a mule ride up to their porch. "Mister Wilson, I'm Leon from over at the Olliver place. Please excuse me for interrupting you all, but it's shore important that I see Mister Thomas."

Lott was puzzled about Leon's need to see Thomas at this time of night, so he walked a little closer. "Maybe, I can help you."

Taking his hat off, Leon nervously answered, "Sir, in all respect, I gotta see Mister Thomas personally."

John shook his head and wondered what Thomas had gotten himself into this time.

Lott pointed to the barn. "I expect you better head that way. He's got a room down there. You best identify yourself when you get to the barn. He is still a might skittish since the war."

Securing his mule, Leon walked down to the barn and headed to the light flickering below one of the doors. "Mister Thomas! This here is Leon from the Ollivers. I need to talk with ya."

Thomas laid the book down he had been reading, picked up his lamp and slowly opened the door. Holding the light where he could see, he recognized the man.

"What you doing out so late and why do you need to see me?" asked Thomas. Thomas saw from Leon's expression that it was a consequential matter so he invited him in and directed him to a seat.

"What's so important that you would come here at this time of the evening?"

Leon took a deep breath and squeezing his hat said, "Sir, this has just got to be between me and you. I'd get in trouble if'n anyone hears about this."

"Well, go on. You can trust me."

"Mister Thomas, Mas Olliver, he knows 'bout Miss Suzanne riding with you, and he got angry as a snake. He told her that if'n she rode with you again, he would send his foreman, Mister Junior Barrett, with her; and if'n you showed, he would kill you on the spot and claim he rode up on you taking advantage of her. Mister Thomas, that Barrett is one mean white man." Leon took another big breath and continued. "Miss Suzanne, she told me to tell you not to meet her no more."

Thomas, shaking in anger that was difficult to contain, muttered, "That man is Satan himself. Who does he think he is? Someday someone's gonna kill him as repayment for all the ones he has cheated and had killed. My Uncle Jake would be alive today, if it weren't for him."

"Sir, I needs to be going," Leon said, getting up from his seat. "I can trust you, can't I?"

Thomas reached over and took his hand. "You can trust me, and thank you for the warning."

As Leon was making his way down the steps, he turned back. "Most forgot, Miss Suzanne say she's sorry, and for you to remember what she said the other day."

There in the silence of the night, the wind began to whip around the corners of the old barn and rain began to pepper the roof overhead as Thomas sat contemplating his dilemma. It angered him the way Frank Olliver belittled his family, but he had known all along that a relationship with Suzanne was as likely as lightning on a cloudless day. But those beautiful brown eyes continued to haunt him as he finally slept. During the night the roll of thunder and flashing of lightning ignited the war demons, and his nightmares returned. Satan was certainly enjoying the ride, and one day Thomas knew the bottomless pit would swallow him and never spit him free again.

5

The Race

In the morning, Lord, you hear my voice; in the morning I lay my
request before you and wait in expectation.

—Psalm 5:3 NIV

Mid-September brought excitement to the Little Rock community. Talk about the races continued to escalate and everyone had an opinion about each facet of the event. Thomas, although infuriated by Frank Sr.'s ultimatum, quickly refused to dwell on Suzanne and put all of his energy toward making the races successful because he knew failure would rob his family of their home and property. Toby, Andy, and Thomas planned to butcher five hogs which Toby would roast, and the women gathered a fifty gallon kettle normally used for making syrup but now would be used to cook the pork stew. They planned to bake at least fifty large rolls of bread.

As October drew near, all plans were completed and autumn swept in crisp fresh air, a reprieve from the sultry, humid summer. The day before the races brought anxiousness and continual lifted prayers that tomorrow the riders and spectators would come. After a day of work in Decatur with Mister Everett, John reined his horse at Walker's store making sure Rebecca's father was prepared for the next day's events. As he stepped from the store, he felt a bony arm reach from behind the door and grasp his neck. Shaking loose, John turned, clenched his fist and prepared to draw back when he heard a familiar chuckle. Smiling in front of him stood Timothy Johnson, his old and faithful friend and fellow soldier. John pretended to swing a punch but grabbed his friend in a big hug instead.

"Where have you been you ole rascal? I thought you had vanished," said John still amazed.

Tim, a slim man, shorter than John, well-groomed and dressed like a Southern gentleman began to laugh. "John, I was down in New Orleans at my business, and word got out that there was gonna be some kind of a big race up here."

"Business!" laughed John. "You mean you were gambling."

"I prefer the term, gaming. You know I am the best at it, don't you?"

"Oh yes, I certainly know that, but why the fancy clothes here in the country?"

"Well, the women seem to relish my new image, and you know I am always available."

John and Tim had a good laugh and headed to a bench on the store porch to reminisce and converse about the coming event.

"Tell me something Tim, did you truly hear of our race down in New Orleans?" asked John.

Distracted by a pretty young woman who had just arrived to shop, Tim got up, tipped his hat and opening the door with a warm smile, he eloquently recited, "Good day, my fair lady. Timothy Johnson at your service."

She smiled self-consciously then cast her eyes downward and mumbled, "Good day, Sir."

Tim swooped his hat down in gesture and said, "Yes ma'am, It is a good day when I see such beauty."

John just shook his head as the woman hurried into the store without a backward glance.

"Yes, the word has reached New Orleans, and yes, Timothy Johnson is strictly up here for business. You know what I mean?"

"I have a pretty good idea that you mean gaming and chasing pretty ladies."

Tim smiled broadly and gave a good chuckle. "You know me well, my friend. I haven't decided which I will pursue first, probably the latter."

John shook his head. "You'll never change, will you? Oh by the way, if you need a place to stay, we have an extra room."

"Thank you, but I ain't seen Mama in a spell so I'm gonna go check up on her."

As he shook hands with John, he paused. "John, ain't nobody around these parts knows horses like you. Do you think you could give me the low downs before the race?"

John shook his head. "Tim, you know me better than that. I'll have no part in cheating."

Placing his foot in the stirrup, he tipped his hat. "Well, my friend, it don't ever hurt to ask. See you at the track."

John watched him ride away as thoughts of their friendship filled his head. *How different we are, but I love him like a brother. Not only did we grow up here in Little Rock, but fighting alongside a friend brings a commitment that never can be separated by dissimilarities.*

As John approached the house, he saw Rebecca and Sister waving vigorously, and Sister quickly ran to meet him.

Gasping for breath, Sister placed her hands on her knees and sputtered, "John, they're already coming."

Holding the reins tightly, John pulled his horse in and dismounted. "What are you talking about?"

Rebecca, a little slower getting there than Sister, reached out and hugged John. "They've been coming all afternoon. Wagons, buggies, folks with horses and even children. John, there's got to be at least a hundred folks down there. Look behind you. Here comes more!"

"Where's Papa?"

Sister caught her breath and began to bubble with excited chatter. "Knowing folks would need fire for cooking, Thomas and Papa have been loading up the wagon with firewood and carrying it down. They told us to tell you to get on down when you got home. We're supposed to stay here and direct folks as they come in. There is so much to do. Can you believe it? Isn't it fantastic? Oh, how God has blessed us. And the weather is great. It's going to be perfect!"

John gave a chuckle, and Sister clasped her hand over her mouth realizing her excitement was spilling over. John put one arm around Rebecca and the other around Sister and walked them back to the house then headed out to help.

All afternoon and into the early night, the procession continued. With all the excitement and constant arrivals, the family could gather little sleep. Thomas finally arrived at ten that night with news of at least five hundred people and rumor of more on the way. He was especially glad to report the fine looking horses that were arriving. With that news Lott lifted his hands upward and prayerfully said, "God has surely granted us a blessing."

A slight westward breeze permeated the morning as dawn broke clear. The men began working to get people to the proper locations. The smell of roasting hogs and the fragrant odor of stew hovered in the air and coaxed the people to the tracks. Toby and his family, working during the previous afternoon and through-out the night preparing the meal, feared that the feast would not be enough.

Lott stood momentarily on the hillside overlooking the swamp bottom below. A low haze of smoke from the numerous campfires hung above the tree tops, and below he saw that a city had risen overnight. Covered wagons, open wagons, buggies, and multitudes of people dotted the campsite. Some were sleeping, some preparing breakfast, and most were just socializing - embracing friends and meeting strangers. Children were running, shouting and playing, and even a band of local Choctaws were camped down by the creek. The most amazing and awesome sight for Lott were the masses of horses receiving brush downs and feedings. Many horses were magnificent thoroughbreds and some just common looking work horses. Lot began to smile and chuckle as he saw the problems of the post war South and the anxieties many were experiencing dissipate as people enjoyed life in Mississippi again. His heart could not contain the joy he felt amidst the laughter, singing and plinking of a banjo. It seemed that the world and its troubles had ceased, and Mississippi was returned to a place of happiness and closeness. The majority of people were not entering the races but were here to forget and frolic, and that was soothing to his soul.

Thomas approached the starting stand with an armload of hickory poles, so Lott called out to him. "Morning Son, you been here all night?"

With a tired smile, he threw the poles down and headed to greet his papa. "Yes sir. You 'bout ready to get this race on the way?"

Lott looked at his pocket watch then mounted the platform to welcome the crowd and begin the races. Thomas handed up their old double barreled shotgun which had been loaded with powder, wadding, but no shot. Cocking both hammers back, Lott pointed toward the sky and let both barrels loose. The loud blast startled the people, and all got quiet except for men grabbing their horses to restrain them from bolting away. All knew that this must be Lott Wilson and the racing was imminent. Men, women and children began to congregate, and Lott cleared his throat before shouting, "Morning folks. It's our pleasure to have you here today. We have some fine horses, and I hope this will be a day you'll never forget."

The crowd applauded and cheered. "Now I know you smell those hogs roasting, and over there in that kettle is some of the best stew you'll ever put in your mouth. After the preliminary race, around two o'clock, you will be our guest for dinner."

This time the crowd roared their approval and a couple of gunshots rattled. "Now, it's about seven thirty. For those racing, you can register and pay your fee to the gentlemen down below at that table. This will also be where the winners will collect their winnings. At this time I want to meet with only those racing in order to go over the rules and procedures."

Lott waited for those racing to step forward. "Men, when you sign at the table, you will receive a number. Due to the width of our track, we can only run five in a heat. To be fair to all, my son Thomas will draw five numbers from a large bucket that contains all the numbers of those competing. When you are riding, you are to be fair. There will be no forcing a horse off the track or using any whips on horses or riders. At the beginning of the race, Thomas will check each rider to make sure no one has a whip, but if someone does use a whip, he and his horse will be disqualified."

Thomas stepped up boldly next to his father and holding a hickory club in his hand said, "Gentlemen, this is gonna be a fair race. And spectators, you too will not cause any disturbances that might spook a horse. If I see any of you taking an unfair advantage, you'll have to deal with me and this here peace stick. You understand?"

All was quiet for a moment as the riders thought over what had been said, and one tall skinny man with a tobacco stained beard and flop-brimmed hat raised his hand. "Mister Wilson. Could you perhaps find you a skinny stick? I plan on being fair, but sometimes my mare has a mind of her own. You know what I mean?"

The grounds shook with laughter as the men moved to the table to register with Mister Walker and John.

Lott shouted out, "Get your horses and riders ready. The races will begin at nine o'clock. If your number is drawn, be prepared to line up, and if your number is not drawn for the first round, stay prepared because it won't take long to race the mile."

At nine o'clock, Lott fired his shotgun again and the drawing began. Thomas drew out the numbers, called them out and then assisted the riders to the track. Once Thomas was sure all was in order on the line, he stood away and watched as his father raised his starting pistol to begin the race.

Before firing the pistol, Lott shouted, "Folks, you need to edge at least ten feet from the track behind those markers. It will be mighty dangerous for anyone who is foolish enough to get close to the tracks. Parents, watch your children closely."

Lott quickly looked at Thomas and received the nod to begin.

"All right, men. Get your horses prepared." Lott pointed the gun upward, hesitated, then fired. The riders bolted their horses forward as people cheered their delight. The horses kicked up dirt as they sped down the track.

Thomas looked over the five horses to pick a winner. He noted that two were American Standardbred and one was a Morgan, but he knew the winners would come from the long legged thoroughbreds. With his knowledge of horses, he could almost predict each winner.

Mister Walker looked over to John. "You won't believe this, but we have exactly seventy five horses registered. You realize what you'll be clearing on this race?"

John thought for a moment then his face brightened with a smile. "Yes sir, we've cleared four hundred and fifty dollars."

Elated, Thomas Walker reached out his hand to congratulate his son in law. "Yep, right on the head."

Beaming with joy, John not only was glad that they would be keeping their land, but was happy that Rebecca's father had actually had some kind words for him. Thomas Walker had wanted his daughter to marry Frankie Olliver because he knew of the wealth that Frankie would inherit. He was upset when John returned home to end the dreams and plans he had for his daughter. John knew that not only had Mister Walker been upset, but Frank Sr. planned revenge on the ones who had caused Rebecca to leave Frankie at the altar. John remembered that in a way, his childhood friend had seemed relieved as he left the church without a word of anger and headed to his grandfather's plantation in Louisiana.

Lot knew that it wouldn't take long to run off fifteen races and was right as they concluded a little after noon. He once again held up the double barreled shotgun and fired into the sky. "Folks, gather round. We have our winners of each race, so now we are going to take a break for a little over one hour. Riders, get your horses rested and ready because we'll begin the grand races at one-thirty. There will be three rounds and from those rounds we'll have a final race for the Champion."

As Lott made his way down the steps, a man approached him.

"Sir, that shotgun of yours is kinda spooking the folks," the man said as he reached into a pouch strapped on his waist and brought out an old tarnished brass bugle that he handed to Lott. "This thing will do the job, and it won't put the scare on folks."

Lott took the old instrument and looked it over. "Where'd you get this horn?"

The gent was ready with his story. "When I was about eight, my father went with Travis to the Alamo. Well, you know that it didn't work out so good. When it was all over, my mama and Aunt Lucy loaded me in their wagon, and we went to San Antonio to give my papa a proper burying. When we got there it was over, and I don't know what them Mexicans had in mind, but they had burned all our Texicans, including my papa. They was still burning 'em when we pulled up. Most of the army had moved on, and folks was loading up the dead Mexicans when I walked over to one of 'em. He had a funny look on his face, eyes kinda glassy, and he had his arm reaching up with that there bugle clinched in his fist. Well, I figured he wanted me to have it, so I sneaked it under my coat, and sir, you got it now."

Lott held it up in reverence. "I don't know how to play this thing."

"Me either." the man said. He turned to look where John and Mister Walker were talking and called, "Hey, sonny boy, get up here and learn how to toot this horn."

John glanced sheepishly at the man, then walked over to him and took the bugle in his hands. He puckered his lips, placed them on the mouthpiece and let out a loud blast.

The man laughed heartily and nodded his approval. "Tis yours, young man."

"Where're you from, stranger?" Lott called out as the man quietly slipped away.

"I was born a Texican, but we moved back to my mama's folks near Vicksburg. So that's where you'll find me these days."

John followed the man with his eyes as he walked away then he studied the old tarnished bugle. "Papa, where'd this bugle come from? It's a little like a cornet that I tried to play one time."

"John, you better hold on to it. It came from San Antonio, Texas, and is bathed in blood. Son, it came from the Alamo."

At one thirty, John brought the bugle to his lips and created the most raucous sound imaginable. Dogs tagging along with their masters began howling while two old mules down by the creek joined in the ruckus. Folks soon realized that the old shotgun had been replaced, and actually as John improved, they began to enjoy the noise the old bugle made. Excitement electrified the air, and people began naming their favorites. Since there were fifteen winners, it was decided there would be five heats of three riders, then the five victors would compete in the final race for the Grand Champion. Soon all five races were completed, and when the dust cleared, five champions were announced and congratulated. "Folks, it is time to rest and enjoy this fine barbecue we've prepared for you. So head on over to the food, and I do hope that there is plenty for everyone that is hungry. After dinner at about five o'clock, we've planned a sprint race prior to the Grand Championship race. Riders, remember this is your time to rest and prepare your champion horses."

A man called out to Lott, "What's that there sprint race like?"

"We've been running a one mile race. A sprint race will be a race on a straight away of one quarter mile. We want to see which horse has the fastest starting speed. You understand what I mean?"

Another man called out. "The thoroughbreds seem to be taking it all."

"A thoroughbred is good for the distance, but that don't mean he's quick on the run," explained Lott.

"Where do we sign up, Mister Wilson?"

"Same as usual, down at the table. Same rules, same winnings."

Mister Walker shook his head as sixteen horses were registered. "Don't say it. You folks just picked up at least another eighty dollars. I know, the Lord does wondrous things."

John patted his father in law on the shoulders and rose to leave. "Got to go get Dusty ready for this next race."

Mister Walker was glad he had agreed to help when Rebecca had asked him. He had wanted to repair the damage he had done when he withheld the letter that had come from John before Rebecca and Frankie's wedding. He really thought that he had done it with her best interest in mind, but now knew being untruthful with his daughter had come close to destroying their relationship. He was glad that it seemed Rebecca had finally forgiven him.

A long line congregated at a large table where Mrs. Walker handed out golden brown, sliced bread, and at another table Toby and his wife Sadie and son Andy served the pork. Finally the line curved to the large kettle of stew being dipped by Sarah, Rebecca and Sister. Like the miracle of the feeding of the five thousand, the food seemed to hold, and everyone who had brought a plate or been able to secure a plate, got a serving.

At three thirty, Lott took the bugle and puckered his lips and did his best to trumpet the folks in. Since only sixteen horses were entered in the sprint race, Lott decided to run four at a time. Thomas again did the drawing and the first heat was in line. After the first race, Thomas drew John's number. As John led Dusty to the track, no one paid any attention to the short, stocky, unusual looking horse. Thomas checked the riders and then came up to John and whispered, "Remember, let him have his rein. Lean low and give him the freedom to run."

Lott fired the pistol and Dusty bolted quickly at the starting line. John leaned low over the horse's neck and within seconds was in front. The spectators were amazed at the victory by the small stocky horse.

After the other two competitions, it was time for the championship sprint race. One of the winners sat high on a long legged thoroughbred which made Dusty seem even smaller. "I'll show you how to race. That squirt won't have a chance," muttered its rider.

John remained calm and patted Dusty on his neck. Thomas checked the riders and again walked to John and whispered, "Loosen the reins. You held him back in the last race. Remember, we want to market these animals. Turn him loose."

Thomas lined the horses up and stepping away, he winked at John.

The spectators were enjoying the new style of race and began shouting to the riders. Lott held the pistol toward the sky and fired. Dusty jumped ahead and sped down the track leaving the other horse behind. At the half way point, he was two lengths ahead and crossing the finish line, he had increased the lead by four lengths. All watched in awe as John reined the little horse triumphantly back down the track, and the crowd began cheering loudly supporting the victor. The man on the thoroughbred headed over to shake John's hand. "What kind of a horse is that?"

John shook his hand and smiling, proudly said, "Sir, this is a mustang from out in Texas, but to tell you the truth, it's been mixed with a horse out west called a quarter horse. Now a quarter horse has a tremendous outburst of speed, so you've got the durability of the mustang and the quick speed of the quarter horse. You got the best of both."

"Beats all I've ever seen. I'd like to have one of those."

John pointed to Thomas. "See that man over there? This is his horse, and one of his mustang mares folded the other day. You might want to talk with him."

John headed to the winner's table. "How'd we do, Mister Walker?"

Walker scribbling down the figures, finally laid down his pen. "Well on the three that you didn't run, you cleared a total of sixty dollars. The one you took, looks like thirty because you had to pay ten to enter. Then on the championship sprint, you made sixty. You just made yourself one hundred and fifty dollars for a grand total today of six hundred dollars. I am proud of you, Son-in-law."

Lott watched the sky deepen with shadows and knew the final championship race must begin. He grabbed the bugle and was able to produce a better sound. The people quieted in anticipation as the riders advanced to the starting line. Thomas carefully checked them over then stepping away, motioned to his father. Lott raised his pistol, hesitated, then fired, and the crowds roared as the race was on. The thunder of hooves echoed down the last stretch as neck to neck the horses fought to the finish line. By a head, a dark red stallion took the victory, and after taking a cantor around the track for people to see, the rider reined him to the platform. Lott welcomed him up and clasped his hand. "Sir, what's your name?"

Elated, the gentleman drenched in sweat and dirt smiled and shouted, "I'm Joseph Peterson from up Memphis way, and that beautiful speedster down there is Hot Fire! Ain't he something!" Once again the crowd reacted with shouts and cheers.

Lott, reached into his pocket and pulled out five twenty dollar gold coins and laid them in the victor's hand. Clasping Peterson's hand in his, he lifted it up and exclaimed, "Ladies and gentleman, this is our champion!" The roar of applause and cheers could be heard throughout the campsite.

Before people began dispersing, Lot addressed the crowd for the final time. "Folks, before you go, I want to thank you for coming and I hope you enjoyed yourself."

A roar of approval, clapping of hands, and smiling faces warmed Lott's heart. "Now don't be too quick to leave. We still have pork and stew left, and about sundown, we have a string band coming in. There's still fun to be had, so stick around."

6
The String Band

I sought the Lord, and He answered me; He delivered me from all my
fears. Those who look to Him are radiant; their faces are never covered
with shame. The angel of the Lord encamps around those who fear
Him and He delivers them. The Lord is close to the broken hearted and
saves those who are crushed in spirit.

—Psalm 34: 4, 5, 7,18 NIV

As night approached, some of the locals made their way home, but most stayed to enjoy a night of music and fellowship. The campfires and lighted lanterns dotting the bottom land reminded Thomas of the many nights he spent camping with the Army of the Northern Virginia; soldiers huddled around their fires, cooking a meal, laughing and soon dying.

John had been so busy during the races, he did not get to visit or rest, so he settled in his hardback chair at the registry table and decided to close his eyes for just a few moments. Lott and Sarah had headed back to the house to have a few minutes of solitude before the music began.

"Hey, Johnny Boy, you alive?" came a voice John recognized. Opening his eyes, Tim stood in front of him holding a large roll of money.

"Where'd you get all that?"

Tim eased down in the chair that had been vacated by Mister Walker, placed his arm around John's shoulder and dangled the roll in his hand for John to see. "You know John, I am a professional and am very good at gaming."

John pushed his arm away and frowned. "Timothy Johnson, you don't know squat about horses. How'd you know how to bet?"

"You be sure and thank your brother for me."

"Tim, you're lying. Thomas wouldn't cheat for you."

Tim laid the roll on the table. "You see, John, when you play poker, you learn to read your opponents' facial expressions. All I had to do was watch Thomas as he examined each horse. When he hesitated and took a second look, I knew the horse was a winner."

John chuckled and shook his head. "Still sounds pretty much like cheating to me."

Tim began to laugh. "Cheating! You cheated too!"

John stared at Tim with disbelief. "What are you talking about? I didn't even place a bet."

"Well, answer me this. You all arranged that sprint race and you rode that mustang. You knew good and well that you'd be the victor. You blew those horses off the track and took the winner's money. Now that is pretty much the same as what I did, don't you think?"

Seeing the race in a different light made John realize that maybe they had planned that race to win, but still there was always the chance that the mustang would lose.

"Tim, I thought you were gonna concentrate on the skirts, not gaming."

As John spoke, a young woman by one of the campfires cast Tim an inviting look. Tim rose and bowed to her. "My friend, you have a lot to learn. One must be able to use his talents and manage his time. There is no reason on this earth that I can't handle both gaming and the fairer sex. You know, I'm very good at both."

John waved him off. "That I know well, but just don't involve me in your shenanigans."

Tim laughed and whispered, "No worry there. Now watch this professional in action."

John watched Tim approach the young woman and heard his melodic voice. "My, why is such a beautiful young lady like you left alone on such an amazing night. You know, the band will be playing in a while, and I would love to have a dance with you. It would truly make my day."

Almost as if on cue the strumming of a banjo, harmonized by a mandolin, guitar, fiddle and bass fiddle, brought the night to life. Tim smiled at the young woman as if he had planned the exact timing and took her arm to lead her to the music. People who had brought chairs and benches carried them to the bandstand while others rolled logs to the area. John, Rebecca and Sister headed in that direction and stood clapping in rhythm as the band lifted their spirits.

Soon John noticed Tim walking his way and alone, John chuckled and quipped, "I guess she didn't care for all those fancy words?"

Tim, surveying the crowd joined in John's merriment. "Now, I think you might be wrong. She seemed to light up to those words, but her boyfriend seemed to have a few fancy words just for me, and I thought it wise to fold that hand and try my luck somewhere else."

As Tim noticed Sister standing beside Rebecca, his eyes widened in astonishment. Sister in a bright yellow dress interlaced with soft white flowers and her long blond silky hair flowing to her waist enchanted Tim. He walked to her and in a melliferous voice began his spill. "Sister, you are like a beautiful red rose opening its petals. Would you care to dance?"

Sister, shook her hand lose, lifted her nose up and answered, "Timothy Johnson, your smooth talk won't work on me. I know exactly what you are after and I am not interested. You take your philandering ways somewhere else."

Tim nudged closer to her and whispered, "Now Sister, you know that I may be a philanderer as you call me, but you are nothing but a gossip and a meddler."

Sister reached back to slap him, but Tim caught her hand and smiling softly said, "Looks like this is one man you will not be able to handle."

Rebecca became concerned with their behavior and quickly turned to John. "Don't you think you need to step in before they make fools of themselves?"

John shook his head, smiling, and to Rebecca's surprise he whispered, "This has been going on for years. You may think that they despise each other, but to tell you the truth, they enjoy this bantering."

Not relenting, Tim eyed her and continued. "You know your problem? You really ain't much of a dancer. That's why the other boys don't ask you."

Sister crossed her arms around her waist in indignation and muttered, "You know that's not the truth. You wouldn't know the truth at all because of all your lying ways."

Tim stepped up in front of her and held out his hand.

For a moment, Sister turned her face away from him and then with a hint of a smile took his hand. "I'll give you one dance, and you better not do any hugging. If you do, I'll kick that peg leg of yours so hard, it'll end up in that creek over yonder."

John watched the squabble and began to laugh so much he could barely contain his shaking, but quickly covered his mouth to keep Sister from hearing.

Rebecca just looked at John totally confused about his sense of humor. She finally asked, "What's so funny?"

"Didn't you observe the whole altercation? Sister played right into Tim's hands. You know, he's a professional skirt chaser and my dear sister just got caught."

Rebecca still did not see the humor and frowned at John for laughing at his sister. "How do you know that maybe your sister didn't orchestrate the whole situation to her advantage. After all, she is dancing, and Tim is a pretty fine looking man."

"You may be right." John continued to chuckle as he watched the way the two seemed to really enjoy each other despite the previous raillery.

As John finally got his laughter under control, Thomas quickly approached John. He had Levi, a friend who was both larger and stronger than Thomas, with him and they both carried hickory clubs. Thomas handed John a club and said, "Come on, we got trouble."

"Is it serious?" Rebecca asked.

"Nothing we can't handle," Thomas said.

As the three walked away, Thomas informed John that there were some men at the south end of camp tipping the bottle. Lott and Sarah, enjoying the music, saw their sons heading back to the track, and Lott knew they might be facing some trouble.

"What's going on?" asked Lot.

"It looks like we are needed at the track." Thomas didn't elaborate, and Lott knew his son could probably handle any disturbance.

"You need me to help?"

"No, Papa. We've got it. You both need to relax and enjoy the rest of the evening."

As Thomas, John and Levi approached the track, they saw a large bond fire and heard loud laughter and shouting. The three advanced toward the partiers. Startled, one of the drunks staggered and fell on the fire and quickly rolled over to the opposite side with his clothes smoking. Thomas grabbed a club in each hand and banged them loudly together. "I'm glad you men came down here for this race today, and it has been a great day, but you ain't gonna spoil it by letting your liquor make you foolish."

All was quiet as Thomas walked around eyeing each man individually. "Now, you can drink yourselves till you fall over dead, but if we catch any of you bothering any of the folks up there, you're gonna get a head smashing. Do you understand what I'm saying?"

Several of the men who had served with Thomas and John during the war stood erect and saluted and with slurred speech, answered, "Yes Sir, General Wilson! If'n we cause trouble, we get us an old fashion head bashing."

Patting one of the clubs across his hand, Thomas stood silently eyeing each man again. Trying not to laugh at the men's drunken, bazaar behavior, he said, "At ease soldiers. You men go on with your business, but remember what I said."

As they were leaving, Thomas noticed that the man who had fallen over the fire was actually catching on fire. Thomas grabbed him and threw him on the ground and began rolling him in the dirt. One of the other drunken men had a bottle of corn whisky and was trying to pour it on the man. Thomas quickly secured the bottle and yelled, "Don't ever put whisky on a burning man, you hear? That stuff is like dynamite. You want to blow us all up?"

Thomas took the bottle, uncorked it and poured it into the fire, and the man watched as the flame quickly rose high and became hotter. "You see what I mean. If that bottle had gotten hot enough, it would have exploded shooting glass everywhere."

John came closer to Thomas. "Well, you definitely took care of this problem."

Thomas shook his head. "Night's early, John. I feel there's more to come."

Rebecca had left Sister to visit with a friend, and Tim headed to get a cup of coffee. Sister noticed five Yankee riders approaching her way. Soon the soldiers were standing near, and she was immersed in the smell of liquor. Ignoring them, she turned toward the music.

In moments, she felt someone touch her hair and as she turned, she saw one of the soldiers eyeing her. "You are just the woman I've been looking for all my life. Let's you and me do some dancing."

"No thank you," she politely said as she took a step backwards.

The soldier quickly reached for her arm. "You ain't turning me down, Missy."

Sister jerked away again and looked directly in his eyes. "Sir, I said that I didn't want to dance with you."

The soldier raised his hand to strike her when suddenly he felt cold steel touch the back of his head. Terrified, the man didn't flinch as he listened to the voice behind him.

"You make one move, and I'll blow a hole through your head. You understand?"

He slowly nodded his head.

"Now you and me are going to take a walk. Whether you live or die depends entirely on you. Now let's walk."

Sister called as Tim led the Yankee away, "Please don't kill him, Tim. It will just get you in trouble."

With the pistol still held at the man's head, Tim called back, "I'll kill him in a split second if he doesn't do as I say."

Tim headed directly to Thomas and John. "Men, I brought you a trouble-maker, and there are four more federal soldiers up by the bandstand."

Thomas was not pleased at the intruders. "This ain't good. You get those Southern drunks down there meeting up with them drunken Yankees, and there'll be trouble for sure. Somebody might get killed. John, you and Levi stay down here and don't let any of those men leave the tracks and don't let anyone else go down there. I'm gonna go see what I can do."

Thomas identified three privates and a sergeant enjoying the music. He recognized the sergeant and quickly went to his side. "Evening, Sergeant."

The sergeant turned and extended his hand. "You're Thomas Wilson. I met you at the depot down at Newton a while back."

"Yes sir, that's right."

"You've had a good day it seems, Mister Wilson."

"Yes sir, we have, but we have a problem now. A big one."

The sergeant squinted up at Thomas. "What's that?"

Thomas cleared his throat. "I hate to say this, but I need to ask you and the other federal soldiers to leave."

The sergeant was not happy about that news. "I understand this is a public gathering and we are public. You have no right to ask such. As an authority, I can stay down here as long as I desire."

Thomas looked directly into the man's eyes. "Sir, it's like this. Down at the south end of the campgrounds is a bunch of Southerners getting drunk as skunks. We just warned, actually threatened them, that they better stay at the tracks and behave. As long as they stay down there, I think all will go well, but if'n your boys wander down to the tracks or if those drunks come up here, I'm afraid someone will get killed. Lot of those men down there were Southern soldiers, and it won't take much to stir them up. We also need to think about all these innocent people enjoying themselves. They might get caught in the crossfire. We've had an outstanding day with no trouble, and I sure don't want it to end with a lot of folks getting killed."

"Wilson, as much as I hate to leave, you are exactly right. I'll round my men up, and we'll be leaving. Thank you for sharing this with me."

Relieved, Thomas took out his handkerchief and wiped his face.

Soon the sergeant returned. "Wilson, I can only find three of my men."

Tim, overhearing, pointed to the starter's stand. "Sir you'll find one soldier that way."

Frowning, Thomas whispered, "Did you have something to do with this?"

Nonchalantly, Tim smiled. "He needed to learn the lesson of how to treat your sister like a lady. That's all."

The sergeant quickly strapped the unconscious man on his horse thinking he was so drunk he had passed out.

Thomas walked to Sister and Rebecca and decided it was time he enjoyed the music. A familiar scent engulfed his senses, and he turned to see two large beautiful brown eyes staring up at him. Smiling, she said, "You miss me?"

Thomas's eyes met hers. "What are you doing here?"

"Is that all you have to say?"

"You know you don't belong here. Nothing good will come of your visit. What about your father?"

Suzanne reached over and placed her arm under his. "Father's out of town. I just got back from Natchez with mother, and I was hoping I would get a chance to talk to you so I had Leon bring me over in the buggy. He's waiting out by the tracks. I need to know if you talked to my father."

Thomas frowned. "Suzanne, you are making no sense. As far as I know, I've never even had a conversation with your father. I am not sure I have ever met him face to face. Are you losing your mind?"

"He just said something the other night that made me think you may have talked to him."

Hearing a slow waltz, Suzanne whispered, "Since I am here, do you think we might have one dance before I leave. You may not ever get another chance."

Thomas stuttered, "I'm really not much for dancing."

"I didn't ask you how well you danced. I asked you to dance with me."

He placed one arm around her waist and holding her other hand gently in his, he pulled her as close as possible. They danced to the slow rhythm, and Suzanne felt safe and complete in his arms.

At the end of the song, Thomas walked Suzanne to the awaiting buggy. He longed to kiss her and hold her but instead quietly helped her up into the buggy. "You know this is goodbye, don't you?"

"I know. I just had to see you once more. I had to let you know in person how sorry I am about my father's attitude toward a man he doesn't even know. But it's best for us both. Good bye, Thomas. Please don't forget me."

John and Rebecca looked at each other questioningly as Thomas and

Suzanne left together. Rebecca whispered to John, "What in the world is going on between those two?"

Leaning over, Sister whispered to them, "They've been riding together early in the mornings for over a month."

"What!" John exclaimed. "How do you know that?"

Sister laughed. "Oh, I have my ways of finding out the news, especially when it comes to my big brothers."

Around midnight, almost all the guests had vacated, and the rest were packing up to leave or heading to the campsites to sleep. John, Rebecca and Sister walked to the house, but Thomas stayed on the porch in a rolled up blanket just in case there was any more trouble. The peaceful night gave Thomas time to contemplate his conversation with Suzanne and the futility of their relationship. Sometime after midnight, his exhaustion welcomed for a first time peaceful sleep void of the usual nightmares. With dawn on the horizon, Thomas suddenly awakened then quietly took his blanket and headed to the barn to continue resting.

The morning sun shone above the treetops, and Lott welcomed the day by nursing a cup of steaming coffee and rocking in a porch chair. Slowly wagons and horsemen began to make their way out, crossing right in front of his house. Lott enjoyed waving a good day to each as almost everyone expressed their thanks and desire for another horse race. Before noon he began to hear the family stir in the kitchen preparing a late breakfast. Lott quickly headed to join his family.

Lott entered the kitchen carrying four cigar boxes. He sat at the head of the table, opened the boxes and begin counting the money collected.

"Papa, I already know how much money is in there," John remarked.

"Well, I plan to count it anyway."

While Lott counted the money placing all the gold coins in one spot, silver in another, then separating the greenbacks from the acceptable bank notes, the rest of the family began to excitedly share all the happenings from the previous day.

Finally, Lott interrupted with the news of the exact amount. "You won't believe this, but we made seven hundred and twenty dollars!"

"Seven hundred and twenty dollars! Can't be! Mister Walker and I counted every bit that came in. It should be six hundred minus the fifty we paid the string band. You might better count one more time." voiced John.

Lott quickly recounted his stacks. "John, I don't know what happened, but I still get seven hundred dollars. That's exactly one hundred fifty more than you and Mister Walker counted."

They could hear Thomas as he swung open the door and entered the house. "Hey, I'm starved; is there anything left to eat here?"

"Come on in, Son. We got a fine breakfast just waiting for you," Sarah welcomed.

As Thomas settled into breakfast, Lott mentally calculated the race money and realized that they had too much money.

"Son, you know anything about extra money we seem to have in our money boxes?"

. "Well, Papa, I did a little betting."

Lott was upset that Thomas had been gambling. "Who'd you bet on, Son?"

Dipping him some grits he replied, "No horse I would ever bet on except Dusty."

Sister whipped back, "Where'd you get money for betting?"

"I kinda borrowed a little from the box when John and Walker weren't looking."

Sarah popped him on the hand and remarked. "Thomas, I am disappointed in you. That is cheating and gambling. You know both are wrong and go against what our Lord teaches."

Thomas laid his spoon down and placed his hand over his mother's and jestingly said, "Mother, you always said that the Lord giveth and the Lord taketh away. The way I see it, is the Lord gave some of those fellows a good bit of money, and I thought it best to take some of it away."

All sat speechless, then Thomas continued, "Mama, I don't plan to keep it. I just thought we could help some of our neighbors keep their land too."

Sarah started to smile, "Son, you know that this noble cause of yours does not make it right to cheat and gamble, but for this one time I am going to forget that you did this because there sure are families in the county that will be grateful for your help come December. I love you, Son, but remember I'm only letting this one time slide."

At that the family decided that the majority of the extra money would be used for any family who could not pay the taxes this year. They felt good that their neighbors would be able to keep what belonged to them. Then Lott reached for the hands on each side as they all united in prayer around the table. "Lord, we feel mighty blessed this day for your mercy and the plan you gave Thomas. We pray that you will help us to give the money wisely to those who are in greatest need. Please help us to follow your Son's teachings and to always serve you first."

When the prayer was finished, Thomas noticed the old brass bugle lying on the shelf next to the stove. He headed toward the shelf, brought down the bugle and examined it. "Where'd this come from?"

Lott told him about the man and the story that he shared about the Mexican bugle from the Alamo.

Thomas shook his head. "This ain't no Mexican bugle. It's too short and curled. This here is one of our own. It's a Texican bugle."

"Not so," John said. "The fellow took it from the hands of a Mexican."

"John, didn't you know some of those fellows who fought in the Alamo were of Mexican decent? As a boy, that man didn't know who he was seeing. I'm telling you, it's one of ours," Thomas assured.

Early on Monday morning, John rode to Newton to catch a train to Meridian while Lott and Thomas headed to Decatur to see the tax collector. Paying their taxes would be like lifting an enormous weight from their shoulders and returning music to their hearts. As they entered the small village, thankfulness pervaded their faces.

Here in Decatur several years ago, General Sherman was almost captured by a group of Southern cavalrymen. Ironically, he was saved by hiding in a corn crib. Now after the destruction he had wrought on the South, Lott felt that even with the chaos caused by the new government, maybe Mississippi could become the safe and secure state it had once been. He had seen the return of love and fellowship at the races yesterday, and it brought back to mind a time before the war had begun when life was hard but very good.

Securing their mounts, the men walked inside the two story frame building and searched for the tax office. They found the sign and saw an elderly woman with tiny glasses sitting at a desk. "Can I help you gentlemen?"

Lott and Thomas removed their hats in respect. "Ma'am, we're here to see Mister Davis."

The woman stood up and said, "You are truly lucky. Mister Davis has been out of the state for the last month, but came back yesterday. I'm Cathy Clarke, and who should I tell him is calling?"

"Tell him Lott Wilson is here to see him."

In a moment the woman returned. "He will see you now."

Mister Davis rose cheerfully and extended his hand to Lott and then Thomas. "Gentlemen please have a seat. I thought I'd be seeing you before long."

Reaching for a box, he continued, "Would you care for a cigar?"

"We're here strictly on business," Lot responded.

Davis pushed his glasses up and smiled. "I guess you gentlemen would like for me to assist you in selling your property. You are certainly fortunate. I think I have a buyer and can guarantee you a fair price."

Thomas looked over to his father and grinned. "Yes sir, Mister Davis, I think you could say we are indeed fortunate."

Lott pulled out a leather pouch and brought out ten dollar gold pieces one at a time and began laying them on the table in stacks of ten. "That's three hundred and sixty dollars."

Lott slid his tax notice to Mister Davis and seeing Mrs. Clarke, he motioned her in. "Now, Mister Davis, if you will write paid in full and place your signature on the form, and Mrs. Clarke, I would like for you to place your signature as an official witness."

Davis reluctantly signed the notice and after Mrs. Clarke had finished, slid the form back to Lott. "Where did you get that kind of money? It's pretty impossible to get that much money here in the South."

Rising, Lott extended his hand to Davis. "Mister Davis, it is good doing business with you. To answer your question, the Lord giveth and the Lord taketh away. But this time the Lord gave it to us, and our new and kind government is taking it away. Bless the name of the Lord. And Mister Davis, when you see the Lord one day, I hope He has mercy on you and all those like you, because you are going to need it. Hopefully, you will repent of your wicked ways because God does forgive."

As the men walked away, Davis called out. "Sir, you gave ten dollars too much."

Thomas laughed. "We want you to have that so you will remember the day that a Mississippian found victory against an enemy."

Lott put his arm around his son, and they left the office knowing that God had certainly granted them a miracle, and hopefully, it would be a miracle for everyone in the county who might lose their land.

As they exited the door, they saw Ed Harmon, one of their neighbors, standing outside the tax office. "You don't look like you're feeling too well. You sick or something?"

The man looked down and cleared his throat. "Well, I ain't too well. I'm sick of this here government robbing us blind. I got a tax notice that I can't pay, and I guess I'm here to plead for mercy. If things keep going like they are, most of us folks gonna lose everything we got."

"How much do you need to pay the taxes?" asked Thomas.

The man remained silent for a moment and then answered, "I've got it all except for forty-five dollars."

Lott and Thomas started grinning. Lott reached in his pouch and brought out the necessary moneys and handed it to Ed. "The Lord has been mighty good to us, and all we ask is that when you are able, you help a neighbor in need too."

Tears began forming in Ed's eyes. "Lott, I don't know if I can ever repay you for this loan. I just don't know how to thank you for what you are doing."

"You misunderstood me. This ain't a loan, Ed. This is a gift from Heaven meant just for you. So the one you need to thank is the Lord."

Ed gratefully smiled and nodded his thanks then headed into the tax office to secure his land.

"Well Papa, looks like we got a few more places to stop and some deliveries to make today."

"You are exactly right, Son. Let's go take some good news to our fellow Mississippians."

7

Bloody Hands

For I am ready to fall and my sorrow is continually before me. For
I confess my iniquity; I am full of anxiety because of my sin. Do not
forsake me, O Lord; O my God, do not be far from me!
—Psalm 38: 17 –18, 21 NASB

This Sunday was dinner on the grounds, and the Wilsons busy with preparations hastily dressed for church. The women carried large portions of fried chicken and a heaping bowl of creamed corn. Loading the wagon, each family member settled into their favorite spot for the ride to church. The leaves had turned a brilliant shade of yellow and gold and were interspersed with the deeper reds and oranges. Autumn brought the crisp cool weather that made the world fresh and new, a reminder of the beautiful world God had created for man.

The church yard was its usual congested, festive gathering filled with welcoming voices and excited chatter softened by the sound of the pump organ calling everyone to cease the conviviality and enter the church. Parents rounded up the children at play and made their way to the church door, each heading to their own family pew. As he entered, Thomas scanned the pews until he located the beautiful brown eyes then quickly nodded at Suzanne and looked away. The shuffling finally settled and the service began.

After forty minutes of singing, the preacher, Rev. Tad Phillips, dressed in a black suit and white shirt, leaned over the pulpit and grasped the corners as his deep voice intoned, "Welcome Brothers and Sisters. Today we will discover why God sometimes answers our prayers with a definite no, but his mercy is sufficient. Let's look at the life of King David. David's greatest desire was to build his Lord, our God, a temple, but God said 'No.' Why does God refuse our desires? In David's case, God knew that Solomon, David's son, would be the one to build the temple because he would be a king of peace. David's reign was one of war, and God knew that the timing and circumstances were not right, so He said, 'No.'"

The tall thin preacher gripped the podium and leaned forward and shouted, "David's hands were of blood!" The congregation sat up a little straighter and began to listen intently.

Again the preacher paused, took a big inhalation of air then calmed his voice. "As a youth, David was the only Israelite with courage to slay Goliath, the Philistine giant, for David had faith that God was with him. David took five stones and killed the giant, then drew the giant's sword and cut off his head to bring victory to the Israelite nation over the Philistines. David began with his hands covered in blood, so God said 'No.' Many years later, David's fame as a warrior had grown and everywhere David went, he heard the people chanting 'King Saul has killed his thousands and David his ten thousands.' Yes, brothers and sisters, David had blood on his hands."

Images of war quickly filled Thomas's mind as the preacher relayed every conquest of David. Smoke was floating over the battlefield; the wounded were crying for relief as they lay dying. Thousands upon thousands were dead. Thomas began to perspire, and his mind took him to the moment he could not find John. As he frantically searched, injured men held out their hands for mercy, but Thomas had none to give. Then he saw a man he had shot, he knelt beside him and shuffled through his pockets. Thomas could hardly breathe as he saw the picture of the man's family. He lifted the picture in his hand, and blood had saturated the picture and was on his hands. The blood of the man he killed covered his hands. Thomas saw faces of dead men and knew each had families who loved them. His hands were becoming engulfed in blood, blood he had wrongfully taken.

Sister could feel Thomas begin shaking and noticed how he stared at his hands, so she quickly placed her hand on his and whispered "Are you all right, Brother?"

Thomas jerked his hands from Sister's and continued to stare at his hands.

The preacher's voice increased in volume. "Worst yet, David, this man after God's own heart, seduced a woman and had her husband killed in battle to cover his sin." The preacher paused, grabbed the podium, leaned forward, and called out, "Once again blood was on his hands."

At those words, Thomas quickly stood and rushed from the church.

Lott looked at his family and nodded for them to come with him. They left the church and saw Thomas heading through the woods.

"What should we do, Sarah? Do you think he will be okay?" Lott considered the option of returning his family to church, but knew finding Thomas was necessary especially since he was evidently distraught.

"Let's go home and see if he's there." Sarah was overcome with concern for her son.

As they began toward the wagon, Suzanne came running toward them. "Is Thomas okay?"

"We don't know. In church, he started shaking and gasping for breath and then just stood up and left," Sister softly said.

"Will it be okay if I come with you?" Seeing the worry on her face, Sarah nodded her up.

At the house, Sarah rapidly searched each room hoping to find him but knowing this search would not solve his problems. The others went to the barn and quickly realized that Thomas had made it home, because Dusty was missing.

John shook his head and frowned. "Thomas probably just needs to be by himself. I think its best we leave him be. That sermon probably just brought back bad memories. He'll come home when he's ready."

Lott replied, "I suppose you are right, Son. He needs to do some serious talking to the Lord, and then we need to find a way to help him."

"Can I borrow a horse? I guess I need to be getting back to the church, or maybe I'll just head home. I'll have Leon return the horse this afternoon." Suzanne wanted to find Thomas but knew her mother would be expecting her at the church dinner.

"You sure you don't want to come up to the house for a while?" Lott asked.

"No, I best get to the church so I can explain my absence to my mother."

Suzanne knew the sermon would probably last another hour and then there was dinner on the grounds, so she decided to ride for a while toward Big Woods to look for signs of Thomas just to make sure he was okay. She took the path often traveled on their morning rides and seeing some fresh tracks spurred her on further. As she traveled down the Little Rock Creek, her head told her that this was probably a bad idea but her heart kept her going forward.

Thomas sat with a pistol in his hands and tears in his eyes. He knew he had blood on his hands and God had answered him "No, no mercy for a murderer like him." He slowly took the pistol in his right hand and raised it, pointing it close to his head as he slowly pulled the hammer back. In turmoil, Thomas held the gun there and hesitated a moment, wondering how it would feel to end all of his nightmares and visions of the families destroyed because of his killing. *Justice demands a life for a life, he thought.* As he continued to seek relief from his guilt, the faces of his loved ones flashed before him and also the beautiful brown eyes. Thomas slowly lowered the hammer and brought the pistol back to his lap.

Where the creek met the Little Chunky River, a high bluff overlooking a series of waterfalls cascaded beautifully over small boulders. Suzanne stopped and decided to turn back toward the church so her mother would not be worried. She whispered a prayer for Thomas and as she finished her prayer, some movement at the base of the creek caught her eyes. Dusty was standing by the creek lazily grazing with reins dragging the ground. Suzanne scanned the area and saw Thomas on the top of a nearby hill overlooking the falls. She pushed her horse upward, and at the crest, she found Thomas sitting crossed legged on the ground, head down and holding a pistol in his right hand. She quietly dismounted and sat down beside him. She took the pistol from his hand and quietly held his hand in hers. After a few moments, she spoke, "Thomas, what can I do to help you?"

The pain in his eyes startled her. He pulled his hand gently away and looked directly into her eyes. "Don't you know there is nothing that you or anyone can do for me? I told you, we have no future. You need to let me be. That's what you can do for me."

"I'm not going to leave you, Thomas. I'll just stay for a while and when you are ready to head home, then I'll go too."

Suzanne and Thomas sat for quite a while in silence until Thomas spoke, "Don't you understand. I am the one who has blood on my hands. I killed men who were husbands and fathers."

"Thomas, the war wasn't your fault. You did what all soldiers do. You had no choice."

"You still don't get it, do you? I did have choices, everyone has choices. I chose to kill; I never saw men as fathers, brothers, husbands, and sons, just as enemies. I gloried in killing the enemy, and I was good at it."

Thomas stood up and pulled Suzanne to her feet. "I'm headed home and you need to do the same. Don't come looking for me again. My problem is not yours, and I don't plan for it to ever be."

Suzanne was crushed by his pain and the words he spoke, but her heart was already prepared to face the futility of a relationship with Thomas, but she had hoped for at least friendship. "You promise me you will be okay and you will head straight home."

"Yes, I promise. And Suzanne, thank you for coming here, but remember nothing good will come from us being together."

"Thomas, I'll send the pistol back with Leon this afternoon when he returns the horse I'm on. Don't ask me for it, because it's staying with me. You talk to your family about this. You need to get some help."

Thomas watched Suzanne leave and then he returned to his spot on the crest and agonized over his life and began explaining to himself each facet.

Even as a boy, I could out shoot everybody, boy or man here 'bouts. When I joined the army, it wasn't long before they knew I had the ability and desire to kill so they made that dream possible. On the firing line, most just aimed and fired toward the masses across the way, not knowing if they hit anyone. Not me, I picked my target, aimed, shot, and watched my target fall. Everybody was giving me recognition for my skills building up my pride until killing became my identity. It wasn't long before the officers noted my skill. One evening, when I was ordered to report to the Colonel's tent where I was given a Whitworth, a scoped musket with a range of over six hundred yards and one of the most accurate muskets made, I knew I had found my calling—a sharpshooter for our regiment. I quickly learned to look for Yankee officers first, especially those on horses, next was the flag bearers who kept the lines in order and then the Yankees manning the cannons. The scope gave me the advantage, but also gave me an image of each man's face, the very faces that haunt me now. I climbed on trees and boulders, anywhere I could get a good look at the white of their eyes never even thinking that these were God's children too. Yes, I was the hero—the hero who killed and killed and killed. Then that day at the second battle of Bull Run, while General Jackson was holding his own behind an unfinished railroad, I was ordered to accompany a regiment of Calvary and move up to our right flank on some high ground. I wish I had never found that large oak tree nor killed that officer on horseback. I can still see him through that scope, see him falling to the ground and hear the cannons aimed in my direction retaliating. And when General Longstreet showed up hitting the federal left flank, forcing the Yankees to run for their lives, all settled, but the bodies and cries for help were all that flooded my eyes and ears. On the field was the man I had killed. The picture he carried made me realize that I wasn't killing the enemy, I was killing men—men who were important to someone back home. That's when I left it all, but those images will never leave me. What can I do to change what I've done? Absolutely nothing. There's nothing I can do to atone for my sins. God will never forgive me because I will never be able to forgive myself. Even if God would have mercy on my soul, I could never ask for forgiveness for what I've done. I don't deserve anyone's forgiveness or mercy. I am beyond all mercy. I am hopeless."

Thomas rose to leave and carried his nightmares with him. He walked toward Dusty and knew that no one could make the images of war leave and that no matter what he did, the blood on his hands would remain.

Had Thomas remained at church, he might have understood that the message had been for him. The Reverend continued his sermon to those remaining in the church. "Yes, David had blood on his hands, and God did not allow him to build the temple, but God did forgive him. Even though David suffered the consequences of his sin, God never left him nor forsook him. God gave David mercy and forgiveness, and today, Christ's sacrifice is sufficient when we have blood on our hands, when we have sinned and hurt others. God will cleanse our hands and restore us. In 1st Chronicles 21:13 it says, 'Let me fall into the hands of the Lord; for great are his mercies.' God told David he could not build His temple, but David was able to prepare his son for the task and was able to collect needed supplies for the temple. David was truly blessed by God, and he continued to live in God's mercy just as you and I must do each day of our lives."

8

Goodbye Again

Unless the Lord build the house; they labor in vain who build it.
— Psalm 127:1 NASB

Lott grabbed his thick woolen coat, slouch hat, and a steaming cup of coffee and sauntered toward the barn. He slowly sipped his coffee as he leaned on the split rail fence overlooking his corral. A white velvety frost glistened brightly on the ground in the early morning sunlight. Crows nosily sang down near the corn field alerting other birds to the copious feast while a lone hound yapped energetically far off in the woods. The corn stalks now brown and shriveled were bare. It had taken a full week, but Lott, Thomas and Toby had loaded wagon after wagon with corn and deposited it into the corncribs until the overflow demanded the building of another crib. Lott loved watching the young colt nursing as the morning peace renewed his spirit with wonder at all that God had fashioned. Warm sun enveloped his face, and Lott knew that the warmth and the joy it brought was one of the many blessings of God in his life.

"Morning Papa," Thomas interrupted the silence and placed his arm around his father. "Great day, isn't it?"

"Couldn't be better, Son. Couldn't be better."

The two stood quiescently for a spell then Thomas said, "You know, with the corn in, I think I'll take me a long ride today, maybe get Mama to pack me some ham and biscuits and make it a day. What do you think?"

Lott smiled at his son. "I'd say, go for it. If my old back didn't give me so much trouble, I'd come along with you. Before you leave, let's talk a little about the horses. This breeding, raising, and training horses takes some time, and I'm afraid at this rate, it'll take years to develop a herd. That man from Memphis who won the races; he wants a mustang now. Since we have a little extra money after helping our neighbors in need and with the good crop of corn, what do you think about investing in some quality mares?"

Thomas shook his head in agreement. "Sounds sensible to me, but for now, I'm fixin' to saddle up and head out."

"One more thing, Thomas. I'm depending on you, Son. You know that John loves law and feels led in that direction. Your mother and I need you, so when you have a problem, you need to come and let us know. We couldn't bear losing you, Son. We love you too much."

"Papa, I love you and Mother. I'll be okay; you don't need to worry about me. Now, I am looking forward to a day of riding. Be back this afternoon. That's a promise."

Thomas saddled up Bet, not an especially attractive horse, but one that definitely showed promise. She was somewhat shorter than Dusty but more muscular and seemed to have great stamina. Once saddled, Thomas cantered her past the fields and then with a kick, they sped toward Big Woods. Thomas kept a tight rein on the mare as he trained her abundant energy by slowing her pace as they made their way to the creek. Even though winter had stripped most of the trees of their leaves and the woods felt more open, wildlife still scampered around with little regard for intruders. When Thomas reached the falls on the Chunky River, he dismounted and led Bet down to the river for water. He let the mare graze on the tender grass nearby while he sat down in his favorite spot to enjoy one of his mother's ham biscuits.

Near noon Thomas remounted and led Bet to the place where the Little Chunky River flowed into the Big Chunky River. Here he planned to head east into a large bottomland forest owned by the Ollivers. Frank Olliver had built a hunting cabin years ago, but word was that he used it more for meeting women and drinking than for hunting. Thomas had only seen the cabin once as a boy and decided to investigate to see if it was still standing. He wandered about the massive oak and hickory trees that dotted the way, thankful for the peaceful day.

Suddenly a shot disturbed the silence, and Bet balked as Thomas listened to make sure a hunter was not near. Several squirrels scampered away to safety as Thomas heard two more shots and then the loud boom of a shotgun. Thomas knew that those were not the sounds of a hunter. As more shots rang out, he recognized the sounds of a pistol, shotgun, and musket. Then an eerie silence made Thomas think that he should head a half mile northeast to check out the situation and to make sure all were fine. Slowly and carefully, he pushed Bet in the direction of the shots and began to smell the faint scent of burnt powder in the soft wind. Thomas rode out of the flat woods and sloshed through a stream and then up a sandy slope until he came in sight of the old dilapidated cabin. At once he knew there was trouble as he pulled Bet to a stop, reached for his pistol and cautiously dismounted. A haze of smoke still hung in the air, and in front of Thomas was a sorrel favoring a bloodied front leg and nearby lay a man face up with glassy eyes. Over to his right another horse lay on its side with a man trapped partially under it and a pistol on the ground next to him. Thomas then saw a Negro man sprawled over a woodpile. In front of the old shack across a grassless yard lay an elderly Negro man and beside him stood a small Negro boy crying. A double barreled shotgun was still clutched in the man's motionless hand.

Thomas tried to catch his breath and regain his composure before slowly heading toward the young boy. Before he reached the boy, Thomas spotted out of the corner of his eye another young Negro boy somewhat older, shabbily dressed and standing near the old woodshed with a musket in his hand.

Raising his pistol and aiming, Thomas shouted, "Better put that thing down! I ain't here to hurt you."

The young boy slowly laid the musket on the ground and took a step backwards.

"You take part in this shooting?" Thomas called.

"No suh. I ain't fired a shot," the boy replied shaking with fear. "Them white folks started the whole thing."

Thomas reached down and picked up the musket, smelled the barrel, and seeing it was not loaded, knew it had not been fired. Pointing to where the small child sat, Thomas said, "Come on over with me. We need to talk."

"What happened here? Are either of you hurt?"

"No suh. We are okay."

Thomas suddenly realized that he had not looked closely at the men and went back to see if any of them were breathing. He recognized the man on his back as Junior Parker, Frank Olliver's foreman. Seeing the bullet hole above his right eye, Thomas knew there was no need to check for a pulse. Then Thomas looked at the horse which was a fine thoroughbred that belonged to Frank Olliver. Thomas shuddered as he realized who was probably beneath the horse. He leaned down and tried to move the horse enough to see if there was a chance the man could be alive. From what he could surmise, the horse and rider were hit by direct shotgun fire, and he was pretty sure he would be looking at death. Thomas was able to get the man free, and his heart beat vigorously as the man's face came into view. Frank Olliver, Suzanne's father, was gone and no matter how harsh Frank Olliver had been, Thomas could only imagine the grief Suzanne and her family would experience.

Thomas turned and found the older boy sitting next to the younger who kept both hands covering his face. Thomas placed his pistol back into the holster and walked to the boys. "What are your names?"

The older one answered, "Jack's my name, and the young 'un here is Seth."

"Do you know the one over there by the woodpile?"

The older boy was close to tears. "That's Clemmy. He's our older brother."

"What about the old man?"

The tears began to roll down the boy's cheeks. "He's our paw."

"What's his name?" Thomas continued to gather information.

"My paw is called Skinner," Jack softly answered.

"Where's your mama? She about?"

"No suh. Master done sold her off four years ago."

"You got a last name?"

"I guess we kinda does. When Mas Olliver owned us, he named us all Ollivers, but when we got freed, Paw renamed us Jackson after Andy Jackson. Paw hated Mas Olliver. Mas Olliver had him horse whupped many a time for no real reason."

Thomas took a long breath and rubbed his chin. "You're telling me that you were Frank Olliver's slaves?"

"Yessuh, we all was his," muttered Jack.

With all the questioning, Seth never raised his head.

Thomas continued to try to get the story straight. "Tell me this, what were you folks doing down here?"

"When we got freed, we didn't know where 'bouts to go. Paw then thought of this old shack, and we decided to move in here 'til we could make some plans. We started a little garden out back, did some hunt'n and fish'n but 'fore long, the food got kinda slack. To eat we started killing some of them wild hawgs in the swamp."

Thomas walked over to an old chair and pulled it closer to the boys and sat down. He rubbed the perspiration from his face with his sleeve. "By the way, my name is Thomas Wilson."

Seth with big brown eyes raised his head up and faced Thomas. "I've heard of you."

"Well, I guess that's a good thing, but right now, Seth, I need to find out exactly what happened down here. Take your time. I want it straight."

"Well, Mas Wilson."

"Don't call me that. You can call me Mister Wilson or just Thomas."

"How 'bout Mister Thomas?"

"So be it. Now, tell me about it?"

Jack took a long breath then sighed and began. "Everything was quiet down here until we heard them horses outside. Peeping through the window Paw seen it was Mas Olliver and his foreman. Feeling the way he did, Paw picked up his shotgun and walked outside to meet him. Mas Olliver was talking hard to Paw about us living down here and killing his hawgs. Well, both talked some hard things, and Mas Olliver up and raised his pistol and shot Paw. Paw fell back on the porch and Mas Olliver shot him again. That's when Paw raised his shotgun and fired it straight at Mas Olliver, knocking both the horse and Mas down. Next thing that happened was Clemmy came up from the wood stack and shot at that other man."

Jack hesitated in thought for a moment, then continued. "Well, I couldn't see it all, but when it was over, both of 'em were down. That's 'bout all I knows."

Thomas walked away from the scene to think about what he should do. Returning to the boys, he asked, "Jack, can you ride?"

"Yes, suh, Mister Thomas. I can truly ride."

"That's good. Now listen to me and listen to me carefully. You take my horse and ride to Decatur as fast as you can and find Captain Jacobs. Tell 'em some men have been killed and that Thomas Wilson needs him here at this cabin as soon as possible. Don't you say anything about you being there and don't answer no questions. You hear me?"

Jack nodded his head. "See Cap'n Jacobs, bring him here, and keep my mouth shut."

Thomas slapped the horse on the back and said, "That's right. Now, get going."

Thomas knew what he had to do.

A small voice reached out to Thomas. "What's I s'pose to do?"

Thomas realized that he had forgotten about one detail - Seth.

"Looks like you are going to have to walk with me." He knew it was two miles to the Olliver place, but he could hardly leave the youngster behind. Thomas reached for the child's hand. "Come on, Seth. You come with me. By the way, how old are you?"

Seth looked up at Thomas with a hint of a smile. "I'm 'bout five. How old is you?"

Thomas smiled back. "Right now, I feel like maybe a hundred." Thomas soon picked Seth up and put him on his shoulders, and as they approached the Olliver mansion, he brought him back down. Taking Seth's hand in his, Thomas sighed as he thought about the news he would be delivering.

Leon could hear the dogs barking and knew someone was coming. He was surprised to see a white man and a small Negro boy walking hand in hand toward the house. As they neared, he recognized Thomas and the small boy and knew that something must be mighty wrong. He hurried to the house for Suzanne and her mother.

As Thomas neared the porch, Suzanne and Judith rushed out to meet them.

Suzanne exclaimed, "Thomas, what is this all about?"

Then recognizing the child, she muttered, "Is that you, Seth?"

Seth raised his head but said nothing.

Judith became apprehensive when she saw Thomas and the boy.

Thomas looked quickly at Leon and held Seth's hand toward him. "Would you please take the boy? I need to talk to Suzanne and Mrs. Olliver."

Judith realizing that she had forgotten her manners quickly spoke, "I'm sorry. Thomas, won't you come inside?" Judith directed them to the study next to the entrance, and they sat facing each other.

With a solemn face, Thomas asked, "What were Mister Olliver's plans when he left the house this morning?"

Judith first looked at Suzanne then back to Thomas and said, "Well, I don't know exactly. We didn't talk much, but I do remember him saying he was going down to the old hunting cabin. Something about someone staying there and killing some hogs. I didn't listen as well as I should have. I just don't know exactly what his plans were. Why do you need to know?"

"There is really not an easy way to tell you this, but your husband did go to the cabin and there was a problem."

"What kind of problem?" Judith was beginning to fear the worse and reached for Suzanne's hand.

"It was Skinner and his family who were living down there, and they had killed some of the swamp hawgs on y'all's property. From what I've been told, there were hard feelings between the two."

"Skinner. Yes, he and his boys were slaves here and there were incidents between the two. What happened down there, Thomas?" Judith asked clasping her hands.

Thomas glanced out the window momentarily and took a deep breath. "Harsh words were exchanged, tempers flared and people were killed."

"Thomas, just tell us. Who was killed? You aren't saying my father killed Skinner, are you?"

Thomas looked at Suzanne and then looked down. "Yes, Skinner and his son, Clemmy were killed as well as your foreman, Junior."

Judith gasped. "Frank is okay?"

Thomas shook his head, "No ma'am, he's dead too."

Judith began to loudly exclaim, "No, tell me it's not true. Surely he didn't kill them. He can't be dead. Maybe you are wrong."

"No ma'am, he was shot and he's dead. I am so sorry to have to tell you this."

Suzanne began to look closely at Thomas. "What were you doing down there? Were you involved?" she whispered, fighting tears.

"No, I was just training a horse and heard shots. I wish I could have gotten there sooner. Maybe it could have been prevented," he answered clearly trying to make sure Suzanne understood that he had not been there.

"Look, I know you need some time. I am going to check on Seth. If I can do anything, you let me know."

Leon and Seth were waiting. Thomas told Leon what he knew and asked him to keep Seth until it was decided where he and Jack would be living. Thomas then asked for a wagon and team to go back to the cabin to meet the captain and also to retrieve the bodies and bring them to the Ollivers.

Captain Jacobs and a detail of soldiers arrived at the cabin just as Thomas was returning in the wagon. Captain Jacobs beckoned Thomas to join him at the porch for questioning. Thomas told him all he knew and when questioned about Jack and Seth, Thomas replied, "Sir, I don't think they were involved, but I do think they saw it all." Captain Jacobs inspected the bodies and then talked to Jack and concluded as Thomas had that the young boys were not involved.

"Thomas, since everyone involved was killed, I don't see how I can take any legal action."

"Men, you get the bodies of these Negroes and help Jack bury them. I think I need to go talk to Mrs. Olliver now. I'll get a written statement from the boys and Thomas later. And soldier, you head out to wire for the undertaker to come to the Ollivers as soon as possible. Thomas, let's get the other two bodies in the wagon and let's head to the Ollivers."

Thomas pulled the wagon near the porch of the Olliver mansion. The bodies of the men had been covered with an old blanket taken from the cabin. Judith and Suzanne stood on the porch arm in arm clinging to each other.

"Which one is Frank?" asked Judith sobbing.

"The one to your right, Mrs. Olliver. You may not want to see him like this," instructed Thomas.

"You don't understand. I have to see him. He's my husband." she agonized.

"I know Mrs. Olliver, but I'm just so sorry you have to see him like this." Thomas understood her emotions and stepped aside.

Judith lifted the blanket, and after a moment, leaned down and pushing his tangled hair aside, gently kissed him on his cheek. She then reached for her handkerchief and softly wiped at the blood on his face. Leaning low, she murmured something in his ear and then clasping the blanket, covered him. She began to speak as if to no one. "You know, even with all the wrong he did, I still loved him. He could be really loving, too. I don't know how my life can continue without him."

Looking at Suzanne, she said, "Do you want to see your father?"

Suzanne wrapped herself in her arms and shook her head. "No, Mother. I want to remember him as he was."

"Captain, can you and Thomas carry Frank to the kitchen table and then take Junior to the table on the back porch?"

"Yes Mrs. Olliver. I've sent one of my soldiers for the undertaker. He'll be here soon."

"Thank you Captain, but I'll get Frank cleaned up and ready now."

Mrs. Olliver looked again at the captain. "I don't know who to tell about Junior. As far as I know, he doesn't have any kin or family here. Maybe the undertaker will know what to do when there's no family known."

Lott and Sarah were beginning to worry about Thomas and were relieved when they saw him riding up at dusk. "Son, where have you been? It's most night."

"Papa, I need to talk to the whole family about something. You think you can get them all in your bedroom. It's really important."

Because Frank seldom attended church, Judith decided to have a small gathering of family and close friends at her home and then carry her husband to her father's plantation in Louisiana for burial. Lott and Sarah felt that for Judith and Suzanne's sakes, they should pay their respects.

Dressed in their very best, the Wilsons pulled up to the front of the Olliver mansion. Leon was there to assist with the wagons. The small gathering had become a large crowd, and the house was filled with those who had come to show respect for Frank Olliver and his family. The Wilsons glanced at the beautiful furnishings in the mansion and then at the people who had come. Most were strangers and extremely well dressed, certainly not common folk like them. Lott knew some of them probably represented the railroad in which Frank had invested and others were perhaps business partners. As for neighbors, there were very few present.

Suzanne quickly met Sarah and took her hand. "It is so good to see you all here. Come on out of this crowd and let's go to the study." Suzanne led them to a room where Judith was greeting people as they entered to view the body of Frank, Sr. The long line winded into the next room. Both Suzanne and Judith were dressed in black and seemed to be handling the death as well as could be expected.

Lott looked at the body of Frank and memories flooded his mind. *You and I came into this country as surveyors. At one time, I thought we were friends, but we seemed to be on different paths. I know you had my brother killed because he wouldn't let you rob the Choctaws of their land. I can't prove what happened and as much as I feel sorry for you and your family, perhaps justice has finally come.*

John and Rebecca saw Frankie standing beside the beautiful oak coffin and were hesitant to approach him. As John's father and mother moved through the line to give their condolences to Mrs. Olliver and Suzanne, John and Rebecca followed. When they reached Frankie, he momentarily paused and just looked at them. He was now taller than John and had wide shoulders. With his clean shaven face, neatly trimmed hair and perfect facial features, he had become a very handsome man.

Frankie reached to grab John's hand and then gave Rebecca a hug. "It's good to see you both. I know it's been a while. I hope we can let the past stay in the past. I want to especially thank your brother, Thomas, for all he did. Before I leave to go back to Louisiana, I'd like to visit with you two, if it would be okay?" Frankie looked again at Rebecca, and his heart warmed remembering the special time they shared in the past.

"I think that would be great, Frankie. I've missed you," John said. John couldn't help but remember the love he had for his childhood friend. They were almost like brothers, camping together, fishing, and riding horseback. He really did miss Frankie and knew that no matter what had happened in the past, Frankie would always be close to his heart.

Frankie's eyes sparkled and his eyebrows lifted when he caught a glimpse of Sister. She was dressed in a dark purple skirt with a white high collared blouse. Her long silky blond hair touched her shoulders, and her sparkling blue eyes met his as he stood amazed. Frankie gave her a hug and whispered, "It's been quite a while since I've seen you. You have become even more beautiful."

Sister blushed as she looked up at him. "Frankie, I am so sorry about your father. If there is any way I can help, just let me know."

"I know this isn't the best time, but I would like to see you before I return to Louisiana. Do you think we might could get together for a ride?"

Sister hesitated then answered, "Frankie, I think it would be okay."

"I'll come see you in a couple of days, and we can go for a ride, if you would like."

As Sister left Frankie to talk to Suzanne, he could not contain the affection he felt for her. She had indeed become a beautiful woman, and he remembered Sister at the party his parents had given Suzanne. Even though then his heart had been captured by Rebecca, he still remembered the special dance he had with Sister. Frankie had known many women over the last years, but there was something about Sister that took his breath. She was definitely different from the others. For the first time since he arrived home, it was as if a bright morning light had lifted his soul. Frankie knew he should be feeling grief about his father's death, but it was difficult to mourn a man he hardly knew, a man who had only demoralized him and made him feel less than a man. His father's death had not really come as a surprise to him. Frankie knew that eventually his father's dealings would catch up with him.

Thomas gave Mrs. Olliver a hug and again expressed his sorrow. When Frankie saw Thomas, he shook his hand and thanked him.

Finally the family reached Suzanne where she stood as far as possible from the coffin. Sister and Sarah gave her a hug. As Thomas approached, Suzanne couldn't help but smile at his stocky build and cleaned appearance. Suzanne quickly took Thomas by the hand and led him to a connecting room.

"Thomas, thank you so much for being there to take care of everything. I really appreciate all you did."

"I'm just so sorry for you and your family and for having to bring you such awful news."

Thomas reached over to hug Suzanne, but seeing her lips he brushed hers softly with his then held her for a moment in his arms. "Suzanne, if you need me, you just let me know."

"This has been a terrible two days. You know, overall my father has always been good to me. There were times when he was difficult, especially when he drank, but there were also times when his love for me was abundantly shown. I know that you and your family must be relieved that he's gone, but I am going to miss him so very much."

"Suzanne, I would never want you hurt in anyway. I hope you believe me."

Thomas held Suzanne close for a few more minutes and allowed her to grieve for her father. "Suzanne, what will you and your mother do in the coming days?"

Tears again puddled Suzanne's eyes. "We haven't made a lot of definite plans yet, but I do know that Mama's heart is in Louisiana with our Papére. I am afraid we will be moving soon because we love New Orleans and the Low Country. There really is not much future here for us."

With a confused expression, Thomas asked, "What are you saying?"

"Thomas, I am sure that we will sell our home and property here and move in with my grandfather. Frankie has developed an interest in both Papa's and Papére's businesses, and he plans to set up an office in one of our suites at the hotel in New Orleans that Papére owns where he will manage both businesses. It's only a two hour ride from New Orleans to the plantation, so this way, the family will all be together."

Thomas felt a sadness creep over him. "What about us, Suzanne?"

Suzanne looked into Thomas's eyes then cast her eyes downward. "It just seems our timing is all wrong. I truly care about you, but I must go with my mother. She needs me now, and I could never let her down. I do hope that you will always consider me your friend."

Thomas gently lifted her chin up. "You know that the feeling I have for you is more than friendship, but I've known all along that what you and I have can never be. I wish you the very best, Suzanne. I am going to truly miss you."

Thomas placed a kiss on her forehead then hugged goodbye the woman he had grown to love and respect.

9

Blood Flows at Walker's Store

I have many aggressive enemies; they hate me without reason. Come quickly to help me, O Lord my Savior.

—Psalm 38: 19, 22 NLV

In a few days Frankie hitched a buggy to visit John and Rebecca in anticipation of spending time with Sister as well. The morning was filled with brilliant sunshine which mellowed the coldness and kept the air crisp. John and Rebecca were sitting on the porch relaxing after a hearty breakfast. When Frankie arrived, they welcomed him to the porch and began to share their lives and reminisce their childhood memories.

"I am really enjoying Papére's sugar cane business, and although I don't much like the actual work on the plantation, the accounting and management is quite rewarding. Since my father's death, I have taken over his business and didn't realize how much he has been overseeing. When I return to New Orleans, I plan to set up an office in Papére's hotel and handle both businesses. My other interest is political; several men in New Orleans have approached me about running for a political position, and I plan to study that possibility. What about you, John?"

"Right now, I am learning as much as I can about law from Mister Everett and am actually his apprentice. If Thomas continues to help Papa, then I plan to devote almost all my time to becoming a lawyer." John smiled at Rebecca then added. "We plan to have a family too. Not right now, but sometime in the near future. Do you have someone special in your life, Frankie?"

"Not really. There are plenty of beautiful women in New Orleans, but I just haven't found one that interests me in that way. I plan to wait until I find the right woman, but for now I plan just to enjoy the company of any pretty woman I find." Frankie chuckled and continued, "No, I really just want to get my life and career in order before I seriously think about the future with a woman."

"Is Sister here today?" Frankie asked sheepishly.

Rebecca raised her eyebrows. "Are you interested in Sister, Frankie?"

"Well, I just want to spend some time with her. She sure has become beautiful."

"I can't believe you think that about my sister. She is still just a baby in my mind, but there have been a lot of young men around here interested in her, so I guess I better start realizing that she is grown up and will be planning her future now. It sure is hard to see how life seems to move on and our relationships change. Hopefully, they will always change for the better. Frankie, I am so glad we can be friends again. I hope you will forgive me if I hurt you." John looked quickly at Frankie to see if their friendship survived all that had happened in the past.

Frankie was still smiling then nodding his head, he replied, "John, you will always be my first and dearest friend. Rebecca was always meant to be yours, and if I had known you were alive, I would have never even pursued her. I hope you both have forgiven me. John, I also am sorry my father paid someone to take my place in the war. You know that it was never my intention to run out on you."

Rebecca and John hugged Frankie, then Rebecca added "Oh, by the way, Sister has walked to Suzy's house. She will probably be on her way home, if you want to ride that way, or you can just wait here for her."

"I think I'll head out that way and give her a ride home."

Frankie climbed into the buggy and drove down the road until he met Sister. "Hello, beautiful. Would you like to go for a ride? Or at least I can give you a ride home."

"Hello, Frankie. It's really not that far from home, and I love to walk." Sister saw that Frankie was disappointed with her answer and added, "But a ride would be nice; it's such a pleasant morning."

Frankie stepped down to help Sister into the buggy next to him. "I still remember the dance we had together. I really enjoyed that time with you."

Sister settled herself on the buggy and moved a little away from Frankie. "The party was one of the best I've ever attended. I guess in Louisiana you attend balls all the time."

"Papére does enjoy entertaining. I would love for you to see his mansion. On the third level there is a large dance floor with a sky light that truly makes you feel like you are dancing under the stars. Maybe one day you could visit us."

"I don't think that will be possible. I am studying now to become a teacher and have a job here teaching. I really love the children and feel like what I am doing is important."

"There is always summer vacation."

Sister smiled and then they both settled into a comfortable silence as they neared Sister's home. Frankie helped Sister down from the buggy and let his arms linger at her waist. "I hope we can go out again soon."

"Frankie, I think that I would enjoy spending some time with you, but I really don't think there is much point in anything more than friendship since you will be leaving soon and I have my teaching job here."

"Friendship is a good place to start." Frankie smiled at Sister as he let go of her waist and thought of what an amazing young woman she had become.

Sister blushed and turned toward the door. She looked briefly back and said, "Thanks for the ride, Frankie. See you at church Sunday?"

Having neglected riding Champ, Thomas brushed him down, threw a blanket over him and then slung the saddle on his back. He stood in awe of the stallion's beauty as he led him from the stall to the open corral. Standing over seventeen hands tall, muscled and with soot black hair, the horse raised his head as if to let the world know he was a champion. As the morning sun showered over him, his ebony hair sparkled across his rippling muscles. Thomas mounted, then reached down to pat his neck and whisper, "My friend, you have got to be the king of all stallions."

Thomas sprinted him on the open road and again at the track and then headed to Big Woods. As noon approached, Thomas, satisfied with the workout, decided to return by Walker's store for a late cup of coffee and to mail a letter to the gentleman in Memphis concerning the purchasing of mares. A smile crossed his face as he saw Leon in the buggy which probably meant Suzanne was inside and he would get to talk with her at least one more time. Thomas dismounted and spoke to Leon as he secured his mount, then he removed his hat and entered the store with Leon to find Suzanne speaking with Mister Walker. Suzanne turned to see who had entered the store and her face begin to glow as she looked into Thomas's twinkling eyes.

"My, what a pleasant surprise," Suzanne said as he reached over to hug her.

"Morning to you. I say you look nice on this cool day."

Excusing themselves, the two walked to the woodstove to enjoy the warmth it emanated and to talk while Leon moseyed to the back of the store and sat on a bench to wait. "It really is good to see you, Thomas. We may be here several months while we try to sell our house and property. Maybe we can spend some time together riding again."

Thomas sipped his coffee and listened as Suzanne gave the details of their plans. Suddenly a harsh voice interrupted their conversation.

"Who in here owns that black stallion out front?"

Thomas turned and saw a federal officer, a tall stone faced lieutenant, standing at the front door with his hands on his hips.

Thomas raised his hand. "That's my stallion, sir."

"I want to see you outside at once," the lieutenant ordered.

Thomas frowned, and as he walked outside to check on this problem, he saw two other soldiers mounted on their horses. One was a young man who appeared to be no more than seventeen and was holding the reins of the lieutenant's horse, and the other was a rusty, mean looking corporal.

The lieutenant walked to Champ and began to inspect the horse. "This is some kind of fine horse. You say this is your horse?"

"Yes, this is my horse. Truth be known, it actually belongs to my father, Lott Wilson." Thomas shuffled uneasily worried about the lieutenant's intent.

"Well sir, the military needs fine horses like this. Yes, this is definitely a horse for our military." The lieutenant loosened the reins from the hitching post and began to walk with the horse.

Thomas quickly walked over and took the reins from the lieutenant's hands. "You are mistaken sir. This horse ain't for sell."

"You are the one mistaken," the lieutenant quipped and pulled the hammer of his pistol back. "I didn't say anything about buying your horse. Let's just say that you are donating this horse to our military. I plan to confiscate him now, and there's not a thing you can do about it."

The other soldiers seemed surprise at their lieutenant's unconscionable actions and were concerned by the determination on Thomas's face, because they knew that whatever happened would probably not be good.

Suzanne had come to the door to investigate. She stood trying to make sense of what was transpiring.

Thomas backed closer to the door of the store with Champ and motioned Suzanne back inside, then said, "There is no way you will take our horse. You are all thieves, and today will be the day that it stops."

Thomas reached in his pocket for a handkerchief to wipe the perspiration from his face, and before he knew what had happened, the Lieutenant had aimed his pistol and fired directly at him.

Thomas heard the blasts of the pistol, felt a gust of air engulf him and felt a flash of pain across his cheek as the bullet whizzed by. Then another bullet ripped into the door casing over his head sending slithers of wood as darts through the air. Without thinking, Thomas reached for the long knife on his hip and taking it by the handle, hurled it at the officer. The knife struck him in the chest and the lieutenant slumped over and fell to the ground. The horses were spooked by the gunfire and as the older soldier tried to gain control of his mount, he reached for his musket. Thomas quickly darted behind the lieutenant's horse.

The pause seemed like an hour as Thomas's life rushed before him. He was in battle now and looking for the enemy. Without a weapon, he would surely meet death today. Thomas glanced quickly around for options and saw the lieutenant's pistol lying on the ground beside the body. He dove for the pistol and lay flat using the lieutenant's body as best he could as a shield.

As a loud burst from a musket deafened him, he rolled, aimed and fired at the soldier. As the soldier was cocking the hammer back for a second shot, the soldier felt a force hit him in his lower neck, and he reeled from the saddle. He was dead when he hit the ground. With smoke in the air and horses whinnying, Thomas saw the lines of Yankee troops advancing in battle. He wildly looked around and focused on a lone Yankee and knew his job well—kill the enemy. Cocking the hammer back, he walked toward the young soldier who was trembling with fear. The young boy raised his hands and pleaded, "Please sir, don't kill me. I didn't have anything to do with this."

"You're a Yankee and a horse thief. This is war and you are the enemy; you don't deserve to live! All of these Yankee troops will die today. We will be victorious." Thomas shouted aiming for the boy.

"But sir, it's just me standing here, there are no troops coming. Sir, I'm only seventeen. Please don't shoot me; I want to see my mother again. In the name of Jesus, please don't do this!" he cried.

Suzanne had come outside and made her way to Thomas, and as she reached softly for his arm, she whispered, "Thomas, don't do this. It's over. Your war is over. He's just a boy."

"No, he's the enemy. I have to kill the enemy. Move out of my way!"

"Thomas, you are here in Little Rock. You're not in the war. Thomas, you're home." Suzanne reached out to hold Thomas in a hug and gently took the gun from his hand.

Thomas awoke from his hell and crumbled to the ground in tears. "What have I done? There is blood on my hands. When will this war end?"

The boy wiping tears from his face with the sleeve of his coat, muttered, "Sir, I'll tell the truth. The lieutenant started this thing. I promise I will tell the truth." He quickly turned and headed away. "Thank you lady, for saving my life."

Suzanne led Thomas to the steps on the porch. She noticed blood on his face and realized he had been grazed by a bullet. She quickly wiped the blood away with the hem of her skirt, hugged him close to her then whispered, "You're going to be okay, Thomas." She quietly prayed that his nightmares would end and that the Lord would hover over him and cleanse his tormented spirit. She continued to pray that this incident would not destroy his life.

In a few minutes, Thomas's breathing eased and looking over to Suzanne he said, "Where did you come from?"

"I've been here all this time. Don't you remember?"

Thomas shook his head. "No."

Thomas became aware of his surroundings, and as he looked around to get his bearings, he saw the two dead soldiers on the ground. His chest tightened and he asked, "Did I have something to do with that?"

"You really don't remember, do you? The lieutenant was trying to take your horse, and you tried to stop him."

"I remember that, but I don't remember killing anyone."

"Thomas, they initiated the whole thing. The lieutenant fired first. You were just protecting yourself."

Thomas seemed to relax and realized that some blood was on Suzanne's neckline. He pulled her collar back and saw a gash across the lower part of her neck. "You've been hit," he whispered.

"No, I think a splinter of wood struck me when a bullet tore at the door."

Thomas shook his head, "I remember everything now. I had to shoot them; that is what I was trained to do. They became the enemy. I could have just wounded them, but I killed them."

Thomas continued, "Suzanne, I know they started it, but you need to stay away from me. I will just bring you grief."

Mister Walker came out when he felt it was safe and was surprised to see Suzanne and Thomas on the porch with two dead soldiers in front of them. Examining the two on the ground, he confirmed that they were dead and then stood in front of Suzanne and Thomas. "You better tell me what happen, and it had better be good, or you both will be in a heap of trouble."

"Suzanne didn't have anything to do with this," Thomas spoke out.

"Well, tell me what you did, Thomas."

"They tried to take my horse, and when I tried to take it back, the lieutenant must have thought I was reaching for my gun. Anyway, he shot first and then a second soldier shot and the third soldier rode away."

"Son, you know this is serious. They will probably convict you even if it wasn't your fault. They are basically the law now."

Realizing the truth, Thomas quickly retrieved his knife, wiped the blood off, then mounted Champ. As he started to leave, he turned to Suzanne. "You tell what happened here and try to get the other soldier to verify it. You won't be seeing me anymore, so don't ever try to find me. It's time you forget me."

Thomas charged Champ straight to his home and ran inside calling out his parents' names. Hearing the panic in his voice, Lot and Sarah both came running down the hall. Seeing blood trickling down her son's face and his frantic state, Sarah asked, "What happened, Son?" Before he could answer, John and Rebecca joined them in the hallway.

"I've got to leave fast." Thomas hastily relayed the events that had occurred. "If I know them Yankees, they will soon be here looking for me. The only thing I can do is leave and find a place where no one will find me."

"Son, wait a minute. Didn't you say the young soldier said he would tell the truth about what happened?"

Thomas shook his head. "He's just a youngster. What if he don't tell the truth? They will sure put pressure on him, because they will want me to pay for those deaths regardless. You know how they feel about Southerners, especially a Southerner who kills two Yankees."

John eyed his father. "He's right. He's got to run to save his life. There's no way they will let him go, even if they know the truth."

"Where will you go, Thomas?" Rebecca asked clinging to John.

Thomas thought for a moment and said, "I can't go to Texas. It's under tight federal control. They'd track me down."

Lott ran his fingers through his scraggly white hair in thought. "I'll tell you where you might find safety until this thing blows over. You go to the Oklahoma territory and to the Choctaw lands. Your Aunt Hatta and her people will hide you. There are not many Yankees there, and the Indians are able to rule themselves. That might be your best choice."

"Well, Papa. I'll make a decision about where to go, but I'm not going to tell you. Don't even let them know I was here or that you know anything about the shooting."

Sarah began packing some food while John collected quilts and oil cloth. Thomas hurried to the barn to get his clothes and buffalo coat. He grabbed his sharps rifle, knife, and two pistols along with plenty of ammunition. When Thomas returned to say goodbye, Lott went quickly to his desk drawer and pulled out a pouch to give to Thomas. "Son, take this. It ain't much, but it will help. You've earned it here around the farm. I love you and am going to miss you more that you can ever know. When you're able, let us know you are safe."

Thomas hugged each of his family members and walked out to mount Champ. "They'll be looking for this horse. I'm taking him with me," he said.

"Son, let's have a word of prayer before you leave." Lott and his family grabbed hands and prayed for Thomas's safety and God's mercy."

"Son, if you do decide to go see Hatta, you know how to get there?" Lott asked.

"Yes Papa, I'll ride northwest and hitting the Natchez trace, I'll head toward Memphis. There I'll cross the river into Arkansas and southwest to the Choctaw lands."

"May God go with you, Son. You will be constantly in my prayers," Sarah whispered as she hugged her son one more time.

Lott could not believe that he was losing his son again. It brought back memories of the time years ago before Christmas when he felt so deserted by God because all three of his sons were gone. He remembered knowing James Earl, his eldest son had died in a Virginia hospital, and he thought John, his youngest had died in battle and had had no word of Thomas. Lott also remembered when John appeared on the doorstep on Christmas Day and Thomas returned that same day at the church. He realized that for now his heart was torn with grief, but that one day there would be hope, and God would return Thomas to his family.

Sarah's thoughts also returned to that Christmas when her sons came home to her. She remembered rocking on the porch and praying for them and knew that she had a lot of praying to do now."

Thomas swiftly rode away carrying his war demons with him once again. This time he felt that the war and killing had won and that his life would never be the same.

Early in the morning, the thunder of horse's hooves brought the Wilsons to their feet, and as expected, a full patrol of federal cavalrymen rode up. Dust floated across the yard and a voice called out, "Circle the house, barn and all buildings and have a thorough search. Let no one escape us." Instantly men quickly covered the grounds and pushed the Wilsons aside as they entered the house.

The captain, a heavy man with a short cropped beard and rigid face barked, "You Lott Wilson?"

"Yes, I am. Can I help you?"

The captain studied John for a moment and turned to a young soldier next to him and asked, "Is that the man?"

"No sir, that's not him," the soldier answered shyly lowering his head.

The captain rubbed his beard, retrieved his pistol and gripping it, pulled it to his waist. "Where's your other son? I believe his name is Thomas."

Defiantly Lott answered, "I haven't seen him since yesterday."

The captain smiled. "We'll soon know, and if he is here, there's no reason for a trial. Justice will come rather quickly."

"Maybe you need to tell me why you want to see him."

"I don't have to tell you anything, but I will say that your son has murdered two soldiers and he will be held accountable."

As the soldiers ransacked the barn and took the house apart, the Wilsons stood huddled together for strength.

An hour later after every inch of the place had been searched, the captain walked up on the porch. Standing near Lott's face, he muttered, "Tell me where your son is."

"As you can see, he ain't here, and I don't know where he might be. I don't believe my son is a murderer, and if I did know where he was, I certainly wouldn't tell you," Lott remarked.

At those words, the captain drew back his fist and struck Lott across the face knocking him backward. In anger, he shouted, "You're nothing but a sorry, filthy southern liar! You know where your son is, and we will find him and make sure he pays for the deaths of our two soldiers."

Worried that the captain would hit Lott again, John reached over to grab the officer by the collar, but crumpled to the floor when the butt of a musket met his head.

The captain straightened his jacket and in a cold voice said, "Like I was saying, we'll find your son, and I hope I can be the one to kill him. My name is Captain Matthew Lowery and one of the men your son murdered was Second Lieutenant Samuel Lowery, my younger brother. Blood runs thick in our family, and believe me, we will find your son and justice will be done."

"Like I told you, my son is not a murderer. You need to get the details, because I think you will find that none of this was his fault."

"You Southerners are all alike, just a bunch of liars and losers."

Lott, wiping blood from his lips, stood proudly and said, "We are Southerners and we did lose the war. It's a pity that men like you were not killed in the war instead of good men like my eldest son. He died a noble death, but you may find out that your brother died a needless death of his own making."

"You might as well forget anything you know, because nothing that happened that day will matter when it comes to saving your son from death. I plan to get my revenge."

As the soldiers rode away, the family was thankful that Thomas had escaped knowing that there would be no justice. They also knew that they would never see Thomas again unless God intervened.

At mid-morning, Suzanne pulled on her thick woolen coat, slipped on her gloves and pulled a knitted cap over her ears, then mounted her Morgan. She had slept little that night and was eager to get news about Thomas. She sped the three miles down the muddy road to Mister Walker's store. "Have you heard anything, Mister Walker?"

"Well, the federal soldiers came late yesterday for the bodies, but they didn't question anyone. This morning I did see about fifteen soldiers heading up the road toward the Wilsons."

Suzanne thanked him and rode to the north, one half mile to the Wilson farm. As she reined in her horse, a strong north wind whipped at her face sending scurries of leaves dancing across the yard while a twisted mass of smoke floated from their chimney and was caught in the wind then quickly vanished. The cold weather had caused the hounds to retreat to the warmth of the barn. Securing her mount, she hurried up the steps and called out, "Anyone home?"

She heard some footsteps approaching the door, and Sarah met her with a hug. "Good gracious child, come on in out of the cold."

Suzanne caught the scent of burning hickory and felt the warmth of a blazing fire. She paled as she saw the large cut on Lott's lip and saw Rebecca hovering near John who had a bandage on his head and was lying on the bed.

Sarah brought a chair to the fire and took Suzanne's coat, hat, and gloves. Suzanne studied the faces of the family, then asked, "Is Thomas okay? What happened up here?"

As the fire crackled away and the old clock on the mantle gave its steady rhythmic beat, Lott told Suzanne all that had occurred. When finished they sat silently, each in their own thoughts.

"I am so sorry. This is nothing but a nightmare. It's simply terrible. What will become of Thomas?" Suzanne softly asked.

Lott ran his hand across his stubby beard and reached over for Suzanne's hand. "Darling, I trust you and I know you care for my son, but if we want Thomas to live, no one must know where he's gone, not even you. In fact, we are not totally sure where he will end up."

Suzanne reached up and hugged Lot. "You know, he needs his family. He blames himself for all the killing in the war. He can't seem to let go of all he saw during the war and seems to take personal responsibility. I wish I could help him. I wish I could make him see that none of this is his fault. And now, he has a new burden to bear."

"Suzanne, I'm glad to know you care so much about my son, but we have to leave this in the Lord's hands and trust that one day Thomas will find God's mercy."

Tears formed in Suzanne's eyes and she nodded her understanding, but her heart ached for the man she had come to love.

10

The Letter

You are my hiding place; You will protect me from trouble and
surround me with songs of deliverance. The Lord's unfailing love
surrounds the man who trusts in Him.

—Psalm 32:7, 10b NIV

January, 1867

Christmas passed quietly with the normal church services and family gatherings, but it was not a festive time for most in Mississippi. Fear of losing property and livelihood had claimed their souls, and the anticipation of harder times consumed their thoughts. Many in southeastern Mississippi gave up and decided to move west. Some considered Texas, while others felt California and the West Coast provided promise. Many had heard that the Oklahoma Indian Territory was soon to be opened for white settlement because Washington felt it only fair to take a large percentage of Oklahoma from the Indians as punishment against the tribes in Oklahoma who had sided with the South.

Suzanne faced a cloudless, cold morning with a gusty wind pushing from the north as she stood in front of her house noting the barren cotton fields that had once flourished. She could imagine the melodic songs floating above the bent backs of the slaves as they labored. The fields were now bare, and slavery had ended. The Southern way of life would never return which was both good and bad. All had changed and change was close at hand again. A gust of wind suddenly whipped at Suzanne sending an eerie chill throughout her body. Tears glistened in her eyes, as she accepted letting go of her childhood home and facing life without the one she cherished.

Frankie joined Suzanne and put his arm around her. "It's sad to leave isn't it? My childhood memories for the most part were special even though father made me feel unworthy and useless." They stood a moment in the silence of their memories until Frankie spoke up. "Well, we have a buyer. A gentleman from New York has met my price. I had actually planned to lower the price, but he got in touch with me and the papers will be signed soon."

"Why would he want to move here, when times are so hard?"

"Well, he's buying low and plans to work it for a few years with some Negro paid workers, and if he can't make a profit, he'll sell it when the economy picks up."

"Frankie, it is sad that we won't own this house anymore, but I guess it's time we began anew. I miss father, but I'm glad that you can be your own man now. I hope that you have learned from the mistakes of papa."

"Suzanne, I have. I certainly have."

Mrs. Olliver waved from the awaiting carriage. "Time to go. Everything is packed." Suzanne took one final look at her home and moved toward the carriage with a heavy heart. "I'm ready Mother, as ready as I will ever be. I love Louisiana, but it sure is difficult to let go and leave our home."

Frankie walked her to the carriage and hugged his mother and sister good-bye, "I'll see you in a couple of days as soon as the paperwork is completed. You be careful. I love you both."

After the shooting at Walker's store, the military placed two guards at the Wilson's home in case Thomas returned. The two soldiers seemed oblivious to the events that brought them to the house and only approached it when they needed water. Posters offering a reward for the capture of Thomas Wilson had been printed at the military office in Newton and were being circulated around the state. Patrols of soldiers covered every county road in the area. Captain Lowery was certain Thomas would return to his caring family, and by offering one thousand dollars, he knew that everyone would be looking for his killer. He also knew with a reward this high, Thomas Wilson would be considered an outlaw worthy of locating. If he would just remain patient, eventually the man would be found and justice for his brother would be served.

"Okay, students. Your homework is on the board. Get your necessary materials ready for home and all of your belongings and line up at the door in the back. Be sure to get your coats, because the temperature is dropping." Sister opened the door, and the children hurried outside to enjoy the rest of the day. She gathered her books and decided to stop at Walker's store to chat and check on the mail. As she approached the steps of the store, Sister could envision Thomas and the shooting that robbed their family of a brother and son. She shuddered as she entered the store and went to the counter to collect the mail.

"Is there any mail for us today?"

"Actually there is one from Texas. How is your aunt doing?"

"Well, she seems to be recovering from her husband's death. I think her son is helping her with the business. I sure wish they would move here."

She picked up the letter from Texas and snuggled into her thick coat and pulled her woolen cap down over her ears before opening the door. As she walked, she thought about her aunt and cousins and how good it would be if they came to live with them, especially now that the house seemed lonely without Thomas. Half way home small specks of sleet began to pepper down bouncing off her cap and coat. Shivering, she quickened her pace and thought of the new baby that would arrive in the months to come. Rebecca and John had given the family a special gift at Christmas with the announcement that another Wilson was on the way. Sister began to think of the special quilt she planned to make for the baby. She could not wait to become an aunt and to hold her niece or nephew.

Captured and confined by the weather, Lot sat leisurely in his padded rocker with his feet to the fire and his eyes on the side window. He sure loved the outdoors, and the months of January and February were difficult for him. The skeleton limbs of the barren oaks outside shifted back and forth and the wind taunted him with its moans and screeches sending his heart yearning for the warmth of spring. On a table next to him lay his Bible, an empty coffee cup and a freshly packed pipe.

As he studied the weather through the window, he noticed the young soldier posted down the road. The cold wind was whipping at him as the soldier pulled his cape up over his head, and he was stomping around trying to keep his feet warm. Lott put on his coat, hat and gloves and headed out the door. On the porch, he paused a moment to breathe in the cold crisp air and then called, "Hey! Soldier boy! If you got to keep an eye on us, you might as well come on in here where it's warm and sit a spell."

The soldier looked up and down the road for a moment and then walked toward the house. Cautiously and timorously, he removed his cap and eased over to the roaring fire holding on to his firearm.

Settling back in his rocker Lott said, "Son, you don't need that musket in here. Lean it up to the wall and get them cold hands to the fire."

His face was blistered from the cold wind, and he reluctantly leaned his musket near him, and shivering, he held his hands as close as possible to the blazing fire. "I want to thank you for your kindness. You didn't have to do this for me."

"I'd do the same for any of God's children. What's your name and where are you from?"

"Gene Watkins. I'm just a farm boy from up in Michigan," he smiled.

"You hungry? I know you are. You been out there all day. Sarah! Can you bring this boy a cup of coffee and a couple of your ham biscuits from breakfast. You hear me?" Lott called out.

"Yes, I hear you. Didn't know we had company. Gonna have to make us some fresh coffee. Be there shortly," Sarah answered from the kitchen.

The soldier had relaxed some, was enjoying the coffee and biscuits and began to share his love of farming with Lott. After a while, he stood up to leave. "Best get back, before my replacement comes. Thanks again for your hospitality and the warmth of your home."

As the soldier got to the door, it opened and Sister bustled inside and removed her coat and cap. The soldier politely tipped his hat to her and smiled admiringly. Noticing her frown, he quickly slipped out the door and back to his post.

"Why was he in our home?" Sister asked. "Why would you let someone who is trying to kill Thomas in this house?"

"Calm down, Daughter. Most of these soldiers don't even know what really happened, and they are just following orders. Besides if I remember correctly, the Bible tells us to love even our enemies."

"Papa, I guess you are right, but I sure find it hard to love those that want to hurt my family."

Sister walked to the kitchen to see if her mother had started the dress she planned for the baby. Sarah shared her work, and Sister loved the lace that her mother had made for the hem. "Mother, do you ever think that maybe if it's a boy, the dress should be made a little different?"

"Daughter, all babies have been wearing dresses like this until they are two years old, and I don't see any reason to change tradition."

"I guess not. Oh, I almost forgot the letter." Sister rushed back to the bedroom where Lott sat before the fire and gave the letter to her father. "Papa, I am so sorry. I forgot about the letter from Texas."

Lott looked over the letter and quickly tore of the edge and opened it. As he read the letter, Sister noticed the concern on his face and knew there was more bad news. She really didn't know how the family could handle more troubles. Sister decided to leave so her parents could have some time together.

Sarah went to her husband and sat on the floor in front of him with her back warming by the fire. "Lott, is it bad news? Is everyone okay?"

"I can't really believe it, but this letter says that my sister is dead. It's from the sheriff of Cass County. He really doesn't give any details."

Sarah faintly asked, "What about the children? What has happened to them?"

"All it says is that Sara Ann has died. Doesn't mention the children," Lott answered. "When John gets in, I need to see him."

Sarah looked up into Lott's teary eyes and said, "We can't leave the children out there by themselves."

"I know. I just don't know what to do. Texas is so far away, and I'm not sure I'm up to a trip like that. We've got some planning to do, and we need to think fast about our options."

John stepped off the train from Meridian and walked over to the livery stable to retrieve the horse he had left in Newton. Buttoning up his thick coat, he wrapped a woolen scarf around his neck, pulled his hat down tightly and mounting, he headed for Little Rock. He knew it would be dark before he made the eighteen miles home. When he reached Little Rock, he stopped at his father-in-law's store where Rebecca often helped out, but since she had already left for the day, John rode on alone. When he reached home, he reined his mount into the barn, took off the saddle and blanket and after brushing the horse down, he turned it into the corral. Shivering from the cold ride, he knocked off his shoes then walked over to the fire totally ignoring his family as he warmed his hands. "Been a cold hard day," he muttered.

"John, I'm afraid it is going to get worse," Lott countered.

John faced his father and saw his distressful expression. As he looked at the rest of the family, who all seemed like stone sculptures, motionless and morose, dread crept in his heart and all he could think of was Thomas.

Finally Sarah spoke to her son. "We've had some bad news, John."

Lott reached to his Bible and pulled out the letter and handed it to John. John silently read "Sorry to inform you, but your sister Sara Ann Lewis has died."

John took his coat off, backed up to the fire and ran his fingers through his hair in thought. He then looked from face to face for an answer. "Papa, what are we going to do about the children? We can't leave them there alone."

"That's right, Son. So now the question is 'How do you figure on getting them back here?'" asked Lott as he got up and joined John at the fireplace.

John just stared at his father knowing he could never leave Rebecca, not now.

Sister finally blurted out. "You both can do it. There's no one else who can."

Sarah and Rebecca glanced at Sister and then back to Lott and John. Sarah knew that her husband could never make the long trip and that John should not leave Rebecca.

The wood in the fireplace sizzled and popped sending out a hissing sound, and the clock ticked away the moments as the family sat in silence. Finally Lott began to voice his concerns. "Texas is a far piece off and the way my back comes and goes, I can't make that trip. God in heaven knows I'm willing, but I'm just not sure my back is."

John now nestled with Rebecca on the sofa cleared his voice. "Papa, we've got a baby on the way. There's no way I can leave Becca. She's going to need me here when the baby comes. I've got to make sure they are both okay. I won't risk losing them."

"This here seems to be an unsolvable problem," Lott solemnly remarked, "It's best we go to the Lord for assistance." Joining hands, the family issued their prayers to heaven, and after praying, they all sat silently in meditation.

Finally Rebecca reached out and took her husband's hand and looking up to his handsome face, said, "Darling, you've got to go. You're the only one that can bring them back."

John dropped his head. "I can't do this, Becca. I can't leave you. With the violence and unrest in this country, I might not ever return. You know I want to see my firstborn child grow up. I just can't do this, not now."

Sarah, distraught, got up and walking into the kitchen exclaimed, "Then I guess we better start praying for God to send someone to help us, because we absolutely cannot leave those children in that awful place by themselves."

Sleep evaded the Wilsons that night as they were haunted by the thought of children all alone without a mother or father. After several hours the house was silent, and sleep had come to all.

In the middle of the night while John slept deeply, he was suddenly awakened by a clear, pure voice that said, "You do it."

John sat up in his bed to listen for the voice, and after a few minutes, he walked to the hallway and called softly near his parents' bedroom. "Papa, did you just call me?"

All was silent, so John returned to bed and then gently shook Rebecca. "Becca, did you just say something to me a few minutes ago?"

She began to arouse from her sleep and rubbing her eyes, she spoke groggily, "John, what are you talking about? I was sound asleep until you just woke me." She nestled herself under the covers and closed her eyes again.

John laid quietly next to Rebecca trying to resolve the matter of the voice. As hard as he tried to ignore the words he heard, the voice continued to resound in his mind until John understood exactly what he had to do. The words were as clear as if God had given him a special message. Deep in his heart, John knew that finding the children and bringing them home was his future. John struggled to find rest, but thoughts of the trip consumed his mind.

Having had an almost sleepless night, John stayed in bed later than normal. As the scent of coffee brewing and ham frying reached his nose, John began to wake to the chatter of the family nearby. He pulled himself out of bed, dressed quickly and tipped over the open hall to the warmth of the kitchen. As John entered, he realized the family had just finished their meal and were enjoying another cup of coffee as they relaxed and made plans for the day. Seeing his tussled hair and tired eyes, Rebecca laughed softly and patted the bench next to her. "Had a rough night did you, sleepy head?"

John poured himself a cup of coffee and eased down next to his wife while his mother fixed him a plate of food. John blew across his cup to cool his drink and then set his cup back down on the table. "I did have a hard night."

John remembered those three words that reverberated in his mind. He looked in Rebecca's eyes and said, "I'll be leaving in the morning to try to find the children."

His family was astonished at his declaration, but Rebecca seemed proud of his words.

"You sure about this, Son?" Lott asked.

John confidently looked at his family. "We can't leave them out there nor can we depend on someone taking them in. They're family. It's our responsibility to care for them."

He then took Rebecca's hand. "In all this talk about our baby, I never asked you when the little one was coming."

Rebecca squeezed his hand and smiling said, "The best I can tell, it will be here sometime in July.

Taking a deep breath and running his fingers through his curly hair, John looked at his father and said, "I don't have the vaguest idea as to exactly what I am supposed to do or where I am supposed to go. I've never been west of the Mississippi and have no idea what this trip will bring or even how to prepare for it."

Lott reached over and placed his hand on John's shoulder. "Well, Son, I've been doing some thinking and praying early this morning, and I think I may have just the plan for you. This morning I found some of my old maps that we used when surveying this country and found one that covered Mississippi and a portion of Louisiana, Arkansas and the Indian Territory of Oklahoma. I remembered that Thomas mentioned that Davis County is now renamed Cass County in Texas, so we can narrow this search down. Since I'm not able to go with you, I think you need to take a train from Newton Station and west to Vicksburg. Board your horse as well, and once you get to Vicksburg, take the road north through the Delta to Greenville on the Mississippi River. Cross the river by barge into Arkansas and head west through the lower part of the state."

The more Lott explained the route, the more it confused John, until he finally interrupted. "Aren't you making the trip longer than it has to be? Isn't that a little bit out of the way?"

"Just listen to the rest," frowned Lott. "When you reach the west border of Arkansas, you'll run right into the Choctaw allotted land."

John's eyebrows lifted and he began to chuckle. "I know your plan now. That is where I will pick up Thomas, isn't it?" A broad smile and a sense of relief flooded John's soul. "I feel a lot better now, because Thomas will know exactly how to find those children."

"You are absolutely right, Son. Thomas knows the country out there better than most, and two is a lot better than one," Lott continued. "Now we got to get you ready because the quicker you find those children, the sooner you can return to your wife."

As John prepared for the journey, he decided to take Bet, one of their Mustangs, for two reasons: Bet had a lot of stamina and she was not pretty, certainly a horse no one would want to steal. John decided it would be best to dress for winter and in his work clothes, so he wouldn't draw attention to himself. He would take the other Sharps rifle Thomas had left behind, two revolvers, and his old hunting knife. In a secret pouch concealed under his saddle, he would carry some extra money for emergency. He then would pack extra clothes, canned beans, beef jerky, coffee and would purchase food only when needed. For warmth, two blankets, an oil cloth and a slicker would be rolled up and tightly tied behind his saddle.

His plans made, John decided to leave at daybreak the following morning. John admitted to Rebecca his thrill of adventure and at the same time his fear of danger. Rebecca tried to be brave, but she knew the next months would be very difficult as she wondered about his welfare and knew she would have to rely on God for her husband's safe return.

John woke early and after a hearty breakfast, he dressed and walked out to the front porch. A smile crossed his face as he saw Toby leading Bet up toward the house. Lott, Sarah, Sister and Rebecca came out as well and pulled their garments close to them in the cold morning air. John loaded the horse with his supplies then pulled off his hat and hugged each family member goodbye. Reaching Rebecca he looked longingly into her deep emerald eyes, ran his hand softly across her cheek and lifting her chin, he kissed her. For a moment, they just stood silently taking in the love they shared, and then she whispered to him, "John, I love you more than you can know, and I don't, I mean, we don't want to lose you." She placed John's hand on her abdomen then hugged him.

John pushed a loose strand of hair from her face. "Lord willing, I'll see my baby being born. I love you too. You take care of yourself and our baby until I return. You are going to make the most beautiful mother, and I plan to return to you, my love."

The family stood close as Lott spoke a prayer for John's safety. "God be with you, Son"

John took the reins from Toby and grabbed him by the hand. "Thank you for all that you do for us. We could never make it without you."

Toby smiled at the young man who had bought his freedom at the slave block years ago. "You take care, Mister John."

As John rode away, the tears began to flood Rebecca's eyes. She whispered to herself, "Oh Lord, I thought I had lost John in the war, but he returned, so please be with him and bring him home to me again. To me and his unborn child."

The posted soldiers watched intently as John rode off. Soon one of the soldiers motioned to the other, and after some quick words, one of the soldiers quickly mounted his horse and took off at top speed.

The morning was still, resting in its wintery frosty coat, awaiting the break of day. There was a light glow in the eastern horizon, and traces of floating clouds were barely visible as John galloped down the road. Reaching Newton Station at midmorning, he purchased a ticket for Vicksburg, and learning the train would not be leaving until noon, John sat leisurely down on a bench at the depot. As noon approached, several soldiers began milling about in search. "Where you going, boy?" growled a crusty grim faced sergeant.

John impatiently but politely replied, "I'm waiting for the train, sir."

"I know that! But where are you going?"

John slowly stood up to his full height and looked down at the beady-eyed soldier. "Sir, where I'm going is really none of your concern."

The sergeant clinched his fist in anger and drew back. As his fist approached John's face, John grabbed it in midair and forcefully pushed it down and twisted it behind the soldier's back. John held it firmly in his brace. "Sir, I don't want any trouble. I just want to be on my way."

Several soldiers quickly approached with muskets drawn.

"Men, at ease," boomed a loud voice from behind them. "Hold off there, men."

An officer walked up to the group. "I think you need to let my sergeant go, young man."

As John released the sergeant, the officer stood close and looked the sergeant in the eyes. "This is a local citizen. Where he goes is none of our business."

Turning back to John who was straightening his clothes, he continued, "I'm sorry for this behavior. Please accept my apology."

"No harm done. I didn't want any trouble," John answered.

After John left, the officer pulled the sergeant to the side, "Sergeant, your only responsibility was to identify the rider. We have someone else ready to track him. Understand?"

Having led Bet up into the cattle car, John removed the saddle, and draping it over his shoulder, he walked into the passenger car. As he settled in the back of the car, he slung the saddle in the seat next to him and looked out the window as the wheels squeaked forward and the clouds of smoke from the smokestack covered the walkway. John noted that the soldiers were intently watching him and reasoned that he was probably being followed. John knew that he was going to have to lose these men if he planned to get Thomas's help.

John was surrounded with constant chatter and a ceiling filled with tobacco smoke, but he tried to keep to himself and enjoy the countryside. Several times passengers would try to start up a conversation with him, but he managed to thwart the attempts. With each mile multiplying his distance from Rebecca and home, his heart became heavy with loneliness. By late afternoon the train pulled into the Vicksburg depot, and John went to the cattle car to get Bet, then saddled her and moved down the walkway heading southward to Natchez to see if he was being followed.

As the sun was setting, John reined Bet off the muddied road and up into a cluster of thick cedar trees bordered by old cypress trees that were draped in Spanish moss. He began to watch the road below carefully, and soon he heard the clomping of hooves on the road and spotted a detail of soldiers approaching. He now knew that they were definitely on his trail. After they passed, he decided to wait until dark and then go back to Vicksburg and hopefully with the aid of the night be able to pass through the city and ride north to the Mississippi Delta. John was completely exhausted by dawn and pulled off the road to eat and try to get some sleep. He figured he was now about twenty miles north of Vicksburg.

Around noon Lott and Toby were splitting white oak for shingles when they noticed a detail of soldiers approaching the posted soldier, and then in a few minutes they rode away. The posted soldier began walking toward them, so they laid down their axes, sat on a log, and waited for him.

"After noon," the young soldier said, shuffling about uneasily. "I'll be leaving you all. They're bringing us in. No more posting here."

"What'd you mean by that? We aren't being watched anymore?" asked Lott frowning.

"No sir." He paused and then extended his hand. "I just want you to know how much I appreciated your hospitality. You're good folks."

Lott decided that he needed a little more information, and it seemed the young man was reluctant to leave. "Why don't you sit a spell. Your name is Watkins, isn't it?"

"Yes sir, Gene Watkins. Thank you." After some small talk, the soldier looked about nervously then said, "You being God fearing people, I think I can trust you."

"Toby and I are men of our word. What you say, stays here."

The soldier cleared his throat. "That report on the shooting isn't correct. Joe Taylor, the soldier that was at the shooting was a bunkmate of mine and he told me what happened. He said that the lieutenant wanted to take your son's horse and that the lieutenant shot first. He said the whole thing was the lieutenant's fault because he was determined to take that horse."

The young soldier continued, "Word is that the captain has friends in Washington. It seems he has a free reign down here in Mississippi, and he's determined to have your son killed."

The young soldier looked down the road again then hastily continued. "I need to warn you that they know your younger son left here packed for the road. Captain Lowery figured he was headed to find your older son. He wired and had three Calvary scouts from out in West Texas and a retired Pinkerton man to meet in Jackson to trail him. There's soldiers trailing him right now, and when those other guys get in, they'll take over, and what I've have heard, they are among the best."

Gene glanced up the road one more time and knew he had better be leaving, so he got up and shook both Lott and Toby's hands. "One more thing, if they catch your older son, they plan to kill him on the spot, and if your younger one is with him, he goes as well. I sure hope that your sons will be safe."

As the soldier hurried away, Lot called out to him. "Where's the boy that witnessed the shooting?"

The young soldier pulled his horse around and answered. "They discharged him and sent him home two days after the shooting. Lives somewhere up in Ohio."

Lott, heavy hearted and worried, dropped his head. "Toby, I just don't know what to do to protect my boys. I just pray that John realizes he's being followed. I don't think I can endure losing them, especially when the truth should keep them alive."

11

Arkansas Bound

I cry to you for help when my heart is overwhelmed. Lead me to the towering rock of safety, for you are my safe refuge, a fortress where my enemies cannot reach me. Let me live forever in your sanctuary, safe beneath the shelter of your wings.

—Psalm 61: 2b – 4 NLT

Sitting in front of a roaring fire with a lap blanket snuggled around her, Suzanne gazed through the floor length French windows to the barren cane fields in the distance. A light breeze shook the limbs on the live oaks out front, but inside all was quiet. Her grandfather's sugar cane plantation covered over two thousand acres and was only a few feet above sea level. It was completely surrounded by water, and a quarter of a mile bridge was the only entrance to the island. The mansion contained a lower basement that housed the carriages plus the maid quarters, while the main floor contained a master bedroom, study, parlor, entertainment room and massive dining area. The second floor was nothing but bedrooms; eight of them. The top level ballroom surrounded by glassed French doors and a shiny polished oak floor had a glassed cupola that allowed the moonlight to filter into the room. Hugh columns and porches encasing the house were connected by open walkways at each level. The view from the top floor was extensive and expanded to the entire plantation which was known as The Empire. The mansion was called The Oaks.

Workers out front caught her attention as they raked the loose leaves and limbs from the yard caused by a strong storm that had swept the area two days earlier. Suzanne had always loved this place and especially her grandfather. She could barely remember her grandmother who died years ago. Suzanne's return was filled with shopping in New Orleans, enjoying two dances given by her grandfather in her honor, and riding horseback throughout the countryside. There was a steady stream of young men vying for her attention, but she could only think of the broad shouldered, troubled, quiet, but loveable man. Questions about his safety and location continued to bombard her mind and even her dreams. She knew the possibility of ever seeing him again was a vague hope, but she would continue to pray for him, and hopefully, one day the Lord would bring him into her life again.

John had heard of the Mississippi Delta with its flat land and rich soil created by centuries of flooding of the mighty Mississippi, but it still was extraordinary. As far as he could see were acres and acres of dormant cotton fields aggrandized with massive mansions. Some were still in use and meticulously kept while others laid unkempt and unoccupied. The war had taken its toll and with the lack of slave labor to keep these cotton empires in grandeur, the plantation life would soon disappear.

Trying to be as inconspicuous as possible, John avoided the eyes of other riders and kept his hat pulled down near his eyes. He only returned greetings in a succinct manner. The first day out of Vicksburg, the weather began clear and crisp, but soon the clouds darkened and hard rain fell in torrents. Finding an old abandoned slave house, he led Bet inside and settled in for the night. Breaking some of the boards from the old shack, he started a fire, and for the first time in days, was warmed. He lay near the fire enjoying the warmth and the sound of the rhythmic beat of rain on the roof. As he thought toward tomorrow and reaching Greenville, he pensively pondered the distance that separated him from Becca and his family. Thoughts of Becca and his unborn baby flooded his mind, and he longed to hold her close and look into her loving face. Closing his eyes, he tried to release all of his worries and think only of his Savior, the only one who could keep his wife safe as well as the children he needed to find. He bowed his head and mouthed, "Lord, I am trusting your protection for my wife and baby. Please show me the way to Thomas and my cousins. And Lord, protect Thomas from those who wish him harm."

John had rested well so he rose early and saddled Bet, led her outside, and mounting, he galloped northward to find a boat heading across the Mississippi. The rain that had fallen throughout the night had now turned to sleet, and the water puddled on the road began to freeze. With the wind sweeping off the Great Plains and whipping across the flat delta, nothing stopped the icy grips of cold that nipped through John's clothing. Mile after mile he pushed Bet onward. Abandoned fields, swamp bottoms, cane breaks and towering trees with hanging Spanish moss slipped by as he rode facing the frigid cold. At mid- afternoon which seemed like dusk, John reined Bet to a stop and glancing down a small rise in the road, spotted what he thought was Greenville. Half frozen, he rode into the river town.

Army Headquarters in Vicksburg

"You men find anything south of here?" asked a short, well-dressed man with slender face, mustache and hair oiled and parted down the middle.

"No sir, we thought he was headed that way, but we found nothing, Mister Stevens."

"You know what the man looks like?"

"I'd say about average. Dark hair. 'Bout six foot and slightly stocky."

Stevens began to laugh. "You just described about everyone around here. How do you think we can find him with a description like that? What about his horse?"

The private rubbed his face and began to frown. "It's kind of a funny animal. Not very tall, muscled and ash grey. I'm not sure what breed it is because I haven't ever seen one quite like it."

Stevens nodded his head, and then gave a big grin to the group. "Now we got a chance. We won't be trailing the man, we're looking for the horse and what you just described is a mustang."

"How'd you know that Mister Stevens?" a man called out.

"Gentlemen, I was a Pinkerton man during the war, and you have to notice those things. The scouts we're bringing in tomorrow from Texas, well they know their horses, especially the mustang. Men, now listen, my thinking is Wilson is headed west, and to do that, he has to cross the Mississippi on some kind of boat or barge. Since you found no evidence of him south of here; that means he's probably headed north where there are few places to cross that river. When the scouts arrive, we will break up in groups and hit every landing in Mississippi from here to Memphis. By riding hard and fast, we'll hopefully catch him in a couple of days. He may be ahead of us, but believe me gentlemen, we'll close the gap. Get a good night's sleep because we will leave at daybreak and may be in the saddle twenty-four hours a day. If the scouts are not here by then, I'll leave a message for them to join us. You're dismissed."

Docking at dark, the scouts arrived on a late steamboat and led their horses down the planked walkway. It was obvious that these three men were frontiersmen. All were tall, thin, long hair, bearded and muscled. One was dressed completely in buckskins while the other two wore regulation black knee length boots, blue trousers with the yellow Calvary stripe running down the outside length of the leg, buckskin jackets and tan Calvary hats.

Daybreak broke with a chilling cold wind and a hint of snow as the men gathered close to the fire and waited for instructions. "Men, you need to be observant and invisible. Be fast on the road but quiet in towns with landings. When you get to any landings, split up and look. Remember, Wilson should never see you. Your task is to trail him not confront him. Don't draw any attention to yourselves, and when you spot Wilson, send one person to me and the rest keep an eye on Wilson until I get there. If he boards a ship, someone needs to board too, but be inconspicuous. Meet me in Greenville if you don't find him."

Two of the scouts were sent on a mad run to Memphis and were told to start at the landings and work their way south until they joined the main party. Stevens sent home all of the soldiers but one that was posted at the dock in Vicksburg just in case Wilson tried to cross there. To Steven's notion, he was sure that if Wilson didn't cross at Vicksburg and he was headed west, then Greenville would be the logical crossing. Wrapped in heavy coats and leading a pack horse, Stevens and a scout named Hank sprinted out of Vicksburg headed north.

John rode into the town, and it was larger than any town he had ever seen in Mississippi. It seemed to be located at the highest point on the Mississippi River. Most of the buildings were burned during the war, but some had been newly bricked and framed. It was surrounded by cotton plantations with some that seemed untouched by the war, and to the west, he could see the muddy Mississippi slowly flowing carrying uprooted trees and debris with it.

Cold, hungry and exhausted, John decided to take a risk and find a stable and grain for Bet and a hot meal and lodging for himself. John left Bet at the livery stable and then put his saddle on his shoulder and walked up the street to a place that the man at the livery stable had recommended.

Few people were stirring on this icy day and even though it was not the cleanest place he had ever seen, it was warm and the scent of food sealed his decision.

"Help you, Son?" a tiny middle aged man with wire rimmed glasses and a slick bald head asked from behind the desk.

John eased the saddle from his shoulder. "Sir, I need a room for the night and a hot meal. Can you do me some good?"

The man slid his glasses down. "Boy, you look most frozen. Where'd you come from?"

John dropped his head, dead tired. "Long story. Can you accommodate me?"

"Sure I can accommodate you. It'll be one dollar and that includes yore supper and breakfast." Reaching inside a drawer he picked up a key, and after John handed him the money, he placed the key in John's hand. "Room eight. Top of the stairs and to the left. Suppers at six. If'n you're late, might not be much left. By the way, where you heading?" asked the man studying John closely.

"I need to cross the river. Going west. Is there a barge or boat crossing any time soon?"

The little man adjusted his glasses and tugged at his vest. "You're in luck; there's a cattle barge coming in here in the morning, and after unloading them filthy animals, it will be headed up the river. Next one won't stop by here till day after tomorrow.

"Think they'll take me and my horse across?"

A hearty laugh erupted. "Sure they'll take you on if'n you got a little money. Look for it about mid-morning. Can't miss it." As John struggled up the steps, the man called out. "Six o'clock, don't be late."

John suddenly stopped. "Do I need to sign my name?"

"Naw, I got yore money. That's all I need."

Good, John thought, didn't want to come up with an alias.

As dark approached and Hank galloped down the road toward Stevens, Stevens knew good news was on the way. Pulling his horse to a sliding stop, Hank shouted, "Got something!" He paused a minute to catch his breath, "Followed a lot of tracks up the way. Most just went to folks' homes, but one kept a steady pace north. Come on, I want to show you something."

Several miles up the road, Hank led them off the trail and to an old shack. Stevens went in and noticed the evidence. He bent down and placed his hand on the charred remains in the fireplace. "Cold. No telling when this fire was made. Could have been days ago."

"Not so. It appears who ever stayed here, brought his horse in with him, and by the freshness of the manure back there, I'd say someone was here last night."

"Let me show you something else." Hank took Stevens back to the road. "Look at this. You notice something."

Stevens began to laugh, "The front right shoe has got a small chunk out of it which means we can track Wilson to Alaska and back. Good work. That's exactly why you are here; you notice things others would never even consider."

Since it was late and the weather had worsened, Stevens knew it would be better to leave at daybreak. As the lone soldier led the horses into the shack, he asked," You want me to stand guard tonight?"

The buckskin clad scout shook his head. "For what reason. Nobody is hunting us, and only idiots would be out on a night like this."

The scout then pulled a pipe out of his pocket, filled it and reached for a burning stick to light it. He took a deep draw and exhaling, directed a question at Stevens. "Who's paying for this hunt?"

"Some captain posted in Newton has connections in Washington, and for some reason he thinks this man we're hunting is going to start another revolution," Stevens said sarcastically. "No, there were a couple of men killed, and they want to find the one who killed them. Seems ridiculous to me because there are killings all over the South. Not sure what makes this one any different."

Hank threw his saddle next to the fire, slid down on the floor while pulling a blanket over him and asked, "Stevens, how much you getting paid for this job?"

Stevens pulled an old box close to the fire and sat down. "You might say I am doing very well."

Hank snorted, "For me, it's just army scout pay. Better than staying cooped up in that old fort all winter. Least I'm out and about. How 'bout you soldier?" Hank asked looking over to the young soldier who was unrolling his blanket. "By the way, what's your name?"

My name is "Clarke, Ken Clarke and I'm just like you. Poor army pay."

John rose early, packed his belongings and moved to the kitchen for breakfast. He threw his saddle and possessions down and sat at an empty table. An old Negro man noticed and walked to his table. "Coffee?" the old gent asked, wiping his greasy hands on his apron.

"That will be fine and some breakfast please."

"Bacon, eggs, grits and biscuits. That sound good to ya?"

John was soon enjoying a breakfast almost good as at home, and he gulped it down quickly and walked to the livery stable. After settling with the keeper, John led Bet by the reins down to the dock. Ice covered the ground as they trudged along trying to keep from slipping. John glanced up into an overcast sky and felt the nip of wind as the mighty Mississippi rolled beneath him. Settling himself on an empty barrel, he scanned the river for any sign of a boat. By mid-morning, he was concerned the old man had been wrong and he would need to head further north, but as he stood to stretch, he heard a horn blow far in the distance and saw a light stream of smoke rising from the river.

Pulling the barge close to the dock, men quickly jumped out and began tying the boat securely to a large support post. A gate was opened, and cattle were herded out and up the street where a corral was located. Once all had cleared, John walked to the man who seemed to be in charge. Large, burly and wrapped in a buffalo coat, the man stood, whip in hand, watching the drive being made.

John cleared his throat. "Sir, I have a question for you?"

Still gazing at the cattle being driven up the street, he peered down at John. "Whatcha need?"

"I need to get over to the Arkansas side."

The man turned his attention back to the cattle being driven into the corral and muttered, "You taking that mustang with you, I guess."

"Yes sir, I am."

"Cost you two dollars. We'll leave here within the hour headed to St. Louis to pick up a load of furs. Give me the two dollars, load your horse and I'll drop you off on the other side."

The man re-focused on John and inspecting him, he asked, "Son, you fight in the war?"

"Yes sir, Newton Country Rifles.

"Carleton head of y'all?"

"Yes sir."

"Tell you what, there's a landing about five miles up the river. I'll drop you off there and don't worry 'bout no fee. You done paid it."

Stevens and his men rode into Greenville a little after twelve, and he quickly ordered Hank to go down to the livery stable while he sent Ken to check out the hotel registers. Minutes later Hank returned smiling. "Grey mustang was stabled there last night. He was picked up a couple of hours ago. The man they described fits your boy."

Ken running swiftly finally reached the men and spoke out, "One man checked in last night. Description sounds like Wilson."

A frown covered Steven's face and kicking his horse in the flank, he screamed, "Get to the river! Quick!"

Reining their horses to a stop, Stevens quickly scanned the river and seeing the barge moving away, tried to focus on the passengers.

John glanced back to Greenville and spotted a group of men near the dock.

He saw a man in buckskins and a gentleman with a dark black coat and dress hat looking at him intently. John knew then that he was definitely being followed, and they were certainly staying close which meant he was going to have to be very careful to make sure he confused his path, or he would have to find the children on his own without Thomas.

Stevens said, "Boys that's him. That's our man. From here on out, we've got to keep our distance. There's no question in my mind, he's searching for his brother, and from the information on the family, I have an idea where he might be going."

Standing on the muddy landing, John watched the barge struggle upstream against the swollen Mississippi. John began planning a change in his route to make tracking him as difficult as possible. In his haste to leave, he had forgotten to restock his food supply and knew it was essential that he purchase items soon. As he mounted Bet, he glanced at the river once more. From his studies, he knew the river basically flowed somewhat north to south and the road behind him led westward. The captain had told him about a town not far from the river called Lake Village, so he decided to ride there, purchase supplies and get information about the towns across the way. At some point, he might have to leave the roads and go cross country to evade being spotted. As long as the sun was shining, he could find his way, but on cloudy days, it would be guesswork at best.

The land looked similar to that of Mississippi with its oak, maple, pine and Cyprus. John pushed Bet up a slope where the branches of long thin barren oaks seemed to take on the appearance of the bony arms of skeletons. John knew that the frustration and loneliness he felt was playing tricks on his mind. Once more the wind picked up and pellets of ice fell. The weather and his imagination were spinning like a perpetual nightmare.

By late afternoon, John rode into the small town of Lake Village. It almost seemed like a ghost town because all the buildings looked desolate and there were no people stirring on the roads. He saw a few shabbily framed buildings, a bank and finally, a general merchandizing store. Securing his horse, John walked up on the plank porch, knocked the mud from his boots and entered. A potbellied stove in the rear of the building roared its heat and beckoned to him. Removing his hat, he held his hands close to the heat and observed steam rising from his wet clothes.

"Help you, Son?" called a large, bearded man behind the counter to his left who was watching John intensely. "You ain't from around here, are you?"

118

John walked over and extended his hand. "No sir. I'm traveling through. Just need some supplies and maybe some directions."

"Well, take your time. Get what you want, and we'll settle up and talk a spell. You look might worn. Care for some coffee?"

John nodded yes and began gathering items from the shelves. When finished, he paid the clerk and the two then settled on chairs next to the stove.

"Son, since you came from the river road, I'm figuring you'll be headed west, but I don't want to meddle in yore business," the clerk said taking a sip of coffee. "Tell you one thing and if'n you're smart, you'll take notice. This here country can be a dangerous place. Didn't used to be so bad, but with the war ending and folks desperate, you can trust no one."

"Not even you?" John said with a smile.

The clerk laughed. "No Son. Not even me. Seriously, you can trust me because I'm a God-fearing man of faith."

For the next hour, the clerk informed John as to the towns, lakes and rivers that lay ahead and advised him on how to travel in safety. "Remember, when you camp at night make sure you notice anyone traveling behind you. When you leave the road, head into the woods and then backtrack about a quarter of mile the way you came and look for anyone that might be following you. Don't make a cook fire at night, and even watch your smoke during the day. With the weather like it is, you shouldn't see too many stirring about, but let me warn you, folks are running scared. You best be careful."

John asked about a place to stable his horse and sleep and was told there was a livery stable on the west edge of town that could accommodate him. That night John stabled his horse and was allowed to sleep there in the barn. It was cold and smelly, but at least he was out of the elements. As he lay resting on a bed of soft hay, he laid out his plan of travel. If it were cloudy, he would stick to the roads and adhere to what the clerk had told him, but if there was sun, he would take to the woods and cover his tracks when possible. He knew he had at least a one day lead if the men at Greenville landing were actually after him. One thing for certain, he wasn't going to make it easy on them. At the first light of day, John rode out.

12

Race across Arkansas

*God says, "Because he has loved Me, therefore I will deliver him; I will
set him securely on high because he has known My name. When he
calls upon Me, I will answer him; I will be with him in trouble.*
—Psalm 91: 14-16 NASB

Stevens and his men warmed themselves beside the crackling fire near
the bank of the mighty Mississippi River. The other two scouts returned from
Memphis with important information about Wilson. "Sir, the captain of the barge
from Greenville arrived in Memphis and unloaded his cargo. We were able to find
out that a man boarded the barge in Greenville and was let off on the Arkansas
side about five miles upriver."

"Well, Wilson sure is making our job easy. With the lack of rain today and
the print of a nicked shoe, we will be able to trail him until he finds the man we
are looking for and then we will move in. Until then, we still need to be invisible."
Stevens adjusted his boots and looked over at his scouts smiling at the names that
the two who had returned were called. One of the scouts was called Bent which
he had earned from a hard fall off a galloping horse that caused his gait to have a
slight forward lean. The other was called Closter, and Stevens was sure that there
was probably a story behind that name too. These scouts were hard men who
knew how to endure pain, push the extremes even to their own endangerment,
and display a clear viciousness when confronted. Of the military men who had
begun with them in Vicksburg, Stevens only kept Ken and had allowed the rest
to return to their unit. Ken had done well retrieving information about the night
Wilson spent in Lake Village and would be a good fit for his group.

With no compass and the sun hidden behind the drizzling rainy day, John
had to stay on the road. On the second day he arrived at Monticello, another small
Arkansas town, but decided to put distance between him and the soldiers, so he
continued without stopping. Finally that evening John knew he had to rest so
he reined Bet off the road into a thicket of cedar trees, grabbed his oil cloth and
slicker, then backtracked a good half mile and hid himself on a rise overlooking

the road below. To keep the rain from drenching him, he found shelter under a low branched cedar and settled in for the night. As he chewed on a piece of deer jerky, he watched the road below trying his best to stay awake. As he was close to sleep, he heard the sound of horses slushing through the road below. Rubbing his tired eyes, he observed five men ride up on horses. All were covered in slickers and had their hats pulled down low to avoid as much rain as possible.

They stopped directly below John's posted location. "Lost him, Stevens," one of the men called out. "Rains covered his tracks."

"Don't matter. I know where he's going. We'll keep riding west and try to get ahead of him. Then we'll wait and pick him up. We are just a few miles out of Fordyce, so we will rest there for the night and see what we can find out."

There was no question in John's mind that he was the one they were following and he must do his best to make sure these men did not find Thomas. John stayed where he was and rested the night, and with the break of dawn, sunlight lit up the countryside sending slashes of light across the woodlands. John's prayer had been answered, and he could easily take to the woods and away from the road. With plenty of food and his ability to hunt and fish, he would continue to head west but would stay away from roads and towns. With the sun on his back, John saddled Bet and wandered off into the dense woods. His spirits seemed to lift with the weather and with his abilities in the woods, he figured he would reach the Oklahoma Territory within the week. The warm sun, fresh smelling earth and scampering wildlife proved invigorating and gave him a nostalgic reminiscence of home. Days slipped by in solitude as John kept out of sight of homesteads and people. He wandered through woods, forded streams and with great difficulty even swam his horse across a small river. To John's disappointment, he could see mountains probably the Ozarks Mountains which meant he had headed too far north. Readjusting, he reined Bet southward and now during cloudy days, he avoided travel altogether. What he had thought to be a four day ride to the Oklahoma territory was now approaching two weeks. Out of food, hungry and exhausted, he decided to find a road and seek a town to resupply and get his bearings. At mid-day, the February weather turned cold, and gray clouds moved across the sky like a slow moving fog. Small flakes began to flutter, and then sheets of snow fell like the heavens had been opened

After three days and with snow almost up to Bet's knees, John rode into the town of De Queen, Arkansas. Exhausted and cold, John was determined to find shelter first, sleep and then look for supplies and directions. Seeing a tiny white church up the way, he reined his horse in, and finding a woodshed out back, stabled Bet. He then took his saddle and blankets and slushed his way to the back entrance of the building. Too tired to think, he flung his saddle down on the floor in front of the pulpit, lay down and pulled his blankets over himself, and soon sleep captured him.

During the night perspiration began to run down John's face, and his body became drenched. He could recognize that same voice calling, "You do it." John opened his eyes and looked frantically for the one who called, but found the church empty. John felt so very tired and extremely hot, as if on fire, but yet his body was shivering. John focused his eyes on the wooden cross that had been placed on a boarded wall behind the pulpit and began to drift off again. He could see a man on the cross with hands and feet nailed solidly. A bloody gash formed on his side, and a crown of thorns was on his head. His body was broken and bloody. His eyes looked deep into John's, and John knew the man could see his soul. The man lifted his arms as if the nails had disappeared, and his bloodied arms were extended to embrace John. John wanted to run into the arms for comfort, but he couldn't seem to move, and then the image was lost in darkness.

"Dang this weather," complained Ken pushing himself away from the table. "The man just up and vanished. Ain't seen hair nor hide of him for weeks. He just vanished."

"Not so," rattled Hank. "He's smarter than we give him credit. The man got on to us and hit the woods. I'd do the same if'n I was him."

Stevens sat there carefully cleaning under his fingernails with his pocket knife. "He threw us a curve, but I'm not worried. In this weather, he's holed up somewhere, and he will come out. I feel like we are right on top of him. A breath away."

Closter, stomping snow from his boots pushed through the door and rubbing his cold hands together asked, "What's plan B, Boss? Oklahoma is just next door."

"When this snow lets up, Closter, you and Bent head north. Check every town, every homestead and every road. I want you back here in four days. Hank, you and Ken head south. I'll be riding west to De Queen. We'll meet up there," directed Stevens.

For the past several days Stevens and his men had been staying at a combination saloon and boarding house in Nashville, a village several miles east of De

Queen. The house wasn't fancy, really not much more than a large shack, but it was warm and dry, and the food was edible. Now the waiting was over, and it was time to get back to work finding the trail Wilson had taken.

John felt a cold object on his face, and he reached up to knock it off. Moments later he could feel the cold object there again. "No!" he shouted as he opened his eyes. Looking wildly about, he tried to determine where he was. The last he could remember was a church, but now he was in a small bedroom with light filtering through an iced, glass window. There was an elderly woman standing beside his bed. The door quickly opened and an elderly man entered.

With a wide smile the old gent said, "I see you're back with us again. My missy and I thought we were gonna lose you."

"What do you mean?" John asked.

The old gent, as round as he was tall and slick bald, settled on a chair next to John's bed while the woman took a chair on the opposite side. "My name is Samuel Jones, or Preacher Jones, and that there is my wife Becky."

Becky, a tiny, thin grey haired woman with a happy face, reached over and patted John's hand. "Don't have no fear, Son. You're in good hands. You're going to be all right."

Still disoriented, John tried to get up but fell back onto his pillow. "Where am I and how did I get here?" he asked pulling his cover back up.

"Son, it's like this. I found you on the church floor unconscious and with a high fever. Me and my missy carried you to the house, cleaned you up and doctored you as well as we could. Yore fever broke sometime last night."

"How long have I been here?"

"You've been here four days, Son."

John's memories were returning, and he also realized he was dressed in a nightgown. "Who put this thing on me?"

The pastor looked over to his wife and then back to John. "Naturally me and the missy."

"She put this on me?" muttered John openly embarrassed.

Becky shook her head and chuckled. "Son, I'm an old woman, and I've seen my share of naked men in my life. You don't have anything to worry about concerning me. I'm just glad we could save you."

John began to feel gratitude for the old couple. "Thank you both." John drifted off to sleep again, and later, Becky and Samuel came back with a steaming bowl of soup. "Try to get this down. You need to get your energy back."

John hungrily spooned the soup down and when finished, asked for more. Regaining a little of his strength and senses made John realize that he had to get moving. "You folks have been mighty kind to me and I am so grateful, but I've got to be going. If you will let me know where my horse is, then I'll get dressed and be gone as soon as possible."

Samuel pointed to the back yard. "I've got him stabled out in the barn. She's fine, but you need to take it easy."

John nodded his thanks and pushing the cover away, slung his legs off the side of the bed. "Can't stay here any longer. I've lost too many days like it is."

"We know, you're on your way to fetch your brother, Thomas, and then you got to find the Lewis children. Your brother is accused of killing two soldiers, but it was self-defense. You have some men trailing you at this moment, and they aim to kill your brother," Samuel said placing his hand on John's shoulder.

"How'd you know all that?" John asked in concern.

Becky smiled. "It was your fever. You did a lot of talking. We know quite a bit about you. Now, I think you realize that you are not strong enough to leave yet. You don't want to get sick again."

John knew Mrs. Jones was right, so he stayed the next two days recovering his strength. After dressing in clean clothes that Becky had washed for him and shaving his beard, he thanked the parson and his wife then saddling up deciding to stop by the church on his way out. Most of the snow had now melted with only hints of it resting under trees and in shady spots. John pushed the doors open and ambled down the aisle to the pulpit area. All was just like he remembered. Boarded walls, benches on either side of the aisle, glassed windows, pulpit and a wooden hand-hewed cross nailed to the back wall. All was still and a sense of peace flooded his body. He remembered the man on the cross in his dream and the comfort those arms had brought. Bending down in front of the cross, John whispered a thanks for his recovery and for the people God had brought to take care of him and keep him safe. He also prayed for Rebecca and their baby and then his family. Finally, John prayed for Thomas and his cousins. "Father please bring your comfort to Thomas, and safely return my cousins and brother to our home."

John returned and saddled Bet and then rode down the slope to the village below. He looked back to study the church once more and to remember the comfort and healing it brought.

The weather had broken and people were stirring. The town was not much, just a couple of small framed buildings, a few modest houses, a grist mill down on the stream that bordered the place and one larger building that appeared to be a general store. With his back to the sun and a brisk cold wind in his face, John slowly moved toward the town. A few people tipped their hats to him, but most had things on their minds other than a stranger. He stopped suddenly as a small boy chased a dog right in front of him. A woman across the road slammed her door open and verbally reprimanded the boy then nodded to John in thanks. John tied Bet to a hitching post and stepped up on the rotted wooden porch. He pushed open the door and a musty odor and darkness met him. Cured hams hung from rafters above, and all kinds of assortments of iron pots and pans were displayed on crude tables. Rolls of cloth were neatly arranged on shelves to his left, and across the end of the room was a long counter. A potbelly stove sat in the middle, yet to be fired.

"Help you with something?" A short, fat, shabbily dressed man rambled in from a back room.

A closer look caused John to hesitate. The man's skin was olive, eyes dark brown and his long white hair was braided down his back. John recognized that he was an Indian, but had no knowledge of the tribe. The Indian wore an old white shirt, red woolen coat and black cotton pants, and to John's surprise, was barefooted.

"Sir, I need some coffee, sugar, beans and some hardtack and jerky, if you've got any," John replied.

The old man waddled about and soon came back with his arms loaded. "Don't know how much you want. You take, then pay."

After John had filled his order, he paid the old man and asked, "Why haven't you fired your stove?"

"I ain't that cold. You cold?"

John broke into a smile. "Naw, I ain't either." Both men laughed. John relaxed and asked the old man some questions and found that he made his living primarily by selling items to the Choctaw and taking in furs that the Indians brought in for trade, and since his store was located less than a mile from the Arkansas, Oklahoma border, his business flourished.

"Can I ask you what the peculiar smell is in here?"

The man's eyes twinkled. "I think you are smelling dried furs and hides from the back storage room, or it could be my special brew, if you would like a sample."

"No sir, I don't think so, but thank you for the offer. But I do need some information. Can you tell me what direction I should take to find the Choctaw land?"

"You look like on the trail long time. Care for some coffee? I want to talk a spell." The old man took his time, but eventually started a fire in the stove and using the flat top as a cook stove, he began to make coffee. After the coffee brewed, he handed John a steaming cup and pointed for him to pull a wooden box up near the stove. For a few moments the two enjoyed their drink and studied one another.

Finally the man began. "You ask about Choctaw lands. Not sure why you want to know, but you stay out if you value your hide. It's like a powder keg 'bout to blow slam up. This here Arkansas is a rough country, but the Territory is worse. During war, tribes took sides; some fought for North and some for secession. They killed each other, and now that it's over, they have hard feelings and still fight. They angry at whites in Washington as well. When war ended, Washington punished all Indians for fighting. They shoved us all here in the Territory years ago, and now, they plan to take a lot of land away from us. I think they want to see us all dead."

The old man laid his empty cup down and reached over for his pipe. After filling it, he lit it with a piece of burning wood from the stove and taking a draw, expelled a large circle of smoke toward the ceiling. Extending the pipe to John, he said, "Want a draw?"

John nodded, "No sir. I don't think so."

"One more thing. If you do go, there is one mean white man roaming about. His name is Cullen Baker. He takes what he wants and kills who he pleases. Folks call his bunch Renegades. You stay away from him. He hangs around the North Texas, Louisiana border. You sure you don't want a draw?"

Trying to be courteous and at the same time inquisitive about the smoke, John reached over for the pipe. "You say the Choctaw land is just west of here?"

"Cross the creek and take the Fakit Road. Choctaw land there."

"Why do you call it the Turkey road?"

The old man raised his eyebrows in surprise. "How do you know Choctaw language?"

John smiled at him. "I was raised among the Choctaw in Mississippi, and my aunt is of the tribe. She taught us her language. I'm actually here to see her."

A wide smile wrinkled his brow, and he reached over and patted John on the arm. "That makes me proud. You just might have a chance to see her, if careful. By the way, they call me Luksi Chitto."

"That means big turtle. Why that?" asked John.

"When I was a baby, my father said that's what I looked like. What are you called?"

"My name is John."

The old man nodded his head. "That's a Bible name. Good name."

Mentioning the Bible, John's mind turned back to the Jones family. "Preacher Jones seems to be a man of faith. Do you worship there?"

"You a stranger, how do you know him?"

"I got sick when I first came here, and they took me in and helped me until I was well."

The old man nodded but seemed baffled. "Sound like them. They were good people and sometimes I would sit in back of church and listen about God. But gone now."

"Well, I really need to get on the road." John began walking with his supplies toward the door.

"Wait," Luksi called and walked quickly to the back storage room and returned with several bottles of liquid.

"You take these. Not for you. You give to any Indian that tries to take your horse or supplies. A bottle of this will help you keep your belongings because Indians would much rather have my brew." Luksi's eyes twinkled again, and he chuckled as he bid John goodbye.

Luksi followed John out the door, and after John mounted, he reached down and clasped the old man's hand and said, "Chi pinsa li ka achukma."

"Good to meet you, too. May God go with you, John."

John decided to return to the church to say one more goodbye to Pastor Jones and his wife. When he reached the church, the windows were broken, the front door was shattered, and the building was leaning to one side. It looked as if no one had been there in many years. In confusion, John walked up the broken steps and walked inside. To his amazement dust covered the floor and many of the benches were gone. The cross that had been on the wall was now lying on the floor. John went out the back and found that the barn and the house were in shambles.

John returned inside and knelt in front of the cross lying on the floor. "Father, I don't understand what happened to me here whether what I saw was a vision or dream or ministering angels, but I thank you for Your wondrous care and healing." John reverently left the church and mounted Bet, then he crossed the creek and headed into the Oklahoma territory.

Music from a string orchestra filled the evening as hundreds of guests laughed, talked and danced across the smooth oak floor of The Oaks. A large meal had been served earlier and now champagne flowed like water, and smoke from tobacco rose to the glass cupola and was pushed out with the slight coastal breezes. Men of means were dressed in formal wear, and women wore lavish evening gowns. As darkness approached, a man in a dark grey tuxedo stepped up on a platform and raising his hand, the merry makers ceased their dancing and socializing and gathered around. "Mister Frankie Olliver would you please come up here and join me." The crowd gave a thunderous roar of applause in approval.

Frankie smiled at the dark haired and beautiful young woman that was his dancing partner for the night and asked to be excused, then making his way through the masses of people, he stepped up on the platform.

Placing his arm over Frank's shoulder, the man exclaimed, "Ladies and Gentlemen, it gives me great pleasure to introduce our new state senator for District Two of the great state of Louisiana."

Once more the people shouted their approval. Cheers, clapping of hands and whistles shook the room. The man continued as Frankie joined him on the platform. "Folks, you know the shape our Southland is in. The House and Senate is full of politicians that have no right to be there. They basically have no qualifications. Decent men can't qualify nor, in some instances, even vote. This Federal Government of ours—this martial law placed around our necks is a burden we have got to destroy. They may think we're all dumb Southerners, but they will find that we know a lot more than they think we do. And so, we found ourselves an intelligent, young man who did not participate in the glorious rebellion; with the death of our late senator from District Two, we managed to get the exact replacement we wanted, and they did not even suspect that we outsmarted them. Ladies and Gentlemen, the Louisiana Senate has recently approved Mister Frankie Olliver as the replacement. Here he is folks, Mister Olliver himself!"

Thunder could not have been any louder than the response that erupted and swept through the bayou country. The people were jubilant that they now had one of their own who could represent them and give them hope for improvements. Maybe soon they would have their homeland returned to them.

Frankie was humbled by the response. "Men and Women, today I promise you that I will work diligently to uphold the laws of the state. I will strive to create more order and do everything in my power to return our state to the stable and prosperous Louisiana it once was. Once again our people will fill the House and Senate, and we will be in control of our state's destiny."

Again the applaud filled the room and Frankie caught the enthusiasm and determined that he truly meant to do all he could to make sure Louisiana prospered in the coming years. After his speech, people began flocking to the platform to shake his hand, give encouragement and their approval. Frankie had never greeted so many people in his life. Finally as the last guest left the platform, Frankie worked his way through the crowd and slipped out to the open balcony to contemplate the evening. He rested his hands on the wrought iron railing to clear his mind in the evening breeze. He knew that his Papére's name and wealth had brought him this new power, but he was determined that he would make a difference in his state and hopefully in this new government. Frankie rubbed his face and took a deep breath of cool, evening air. *Yes, I plan to do whatever I can to heal this broken land.* For the first time in years Frankie felt he truly had a purpose and that his future was going to be better. He no longer would let his father's negative and hurtful words define him as a man. He would be confident, and he would strive to be honorable in every circumstance. Even though he would never enjoy the approval of his earthly father, he would strive to be a man who honors his Papére, his family, his state, but most importantly, his Heavenly Father. This was his new beginning; this was his destiny.

Mister Carden Baudin of Baudin Shipping in New Orleans was twenty two and stood six foot three, had broad shoulders, dark short curly hair and a charming smile. He was gazing at the most beautiful girl in the room and felt such gratitude for the chance to be her escort. He had met Frankie two months earlier at a fund raising event in Baton Rouge and instantly developed a friendship that led to his invitation to The Oaks. Although he was thoroughly impressed with the plantation and the festive event, it was Suzanne who took his breath away. Her dark complexion and soot black, silky hair was complimented by the deep purple evening gown that was revealing but modest. He loved the way she glowed with pride at the response her brother had received. Dancing with her had been a delight, and he was reluctant to let the evening end before insuring he could spend time alone with her before his stay ended.

As the party broke up in the early morning hours, Frankie invited Carden to go downstairs to the study to see his grandfather's collection of antique arms. Carden turned quietly to Suzanne. "Suzanne, this has been a wonderful night for me. I have truly enjoyed every minute of our time together. Since I will be here for a few nights, would you be able to take me on a tour of your Papere's plantation?"

Suzanne released his arm and smiled "Thank you for tonight and it would be my pleasure to show you The Oaks. We can meet about ten o'clock in the morning."

Suzanne walked out to the balcony as Carden left with Frankie. She sat down on a padded couch and removed her shoes and felt instant relief from the hours on the dance floor. Off in the distance an owl sang his lonely tune, and a light fog hovered over the low lying fields. A full moon showered its light down upon her, and fluffy clouds floated carelessly across the heavens occasionally caging the moonlight. Since returning to her Papere's plantation, this was the first time she had actually enjoyed the company of a man. All the others who had approached her could not make her forget the one she left in Little Rock, but she had actually enjoyed Mister Baudin's company, and looked forward to the next day and her date with him. As she recalled his humor, gentleness and sweetness, Suzanne was glad that someone had come that could make her empty heart feel a little lighter.

13

Choctaw Territory

*Consider it pure joy, my brothers, whenever you face trials of many
kinds, because you know that the testing of your faith develops
perseverance. Perseverance must finish its work so that you may be
mature and complete not lacking anything.*

—James 1: 2-4 NIV

John left the sparsely inhabited southwest Arkansas, pushed Bet across a
rippling stream and entered the Oklahoma territory. The old trader had told him
to look for an Indian agent at Broken Bow, about sixteen miles to the west. Even
though he would be able to find his kin through this agent, John still decided to
take precautions by following a seldom used narrow road instead of taking the
main thoroughfare to Broken Bow. He pushed his long coat over to the side where
his revolver was in easy reach and placed his Sharps rifle across his lap. John knew
that letting folks understand his alertness and readiness was a great deterrent to
crime.

Dense woods bordered the road as far as he could observe, and homesteads were close to non-existent. A few Indians were milling about their cabins,
but they paid little attention to him; most just gave him an intense stare. John
constantly scanned the landscape for any movement as he slowly followed the
path. John's first interruption was a trio of deer bounding from the underbrush.
Even when he jerked his rifle up toward the sound, the deer just paused, ran a few
yards, turned back to look at him and then lowered their noses to the ground in
search of acorns. The next interruption was a little more unsettling. While watering Bet at a small creek, a couple of Indians rode by and momentarily stopped.
When they saw John's rifle, they spoke some words, kicked their horses in the
flanks and galloped away. John hoped the words spoken did not mean trouble
later on down the path.

At mid-day John saw in a clearing a small house with a covered front
porch. John rode to the cabin and found an old man sitting in a straight back
chair whittling on a stick. He looked rather thin and wore a dark blue army jacket,
brown sloop hat and black woolen britches. Wrinkles told of his age, and the long

mustache that ran down each side of his mouth stained with tobacco juice gave its own story.

John came closer and sheathed his rifle. "You the Indian agent?"

The old man dropped his stick and eyed John for a moment. "You lost, young man?"

John slid down from his saddle and fastened the reins on a hitching post. Bet shook her head and rattled her harness as she tried to nibble a parcel of grass below, and John stepped up on the porch. "Sir, I need directions. I have family somewhere abouts."

The old man reached into his coat pocket to bring out a chunk of tobacco; then he bit off a piece and pointed to a chair leaning against the wall. "I'm Captain Johnston, retired, and some folks in Washington thought this here would be a proper place for me. What's your name?"

John extended his hand. "My name is John Wilson."

"You sure you're in the right place? This here is Choctaw land, and it can be dangerous. There's a lot of hatred bound up here. Indians hating Indians and no love for whites. Who you want to find?"

"I'm looking for my Aunt Hatta. Hope she's still alive. I haven't seen her since I was a boy."

The captain leaned over and spat a large blob of slavered tobacco off into the yard. "Ain't ever heard of the woman," he answered, rubbing his mouth across the sleeve of his coat.

John pursed his lips in thought. "How about a Hatta Wilson who has a son named Homer?"

The old man's eyebrows lifted, and a smile formed. "Why didn't you give me their full names? I know both of 'em. Saw Homer and some other white fellow about a week ago. What do you want with them?"

John sighed in relief as he figured that Thomas was the white fellow with Homer and that Homer and his aunt were alive and well. All the harsh and lonely weeks on the road were finally coming to an end. "They're kin. You might say this is a homecoming," John answered. "Can you tell me where to find Aunt Hatta?"

"Let's go inside where I can get to a map. I think I can locate the place," The captain pulled himself up from the old cowhide covered chair. Once inside, he lit a lantern and shuffled over to a cabinet to pull out a rolled map. Spreading it out on a dilapidated table, Johnston smoothed the edges down and began running his fingers across the map in search. Finally he stopped and pointed to a spot and directed John to pay close attention. "Son, here's where you are now. You ride northwest for about twenty five miles, and you'll run slap into what we call Little River. From there follow the stream north for about forty miles, and you'll find a road that runs east to west. Turn east for about three miles and cross a small creek. There'll be a path leading north, and their place is about three miles down that path. Beautiful country there. Foothills of the Kiamichi Mountains. You got it?"

"Yes sir. It seems like about a three days ride," added John. "I was told that this was dangerous country, but I've met no trouble so far."

"Come on out front, and if you'll sit a spell, I can shed some light on that statement," shrugged the old man walking back to the porch. Settling in his chair, he reached for another chew of tobacco. "It's like this, you ain't very far into Indian country, but these Indians had a hard time with each other when they were spread out all over the country. Now that they are crammed into this one area, it's a lot worse. With the war, they took sides, and believe it or not, they are still killing each other. North of us is the Creek, Osage and Cherokee, to the west we have the Chickasaw, Kiowa, Cheyenne, and to top it off, they brought in the Apache. Them Apaches are a rough tribe and mad as hornets about being forced here. As long as you stay with your kin here in Choctaw land, you'll probably be fine, but stay out of the other lands. What is really sad, is that since the war ended, the government is gonna strip land from the Indians which will shove them even closer, and believe me, there will be trouble."

John shook his head in thought. "What about this man called Cullen Baker?"

Placing his hand on John's shoulder, he muttered, "If you come across that scoundrel, stay clear. He's one mean, crazy white man, and along with his pistols, he carries a double barreled shotgun. He hates Yankees. I heard he killed most of a small patrol weeks back, but it could have been government men instead of soldiers. Not really sure. You fight with the South?"

"Yes sir, I did."

"You might have a chance then, but don't count on it," stammered Johnston. "You seem to be a good man. Just be very careful."

All of a sudden a question formed in John's mind. "You ever run across Baker?"

The old man laughed. "Yep, he came through here one time and scared the pants off of me. He pointed that shotgun he always carries right in my face, and I was so terrified I couldn't even blink my eyes. He held it there for it seemed like a day and began to laugh. He lowered his gun and told me I was too old and ugly to kill. And then he just rode on off."

John thanked the captain for his help, and saddling Bet, he rode with the sun to his back and the dense forest in front of him. In a lot of ways the terrain and woods were much like that of southeastern Mississippi, but some of the vegetation and trees were new to him. Weaving his way through the forest was time consuming, but he felt safer with no trail or road. When he did come upon a homestead, he veered out of sight and continued. A little past noon John had still not come to the Little River, so he spurred Bet up a steep, leafed hill and when cresting, he saw the rippling waters of the river below. As he carefully descended, he found a well-used trail that followed the eastern bank of the river. After traveling this trail for a while and with the sun setting, John knew he needed rest, so he reined Bet up a hill from the road and dismounted. John made camp out of sight of the road, then gathered wood for a fire and began preparing for the night. Breaking pine and cedar limbs, he built a windbreak for shelter and gathered pine straw for bedding. John opened a can of beans and cut small hunks of deer jerky to mix with the beans. After his tasty meal, John threw down his saddle and saddlebags, rolled out his oil cloth and resting his head on the curve of his saddle, he was soon asleep. His feet were near the fire which in his exhausted state he had forgotten to extinguish.

In the middle of the night John felt a hard jab to his stomach, and as he began to awaken and get up, a blow to his head sent him back to the ground.

Before the blow, John heard someone say, "Katima hon hahullo kmat minti?" (Where did this white man come from?)

"You be still white man," a voice muttered in English. "You listen, and we might not kill you."

As John tried to overcome his dizziness, he could smell the odor of an unwashed man. As John's vision returned, he could see a man with long unkempt hair crouched away from the fire and holding an old musket pointed directly at him. Another man was sitting cross legged next to the fire warming himself and holding a pistol in his hands. John thought both were probably Choctaws.

"What do you want from me?" John asked, rubbing his head as he tried to sit up.

The Indian laughed as he held John's pistol "I think it would be good to take your pistol and then that nice Spencer rifle. Maybe the horse as well, even though she is a sorry lot."

Sitting up and less than confident, John thought for a moment, then smiled over to the Choctaw. "I'll tell you what, I've got something you might rather have, and as John reached for his saddlebags, the Indian knocked him back down and grabbed the bags from John's hands and hastily reached inside.

"Ohee!" he shouted as he danced around the fire holding a bottle of whiskey in each hand. "The gods are blessing us, Isi," he screamed to his companion. "Now we have pistol, rifle, horse and spirit water. What a day!"

The day actually was in John's favor as they began to drink whisky, laugh and then sleep.

With the breaking of dawn and the snoring of the men, John quickly and quietly rolled up his blankets, gathered his belongings and saddled Bet. Before he left, he rekindled the fire, covered the drunk Choctaws with the blankets he had retrieved from their two horses and then rode away.

Yes, this had not been one of his better nights, he thought, but God was in His heaven and peace was on the earth. John was not only thankful to his Lord, but he was very grateful for the insight of Luksi at the trading post. Because of it, God willing, he would see his kin soon.

"Bout time you got here!" barked Stevens to Closter as he rode up to meet the group. "Bent and Hank got here last night."

"Sorry about that. I searched every road and trail north of here and found nothing. No sign of 'em," stammered Closter taking his hat off and pushing his long hair back.

"Don't worry about that. I caught his trail about a mile back where he finally came out of the woods. No way to get in touch with you," informed Stevens. "Hank's gone on ahead trailing. It won't take us long to catch up with him."

That night as the men prepared a campfire, Hank returned, tethered his horse and walked slowly to Stevens to give his report. "Well, not only have I managed to see where Wilson has been, but there is an Indian agent up the way, so we will be able to get some information on where he's headed."

Stevens was elated over the news and quickly decided it was time to leave in the fog laden dawn. At mid-morning Stevens and his men rode up to the agent's cabin "Hank, go see if anyone is there."

Hank dismounted, walked on the porch and pounded the door several times, and finally after hearing no one stirring, called out, "Hey, in there! Anybody home?"

Frustrated, Stevens drew his revolver and cranked off a shot. Smoke floated across the porch covering Hank, and off in the distance, they heard it echo.

"Hey!" shouted a voice out back. "Is that necessary? A man can't even relieve himself in peace this day and time." Pulling up his suspenders and tucking in his shirt, Johnston slammed the door of his outhouse and walked to where the men waited. "I'm Johnston. What do you gents need this early in the morning?"

Stevens cleared his throat. "Sorry to bother you, but all we need is a little information. We're following a fellow from Mississippi that came through here perhaps yesterday. Medium height and riding a grey mustang. You seen 'em?"

Johnston rubbed his hand across his chin and carefully studied the men eyeing him. "Sir, I'm just an Indian agent, retired military. My job is to look after the needs of the Choctaw here. I don't give out information."

Stone faced, Stevens nodded over to Hank who slowly slipped his revolver out and leveled it on Johnston. "You either talk, or I'll blow a hole right through your head."

Stunned, Johnston took a step back and raising his hands, muttered, "Now wait up boy. Ain't no call for this. Now what exactly do you men want?"

"I want to know what you know about the man we're after. His brother murdered two federal soldiers, and we believe the man we are trailing is going to meet up with his brother," informed Stevens as he dismounted.

"You say this man's brother killed two federal soldiers?" Johnston asked.

"He did and we want to bring the killer in," Stevens answered extending his hand. Turning to Hank, Stevens breathed, "Put the revolver down, Hank."

Johnston invited the men in and quickly told all that he knew about his visitor. He showed them the map and the location of the cabin of Homer and Hatta Wilson. A big smile crossed Steven's face and reaching inside his inner coat pocket, he took out a bag and pulled out five gold coins which he laid on the table. "Gentlemen, we have finally reached the end of our search. By leaving now, we should have him in custody by tomorrow. This has been one long ride," chuckled Stevens.

"Are we to take him dead or alive?" Closter asked making his way toward the door.

"Doesn't matter. It will be entirely left up to Wilson. If it comes to violence, we'll do what is necessary even if it means killing the whole group. That would be easier than carrying him all the way back to Mississippi. It really don't make any difference," Stevens said as he walked away. "A Pinkerton always gets his man."

The sun was glimmering through the trees, and spring was finally approaching. Grass was turning green, trees were budding new growth and birds sang sweet melodies. A warm sun touched John's back as he rode north. John soon found the road, and turning east he had no trouble finding the stream which meant he was only three miles from seeing his aunt and cousin and hopefully, brother. He reined Bet north and followed the narrow trail along the creek bank. The old oaks of centuries past stood tall, massive and commanding, creating a canopy with their fully leafed size and allowing little direct sunlight to reach the ground The stream below bubbled and tumbled over stones and fallen trees as it rushed past. In the far distance he could now see a trace of the mountains. Both joy and peace filled his heart as he beheld the most beautiful and serene place he had ever seen. His mind went to visions of Rebecca with their new born child as he held its little fingers in his and kissed its cheek at her side. He was lost in the glow on Becca's face as she held the baby and that glow haloed her as an angel.

Finally an open field lay ahead bordered with split railings, and horses lazily grazed as chickens clucked and cackled in search of their morning meal. Beyond the field was a log cabin with smoke curling from the stoned chimney and clusters of cedar trees surrounding the place. The hounds bounded from the porch and raced out toward the intruder. John laughed to himself. "Homer always loved his hunting dogs, the louder, the better,"

As John rode closer to the cabin, an old woman got up and reached for her musket and walked quickly to the edge of the porch. "What do you want?"

John removed his hat and smiled. "You don't know me, do you?"

"Can't say I do, young man," she answered turning her head to get a better look at the stranger. The woman tall, thin, dark complexioned with her long white hair rolled in a bun stood eyeing him. "You do look somewhat familiar."

"What if I call you Aunt Hatta?"

The old woman's eyebrows lifted, and a faint smile formed as she recognized the man before her. "You can't be my little John, can you?"

"Yes ma'am. I'm John."

John quickly dismounted and wrapped his arms around his aunt. Tears began to flow as they greeted each other. "It's been such a long time. It is so very good to see you. I guess you were just a child the last time I saw you."

After another hug, Hatta stepped back and said, "Well, I think I need to get some food out for you. Have you eaten?"

"I really am not hungry right now. Maybe later. I just want to find out all about you and tell you about home. We sure do wish you were with us." After John stabled his horse, he returned to the porch and they continued to share stories. For hours John informed his aunt of all that had happened to the family since she and Homer had left. Sometimes they laughed, and other times sat quietly in tears.

"I'm glad your mama and papa are doing fine. But I sure am sad to hear about James Earl. The war took a lot of good men. I sure will miss seeing his sweet smile."

"I have some good news too. Do you remember Rebecca Walker? Well, we are married, and in July we have a little one coming." A glow formed on the old woman's face as John told the details of his marriage to Rebecca and the coming of the little one. "Is Thomas here? Will Homer be home soon?"

"They've been gone the past few days but should be home before dark today." Hatta looked at John in question of his need to see them.

"Aunt Hatta, I hate to bring bad news, but Uncle Jonathan was murdered and Aunt Sara Ann got sick and passed away. I've come to get Thomas so we can locate our cousins and take them home with us. You know, it would just make our family complete if you and Homer would also come home."

Tears formed in Hatta's eyes as she heard about her husband Jake's sister's death and about the children who no longer had parents. She stood and gave John a hug. "Let's head inside, John. This breeze has become cold."

John grabbed his belongings and was soon warming himself at the fireplace. The cabin was soundly constructed of logs ten inches wide and tightly chinked with red clay. The right side of the house served as a dining and living area with the fireplace used for cooking. To his left were two bedrooms and at the opposite end was a ladder that led to the loft which served as a guest room as well as for storage. Climbing the ladder, John threw his belongings up above and noticed the warmth rising from the nearby chimney.

As the sun was creeping behind the hills, John heard approaching horses and excitedly headed to the porch. John recognized his brother and a man slightly larger than his brother with the dark skin of the Choctaw. Soon they were close and the deep blue eyes and short cropped light red hair proved that this was indeed Homer, his Uncle Jake's son.

As they rode closer to the porch, Homer frowned and softly voiced, "Wonder what that fellow is doing here."

Thomas chuckled and called out so John could hear. "Well, I can tell you this, I definitely know him, but don't know what in the tarnations he's doing here." Thomas jumped off his horse and grabbed his brother in a big hug. "Homer, meet your cousin and my brother, John Wilson."

Homer sat speechless thinking about the skinny, curly headed boy he knew as his cousin who now had grown into a man with that strong Wilson semblance.

Homer just shook his head, and a smile soon appeared as he dismounted, patted John strongly on the back, then gripped him in a bear hug. "Welcome Cousin. It's been a long time, and you've become a man."

After all the greetings and talk, John volunteered to take the horses to the stable out back. He removed their gear, brushed the horses down and turned them loose in the fenced field. John quickly walked to the house anxious to spend time with his family. Hatta was cooking a pot of venison stew over the fire while Homer and Thomas held steaming cups of hot coffee. Homer pulled a chair up for John, poured him a cup of coffee and the three settled down for a long conversation.

A nervous frown appeared on Thomas's face, and he laid his coffee down to direct his eyes toward John. "Okay, Brother. It is really good to see you, but I have a feeling that this isn't a social call. What is the problem? Is something wrong with mama and papa?"

John nodded no and began at once to repeat the story about the Lewis children to his brother and cousin. "Thomas, there is one more problem. There is a group of men following me." John continued to relay the events of the past weeks.

After he had finished, Thomas got up and backed up to the fireplace. "John, you say one man was well dressed, one a soldier and three wore Calvary pants, tan Calvary hats and buckskin jackets," Thomas mumbled to himself. "Is that right?"

"That's exactly right."

Thomas rubbed his beard in thought. "Tell you what, the well- dressed man is some kind of a detective. The soldier is not really a threat because he is just representing the military. Now, the other three fellows concern me. To my thinking they are army scouts from out west. I recognize their apparel since I used to wear the same myself. If this is so, we have got us a problem."

All grew quiet as Thomas continued to evaluate the news. "You said they tracked you from Vicksburg to the Oklahoma territory. If they did that even when you were trying to evade them, then there is no question that it is just a matter of time before they'll track you here. Those scouts are used to tracking Indians, so you, John, were probably easy prey for them."

Hatta stopped stirring her stew as she pondered the predicament. "What are we gonna do then?"

"I ain't running no more. I say we take a stand," Thomas stammered.

Homer furrowed his eyebrows. "Not so hasty, Cousin. Let me do some thinking before we start shooting."

Even though the men were tired after their three day journey, they talked deep into the night. At early light, Homer saddled his horse and rode away. He returned later that morning and told everyone to stay near the house and keep their rifles close. Hours crept by as they nervously waited and dusk became darkness. A couple of hours past dark, Homer gathered them all together. "Thomas, you need to put out the light of the lantern, and we are all going to be very quiet and pretend to be asleep. I will take the first shift while you two actually sleep."

Hours slipped by, and the three men took turns sleeping. As dawn approached, the men were awake but continued their vigil. Soon they heard a shot, and a voice from outside called, "We've got the place surrounded! All we want is Thomas Wilson!"

"How do you know he's here?" Homer yelled back.

"He's here. We tracked you two as you rode in yesterday. Just turn him over to us, and no one will be hurt."

"And if we don't?" Homer yelled back.

"We'll burn you out and kill all of you. The way I see it, is you just don't have a choice."

Homer quietly slipped to the back porch and grabbed the hunting horn he had hidden behind a large fifty gallon barrel. He pulled it to his mouth, blew a deafening blast, and echoes resounded across the mountains. All was eerie quiet for a moment, then the yells of hundreds of Choctaws filled the air. The Choctaws had earlier encircled the cabin and allowed the intruders to come into their trap.

Hearing the myriad of screams, Stevens and his men were gripped in total surprise and fear. Homer blew his horn again and stepped out onto the front porch. "You have two choices. You can throw down your weapons and come out, or I'll turn you over to some of my friends. The choice is yours. You've got exactly sixty seconds to consider your fate."

For a moment silence pervaded the air, then one by one the men moved from behind their cover with hands held high. Thomas, John and Hatta joined Homer on the front porch with muskets and rifles in hand. As the intruders gathered humbly before the Wilsons, Homer studied them carefully. "You know I could have you killed right here and no one would ever know, but you need to know the truth about my cousin."

The young soldier was shaking with fear while the three scouts used to facing death, stood straight and calm. Stevens, obviously nervous took a deep breath. "We were sent on this mission to fetch Thomas Wilson who murdered some military men. We are just following our orders."

Thomas walked up and looked Stevens in the eyes. "Well sir, you have found him, but I'm not a murderer. If you had taken time to seek the truth, you would know that I didn't start that fight and I was just defending myself. But I guess now, that mistake may just cost your life and the lives of your men."

Stevens realizing his fate began to tremble. "You can't just kill us because we are doing our job."

Homer called to Hatta's brother. "Minsa, have these men tied up, bind them to that old oak out back, and have someone keep guard. Any of your men bring your hatchets? How about bows?"

Fearing death, Stevens and the young soldier began to plead for their lives while the scouts stood solemnly accepting their fate.

After the men were taken away, John turned to Homer, "Do you plan to kill them?"

"It would solve my problem," stated Thomas throwing a log on the fire.

"No, we can't do that. We'd have too many Federals hunting us down," answered Homer. "What I plan to do is put the fear of God in them tonight, then escort them to the Arkansas line. Once there, Minsa and our people will strip them of their money, take their horses and leave them on foot. He will warn them to leave, never come back, and to keep their mouths shut."

"What if they do come back?" asked John.

"Well, I'll only spare their lives once."

"When did you get so bold and blood thirsty, Cousin?" laughed Thomas.

A calm came over Homer. "White men murdered my father, drove us from our Mississippi home, and now Washington plans to take more of our land. And today, a white man has threatened to burn my house and kill my loved ones. Can you not understand why I plan to protect my family even if I must kill?"

With a band of over forty Choctaws, Hatta quickly brought out her iron kettle and began preparing a stew of venison, beans, potatoes and onions complimented with cakes of cornbread. As the night drew on, the Choctaws built a large bond fire and with several gallons of corn liquor, began to party. As the spirits took hold, laughter, shouting and singing filled the evening. Eventually some of the Choctaws started throwing their hatches and shooting arrows into the tree above the prisoners terrorizing Stevens and his men. Minsa had ordered his people to scare but not hurt the prisoners, even though there were some close calls. Once every hour Minsa would go outside and check on the night's activities and would come back with a smile on his face.   To John's surprise, two of the Choctaws were the same ones who tried to rob him earlier. When they saw John, they just smiled apologetically and thanked him for the spirits they consumed.

As daylight approached, Homer and Minsa strode out to the bound captives who expected death. "Minsa, keep them bound, saddle them up and take them away," Homer said expressionless.

Trying to get on his feet, Stevens gaspingly said, "You're smarter than I thought. You don't want to kill us on your property. You plan to take us out into the woods and dispose of us."

"Take them away, Minsa."

Saddled, Stevens looked back to where Homer stood. "You'll pay for this, Homer Wilson."

"If you are smart, you will keep your mouth shut. You will forget you have ever seen Thomas Wilson. If I ever see you again, your fate will be worse than death. Do you understand what I mean by worse than death? Minsa, get 'em out of here. If they give you trouble, you know what to do."

Walking back to the house, John met Homer on the porch and asked, "What if they do come back?"

Homer smiled and slapped John on the back. "Don't worry. They won't come back here, but even if they do, you and Thomas will be somewhere in Texas looking for the Lewis children."

14

Texas Bound

My soul waits in silence for God only, for my hope is from Him. He
only is my rock and my salvation. My stronghold; I shall not be shaken.
—Psalm 62:5 NASB

Realizing that John was extremely exhausted, Thomas decided to give his
brother several days rest before heading into Texas which also gave them time
to prepare for the search. Supplies of food and ammunition were essential, and
hopefully, the Lewis children were in good care. Thomas planned to ride south
and within three days reach the northeastern section of Texas where Jonathan
Lewis had run a ferry on the Sulfur River in Cass County. There the search for
the children would begin. Thomas worried about leaving the protection of the
Choctaws and facing the military presence in Texas. If caught, he knew he would
be taken back to Mississippi, although he knew there was less military activity
in northeast Texas. Thomas hoped that finding the children would give his life
purpose because, for him, despair and guilt consumed his every moment. If he
could sacrifice his life for the safety of the children, then maybe his death could
cover some of the deep sin that pervaded his soul. He looked forward to his death
and a release of all the nightmares and emptiness caused by the killings that he
had committed and relished during the war.

Stevens stood under the porch of a boarding house in Nashville, Arkansas,
and brooded over the harrowing and embarrassing event of the past week. As he
watched the rain pounding down on the muddied street, he deliberated about
how he, a Pinkerton agent, could have been so easily trapped and man handled.
He pulled up a chair, sat down and proceeded to pack his pipe for a smoke. He
was thankful he had been able to conceal a money belt secured around his bulging
waistline which had enabled him to fund lodging and food for their return. Now
the decision that haunted him was whether to give up the hunt and admit defeat
or complete his mission. Continuing would not only be dangerous, but they would
need extra funds for mounts, supplies, and salaries for his men. He finally decided
to confide in Hank for direction.

"Hank, I've got a job for you. I want you to ride up to the capital where there is wire service and send a message to Mississippi. Briefly tell them what has happened and if they want us to continue, extra funds will be needed. Take the horse I just purchased and ride out as soon as possible. If you leave this morning, you should be back by late tomorrow, and on your return, we'll have a meeting to discuss our options. Time is important because Wilson will be on the move."

The fire crackled and popped as John sat relaxing in its presence. Outside a cold northwardly wind howled and whistled as it pushed against the old log house. Shadows of flames danced across the walls to his back as the smell of burning hickory wafted through the air. With the dim light of a candle, Hatta was struggling to knit some socks. At the back of the room, Homer at a small desk prepared a document while Thomas on the floor near the hearth with file in hand, repaired the trigger mechanism for his Sharps rifle.

John loved the quiet warmth and companionship of his family. He was thankful for these few days to recover his strength. His heart ached for Becca and he wondered if she and the babe were healthy. He worried about his father and Toby being able to handle the spring planting without him? He was amazed by the inexplicable dream in the church and its mysterious meaning.

Suddenly, he remembered the message for Thomas. "Thomas, before I left, Suzanne asked about you. I could really tell that she cares for you."

Thomas just raised his head acknowledging John's words then returned to his work.

Homer turned in his chair. "You mean Suzanne Olliver?"

"Yes," John replied.

"What is that woman to you, Thomas?" Homer stated harshly.

"Just drop it. It's none of your business, and she is not in my future," muttered Thomas.

"None of my business! That girl's father had my father killed, and you say it's none of my business," Homer answered in anger.

John walked close to Homer. "You don't know that for sure, that Mister Olliver had Uncle Jake killed."

"That's where you're wrong. Some of my people tracked one of the men who was in on the killing, and he admitted that Frank Olliver, Sr. paid them each one hundred dollars to kill my father. One day, I promise you, Mister Olliver will meet the same fate. If I ever see him, he will exist no longer."

Hatta looked up and removed her glasses. "Boys, that's enough of this hard talk. Suzanne and Frankie were always welcomed at our place as children. You can't blame a child for what a parent does."

"But Mother, the man killed my father."

"Yes Son, and he killed my dear husband as well."

Thomas quietly spoke, "Well, Homer, you won't have to kill him. Someone has taken care of that task for you. Cousin, you need to know that Suzanne loved her father, but she did not condone his behavior, and Frankie hated his father and moved to New Orleans to be away from him."

The next morning was bright and the weather had cleared, so Thomas and John packed, mounted their horses and prepared an additional pack horse for the journey. They waved to Hatta, but Homer was nowhere to be seen. As the two turned to begin their journey, they heard a loud voice thunder out.

"Hold up! You ain't gonna leave me behind," shouted Homer, galloping from the barn riding a mustang. John was surprised, but Thomas smiled widely as he thanked his cousin knowing that the sheer size of the three together would be a force to reckon with and be avoided.

"We should be at the Texas border in about a day or two, and Cass County is just south of there. Since there aren't many ferries on the Sulfur River, we will find them quickly," Homer informed them as they galloped away.

The trio made excellent time as they followed trails and roads as much as possible. Often mounted Choctaws would approach them and call for Homer, and after a short conversation, would ride away. The weather cooperated, and the woods were turning into a glorious introduction of spring. The dogwoods were sprouting their white blossoms, and spring flowers dotted the woodlands generating peaceful serenity. By noon, the men removed their heavy coats and breathed in the cool, crisp, clean air. *If all goes well*, John thought, *I could be home in a couple of weeks.*

At dusk, Homer led the group to a knoll overlooking a small stream, and the men began to make camp. A fire was built, bed rolls laid out and a pot of coffee brewed on the coals. Saddles were removed, and the men brushed the horses down and tethered them to graze on the young grass. As the sun was waning below the horizon and streaks of golds and purples laced the clouds, the men prepared their bedrolls.

A soft wind blew the bare branches above and flickered the fire as the men lay reflecting on the day. John glanced at Thomas thinking that he had changed since the shooting; he seemed impassive and detached, accepting of his bleak future. John knew little about Homer because he had been just a boy when Hatta, Homer, and many of the Choctaw had left Mississippi.

John deep in thought, raised up on his elbow and woke Homer who was almost asleep. "Tell me something. What's gonna happen to the Indians out here?"

"John, that's a good question. First, we ain't Indians. That's what the first explorers called us. I call us the People. We were here first but that does not matter. There is little hope for the People."

"What do you mean, no hope!" resounded Thomas gaining interest in the conversation.

"Listen to me. The white man is like locusts that destroy and consume everything as they advance across the land. The white man preaches peace and the love of Jesus, but he lies, cheats, steals and kills to get what he wants. The People have been swept across the Mississippi and herded into a small land. And now there is word coming from Washington that they will take more land from the People and give it to the whites. The Negro at least had worth as slaves, the People are considered less than human. We are looked upon as nothing more than animals. Our way of life demands lots of land, and so our way of life will soon be gone. Our future is death. A hundred years from now, we will be no longer."

All was quiet for a moment then John softly asked, "Do you hate the whites? You know that you are half white."

"Homer shook his head. "I don't hate the whites. I hate what they are doing to my people. How can I hate my kin? I can't. I am a half-breed, but my heart is completely with my people. They are my peace. They are my home." All was silent as each man contemplated the fate of the Indian.

"You know I really haven't learned a lot about you, but I do know farming, and your farm doesn't seem to be very productive. What do you do for a living? What's your trade?"

Homer winked to Thomas and laughed. "Well my cousin, you are full of questions tonight."

Turning his attention to John, he replied, "When we got here, I attended an Indian or People's school. Because I was a good student, I received an appointment to West Point. Some politician thought that would be a good gesture, or should I say joke, but the joke was on him. I did well at West Point, and when the war broke out, they sent me to Texas to command a regiment of Union troops. Because my people were taking sides, I decided that I couldn't fight against my own people. I resigned and stayed out of the war."

"That still doesn't explain what you do now to make a living." John continued to query.

Homer reached to his leather jacket and turning the collar out displayed a gold badge. "I'm an Oklahoma Ranger. Me and about a dozen others are trying to keep peace in the Territory."

John shook his head in amazement. His cousin was working in the military as a ranger to his own people. How ironic.

March in Mississippi brings preparation for the upcoming farming season, and Lott and Toby were busy at work. They had already done some breaking of the soil, but with the absence of Thomas and John, had decided to reduce the acreage. Corn had brought them a nice profit last season, so they decided to add twenty acres in cotton. After the shooting at Frank Olliver's cabin, Toby and his wife, Sadie, took Skinner's two young boys into their home. Lott helped Toby add an extra room onto his house, and the boys were adjusting well despite their memories of death. Jack, the older of the two, was interested in farming with Toby while Seth, the younger boy, helped Sadie around the house with the day to day farm chores.

One day when rain had prevented further work on the farm, Lott rested on his front porch enjoying the peaceful sound of raindrops on the roof. His peace was soon disturbed by a lone rider. Lott recognized a Union officer, and with wariness waited for the bad news.

The officer pulled his horse to a stop in front of the porch. He removed his hat and spoke with a slight smile. "Good afternoon, Mister Wilson. I'm Captain Jacobs. Would you mind giving me a few moments of your time?"

Lott nodded his head in agreement. "Won't you get on down and have a seat? How 'bout a cup of coffee?"

"That sounds good to me."

"Sarah, we got us a guest. Will you make us a fresh pot of coffee?" Lott called out.

Shortly Sarah brought the men steaming cups of coffee and asked to be excused.

The captain blew across his cup then looked over at Lott. "I guess you are wondering why I've come, and I must ask you to keep what I share with you in confidence, otherwise it could cost me my career."

Lott shook his head and sighed in concern. "I'll give you my word. What you say will remain here on this porch."

The captain cleared his throat. "Mister Wilson, I know a lot about you and your family, and I am confident that you are honest, God fearing people. I also have had brief dealings with your son, Thomas, and find in him of the same stock. The truth about the shooting at Walker's store is a sham of injustice. I know the truth but am not in a position to help. May the Lord forgive me. But I do have some information that in some way might give you some relief."

Lott's heart leaped in hope for any news that could give his family comfort.

Captain Jacobs got up and walked to the edge of the porch to stare across the way. "They are on to Thomas. When your son left here, they hired a professional agent and three army scouts. They tracked him across Arkansas and into the Indian territory of Oklahoma and located him on the farm of Hatta and Homer Wilson. At that location, there was some kind of altercation, and the pursuing party was captured, stripped of their horses and led back to the Arkansas line."

Lott took his handkerchief out and wiped his face. "Did anyone get killed?"

"No one was killed, but the man in charge, a Mister Stevens, wired back to our office and asked to continue pursuing your son. Washington wants him to pursue at all costs, and if accosted, kill your son and anyone with him. In other words, if your younger son is with Thomas, his life is also in danger."

Lott, relieved that his boys were alive, now struggled to breathe with the realization that the search would continue until Thomas was found and killed. "I just don't understand why this is happening. Why isn't the truth revealed and Thomas cleared?" he whispered.

"It's all about hate, Mister Wilson. When Lieutenant Lowery was killed, his older brother, Captain Lowery, seemed to lose his mind. In his hate, he didn't look for the truth; he only wanted vengeance. The Lowery's father was a general in the war and now sits in the United States Senate as a fire-breathing Republican. He lost one son at Petersburg and was severely wounded himself during the Wilderness Campaign. As you might see, he has no love for the South and its people and is a strong Washington connection."

Both men stood silently for a moment, then the captain reached out his hand to Lott. "That's really all I know right now. I plan to keep giving you the news

149

as I know it. I'm really sorry and hope that someday and in some way I can help bring peace to this country and to your family."

Lott bid the captain goodbye then eased down into his chair trembling. He had lost one son during the war and at one time thought he had lost John and Thomas. Was the hatred from this war going to rob him of all his sons? Lott got up and headed to the barn to be alone. In Thomas's room, he dropped to his knees and prayed fervently for his sons. "Lord, I don't know what to think or do? Do I tell Rebecca that she may never see her husband again? Lord, please protect Thomas and John and bring them safely home. Please see that justice prevails. Protect Rebecca and the babe. Please allow John to see his child. O Lord, I place my sons into Your protective arms and trust You with their lives. Help me to rely and trust in Your great mercy."

As the full moon filtered into Rebecca's bedroom all was quite except for the occasional lonely cry of a whippoorwill down near the creek. Unable to sleep, she eased over to her bedroom window and curled up on the floor to enjoy the full beauty of the evening glow. Unconsciously, she reached down and let her hands enfold the curve of the baby in her womb. Tears began to swell in her eyes and trickle down her face. She remembered the time when John was reported missing after that terrible battle. When others proclaimed his death, she continued to believe and hope for his return, and finally, when all her hope had vanished, she had agreed to marry Frankie and try to begin a new life, a life without John. She remembered her wedding day and the love in the eyes of the man who entered the church late. John had returned to her, and she had to believe he would return again. With a heavy heart, she took her pain to the Lord and wiped away her tears as a heavenly peace settled deep within and covered all of her fears.

15

Entering Texas

Do nothing out of rivalry or conceit, but in humility, consider others as more important than yourself.

—Philippians 2:3 HCSB

In the March wind, the trio slowly pressed up a piney slope leading the balking packhorse, then topped the crest to gaze down on the Red River, the northeastern border separating Oklahoma and Texas. The morning sounds of crows squawking for food in the distance and geese honking in northern flight were invigorating. As the trio carefully moved down the steep riverbank, they found a shallow crossing upstream and fording, entered Texas. Since they knew the forest along the Sulfur River was a dense tangle of swamps, sloughs and quicksand, the men traveled south to a nearby town for information on the safest route to the ferry.

"John, you ride ahead of us and see if you spot any military troops. If you see any, double back to warn us."

At mid-morning John rode hastily back to the waiting men. "There is a small village about twenty miles to the south, and I've not seen any soldiers."

A little after noon the group rode into Clarksville and carefully scanned the village finding only a general merchandizing store, a livery stable, small church, an abandoned shack and a building with a shabby sign that said First Stop—Food and Spirits. Few people were seen, so the men secured their horses to a hitching post out front. "Bring your Sharps in with you," Thomas said as he looked up and down the dry dusty street.

"What for? We haven't seen any Federals," John commented as he reached for his Sharps.

"Well, let's just say we plan to be ready to make a point if we need to. Kinda like a good insurance policy," Thomas answered as he pushed the door open.

As their eyes grew accustomed to the darkness, they could see a bar down the left side of the room. Tables were scattered, and an old dilapidated piano sat in the corner next to a window in the front. Tobacco smoke hovered about the low ceiling, and the smell of fried bacon settled in their nostrils. As hungry as the men were, the dark filthy place dullened their desire for food. The men walked to the bar perceiving the menacing eyes of the man at the bar and those at a table near the back door.

Thomas nodded to John and softly said, "Watch the street for Feds." John with rifle in hand walked to the door, while Homer stood next to Thomas discreetly observant of the men at the back table. A tall man with dark hair, piercing brown eyes and a black slouch hat eased a double barreled shotgun on the table. The other two were lean, trail dirty, bearded, hardened and definitely spelled trouble.

"Can I help you men?" the man behind the counter nervously asked.

From the corner of his eye, Homer saw the man at the back table rest his hand over the handle of his shotgun. Homer slipped his hand down to his pistol and looked directly at the man in the back. "Mister, we're not here to cause any trouble, and you are making me mighty uncomfortable by keeping your hand on that gun. You may want to reconsider your intentions because you and at least one of your friends will be dead before you get the gun off the table. So just let us get our business here done, and then we'll be gone."

Silence swallowed the saloon as the men studied each other intently. Suddenly hoof beats interrupted, and John cautiously looked out the door. Quickly he turned to Thomas and whispered, "Yankees."

Thomas moved behind the bar, rested his rifle against the back wall, grabbed an apron and quickly tied it around his waist. He removed his hat and waited.

"Let's make this quick," came a voice from outside. "The sergeant will be looking for us if we don't show up soon."

"Yeah, but a drink of liquor sure will quench a dry throat," laughed another. "Don't worry 'bout the time; the sergeant isn't going to miss us."

Two dusty cavalrymen pushed the doors open, shook the dirt from their hats and lumbered over to the bar where Thomas and the bar keeper stood.

"Can I help you, boys?" Thomas asked.

"Whiskey. A shot each."

Thomas reached under the bar, found a bottle and before pouring their glasses, said, "I tell you what, I'll pour each of you a double and have it on the house if you will enjoy your drink then get on you horses and leave."

Surprised but taking no offense, the soldiers smiled at each other and one of them said, "Sounds like Christmas is coming early this year. Thank you, sir." Gulping it down, they slammed their glasses on the bar, nodded to Thomas and walked out.

"That was mighty generous of you," the bar keeper said as Thomas dropped a coin on the table to cover the drinks."

"Generous," Thomas muttered. "Those men don't know it, but I probably just saved their lives."

The stranger in the back pushed on his hat and moved his hand away from his shotgun. The other men with him also seemed to relax. "I see you don't care for Blue Bellies."

Thomas took the apron off, picked up his rifle then walked toward the men looking intently as he staidly replied, "I certainly can live without them, mainly because they plan to see me dead."

The men began to smile and relax as they looked at each other. "You men pull up chairs. Let's talk."

Thomas shook his head at John. "No, you stay on watch. They might come back."

Homer and Thomas grabbed chairs and joined the men at the back table.

"Where you men from?" the dark eyed man asked pouring himself a shot of spirits.

"Basically, we're all from Mississippi. Homer here was from Mississippi, but when the government removed the Choctaw, he moved with his mother and uncle to the Territory. We're all cousins."

"What are you here for?" the man resounded wrinkling his forehead.

"A while back we got a letter informing us that our uncle was murdered, and five months later another letter came telling us that his wife, our aunt, died, leaving their children out here in Texas. We've come to find the young 'uns and take them back to Mississippi."

The man cleared his throat. "What was the man's name?"

"Jonathan Lewis. Do you know of him?" Thomas asked, raising his eyes to look for a reaction from the men.

The man nodded his head in recognition. "I know him. Well, I did know him. He ran a ferry down the way on the Sulfur River. Good man. We rode together during the war with the Texas Calvary. That is 'fore I quit that unit. You boys fight with the South?"

Homer remained silent as Thomas continued. "John over there did, and I fought as well till I got fed up and quit in sixty-three. I ran from the regulators and ended up in west Texas and the Arizona Territory as a ranger fighting Indians. I finally quit that as well." Thomas shrugged, saddened by the thought of what they as rangers had done.

"You fought them Apache, didn't you?" whipped one of the men.

A surprise covered Thomas's face. "How'd you know that?"

The man laughed. "You're none other than Thomas Wilson, ain't you? I heard about your precision shooting there across the border in Arizona Territory, and the word is out that you is a wanted man."

Thomas rubbed his hand across his face and carefully reached down to his pistol.

The dark-eyed man realized what Thomas's movement meant and shook his head. "Ain't no call of fearing us. We're on the same side. Just relax. What do you want to know about Lewis?"

"We need to know where we might find the location of the ferry and if there is any news about the children," Homer stated beginning to relax but still cautious.

"There were a couple of men who Jonathan took across that didn't think it was necessary to pay, and after some harsh words, one of the men took out his pistol and shot him. After that his youngest son ran the ferry for a while until his mother got sick and died. Heard tell after her death, the boy sold the place. You know, come to think, I heard the boy actually witnessed his father being killed."

"Where can I find this crossing?" Thomas asked.

"The Sulfur River runs south of here. You could say it flows almost parallel with the Big Red. Take the road south for about eighteen miles, and you'll find a sign saying, crossing. Follow it east fer 'bout three miles, and you'll run slap into the Sulfur. The ferry runs there. This road carries you to another small village, Bogata and from there it runs to Mt. Pleasant. It's a good sized town, and you will come near to finding Yanks there. You'd better stay out of that place."

Thomas continued to tell about all that had happened to him since the shooting in Mississippi. Cullen and his men listened carefully to the details and were amused at the handling of the scouts by the Choctaw.

Thomas got up and extended his hand. "Thank you. By the way, in all this talk, I never got your name."

A smile crossed the man's steeled face. "I'm Cullen Baker."

Thomas's eyebrows lifted and he nodded his head in surprise.

"By the way, Thomas Wilson, what you gonna do after you find them children. You come back and see me, and we might have us some dealings." Baker called out.

"I plan to send them home with John, and then I suppose I'll go looking for the men who killed my uncle."

"No need for that. Jonathan was a comrade and friend. I found them men myself, and I do say that you don't have to worry about looking for them," chuckled Baker.

"Why's that?" John called out pushing the door open.

"They don't exist no more."

As the Wilsons rode out of town, Homer divulged to Thomas and John. "Cousins, you know what? If them Feds hadn't walked in when they did, there would have been some deadly shooting."

"How's that?" question Thomas.

"From what I have heard about Baker, it don't take a lot to rile him, and it's said that he usually shoots first and asks questions later. We owe those soldier boys a big thank you for saving our lives."

"'Bout time you got back. You're a day late," grumbled Stevens chewing on a cigar.

"Sorry 'bout that. It took time to get an answer to your request," complained Hank, tiringly dismounting.

"And!" Stevens scowled.

"They said for you to continue the search, and if necessary, they could add a military presence for you. Also, if Wilson is captured and brought in, there would be bonus pay awaiting."

Stevens stood silently in thought for a moment. "Bonus sounds good," he mumbled to himself. *Military presence, that's a joke. The one soldier I do have is worthless. Soldiers won't catch Wilson; only a Pinkerton can*, he thought. "Hey boys! Come on out here!"

As Clarke and the scouts lumbered out, Stevens revealed his information. "Men, the government wants us to continue our search. I want you to know up front that I appreciate your good service, but I'll certainly understand if you decide you have had enough. If you do decide to continue with us, there'll be a bonus from the government for the capture of Wilson."

Private Clark lowered his head and shuffled his feet as he contemplated his words. "Mister Stevens, when I volunteered for this hunt, I didn't know much about this mission. If I have a choice, I'd rather go back to Mississippi and join my unit. I don't plan to get involved with those Choctaws. Almost being killed by Indians once is enough for me."

Stevens and the scouts sneered at the soldier's words, then Hank contumeliously remarked, "Almost being killed! Those Indians had their chance and you see what happened. You gonna miss out on one big bonus cause of your fear. That's all right, you go home soldier boy. We don't need spineless wimps tagging along with us."

The soldier knew that a bonus was not worth his life and he had made a wise decision, so he waited for the laughter to end then quietly spoke to Stevens. "Sir, right now you think the joke is on me, but if those Indians do find you chasing Wilson, then the joke is going to be on all of you."

Stevens paused a minute as the soldier walked away. "All right men, let's pack up and move. Time is wasting," ordered Stevens. "I feel that in the next few days we will find our man and get our reward."

John pushed Bet at a gallop down the narrow, muddy road. In a couple of hours, they should be at the ferry crossing, get the children, and make rapid plans for the return trip to Mississippi. The afternoon sun shone brightly across his back, and to his relief, no soldiers had been seen. In fact, he had met very few travelers. As the swamp closed in with dense foliage and the scent of damp undergrowth increased, John knew the river was minutes away. He soon saw the sign posted on a tree—Ferry Crossing. To his surprise, the road headed east skirting the swamp to his right. After a couple of miles, John heard men shouting to one another, and making the bend, he saw a clearing that led to the operating ferry. On a slope away from the landing, a rather large framed house stood with smoke curling from the chimney. Reining Bet in, John carefully scanned the area below seeing no evidence of the children. Several men were preparing to carry a loaded wagon across the river and never looked up. There was no sign of soldiers, so John reined Bet and turned around to get Homer and Thomas. He hoped this would be the end of the search, but it looked doubtful.

The trio returned to the ferry and waited cautiously before descending. When there was no evidence of military men, the three rode down to the landing.

As they approached, armed and intent, a man quickly secured the ferry and reached for his rifle that leaned on a post nearby. "Stop where you are!" shouted the man raising his rifle. "What brings you here?"

Thomas noted the fear in the man's face and motioned for Homer and John to stay, then he rode forward. "You can put your rifle down, sir. We mean you no harm; we're just looking for some of our kinfolks."

The man squinted his eyes as the afternoon sun fell across his face. "Go on," the man replied still rifle in hand.

Thomas quickly decided that using his real name could cause a problem since the men at the saloon had heard of him, so he answered, "I'm James Wilson. The other two are Homer and John Wilson. From what I've been told is that Jonathan Lewis used to run this ferry. He's our uncle, and after what has occurred, we are here to take the children back home to Mississippi."

The man lowered his rifle and relaxed. "Tell the men to come on down. By the way, I'm Robert Holman, and I bought this place from his wife right before she died. They were both good people. It sure was a tragedy."

John and Homer rode up and dismounted.

After shaking hands, Thomas looked about the place. "Are the children here? We're anxious to see them."

The man solemnly dropped his head. "After their mother died, I asked Tommy, the oldest boy, what they were gonna do. He said they were gonna load up some of their belongings and head for West Oklahoma."

"West Oklahoma! What in tarnations for?" Homer remarked.

"A party of government men and surveyors came through here a while back and told us that Washington had decided to open up sections of the Indian country for white settlement. They said the land was free for the taking. The boy thought with the money his mother had gotten for this place and the ferry, he had enough funds to start their own farm."

"Well, thank you sir for the information. We sure were hoping we would find them here. Looks like our search has just begun." Thomas looked at John and realized that now his brother would be later in getting home to his wife.

Homer quickly asked, "How long ago did they leave?"

""Been well over a week at least."

"How many children are there?"

"There's five of 'em. Three boys and two girls."

"You sure they said Oklahoma?"

"That's what the boy said, and they left out of here the same way you folks came."

"Thanks again. Looks like we better be on our way."

The men remounted and seeing a nearby stream, they decided to make plans while the horses watered down. After a moment of silence, Thomas looked at John. "Well, we didn't plan on this, but John, I think it best that you go on home. You got a young'un on the way. Homer and I will try to find the children. The wagon can't make good time, and with us on horseback, we should be able to track them."

John shook his head. "Can't do that, Brother. I gave my word to Papa that I'd bring those children home. Wilsons keep their word."

Thomas and Homer smiled at him. "Well said, well said. Looks like we'll find the children together."

Homer sat down on the grassy ground, crossed his legs and shook his head. "West Oklahoma! Doesn't make any sense at all," he mumbled. "I did get wind of what Washington is doing, but that free land is several years away. If those children even make it to the Territory, they're gonna run right into the Apache lands. They're the last to be brought in, and they're volatile and vicious. If the Apache don't kill them outright, they'll either make them slaves or sell them down across the border. So, Cousins, we don't have time to wander off aimlessly. We better make a good plan," Homer stammered.

Frustrated, Thomas frowned over to Homer. "Why in tarnation would those children do something so ridiculous and dangerous?"

"Cause they're just children. That's why," Homer replied.

The men thought of options and finally Homer spoke, "They probably are moving northwest and that's a wide area. Traveling together, we could be on a completely wrong trail and never catch up with them. In order to cover more ground, I will ride north to the Red River and follow the south banks for three days. Thomas, you take a southerly route where there'll be fewer military, and John, I'll get you on the road that leads from Clarksville through Paris. On the fourth day, we all meet up at the town of Sherman. If I'm right, those children took the easier, closest route, and so John, you need to keep your eyes opened because you will probably be the one to find them. That sound all right to you both?"

"You know this country Homer. I think it'll work," Thomas affirmed.

Homer mapped out the path for John and reviewed the way he and Thomas would go. He gave them instructions about the land and what to expect.

"All right cousins, let's ride west!" shouted Homer as they raised their hats to each other and galloped away.

16

Apache Lands

Do not be anxious about anything, but in everything by prayer and petition with thanksgiving present your requests to God. And the peace of God which transcends all understanding will guard your hearts and minds in Christ Jesus.

—Philippians 4:6-7 NIV

John was the first to enter Sherman, so he asked about the children at the general store. As John carefully questioned the merchant, he discovered that some children in a wagon had stopped in Sherman over a week ago and had purchased items and that the eldest boy indicated they were headed west to Wichita Falls. Even though the government was planning to take large tracks of land from the tribes in Oklahoma, Homer had disclosed that transactions would not transpire for several years. When the children did cross the Red River, there would find no free land; they would only find Apaches who were hostile toward whites coming to secure their land. John was both frustrated and disappointed that the children had not remained in Sherman longer. It seemed they were always just out of reach which made their safety settle down heavy on him, so he whispered a quick prayer, "Lord, we sure need your help to find these children before they reach Apache land. And Lord, I hope it will be soon so they will be safe and I can get home to Becca."

While the Wilsons were meeting in Sherman, Cullen Baker and his men were waiting for a fellow roadman to join their party. A hard spring thunderstorm had just swept through the little village, and a mist rose from the muddied street and sidewalk that led into the tavern. Bo, one of Baker's gang called out, "Cullen, looks like he ain't gonna show. Either the law got 'em or the Yanks. I say we move on without him."

Cullen, nursing a shot of whiskey while standing next to the bar, took a sip. "We'll wait until morning. If he don't show, we'll do the job without him."

The men heard approaching horses, so Bo stepped to the door for a better look. "Cullen, we got four men riding up, and several of them look like army scouts. What do you want us to do?"

Cullen rubbed his hand across his upper lip and down his chin then reached for his shotgun. "Bo, you stay over there next to the door. Colt, get to the back next to the piano. Curtis, be the bartender and have your scatter gun handy. We'll just see what they want."

Stevens and his men glanced down the streets as they approached the tavern. "Boss, this place is shore 'nough a dump if'n I've ever seen one," Hank remarked reining in his horse.

"Makes no difference, we need information. Let's see what we can get out of these folks," Stevens ordered while dismounting. Securing their mounts to a hitching post, the men ambled into the building. The place was dark, damp and smelly, and it took a few minutes for their eyes to adjust. "What kind of a hole is this?" Hank remarked walking to the bar while shaking water from his hat.

"It's the place where I make my living," Curtis answered coolly, readjusting his apron. "Can I help you?"

"Whiskey for the boys if you got anything decent, which I doubt," smiled Stevens.

Cullen and his men stood motionless carefully observing the intruders while Hank and the scouts sauntered to the bar. Stevens, winded, chose a table next to the window and settled there. Looking directly at the bartender, he voiced quietly, "Looking for a man who we believe is riding a black thoroughbred. He might have a couple of other men with him."

"What's the man's name?" Cullen interrupted, eyeing Stevens while taking another sip.

"Name is Wilson. Thomas Wilson."

"What you want him for?"

"Murder. He killed two soldiers back in Mississippi."

Cullen cleared his throat and calmly stated. "You chasing a lie, mister. The lieutenant down there pulled first. If'n you men were smart, you would have gone on home after them Choctaws got you."

Startled that the man knew about the incident, Stevens quickly got up, and expecting a conflict, Hank and the two scouts laid their glasses down and looked toward the men.

"You seem to know a lot about Wilson. I aim to catch him and kill him and ever who is riding with him," Stevens smiled rubbing his top teeth against his bottom lip. "I'm working for the government, and mister, you will tell me what you know about Wilson."

Baker, his face flushed red in anger, nodded over to his men and leveled his shotgun at Stevens. Before Stevens could react, an explosion erupted sending him flying over a table and through the front window. A cluster of shots followed and gun smoke filled the small room. Cullen calmly walked away from the bar and nudged each man with his boot to make sure death had come. Outside, he found Stevens lying prostrate on the wooden walkway. Buckshot had riddled his chest and lower face. Cullen pilfered through Steven's clothing, then mumbled to himself, "Sure didn't expect this money belt."

"Hey boys, we just robbed us a bank!" Cullen shouted. "I never could stand arrogant, stupid government men."

Cullen held the money belt for his men to see, then looked snidely at Stevens as he called downward, "Mister devil, I'm sending one more down to ya. Try to make him comfortable as possible." Cullen looked down the street and saw nothing but a terrified dog with his tail tucked and headed to a vacant house.

Cullen and his men returned inside. "Curtis, get someone to clean this mess up and have them take these bodies down to the swamp to the quicksand. Search each man for valuables, then sell the saddles and horses and you keep the money. As of today, nobody will know what happened to them. They simply don't exist. Now remember men, we've been friends a long time, but if your tongue waggles even one bit about these men and what happened, then you will meet the same fate. You understand me?"

"Yes sir, Cullen. We have a clear understanding. These men never existed to us, and we know nothing about them."

Sitting under a leafed oak tree growing next to the Little Rock Baptist Church which was also the school, Frankie patiently waited. The warm afternoon sun filtered through the leaves causing him to remove his jacket and roll up the sleeves of his shirt. A butterfly danced around a flower and finally rested on a petal while rhythmically fluttering its wings. The soft breeze gently tossed Frankie's blond hair, and he settled into the serene peace of nature as he waited for a special woman.

Inside a woman was tirelessly teaching. At three o'clock a student hurried out to ring the church bell, then like an explosion, the front doors burst open, and children ran down the steps and across the yard. Laughter and talking filled the air. One boy grabbed a girl's dress, flipped it up, then laughed as he ran away. The girl feigned anger and picked up a rock to hurl at the sprinting lad. She missed her mark and with her hands resting defiantly on her hips, smiled after him.

Frankie chuckled at the scene remembering similar incidences when he attended school. Flashes of running around the church, swinging on the old hickory tree, squirming through lengthy preaching services, teasing the girls after school, and hurrying to go fishing and hunting with his best friend John returned to his mind. Then he recalled the most important moment of all when he gave his life to Christ at a two week revival he had attended at the age of eleven. He had made the decision in early spring and had to wait two months for the creek to be warm enough for his baptism.

Then there was the day at the altar when he waited for Rebecca to become his wife. She was radiant and his heart sang out to him, but as she approached the altar, a bearded stranger entered the church and stood in the aisle. That stranger changed everything in his life for the better. John had returned in time to keep him from marrying Rebecca. Even though he had thought he was in love with her, he knew now that it was more about emulating his best friend, John, than having Rebecca as his wife—a woman who would never love him the way she loved John. God was merciful.

At last his thoughts turned to his father, who seldom entered the church doors. He wished that his father had been a real father, but he never felt loved by him, just criticized and degraded. Even now, he only felt emptiness and disappointment when he thought about Frank Senior. Thank goodness his grandfather had shown him the love of a father, and because of this, he could understand the love of his heavenly Father better.

Frankie's gaze fell on the beautiful blond hair of Lucretia, known to all as Sister but to him just Cretia. Her hair seemed to dance and sparkle in the sunlight as she stood on the steps closing the doors of the school for the day. His heart came alive as he observed her pure beauty. Who knew he would feel this way about his childhood friend's sister.

"Hello beautiful!" Frankie called out.

Sister shaded her eyes with a hand and glanced at him saying nothing. Finally she called out, "What are you doing up here?"

"Is that all you can say to an old friend?" smiled Frankie.

Sister stood on the step studying him. He had certainly filled out a lot since she last saw him at his father's funeral, and he was definitely handsome. "Well, I could say good afternoon Frankie, but then I still say, why are you here in Mississippi?"

Frankie laughed and jumped down from the buggy giving her an exaggerated bow. "Do you know that even though you do not seem happy to see me, you are the most beautiful woman in both Mississippi and Louisiana, and I am here to take you to Meridian for supper."

Sister shook her head, but managed a smile. "Frankie, now we both know that you are exaggerating my beauty and also that I cannot go anywhere with you. My father will certainly not allow me to accompany you tonight on such short notice."

"And if he did?"

"He wouldn't."

"But, that my dear, makes you wrong on two accounts. The first is that your beauty surpasses what even you realize, and your father has already given me permission to take you to Meridian. So we leave now to catch the train at Newton at five, dine at six and be back by ten tonight. Are you ready?"

Sister frowned at the revelation. "Well, I see one problem with this plan of yours. You really haven't asked me if I would like to go."

Frankie looked at Lucretia and then knelt beside her and grabbed her hand. "My dear Cretia. Will you please do me the honor of accompanying me to supper in Meridian. I have looked forward to the pleasure of your company for months."

Sister could not contain her laughter. "You are very fortunate that you made me laugh because I had planned to turn you down, but now I guess I will consider your request. After all, I am mighty hungry. I was so busy today that I forgot to eat my lunch."

"Well, I can't have the most beautiful woman in Mississippi fainting from hunger." Frankie helped Sister into the buggy and headed south directly opposite of her home.

"Frankie, you must turn around because I will go nowhere with you until I have made myself more presentable."

"Cretia, you cannot improve on what I see right this minute, and if we don't leave now, it will be difficult to get you home at ten."

Sister nodded her head. "Okay, but I want to know how you got my father to agree to this, and you better be telling the truth."

Frankie in a teasing voice spoke, "Well, first you have to come a little closer in the buggy so you will be able to hear every word I say."

Sister chuckled and moved about two inches closer. "That is about all the length I am going to move. So get to talking."

"Well, I guess I will be satisfied with that tiny bit of a move for now."

They both settled into the ride before beginning to share with each other. "Cretia, I came back here to close out the sale of our place and to see you. I had dinner with your parents and spent hours talking with them. I also promised Suzanne I would find out as much about Thomas as I could. I was really hoping you would be glad to see me."

Sister studied him for a moment and fearing he could hear her heart pounding said, "You know I'm glad to see you, but Frankie, I'm not like all the women you are with in New Orleans. I am just a country girl with some pretty high principles."

Frank smiled at Sister. "That is exactly why I want to spend time with you."

"You know, Tim keeps me informed about your escapades down there, and I really don't think we can be more than friends. I'm just not going to fit in with your ways."

"Timothy Johnson! You listen to what Tim says about me?" Frankie countered. "He's too busy gambling and chasing skirts to keep up with me. Do you really think I have time to spend on wild women?"

"I just know that you and I are so very different."

"Cretia, you don't really know me anymore. You remember how I was when John and I were best friends. I know I got in a lot of fights, and John had to come to my rescue. I know that I talked like I was big and bad, but that was just because John was so perfect in every way. He was the best student, the best in sports, and everybody loved him. I was always trying to live up to his reputation and never could quite get there. But I've grown up, and I am happy with the man I've become. I don't need those things I used to think were important. I really hope you will give me a chance to get to know you better."

Sister looked deep in Frankie's eyes to see if he was just teasing with her, but found that he seemed to mean the words he had spoken. "Frankie, I think I would like to get to know you better, and I'm sure looking forward to getting to eat with you. After all, I am ravenous."

Frankie and Sister smiled at each other and then began to share the last few month's events. Even though Sister knew that Frankie had had numerous relationships with women, she was attracted to him and decided that maybe it was time to consider giving him some serious thought.

Frankie took in Cretia's beauty and regretted all the numerous relationships he had had with women and hoped he would have the chance to show her how much he had changed. Cretia was so beautiful, innocent, exciting and challenging, and she consumed his every thought, but oh such a chasm divided them. For now, he was determined to enjoy every moment with her and try to forget his past.

The evening swept by as hours seemed like minutes. The meal at Weidman's was superb, and the conversation and laughter flowed. On the trip home, he was surprised and pleased that when he took Cretia's hand, she let it remain in his grasp. As they arrived at her home, the lamp in the window indicated the family was waiting up for her. At the door, Frankie took her hand and looked deep into her blue eyes. "Cretia, you don't know how much this evening has meant to me. Thank you for trusting me enough to accept my invitation."

Sister blushed and catching her breath whispered, "Thank you for thinking of me."

Frankie reached under her chin and gently lifted it and lightly touched her lips. He looked longingly at her and saw a return of that longing. He tenderly touched his lips to Cretia's again and felt her responding as the kiss deepened.

Sister pulled away and shook her head a little. "Frankie, I think I need to head inside. Thanks again for the meal." Then she tilted her head and quipped, "I really was ravenous for the food, and the attention was wonderful too."

"Don't go yet. Can I see you again?"

Sister chuckled, "Don't you mean, 'May I see you again?' Sorry, couldn't help the correction. Can implies you are able and may implies permission."

"Okay, teacher. May I see you again?"

"I would really like that."

"Do you think you could visit me in Louisiana one day?"

"No, Frankie. I have commitments and just can't leave my students or my responsibilities here at home."

"Don't say no yet. Think about it, and next time I am here, we can make plans so that you won't neglect your responsibilities."

Sister smiled and as she started toward the door, she tipped up on her toes and gave Frankie a quick kiss on the cheek. "Thanks again for the evening. Good night, Frankie."

"I am so glad you said good night and not goodbye. I do plan to spend time with you again, Cretia. Whoever knew the scrawny sister of my childhood friend would become such an amazing woman."

Sister laughed. "There you go again with those fancy words that I do not believe, but thanks anyway." Sister open the door and embraced the family that waited for her.

The next day Frankie stood on the bow of the riverboat, The Queen, as an evening breeze whipped across his face. Massive paddle wheels churned the muddy water of the Mississippi sending waves rolling to the banks and splashing against the shore. Here and there birds seeking a meal swooped down from the old Cyprus trees that bordered the river and often, without success, flew back up for another chance. Never had he felt such loneliness and despair. Then Frankie remembered her smile, the touch of her hand in his, and the girlish outburst of laughter when he held her in his arms. A ray of sunlight scattered his sadness and he knew that her love was his desire, but he also knew that a relationship with Cretia would be difficult to attain. Even as a boy, he had heard rumors that his father was instrumental in the death of her Uncle Jake. With time and investigation, he found it was true, and if he knew the truth, then the Wilson family probably did too. His father's dealings would mar any true relationship between Cretia and him. No, the Wilsons would not forget all the evil his father had committed. How could they?"

Later that night as he tried to sleep, his mind dwelled on the conversation he had with Tim at Newton Station. Tim had spoken of a secret organization led by General Nathan Bedford Forrest that planned to recover the Mississippian government by running out the carpetbaggers and creating fear for voting Negroes who supported the Union candidates.

Next his thoughts turned to Thomas and the lack of information on his safety. He realized that he had little to tell Suzanne and she needed to move on with her life because Thomas would no more consider Suzanne than Cretia would consider him. They would and should be held responsible for their father's wrongdoings. Exhausted, Frankie tried to make his mind calm but settled instead into a sleepless night.

North Texas

Dark clouds rolled in from the western plains as a rumble of thunder broke the silence over a covered wagon which creaked and rattled down a well beaten road leading to the Red River. The large trees that covered eastern Texas were far beyond, and open grass meadows dotted with dwarf trees covered the land like a sea of grass. Clouds now shut out the sunlight as swirls of wind swept across the

166

fields shaking the old wagon. A young man, Tommy Lewis, lashed his whip and screamed over the sound of thunder, "Get on you beasts! A little rain ain't gonna hurt you."

A lanky lad at thirteen with dark brown hair looked over to his older sister, Sally, who had pulled down her bonnet to avoid the thrashing wind and said. "Sis, I think we need to look for cover. Don't like the looks of this."

Keeping her head turned from the storm she groused, "Where! It's all the same out here. Ain't no shelter to be found."

In the back of the wagon loaded with family items, sat ten year old Mary watching over her two year old brother, Lonnie, who was fast asleep. Richmond, age six, sat on the tailgate with his feet dangling and so happy in his fantasy world that he was unaware of the approaching storm.

With the storm intensifying, Tommy finally reined the horses to a stop, and he and Sally crawled inside and closed the front cover of the wagon. Two horses, one solid white and the other dark brown with white stockings shivered in the cold. The lone mule, brayed a few times and then being thirsty, accepted the rain readily.

Sally quietly observed and worried over the change in her brother Tommy. He no longer was the happy, mischievous boy he had once been, but had grown silent after their parents' deaths. He had witnessed the murder of their father, and Sally was afraid that Tommy might never be the same. She knew how difficult it had been for her heart to begin mending, and it seemed Tommy had a lot more on his shoulders than she did. Hopefully their decision to use the money from the sale of the ferry and property and move west would help them begin afresh.

As they sat quietly waiting out the storm, Sally, the eldest, pondered the decision they had made to move west. She wondered if they should have considered finding their relatives in Mississippi instead, but the news of free land in western Oklahoma had clinched their decision. With a free grant, their money and hard work, they could start a cattle ranch, but doubts disturbed her thoughts. What if the men were wrong and there were no homesteads, and what if the land was dangerous because of the Indians. But then, what choice did they really have? They couldn't afford to stay, and they had never even met their Mississippian relatives who surely wouldn't want five more mouths to feed. In a matter of days, they would reach the Red River and beyond that, Oklahoma and their new home. They saw no other way.

In the dark of night with only drips of rain tapping on the canvas cover,

Sally whispered to Tommy, "You sure this is right? There ain't nothing but grass out here, and we ain't seen nobody for days."

"Sally, cows eat grass and there's plenty here. We ain't seen people 'cause we got here first."

"Tommy, it might be raining now, but this place is dry country. Cows gonna need water."

"Yep, I thought about that. When we cross the river into Oklahoma, we'll travel either up or down the river until we find a good stream and go from there to locate us a place."

"I hope you're right, but I still say it's strange that there ain't no settlers out here. Seems like free land would bring lots of settlers."

The Wilsons, trying to save their meager funds, camped outside of Sherman. They decided they would ride from daylight until nighttime until they caught up with the children. Their optimism grew with the hope of finding the Lewis children in a few days.

After a hard days ride, the trio gathered around the evening campfire for rest, relaxation and conversation. The fire dwindled as the men finished their last cups of coffee. John, as usual, was the conversationalist, and as he poured out the coffee grinds from his cup, he sat down on his blanket in thought. He looked up into the clear night and was amazed at millions of stars that twinkled their light to earth, and in the east, the full moon rose over the horizon displaying God's wonders. As John enjoyed the grandeur, he glanced back to Homer. "Homer, you never talk about it, but what is your belief about our Creator?"

As the silence grew, John knew he had probably overstepped his place and had tread on personal ground. "I'm sorry. It's really none of my business."

John was almost asleep when Homer finally spoke up from the darkness. "That's all right. It's taken me a long time to reach a conclusion, John. I do believe in a Creator, as my people do. We look at the stars and moon, plant life and animals, the rain that nourishes the earth and the newborn child. The Creator is obvious."

Silence again filled the campground, and John closed his eyes to sleep, but soon Homer continued. "Do I also believe in Jesus, God's son, and his redemption of mankind? Yes I do, but do not believe that some of the white men truly believe. They talk of loving your neighbor as yourself, but yet refuse to help all men. My people have been driven from their lands by men in Washington who claim to be followers. These followers seem to talk of Jesus but act of the devil. They are a scar to the face of Christ and to his message of love. My people find it difficult to follow the white man's religion when their cruel actions speak so loudly. So do I believe in Jesus? Yes, but my Jesus is not the white man's Jesus."

The embers in the fire was now only a glow. John called to his brother, "How 'bout you Thomas?"

Thomas pondered Homer's words before answering. "John, I accepted Christ when I was twelve and thought I knew all the spiritual answers, but, to tell you the truth, I think Satan has claimed my soul."

"Thomas, that's not true."

"I'd rather not talk about it. The Lord don't want none of me."

"Thomas, when you receive the Holy Spirit, His power is stronger than the devil. I thoroughly believe that when you received Christ in your heart as a boy, well He's still there. If you don't believe me, think of David, a man after God's own heart. Returning from a battle the Israelites sang, 'He killed his ten thousands.' He also took another man's wife and had her husband killed, but Thomas, he repented and was Israel's greatest king. Now, can you beat that?"

"I killed two men months back and see where I am now," Thomas softly replied.

"It was self-defense and not near the ten thousand David killed. Think about that, big Brother. You are still saved and forgiven."

Thomas quietly got up to check on the horses that had become restless. John lay listening to the low fire pop and sizzle. Homer unfolded his roll and resting his head on his saddle, tried to find comfort. Leaning up on an elbow, he looked over to John. "Something's wrong with that brother of yours."

"Why do you say that? " John answered, coming to a sitting position.

"Well, it seems he has to stay busy all the time. I'll go to bed late at night and still hear him rumbling around in the wee hours, and when I get up about daybreak, he's already gone outside looking for something to do. He never sleeps. You know, I think he literally chooses not to sleep at night."

John looked into the fire in thought and momentarily answered, "Homer, he ain't been the same since he came home from the war. He acted this way at Papa's and sometimes, even stranger. He hates sleep because I think it's at those times, he has haunting dreams. I've walked in on him screaming and crying like someone insane. But you know there was a while when he was seeing Suzanne, he appeared to be returning to his old self, but with that shooting down at Walker's store, I just don't know."

"Another thing is that if you notice, he is always mumbling to himself. Almost like he's talking with someone. I mean a real person," Homer softly said seeing Thomas approaching.

"Like I said, I don't have any answers, Homer. But I do know that I plan to pray every day for my brother and then leave the rest to the Lord."

After not hearing from the Steven's party for over a month, the federal authorities became concerned and sent out numerous Calvary units in an extensive search covering northeast Texas. The only news came from an old woman who thought she saw the men described about a month earlier. She had described two to be in Union trousers with leather jackets and one man well dressed and the fourth's apparel evaded her memory. With no other sightings, the Agency feared the worst because Steven had consistently reported his whereabouts. The Agency decided that the Steven's party had met up with the Wilson boys and the latter had prevailed. If no word was received from Stevens in the next week, a generous bounty would be placed on Thomas Wilson and anyone else who rode with him. If needed, a full regiment would be called and every stone and bush would be turned over until either Stevens or the Wilsons were located.

17

Summer in the Bayou Country

The Lord is my refuge and my fortress, my God, in whom I trust. He will cover you with His feathers and under His wings you shall take refuge. You will not be afraid of the terror by night or the arrow that flies by day.

—Psalm 91 2, 4-5 NIV

The heat intensified on the freshly planted sugar cane, and the humidity stifled the air. Birds, seeking shelter from the heat, hovered on the shaggy, moss-draped cypress tree limbs that bordered the creeks and sloughs. With the cane in the ground, workers now had to keep the weeds away in order to walk between the rows of the ample thick branches. The hardest toil was completed until harvest time again brought heavy labor for all. The Oaks Plantation was placid with its workers taking time to tend their own gardens and valued livestock.

Suzanne enjoyed the contrast from inactivity in Mississippi to a complete and full social life at her Papére's plantation. Her weekly trips to New Orleans to shop and mingle brought some excitement into her life, and everywhere she went, young men were captivated by her beauty. Soon they referred to her as the Belle of New Orleans, the Uncatchable Lass. Whether in New Orleans or at The Oaks Plantation, young men invited her for dinner, horseback rides, dances, and even to church services. She declined all invitations to church because this was her special time with family and in worship of her Lord. Suzanne realized that where there should be emptiness after the loss of her father, that in actuality, for once peace had settled over her family. With the death of her father, harsh words and anxious expectations of condemnation had disappeared. Her grandfather gave her unconditional love and acceptance, the total opposite of her father's disposition. Her mother had taken over the management of the maids and house workers and seemed truly happy. Both she and her mother took great pleasure in planning the social calendar adding gatherings, teas, and balls.

Frankie seemed content and had grown into a mature and honest business man and appeared to thrive as he worked on the financial end of the Bourdeau business. To the family's surprise, he was assigned a political seat in the government, and he flourished in that role. He was chosen because the Republicans in the capital knew he had not participated in the recent rebellion and also because his family was among the richest in the state, but what they did not know was his political intentions, for he kept them to himself for the moment. In his heart, he abhorred the behavior of the Republicans in office, and he planned to find a way to help the old South as it struggled under the shackles of this new government. Suzanne realized that since Frankie had returned from his visit to see the Wilsons, he was happier than ever before, and she planned to find out more about the visit.

As dusk covered the land and gave relief from the early summer sun, Suzanne wandered up to the open balcony that surrounded the top floor ballroom which was called the Dome because of the glass cupola over the dance floor. A thunder cloud gathered in the west, and cool refreshing breezes swept through the tops of the oaks that surrounded the home and then across Suzanne's face as she gazed over her Papére's land. She watched the tops of the young cane branches sway and dance in waves as her mind returned to her life in Mississippi. Even though she had been happy, the constant fear of the changing moods of her father and all the turmoil he created had kept true contentment away. She was beginning to be able to accept her father's death, but it seemed more difficult to forgive his ways.

When the wind swirled her summer dress, her thoughts turned to Thomas, sweet and kind and good. Even though the attention from the men in Louisiana was exhilarating, Thomas was the only man who had touched her heart. How she longed to see him again so she could forget the last time when his eyes had been so sad and his clothing was covered in blood. She could still remember the love that was in his eyes. How she longed for those eyes and his touch.

Suzanne turned as she heard footsteps behind her. "Hello Papére. Come on out and enjoy the evening."

As Suzanne and her grandfather moved to the cushioned sofa, he handed her a glasses of tea. "Beautiful, isn't it?" He paused as his eyes swept over the land beyond. "You are looking at my life out there," he sighed pushing his wind swept white hair from his face.

"I know, Papére. You've worked hard on this land. I just wish Mamére could be here with us."

Tears welled in the corners of his eyes as he remembered his beloved wife. He nodded his head as he placed his arm around Suzanne's shoulder and pulled her to him. Finally, he whispered, "You know, she would be so proud that your mother and Frankie, and best of all, you are right here with me. I do miss the love of my life, but I can just see her smiling down on us all, so happy her family is together."

Streaks of lightning bolted from the dark rolling clouds as the storm moved closer.

"Papére, how do you know if you're in love?" Suzanne smiled at her grandfather as he glanced out over the land.

His eyes twinkled and his brow furrowed as a smile erupted on his face. "You in love, girl?'

Suzanne blushed and her face reddened. "I don't know Papére. I've never been in love, but I have a man that I can't get out of my mind, and it just doesn't make any sense. Anyway, even if I do love him, it will never work out for us."

Her grandfather roared in laughter. "Your Mamére's folks said the same thing about your grandmother and me." Taking her hand, he escorted her away from the approaching storm and toward the door. "When the time is right, you'll recognize real love. At your age it's important not to confuse infatuation with love. You pray about it, and I'll pray for you."

"But Papére, what can I do about it, now?"

"Sweet granddaughter, just give it time and ask for the Lord's guidance and let Him work out the details. Now let's get into the house before we both get struck with a bolt of lightning and never have a chance to solve your problem."

"You didn't really answer my question, Papére."

"Yes darling, I did."

By late evening the storm had passed bringing in a cool evening breeze, and with the breaking of day, the earth seemed replenished and fresh. The humid conditions that plagued the low country were temporarily pushed aside, and the birds sang their love songs in the live oaks that surrounded the mansion. Suzanne decided to relax at home, curl up in one of the rockers out on the back patio, and delve into a book. Some women loved to read and discuss poetry, but to her, a challenging mystery was more entertaining. Suzanne was intrigued by her book and didn't hear a rider approach nor the call from their butler that she had a guest.

"Miss Suzanne, you have a visitor," George called out as he walked about the house looking for her. "Where 'bouts is you?"

George, a soft-spoken elderly Negro who was born on the plantation, had decided to remain after the slaves were freed, but no longer was able to work in the fields and had assumed the position of butler. His job was to meet visitors and take care of the horses, carriages and the Bourdeau livestock. When at the mansion, he was always dressed in a black suit, white shirt, and black bowtie.

Finally hearing her name called, she lifted her eyes. "I'm out back George. I can barely hear you."

George opened the back door that led to the open patio where Suzanne was sitting. "Miss Suzanne, it's a Mister Carden Baudin. Should I escort him to the parlor or to the patio or are you not receiving guests today?"

Closing her book, Suzanne quickly rose from her seat, straightened her skirt and pushed her hair back from her face. She had spent time with Mister Baudin on several occasions including a night at a theatre in New Orleans and two balls held at The Oaks, and she had given him a tour of the plantation on horseback. He was attractive, polite, well- mannered and humorous, but she had not heard from him in several months. Of all the gentlemen who had entertained her, this man caught her attention and intrigued her enough that she wanted to get to know him better.

"Yes, I'll see the gentleman," Suzanne whispered back to George.

George returned with Mister Baudin and formally presented the visitor. "Miss Suzanne, Mister Carden Baudin," George walked silently back inside the house and out to the front where Mister Baudin's horse was tethered.

Dressed in a light tan suit with an open collared shirt and riding boots, Carden hesitated momentarily admiring the beautiful woman. With his ebony hair neatly combed back and well groomed, his six feet and five inches appeared even taller.

Suzanne looked up and politely stated, "Mister Baudin, it is a pleasure to see you again. Won't you join me?"

Baudin shook his head and laughed, "Not until you start calling me by my first name, Carden."

"Then Carden it will be. Come join me, Carden" Suzanne answered, as her eyes twinkled with amusement. "Macy, will you bring Carden something cold to drink," Suzanne called.

"Yes'm, I'll bring it right out," came an answer from inside.

"It's been quite a while since I've heard from you, so I thought someone else must have caught your fancy—some Southern Bell." Suzanne cocked her head in anticipation of the answer.

"You certainly get to the point, Suzanne. As for Southern Belles, why would I pursue them when I have the Belle of New Orleans here in my presence? That would make me a foolish man, wouldn't it?"

"I am sure there are plenty of beautiful women in New Orleans, and you still haven't explained why it has been so long since you've called."

"Well, I've been in Brazil with my father purchasing goods. You would not believe the quality of craftsmanship in furniture and jewelry we found down there. In that trip alone, we'll make a fortune in the New York market."

"Brazil! That's amazing," breathed Suzanne, thinking how wonderful it must be to travel to a foreign country. "Such exciting adventures. Do sit and tell me more about you and your family. Where did you spend your childhood?"

Soon fresh lemonade was brought, and as Carden sipped his drink, he took her hand in his. "Well, my childhood was spent in Baton Rouge until father sent me to Saint Andrews Catholic School in New Orleans when I was twelve. Since we had a business there, he moved to the city with me. When I finished my studies, he insisted that I go east and attend Harvard."

"Harvard! That is one of the best academic colleges."

"That's true. It was plenty difficult, so after a couple of years, I told father that I had enough education and wanted to return home to work with him. Since I love adventure, he then introduced me to the import business and taught me how to value a product, to estimate the profit and to market it. We traveled to South America, all around the Mediterranean Sea and also Japan, China and India."

"How wonderful to visit all of those places. What about the war years when the Yankees had the ports blockaded? What did you do during that time? Did you fight for the South?"

Carden got up, walked to the rose garden that bordered the patio and plucked a rose. He brought it back and tucked it gently into the side of Suzanne's long hair. Leaning down, he softly placed a kiss on her cheek. "Beautiful rose for a beautiful woman."

Sitting back down beside her, he confided, "Father wouldn't let me fight in the late war. He felt the South did not have the men or resources to win and that my life was worth more than a useless sacrifice."

Taking another sip from his drink, he continued, "During the war years we sailed to all those foreign ports searching for items that could be sold once the war ended. We sold to people of means in New York, Philadelphia and some of the larger eastern cities."

Suzanne looked into Carden's eyes and smiled. "I am amazed at the exciting life you have lived. It seems much like the fiction I love to read. Is all of this really true, or are you just teasing me with fairy tales?"

"Suzanne, my life seems a fairy tale, but no, all that I've told you is true. In fact, if you will, I would love for you to accompany me to Italy. We would be gone for three weeks and will be well-chaperoned. Do you think you might like that?"

Suzanne could imagine the trip and longed to say yes, but instead replied, "My mother would never allow me to travel that far away, and I am not sure that I would be brave enough to leave my family."

Carden stood and reached for Suzanne's hands then gently pulled her to her feet. "Let's go inside and inquire as to the possibility of your visit to the Mediterranean. I promise you a voyage you'll never forget. Shall we?"

Taking his hand, she could not comprehend this amazing opportunity. She had read about the Roman Empire, the grandeur of Rome and the beautiful Mediterranean coastline, but to think about visiting Italy made her heart beat with fascination.

The Lewis children had seen no sign of travelers since the last rain. As they approached the Red River, they were amazed at the breadth of this muddy body of water and the flourishing bushes and trees on its banks. They had definitely left the desolate grasslands and found bountiful vegetation. As they stood considering the hazardous and boggy flowing dirty water, they realized crossing would be both treacherous and foolish. For over an hour, Tommy and Sally waited trying to decide the best way to safely cross. Mary, their ten year old sister, had grown tired of sitting, so she took six year old Richmond, two year old Lonnie and a blanket to a cottonwood tree. She spread out the blanket to relax in the fresh air. She began teasing, entertaining, and playing games with her brothers, and soon they were laughing and having fun. Finally Tommy got down from the wagon, walked to the bank of the river and removed his shirt, socks and shoes then called back to Sally. "I'm gonna wade out and see how deep it is and what kind of surface is under all this muddy water. This road led us here and way across there I can see where others have made it out."

"I don't know, Tommy. It sure doesn't look safe. You be careful. If it gets much over your waist, I wouldn't go any further," Sally exclaimed pulling off her bonnet while getting down from the wagon to follow him.

Mary watched Tommy approach the water then screamed from the cotton-wood tree, "I wouldn't do that Tommy!"

Tommy glanced at the children under the oak tree and saw that Richmond had moved close to the woods. Angered, he shouted, "Richmond, you get back near Mary!"

Richmond calmly waved to him. "You ain't my boss. If'n you are gonna boss, stay over there on the other side of the river." At the young age of six, Richmond had a mind of his own, and Tommy knew he would have his hands full trying to be a father to him.

Tommy just shook his head and remarked, "You heard what I said. I expect you to do like Pa would want, and he would want you to mind me."

Cautiously wading into the slow moving water, Tommy took one step at a time then stopped to observe how the bottom felt to his feet. The wind whipped down the river and rippled the water as crows cawed in the tree limbs across the way. Off to the north Tommy noticed a circle of buzzards zeroing in on a meal. He returned his concentration to his task and realized that although the first steps had been oozing on his toes, the next steps were on firm ground. A weaving movement to his left caught his eyes. Tommy froze in the water terrified. A limb swept in front of him, so he quickly grabbed it and began thrashing the snake on the head. The snake ducked into the water and swam away from him.

Breathing easier, he tried to relax and regain his composure before continuing across. At a slow pace, Tommy would step, pause, step, and pause until he eventually reached the other side. On the return trip he noticed the coloration and variation of the shoreline had changed which meant the water was dropping. Tommy headed to the cottonwood and told his siblings about his encounter with the snake. "The river is falling, so let's camp tonight, and we will make a late morning crossing tomorrow. I am going to get us a rabbit. Sally, you and Mary get a fire started." Tommy grabbed his shotgun and soon returned with fresh meat.

"The river bottom has lots of wildlife. Looks like we are going to have a good meal tonight."

Tommy cleaned the kill and gave the rabbits to Sally who began roasting them on sticks she had placed over the open fire. Even though the rabbits turned out rather tough, the children enjoyed the taste of fresh meat.

Tommy remembered the buzzards and wondered what had attracted them. He didn't realize the buzzards were a warning of danger. Earlier that day, the buzzards had found the tortured body of a buffalo hunter who had been headed to Wichita to make profit from the sale of furs but had encountered Apaches who felt the furs belonged to them.

At mid-day, the river had dropped to about two feet, so Tommy forced the horses and mule into the water, and they were able to cross without a problem. As the children looked across the river, it seemed to be a mile wide. They decided to travel southeasterly along the river bank until they could find a stream flowing into the Red River. If it had a good flow and decent water, they would proceed up that stream until they found the perfect spot for their home and barn. They knew that to build a house and barn, they had to locate an area that contained trees and a fresh spring of water. How to accomplish all of this was presenting an enormous problem for Tommy.

Finally after two days wandering down the river, they found a stream that flowed into the Red. They followed the stream three more days until they found a valley covered with short, but useable trees and surrounded by enough grass to support cattle. To their surprise, a small trickling stream flowed into the creek, and after following it, they discovered water seeping from the ground at the base of a large bolder. They had found their spring of fresh water, and they thought by God's grace, they had found their new home.

Elated, they made camp and sat around the campfire, laughing and planning their new life in Oklahoma. Of course, first on the agenda was to construct a house before the cold weather came.

"Well, I plan to start a garden as soon as possible so we can have vegetables to eat." Sally was excited and soon her thoughts turned to the ranch. "Tommy, where are we going to purchase the cattle? We didn't see a single soul on the trail."

Doubts again troubled Sally as she contemplated their ability to manage a cattle farm. Would it be necessary to return to Texas for the cattle, and how could children drive cattle back over the plains and the river, a task that would be difficult for experienced cattlemen? Her unease would have become terror if she knew that they were now on Apache land and that an Apache camp was located only a day's ride north of them. Even though the clan was supposed to be friendly, other clans were using this area for refuge as they raided ranches and wagon trains in north Texas and the Arizona Territory.

The children held hands and thanked the Lord for bringing them to a new home and then snuggled in for a good night's sleep. Late in the night, Tommy awoke to the sounds of restless horses shuffling and fearing some kind of animal, took his shotgun and tipped out to the tethered horses. Slipping quietly across the damp grass, he approached the animals.

Suddenly Tommy saw a figure leap from the darkness and felt a sharp pain shoot through his head. As he crumpled to the ground, he heard the man speak in an unknown language. Then all went black and silent.

The Apache spoke to two others with him, "We take the children and sell them across the border. The horses are now ours, but the wagon is of no use."

Another cantered, "What about this boy?"

"He looks strong. We take him as slave. If he does not work or causes us problems, we kill him."

Leaving the camp outside of Sherman at dawn, the Wilsons fanned out heading west toward Wichita Falls. Homer rode along the Red River and looked for the best crossing into the Oklahoma territory. Thomas made a southern swing through the woods, and John took the main road toward Wichita Falls. Along the trail, John saw several wagon camps filled with people heading west. He knew that since the end of the war, many Southerners had been forced from their homes by a corrupt government and were no longer happy in the South. John checked every wagon in hopes of finding the children. After noon the Wilsons planned to meet together outside the town of Gainesville to regroup. Homer was the last to arrive and like the others was exhausted and frustrated. Dropping to the ground, he lay there too tired to talk.

"Nothing?" Thomas asked handing Homer a cup of coffee.

Homer reached up to grasp the cup. "Nothing. They seem to have vanished."

"Same for us. No telling how many wagons and campsites I've searched," John answered walking toward Homer's horse to tether, water it down, and feed it.

After a lunch of beans and jerky, John and Homer collapsed on their bedroll and fell into a deep sleep. Thomas stayed up and kept guard while the two napped.

Days had become weeks as the men diligently searched for signs of the children and the route they had taken. It was now summer, and Thomas knew that soon the heat would be intensifying. Leaving the woodlands of east Texas, he had seen the hills evolve into rolling plains and only small clusters of dwarfed trees dotted the grasslands. Where streams flowed, cottonwoods and plush vegetation thrived, but from now on, it would become unbearably hot. Oklahoma would be a wilderness with few inhabitants. Cattle ranches would be few in number and spread across the vast grassland. Thomas, a west Texas Ranger, knew the importance of knowing the land and where water could be found.

When Homer and John finally began to rouse, Thomas had a grin on his face. "'Bout time you two woke up. We need to get to searching again."

"We'll need to continue on to Nocona, a small village that is about halfway to Wichita Falls. I'll follow the Red River, John, you keep to the main road, and Thomas, keep to the south, and we'll meet together again about supper time," Homer instructed.

As John gathered the horses, he suddenly stopped and turned to Homer and Thomas, "I forgot to tell you something I remembered while I was riding this morning. We've been looking for children manning a wagon and we've gotten nowhere, but I think I know a way to find them. Most folks don't pay a lot of attention to who is driving the wagon, but they do consider horseflesh. The man at the ferry told me that the Lewis children left here with an old wagon pulled by a solid white horse, a dark brown one with white stockings and here is the clincher; an old black mule. Now, won't that make it easier for us to find them?"

As Homer and Thomas readied their horses and swung into their saddles, Thomas cocked his head at John and said, "I wish you'd thought of that sooner. Experienced drivers never mix a mule with horses. Let's hit the trail men. We've wasted too much time already."

Homer skirted the lower bank of the Red River while Thomas swung south in a less populated area in order to evade soldiers who might be searching for him. John took the main road leading west. The men had abandoned their winter clothing months ago and replaced it with cotton shirts, hats pulled down for protection from the sun and torn strips of cloth shielding their necks and face from the dusty wind. As each day passed, John became more anxious over the coming birth of his child and knew if something didn't happen soon, he must turn back and head for Mississippi without the children.

John met an old prospector who had camped off the road, and when John questioned him, he discovered that the old gentleman knew the area well. With the old man's help, John drew out a crude map that gave locations of fresh water on the road ahead and also some of the safest river crossings.

The Wilsons made camp outside of Nocona, and soon Homer and John were sound asleep. Thomas was unusually quiet and sat by the fire peering into the dancing flames. Late in the night John was awakened by mumbling, and when he slowly raised up, he saw Thomas still sitting by the now ember fire. He had his knees tucked to his chest with his arms tightly clutching them. He was continuously rocking back and forth and mumbling to himself.

John moved over to his brother. "Thomas, you all right?" he asked as he placed his hand on Thomas's shoulder.

Thomas jerked his head around, jumped up and drew his knife. John could see the crazed expression on his brother's face and his piercing eyes. In one motion, Thomas threw John to the ground and raised his knife to strike.

"Thomas, it's me, John." John watched as Homer grabbed Thomas by the arm.

"Woah now! Just take it easy!" shouted Homer twisting the knife from Thomas's hand. "It's gonna be all right."

Thomas blinked his eyes several times and then looked at John who had scrambled up and away from Thomas. "Where are they?" he asked. "Where'd they go?"

"Who you talking about?' John asked.

"Those men. The ones who are trying to kill me."

Homer reached over and handed Thomas a cup of water. "There's no one here but us. It was only a dream. Now, you lay down over there, and John and I will keep guard."

Thomas was confused and extremely exhausted, so he lay on his bedroll and was soon deep in sleep.

John spoke quietly to Homer, "If you hadn't stepped in, do you think he would have killed me?"

Homer shook his head. "John, I'm afraid he would have. I'm worried about Thomas. He seems filled with worry, fear and guilt, and he is just not getting enough sleep. If he keeps this up, I think he may lose his grip on reality, if he hasn't already."

"What can we do?" John asked.

"You're the praying man. Pray for him, and in the meantime, we need to constantly be on the watch."

When morning broke, Thomas awoke and acted as if nothing had happened. John and Homer decided it was best to refrain from mentioning the incident.

18

Terror in Apache Lands

*For to Thee O Lord I lift up my soul. For Thou Lord are good and
ready to forgive and abundant in mercy to all who call upon Thee.
Thou O Lord are a God full of compassion and gracious, longsuffering
and abundant in mercy and truth.*

—Psalm 86:4b, 5,15 KJV

"Okay Cousins. Let's head into town and see if we can gather some information about the children." Homer knew they must replace needed supplies and hoped Nocona would have a general merchandizing store. Riding down the rutted, dusty street, they saw a blacksmith shop, livery stable, a couple of small framed houses, and to their delight a store with a sign that stated, Best Goods in Texas—Merchandizing and Saloon. Four wagons were pulled up in front while several more could be seen coming in from the east. It was quite obvious that this settlement catered to the pilgrims moving westward.

Homer dismounted and shook the dust from his hat and walked up the steps into the establishment leaving his cousins to tether the horses. He quickly pushed his way through a crowd of people and saw that the store was well-supplied then walked to the saloon located in the adjoining room. There were several tables and chairs, an old piano and an unusually short bar with a mirror to the back. Dust covered the entire room indicating that sobriety was a value of the westward pilgrims. Homer walked back to the store and joined John and Thomas at the counter where a tall man with gray hair and mustache was placing money in a drawer under the counter.

The man appraised the three, then asked, "Can I help you?"

Homer took off his neck cloth and wiped his face. "We're going to need some supplies, sir. And we are also looking for some of our kin who might have come this way. Have you seen three boys and two girls traveling in a wagon all by themselves with no adults?

The old gent shook his head. "Son, I see a lot of folks coming in here and lots of children. Seems like the whole east of our country is headed west to somewhere. Wish I could help you."

Thanking the old gent, Homer left John and Thomas to get the supplies and decided to see if the blacksmith could fix the loose shoe on his horse. Homer led his horse to the edge of the blacksmith shop and called out, "Anybody here?"

The side door opened and a large, bald man with an apron tied about his waist, walked through. The man's arms were as large as Homer's thighs and stockiness marked every inch of his body. Homer chuckled thinking how he hoped this giant would always be on his side of an argument.

"Sorry. Didn't have time to eat my dinner, so I was in the back trying to get a bite," the man said walking toward Homer. "You need help? By the way, folks call me Big Dave."

Homer extended his hand. "Name's Homer, and I've got a loose shoe on my horse."

"Bring him on in. Won't take me long to fix that."

While Dave was working on the shoe, Homer suddenly remembered what John had told them and thought that the blacksmith who worked in this open shop might have observed wagons and horses as they passed. "Dave, my cousins and I are looking for some kin that might have come through here traveling in an old wagon."

Dave kept pounding his mallet against the red hot shoe and only grunted.

"Their rig was pulled by a solid white horse, a dark brown one with white stockings and led by an old black mule," Homer said, shuffling his feet.

Dave laid his mallet down and scratched his chin in thought. "You know, that was the most ragged, dang thing I ever seen. Who in their right senses would team up like that? I told the young man what I thought about such. You just don't match horses and mules."

"You've seen them!" Homer exclaimed.

"Yeah, they come through here a while back. Said they was headed north into the Oklahoma Territory. I told 'em it was Injun country and they was fools to go in there. I heard one of the girls say, he don't have the information we do. Didn't make no sense to me"

"Did you notice which way they went?" Homer asked.

Dave took out a handkerchief and wiped the sweat from his face. "Well, I told 'em that if their minds was made up, then they should take the old trail 'bout three miles up the main road that heads north, and they would find a good river crossing there. I told them the only ones who used the trail was Buff hunters, Indian traders, and outlaws, and it certainly wasn't safe for young 'uns. But they seemed determined, and so I warned them again that it was mighty dangerous to cross the Red River and head into Apache land. They didn't heed the warning and set out toward the old trail."

As soon as the shoe was fixed, Homer excitedly hurried to find Thomas and John. For once he knew where to go, and the days it had taken for them to search for signs was over. Finally they were on the right trail.

Thomas and John were waiting outside the store, and Homer ran quickly to them to share the news. The trio finished packing the supplies and rode down the old trail as the sun was setting. They planned to be at the river by dark, camp there and cross over in the morning. As dusk approached, the party picked up the trace of wagon wheels on the trail and felt with luck, they would be able to easily follow the party the next morning. For the first time in months, the men felt optimistic about finding the children and sleep came easily, even for Thomas.

Dawn came early for the Wilson's, and they were on the north bank of the Red River before the sun rose. They found wagon tracks, and after a couple of miles when the tree and bush laden river bottom gave way to grasslands, the wagon veered to the east where traveling would be easier. At noon, the group reached a stream that flowed into the Red and at that point, the tracks turned upstream. Studying them closely Thomas said," They're looking for a good place to settle, and I have a feeling, it can't be far from here. As slow as they must be traveling, we should catch up with them soon."

As the sun was setting, the group rounded a bend in the creek, and an abandoned wagon with the tongue resting on the ground met their eyes. Some furniture was strewn across the grass, and clothes were on nearby bushes. Up the way, an old mule was lazily grazing. The men were devastated by the sight and stood silently contemplating the dilemma.

Thomas finally spoke, "Y'all stay here, and I'll go down and check for signs. If we all ride in, we could ruin tracks." Thomas dismounted and carefully edged down to the wagon. He began to study every track made and then called out, "Come on down and bring my horse with you."

John and Homer walked the horses to Thomas who was squatting on the ground diligently studying the evidence.

"What do you think?" John asked.

With a frown, he replied, "From the unshod horse prints and moccasins, I'd say three Apaches sneaked in and took not only the children but their horses as well."

"Why did they leave the mule?"

"They didn't need or want the mule nor wagon."

Homer leaned down to examine the prints below. "You think they killed the children?"

Thomas wiped the perspiration from his eyes. "Naw, they didn't kill 'em. If they had, we'd be seeing buzzards."

"Then what are they going to do with them?" John asked.

Thomas stood up and shook his head. "They'll either keep them as slaves or sell them down across the border in Mexico."

"That can't happen," exclaimed John. "We've got to find 'em."

Thomas thought for a moment and then said, "There are many different clans of the Apache in this land, and it could have been any one of them. To find the right one will take too much time. We can't afford to lose time, so I say we try to bring them to us."

"What do you mean, Thomas?" Homer asked.

"Well, we'll camp right here tonight and keep a big fire going. We'll take our winter clothing and wrap it inside of our blankets, place our hats where a head should be so it looks like we are asleep. Not only will we tether our horses but hobble them as well. If we're paid a visit, the first thing that the Apache will want will be our horses. By tethering and hobbling them, it will give us enough time to get ready."

"What next?" Homer asked impatiently.

"We hide outside of camp, hide the best we can and wait. If they come, they'll probably be from the same clan that took the children and will likely live close by."

"Do we kill them?" John asked.

"That's the last thing we want to do. That would be like stirring up a hornet's nest. No sir, we try to capture them alive, and maybe, just maybe, we can get some information from them."

Pleased with the plan, the men built a large fire, prepared their bedrolls with lumps and hats and after taking care of the horses, found secure hiding places not far from the animals. Dusk gave way to darkness as night settled in. A half-moon silvered the sky, and the sound of croaking frogs from the stream and a hoot of an old owl serenaded the night. Hours crept by as the Wilsons sat in waiting.

About an hour before dawn, the old mule that had wandered back up the stream began to shuffle nervously. Thomas threw a small rock toward Homer, alerting him to visitors. With pounding hearts and alert eyes, the men waited.

Finally they saw two figures emerge from the shadows and sneak into the camp and over to inspect the bedrolls. Confident that no one was stirring, the two crawled to the horses and pulling out a knife, began to cut the ropes tied to the horse's hooves.

Quietly, Thomas and Homer rose up and in the Apache language, Thomas shouted, "Stop! Lay down your knives or you die now!"

Completely surprised at the sound of their own language, the two froze in their tracks, dropped their knives and stood up. Thomas and Homer approached them with rifles drawn and quickly secured their knives, then searched them for other weapons. "Go to the fire," Thomas ordered.

John quickly rushed in to help.

As Thomas ordered them to place their hands behind their backs, John tied their wrists tightly. The Apache had their hair at shoulder length with a headband tied above the brow. Knee length moccasins protected their feet and legs, and only loincloths were worn leaving their upper body bare in the summer heat.

To John's amazement, the two prisoners sat crossed legged and showed no fear at all. They kept looking at each of the Wilson men. Finally one called out, "You kill us?"

Thomas walked over and placed his knife blade against the throat of the one

186

who had spoken and said, "That depends on what you tell me. You tell me what I want to hear, and you will live."

"We did not try to kill you. We only wanted the horses," the other Apache barked out. "What do you want from us?"

Thomas sheathed his knife and placed the barrel of his pistol on the Apache's forehead. "I want to know what happened to the children taken from this wagon and if they are still alive. You lie, then you die."

Showing fear for the first time, the Apaches talked quietly to each other, and finally the older of the two spoke. "They walk on Apache lands uninvited. We take horses and children but no mule. Take children to my camp. Maybe slave or sell in Mexico."

"I'll tell you what. You take me to your village and to the children, and you will get back with your lives. If, not. I'm gonna shoot both of you."

"Why you interested in children?" the older man asked.

"They're my cousins, and I want to carry them home to Mississippi."

Seeing no way out, the two once again murmured to each other, and the older man spoke. "We take you to village but cannot guarantee your life once there."

"Fair enough," assured Thomas.

Before leaving, Homer made some coffee and breakfast while they discussed the best way to get the children out safely. Thomas finally outlined his plan. "When we get near the village, I want to go in by myself."

"By yourself!" exclaimed Homer. "We can't let you do that, Thomas."

"Listen to my plan. I'm going to try to strike a trade. John, I need your Henry rifle and knife for trading. I will ride your horse today to protect my thoroughbred. Papa's going to need this horse on the farm, and I don't intend to lose it. If they should kill me, then you two may be able to get away and plan another way to rescue the children. You shouldn't approach the Apaches again because if the children cause them too much grief, they will murder them. Your best bet would be to trade for them once they've been sold as slaves in Mexico."

The trio rode for several hours leading their captives. About noon they caught a slight smell of smoke, and as they gazed across a grassy field, they saw a large herd of horses indicating the Apache camp was near. Thomas led the two bound Apaches up the clearing just beyond the trees then walked a few steps back to his cousins and spoke, "Look for good hiding places while I'm gone, and if you sense any trouble at all, run. If the children come out here, you get them ready and head home at once. If the children don't come and I'm not back in two days, then John you go on home. Homer, you stay and try to find out if the children will be sold."

Thomas mounted John's horse and placed his rifle in ready position then turned back and called, "Cousins, now is the time to lay your requests before the Lord. Pray He will keep the children safe so you can return to Mississippi with them." Thomas turned and followed the two captive Apaches as they led him toward the camp.

John turned to Homer and remarked, "Did you notice that he didn't ask us to pray for his safety? Well, doesn't matter. I intend to keep praying for my brother."

Homer nodded in agreement, and both men settled down in a hidden spot to wait.

Thomas placed the Apaches in front of him while he followed with his rifle resting on his lap. Realizing he was probably facing death and even though fear coursed through his soul, he also felt relief knowing that his trials might soon be over. He hoped he could get the children safely away, but as for his life, it really didn't seem to matter anymore.

As he contemplated his death, he heard a verse spoken softly within his heart, and soon he was whispering with the voice, "The Lord is my shepherd, I shall not want. He makes me lie down in green pastures; He leads me beside still waters. He restores my soul; He guides me in the path of righteousness for His name's sake. Even though I walk through the valley of the shadow of death, I fear no evil; for you are with me. Your rod and your staff, they comfort me. You prepare a table before me in the presence of my enemies. You anoint my head with oil; my cup overflows. Surely goodness and mercy will follow me all the days of my life and I will dwell in the house of the Lord forever."

Thomas wondered about the inner voice and the words that seemed to flow from his lips. Was it the voice of God, and why would God send comforting words after all he had done? Thomas breathed a prayer for the first time in years, "Lord, I know we have not been on speaking terms lately, and I know that I have sinned so much in these past years that forgiveness is impossible, but I do pray that these children will be safe. Lord please help me to know the way to get these children to John and Homer, so they can take them home. If anyone has to die, let it be me."

As Thomas came upon the Apache village, he could see a field full of crude grass structures made from bended stripped limbs fastened together with grass piled on the top to keep the sun's heat from penetrating. Thomas knew this to be the typical easily constructed summer home that gave comfort. He could see men sitting in the shades of trees talking while women were on their knees scraping the fat from buffalo hides. He knew the women would follow the scraping with tanning, and the hides would make fine winter clothing and covering for their shelters. Off to the creek some women were washing while children were scampering around the camp, but there was no evidence of the children he sought.

As they grew closer, one of the children began screaming, "Tsayaditl-ti!" (white man) The whole camp came alive, and all began arming themselves as they walked toward him and his Apache captives. Women picked up limbs while the men retrieved their rifles and bows. Shouts and screams broke the silence of the afternoon, but the only word Thomas recognized was Tsayaditl-ti.

Tommy, battered and bruised for his open defiance and fearing an attack from a rival tribe, dropped the limbs he had been collecting for firewood and ran toward the camp. He pushed his way through the crowd and was startled to see a white man leading two Apache captives.

As the angry Apaches approached, Thomas called to his captives, "You keep them away from me, or you'll be the first to die. I want only to see the clan leader."

The captives began shouting to their people, and soon silence swallowed the camp. Their clansmen began to step back, but Thomas noted the deep hate and resentment in their eyes. As they reached the center of the camp, the captives pointed to a shelter and the older said, "He's in there."

"Tell him I only want to talk." Thomas ordered.

Thomas reached for his knife and dismounted. He walked to the captive Apaches sitting in their saddles and cut the ropes thus freeing their hands. "You are free to go now," he said.

As Thomas turned, he saw an old Apache with dark, glazed eyes, wrinkled aged skin, and a definite stoop in his shoulders. Momentarily they stood in silence meeting each other's gaze. Thomas spoke in Apache. "I come in peace. I want to talk with you."

Surprised to hear a white man speak his language, he nodded his approval and pointed to the opening of his shelter, directing Thomas inside. Once seated, Thomas told him why he had bound the Apache and that he wanted to trade with him. He stated that he knew he was holding five white children, and they were his clansmen. He only wanted to carry them back home to Mississippi.

The old man thought for a while and then spoke, "They were on our land

and we have been feeding them. If you want them, what will you trade?"

Thomas laid the Henry rifle on the rug between them and gave his massive hunting knife to the man. "I'll give you all of this and fifty rounds of shot."

The old Apache picked up the rifle, held it as if shooting then laid it back down. "Not enough. They cause us lots of trouble," he bantered.

"Not the trouble that could occur." exclaimed Thomas. "When the white soldiers across the river hear that you are holding five white children as captives, they will come in here like a storm and burn your camp, take your horses and kill most of you before you can run and hide. Do you want that to happen to your people?"

The old man dropped his head and tightened his lips knowing what Thomas said was true. "You give me the rifle, knife and the pistol you carry and they will be yours."

"Is your word good?" Thomas asked extending his hand. "We will need horses for the children to ride. What is your name?"

"I am called Dahkeya."

"I've never heard that name before. What does it mean?"

"The old man smiled. "It means nothing. My parents could not decide on a name, so they made up the word Dahkeya. But I give it meaning of Great Hawk."

Both men laughed. "What's your name, white man?"

"My name is Wilson."

"Well Wilson, may the gods curse me if I lie. Before the sun sets, the children will ride out. "Lacomba," he called to a man outside. "Bring the children here."

One by one the children bent down and walked inside. All were dirty, ragged, but grateful and apprehensive to see a white man "Sit down children," Thomas said.

Tommy, taking authority, asked," Who are you?"

"Thomas smiled at the boy. "I'm Thomas Wilson, your cousin from Mississippi. We've been looking for you for months, and the head of this Apache clan has agreed to let you all go as of this evening."

Smiles erupted on the children's faces, and they ran over and hugged Thomas pushing him to the ground as tears of joy flowed down their cheeks. Even Tommy found tears on his face. Sally began making introductions one by one beginning with Tommy. Each gave Thomas a hug as they were introduced. Mary, Richmond, and Lonnie were last, and Lonnie returned quickly to the rug to play with a puppy that had waddled in.

Thomas quietly spoke to Tommy and Sally, "Cousins, you have two more cousins waiting outside of the camp down by the creek. Now listen carefully. If there is any commotion or trouble when we start to leave, you are to get as quickly to your cousins as you possibly can. Do not look back, just keep riding that way. Go get all your belongings, and let's get ready to head out. We need to go as quickly as possible while the chief is still willing to let you go."

The children left, and Thomas crawled outside the shelter to wait for them. No sooner had he stood, than a group of about twenty Apaches came riding into the camp from the west sending swirls of dust in the air. Cheers of welcome shattered the evening as the men arrived. Dahkeya stood beside Thomas and muttered, "Geronimo. He always bring trouble."

Thomas watched as the lead warrior of the Apaches approached. As a custom of respect to a clan leader, Geronimo brought his men into the village and up to Dahkeya and Thomas. Thomas recognized Geronimo from a treaty meeting he had attended out in Arizona. He was a rather short man, typical of the Apache, and had slightly crossed eyes and was extremely dangerous. Thomas felt he looked even more confident and vicious than at the meeting in Arizona.

As Geronimo's men dismounted to visit with old friends, Geronimo spoke quietly with Dahkeya. Thomas decided to walk toward the edge of the camp and wait for the children. He noticed as the two Apaches talked, Geronimo kept glancing at him and a sense of trepidation gripped his heart.

Finally Geronimo walked to Thomas. "I know you. You were Ranger down south of here. You were with the ones who burned one of our villages and killed men, women and children. You deny that?"

Thomas tried to calm the panic that arose from the hidden threat in Geronimo's words. He knew he needed to explain, but fear seized him. After a few moments of silence, he spoke, "I'm not gonna lie. I was there, but -"

Before Thomas could utter another word, he felt a swift blow to his head which sent him sprawling to the ground. As Thomas tried to stand, Geronimo again took the butt of his rifle and struck Thomas in the back of his head. Blood poured down his face as the blows continued and shouts filled the air. Darkness engulfed him.

Geronimo and his warriors soon rode from the camp and headed to north Texas on a raid. Before he left, he gave instructions to Dahkeya that Thomas must face death.

When Thomas awoke, he was sitting on the ground with his back to a hitching post and his hands tied behind him. Both feet were staked to the ground in front of him. Intense pain engulfed his whole body, and one eye was swollen so badly he couldn't see from it. A large group of clansmen were standing nearby while Dahkeya was squatting silently observing him.

"You lucky to be alive, Wilson. Men who kill our people no matter white or Apache, must die. You fool to come in here," muttered Dahkeya.

Trying to clear his throat, Thomas whispered, "You gave your word. The children…"

"I not like white man. I don't lie. Children have already gone. You stay and pay for what you did to my people. You live till morning."

All during the night, fires burned while Apaches danced and sang Thomas's death song. On occasions a warrior would fire his rifle or shoot arrows at Thomas. One shot tore through his shoulder, and an arrow nipped his neck. A drunken Apache walked close and took his knife to Thomas's neck and made a slice. Dahkeya noted the attack and rebuked the warrior then sat down next to Thomas.

Dahkeya was surprised that in all the inflicted torture, this white man seemed to welcome death, so he asked, "Are you not afraid to die? Why do you have no fear?"

Straining to talk, Thomas whispered, "You don't fear death when you don't care whether you live or die."

The old man shook his head. "You are too brave, Wilson. You die with honor when sun rises. Your spirit strong. I only wish I was that brave."

"It is not bravery. My death is what I deserve for the sins I've committed."

As the darkness grew, the Apaches eventually retired for the night and an eerie quietness settled in the camp. Thomas watched as a full moon crept into the upper sky and fluffy clouds danced across the heavens. As Thomas faced his own death, he began to think of the significance of his life. He remembered his boyhood days and the happy family times he had experienced. Next he remembered volunteering for the war and the pride he felt when he was noted as a sharp shooter. Then his life was forever changed, and his joy melted into hatred of an enemy with no face. He killed and killed and killed. When he received the scope, his enemy's face was clear, and he realized that the enemy was men just like him with families that loved them, and he knew that he had become a murderer. He no longer deserved to live, and death was justice.

Thomas remembered when he had given his life to Christ and how he had lost sight of that commitment during the war. He began to pray, "Lord, into your hands I commit my soul. I have sinned, and I pray you will forgive me of the terrible things I have done. I pray that you will welcome me home. I know that I don't deserve your mercy, and I'll understand if I am beyond mercy, but Lord, I just want to come home to you."

Thomas felt the peace that had evaded him since leaving the war and knew he had been forgiven. "Thank you Lord," he smiled. "I now can die in peace knowing I have been forgiven."

For the first time a peace came over him, and he felt he had finally been freed. Before he drifted off to sleep, his thoughts turned to Suzanne. Her beautiful smile, the dark sparkle of her brown eyes and the touch of her skin seemed so close. He struggled as he realized that he would never get the chance to tell her how much he loved her.

As day began to break, the village came alive. Women gathered bundles of limbs and bushes and piled them around Thomas, as he sat silently in peace. When the sun touched the eastern horizon, Dahkeya came to Thomas. "You seem too calm too brave as you face death."

Thomas looked at the sun steadily rising over the eastern horizon and struggled to smile. "Old man, you can have this courage in my Lord Jesus Christ. Anyone can."

A worried look crossed Dahkeya's face. "I wish I could know this Christ."

"You can. Just call on Him, and He will come to you in spirit. You will hear His voice in your heart."

Dahkeya rose and called to his people. The men began removing their moccasins and sat crossed legged, facing Thomas while the women settled further back. The children remained in the dwellings. Motioning, Dahkeya beckoned for one of his clansmen to bring a torch, and he took the torch and stood before Thomas.

Thomas waited silently for his death.

Dahkeya held the torch high, reached toward the sky and began chanting Apache words. Then he looked at Thomas and back to the sky. "Today, we send this brave soul to you in honor." With those words, a hissing sound filled the air as the clansmen exhaled all the air in their lungs.

As Dahkeya leaned down to torch the brush, a cloud of dust was seen rising from the west. He dropped the torch in the dirt and shouted for a rider to investigate. Dahkeya knew if soldiers were arriving, he would have to quickly hide Thomas.

"Jicarilla Apache coming," spoke the rider who had been sent to investigate.

As the tribesmen arrived, they silently approached the Apache camp and dismounted in front of the chief. "We have travelled from the reservation in San Carlos. We grew tired of it and have escaped the white man to seek safety with clansmen."

"You will have this safety. Join us. We are sending this brave man to his maker."

The Jicarilla Apache removed their moccasins and took position with the clan. As Dahkeya again called for a lighted torch, a young boy from the new arrivals walked toward the brush and looked ardently at Thomas. An older man rebuked the boy and jerked his hand to lead him away, but the boy broke free and ran to Thomas and began pulling the limbs away. The Apaches watched the odd behavior of the young boy.

The boy leaned down, pushed Thomas's hair from his beaten face and with his shirt sleeve, began to wipe the blood from his face while speaking gently to him. To the tribe's amazement, he squatted down on Thomas's lap and crossed his arms. For a child to do such was not the way of the Apache. Dahkeya, feeling the gods had rendered some kind of spirit to this child, walked toward the boy. "What does this mean, little one?"

The boy turned to Thomas. "When our village was raided by the white soldiers, this man picked me up and rode me to safety. Two days later, he handed me to my mother who had hidden during the raid."

A soft mumble arose from the Apaches as they pondered what had been revealed.

"Can anyone support this boy's claim?" Dahkeya shouted.

A young woman rose and walked to Dahkeya to study the man holding her son. Finally she said, "He is the one who struck the soldier who was going to kill my son. I was afraid and had hidden when the soldiers first came. Two days later, this man tracked us to our camp and gave me my son. He stated that he was tired of killing innocent people and was going home."

Nodding his head, Dahkeya took out his knife and cut the ropes that bound Thomas. "You can either stay with us or go as you please. Your Jesus God has favored you."

Thomas tried to stand, but did not have the strength. Dahkeya motioned for two of his clansmen to assist Thomas. They lifted him to his saddle and led the horse southward then gave the horse a sound whack as Thomas slumped over and held on as best he could.

19

Homeward Bound

*You have turned my mourning into joyful dancing. You have taken
away my sackcloth and clothed me with joy that my soul may sing
praises to You, and not be silent. O Lord my God, I will give You
thanks forever.*

—Psalm 30 11-12 NASB

"Are you our cousins?" Tommy asked the two men he saw by the creek.

"Yes. We are." John quickly helped the small children from the horses and looked back toward the camp for Thomas.

"Are you all right?" Homer asked.

"Yes, but we don't know what happened to Thomas. We were supposed to meet him at the edge of the camp, but before we could get there, some of the Apaches came for us. They slipped us out of the camp away from Thomas, put us on these two horses and motioned for us to ride out, so we rode as fast as we could." Tommy knew the news must be difficult for his cousins.

Sally added, "We didn't even get to thank him for getting us released."

After welcoming their cousins, John and Homer had the children remount, and together they rode back to the other side of the Red River for safety. After reaching the river, they decided to wait several days in hopes that Thomas would return.

The next morning John and Homer prepared breakfast, and John begin to share with his cousins. "You are going to love your Aunt Sarah and Uncle Lot. My parents are wonderful people and have been so worried about you. They wanted your mother and all of you to come live with us when they first heard about your pa, but your mother didn't want to leave her home."

As the children cleaned up in the river, Homer and John decided what to do about Thomas. "John, I'm going to ride back to the Apache camp to see what has happened to Thomas. You keep the children near here, but make sure you find a safe place to hide in case trouble should come. I'll find you by nightfall. Here you keep my rifle; you may need it."

Homer mounted his horse and rode toward the Apache camp. John sat on a boulder to watch the children play by the edge of the river. Later he gathered them and headed to the woods to make camp.

As the Apache camp became visible, Homer dismounted in the nearby woods and was amazed to see two Apaches put Thomas on John's horse and whack the horse on the rump to send Thomas headed directly toward him. He was able to catch the horse by the reins as it cantered by. "Woah boy. Woah." Homer soon had the horse calmed beside him.

Thomas slowly raised his head, but then collapsed down on his horse.

Homer saw the blood caked on his face and neck and hoped his cousin would live. He quickly tied Thomas in the saddle and gently took the reins and rode away from the Apaches.

With the sun creeping low, Homer began to worry about Thomas who had not uttered a word for the entire trip. He slowly moved toward the Red River hoping that Thomas could stay astride the horse until he found a safe place to tend his wounds.

As John and the children waited at their camp hidden in the woods, Tommy thought about their belongings at the wagon site and confided in John, "We have some money hidden under the wagon on the other side of the river back at the creek. Is it okay if I cross over and retrieve it?"

John got Sally to keep the children hidden with her while he took his rifle and Tommy then headed across the river and back to the wagon site along the creek. Tommy found the money, and John decided to hitch the old mule to the wagon to take back with them. Tommy gathered all of their belongings and loaded the wagon, but as they moved toward the river, they heard a horse, so John motioned for Tommy to follow him into the woods for cover. Creeping silently, the two found a place to hide in the brush. As two horsemen approached, John got his rifle in ready position anticipating Apaches. When the men came nearer, John's heart pounded fiercely, but then he noticed that one man was hurt and recognized Homer. John and Tommy pushed out to meet them.

"Homer, is that Thomas with you? Is he alive?"

"I'm not sure. He hasn't spoken at all. The Apaches sent him on your horse into the woods, but it looks like he is pretty badly beaten."

John and Homer lifted Thomas from the horse and laid him on the ground. Homer leaned down and put his ear to his cousin's chest and then checked his breathing. Turning to John, he muttered, "He's alive, but barely."

"I can hardly recognize him."

Both of Thomas's eyes were swollen shut, and his face was severely beaten. Blood covered most of his shirt, and cuts were evident on his neck and shoulder.

"What can we do?" asked Tommy leaning down.

"Tommy, go get the mule, and we'll place Thomas in the wagon and use our horses to pull the wagon. We need to get him to camp as soon as possible to keep him alive."

The men were able to get Thomas to the other side of the river without incident. Sally had already gotten the children to sleep, so the men eased Thomas down upon a blanket, and Sally started boiling water on the fire that she had built earlier. Before long she was able to clean Thomas's wounds, then Homer and John skillfully stitched the cuts on Thomas's face and shoulder. Early the next morning, Thomas began to moan as he regained consciousness.

Sally lifted his head up and began dripping water into his mouth.

"Sally, is that you?" he murmured.

"Yes, Thomas. We all made it away from the Indian camp thanks to you."

Thomas smiled at her. "I am so glad you are safe."

Sally continued to drizzle water into his mouth. When he seemed to quit swallowing, she retrieved some of the boiling water that had cooled and again cleaned around the wounds. His breathing became steady, and soon he was sleeping again. Homer, John and the children now awake hovered over Thomas as he slept. It seemed their prayers had been answered.

"Do you think he will be able to see when his eyes heal?"

"We just have to keep praying for that, Cousin."

Two days passed, and Thomas began to recover. He had no trouble with the sight in one eye and was able to eat and drink by himself but experienced excruciating pain when trying to sit or stand. Homer decided to split up a piece of the old canvas from the wagon and bind it tightly around Thomas's chest in case there were cracked ribs.

"Do you think it will be long before Thomas can travel?" John anxiously asked.

Homer knew that Rebecca and the coming babe was on his cousin's mind. "Let's give him five more days to mend, then I think he will be able to ride in the wagon or double with one of us. We really need to get you home to your wife, and these children need to start their new life with your family."

Thomas had recovered enough strength to handle the bumps of the trip so they set off early in the morning, and a little before noon arrived in Nocona. They planned to resupply, purchase saddles and gear for the two horses, and sell the wagon. They would rely on the horses to carry them home, riding double with the small children.

Big Dave watched the unusual group ride into town then laid down his hammer, wiped his hands on his apron and walked out to meet them. "Mercy, I never thought I'd see you folks again," he called out. "Yep, that's them chillun I warned to stay out of the Territory. With the way the Apache has been acting up, I just think I've seen a miracle."

Homer dismounted and motioned for John to help him with Thomas. "Miracle. You can surely say that."

As they struggled with Thomas, Big Dave walked over and gently lifted him from his saddle as if he were a bag of feathers. "This man looks like a herd of Buff ran over him. Let's get him inside."

Tommy helped his brothers and sisters down. "Weren't buffalo. Apache did this to him."

Thomas looked back at Tommy and smiled. "We got you out of there. That's what matters." They all began to share the events of the past few days with Big Dave.

During the next two days, they replenished their supplies, purchased saddles for the two Lewis horses, and sold the wagon. They decided to keep the mule as a pack animal, and the children only kept the necessities that could be carried on their horses.

They camped on the outskirts of town by a small stream and waited for Thomas to grow stronger. Tommy was naturally drawn to the men, while Sally became Thomas's constant nurse. Mary prepared the meals and assisted Homer as he packed supplies for the journey home. She also managed to watch her younger brothers. Lonnie and Richmond loved playing at the stream and were able to catch fish and crawfish for the stew Mary was cooking.

In a matter of days, they were becoming a family who enjoyed sharing not only the chores but also stories about their hardships and adventures.

One evening, Thomas watched Sally chew a mouthful of beans and beef jerky and then spoon it into Lonnie's mouth. Thomas cocked his head and asked Sally, "Why you chewing his food up like that?"

Sally laughed. "The baby's only got four teeth."

The whole clan roared in laughter. "Didn't you ever watch Mama at all, Thomas. You don't seem to know anything about caring for a baby, do you?"

Thomas smiled. "You are right about that, Brother. Taking care of babies was not an interest of mine. I don't expect it ever will be."

Homer observed the children and noticed that all were tall for their ages with greenish eyes and brown straight hair. "I'll tell you one thing. You children sure do favor."

Mary laughed. "Folks say we look like our parents. I'm not sure we favor though. I think Tommy is a little on the ugly side. Don't you?"

"Ugly! You ought to look at them buck teeth of yours before you start talking about my looks," teased Tommy.

Mary's laughter turned to tears. "Papa said I look just like Mama."

"Looks like you can dish it out, Sister, but you sure can't take it."

Thomas cleared his throat. "Now that's enough teasing. You all look mighty fine to me, and if'n I hear another thoughtless comment, you might just get introduced to my belt."

John winked at Homer. "Sounds just like a family, doesn't it?"

Homer enjoyed a good chuckle, and the rest of his family joined in.

On the third week of July, the Wilsons rode out of Nocona with Homer leading the way followed by John cradling Lonnie, Thomas, Tommy doubled with Richmond, and Sally with Mary. Homer had placed Tommy in charge of the pack mule which was roped behind him, and he was also given the responsibility of setting camp. Homer knew Tommy was distressed about seeing his father killed and leading the family into a dangerous debacle, and his confidence would need to be restored. The men had shared accounts of their failures and how the failures led to experience, wisdom, and strength. Tommy soon accepted his failure and was ready to meet new responsibilities.

Homer, who was leading the group, wanted to make at least twenty five or thirty miles per day, but with Thomas's condition, they were struggling to make ten. At the end of each day, John became more anxious. In about a week, they had reached Sherman and set up camp outside of the town. As they gathered around the campfire, Homer decided to call a family meeting.

Homer took a quick sip of coffee and cleared his throat. "The way I figure it, if we continue at this speed, John will miss the birth of his baby. We can't risk Thomas's healing by riding longer or faster."

"Now wait a minute," Thomas interrupted, "I can push it more."

"Naw you can't, and you shouldn't," Homer parleyed. "Now, this is what we're gonna do. It should be safe riding from here to Mississippi, so John, you take the children in the morning and push as hard as you can each day. As soon as you reach the first town that has wire service, you send Uncle Lott a message letting him know you have the children and are on the way home. If something happens on the way, they will know where to find you."

John added, "Our folks definitely need to hear that we are safe. I know it will ease their minds, plus they will be excited to begin preparing for our new family members."

When the children heard the word family, they began to smile at each other as thoughts of a home where they would belong warmed their hearts. They knew that the sufferings faced in the past year would be replaced with joy and family.

"What about you and Thomas?" John asked. "Where will you go?"

Homer smiled at Thomas. "Well, I'm going back to the Territory, and I think Thomas is headed for Louisiana. Ain't that right Thomas?"

Thomas rippled his brow then chuckled. "Well, I guess you are right. I certainly can't go back to Mississippi. This might be the perfect time to visit the Low Country before heading to California."

A smile crossed John's face. "Unfinished business, I presume."

"Yep, unfinished business."

Early the next morning before the sun had peeked over the horizon, John and the Lewis children rode east while Homer and Thomas took their time breaking camp. Two weeks later John rode into El Dorado, Arkansas, and located a wire service. He quickly sent a telegram to inform his parents of their return in less than three weeks and that his five cousins were safe and with him.

After three weeks of riding, Homer and Thomas rode into Clarksville. Thomas had completely healed and they could go separate ways. Homer would return north to Oklahoma, and Thomas would head south to New Orleans. They decided to share a meal together before departing and returned to the establishment where they had earlier encountered Cullen Baker. They dismounted and shook the dust from their clothing and pushed open the door. It was still dark and dusty, and behind the long bar, the bartender labored cleaning glasses. "Kinda early for drinking, ain't it?"

"Don't need spirits. How 'bout some hot food?" Homer asked, wiping the dust and perspiration from his face with his handkerchief.

Curtis frowned at the two. "Don't I know you men? Weren't you in here a while back?"

Thomas nodded. "We came by to resupply and grab a bite to eat. It was kind of interesting meeting that Baker man."

Curtis raised his eyebrows and dropped his towel on the bar. "Let me tell you what happened after you left here. A few days later Baker and a couple of his buddies were here when four men rode up. Well, they made some remarks about how nasty this place was and how they were tracking some men. Well, one thing led to another, and before I knew it, Baker and his friends had killed them all."

"Was one of 'em dressed up and two others appeared to be army scouts?" Homer asked.

"Yeah, how'd you know that?"

"Was there another man with them as well?"

"Yeah. You know something I don't?" frowned Curtis.

Homer shook his head. "Don't know a thing."

Curtis squinted his eyes at the two, then relaxed. "That ain't all the story. Several days after the shooting, Baker was found dead. Word was, he was poisoned."

"What about the bodies?" Thomas asked.

"Well, what I'm gonna tell you, I would never talk about if Baker was alive, but after the shooting, he had the bodies carried out into the swamp and dumped into quicksand. Nobody will ever find them, and the military sure did try. I ain't ever seen so many soldiers roaming around here. I heard tell the military blamed the killing of them men on the one they was tracking, not Baker."

"Why didn't you set 'em straight?" Thomas interrupted.

"Set 'em straight! Not while Baker was alive. I value my life more than that."

"Why not tell now?" Homer asked.

"Well, after a few days, the military was gone, and to tell you the truth, Baker still has some friends around here," explained Curtis. "As for something to eat, I'll get my cook going, and we'll see what we can round up."

After a late breakfast of fried ham, eggs, biscuit with gravy complimented with steaming hot coffee, Homer and Thomas thanked Curtis and wandered outside. Before mounting, Homer extended his hand to Thomas, then grabbed him in a tight hug. "Been great riding with you, Cousin. I haven't met many with the grit and stubbornness you got. If you ever want to come to the Territory, you've got a home waiting."

Thomas clasped Homer's hand firmly. "Same to you. If I ever got in deep trouble, you'd be the man I'd seek."

Homer laughed. "You mean you ain't in deep trouble now! Just watch your back and stay clear of the soldiers. May the Lord direct your path."

Thomas mounted and then looked at his cousin, "Looks like John's preaching must have sunk in."

"Well, he sure does keep hammering, doesn't he? Glad you're on speaking terms with the Lord again." They both took a long look at each other and broke into grins, then they tightened the reins and signaled the horses to move.

"Love you, Cousin." Thomas called back as he galloped away.

Thomas had ridden hard for two weeks and was almost out of funds. He would be in New Orleans in a matter of days and decided to seek temporary employment until he had enough for his journey to the west coast. He let his beard and hair grow to help conceal his identity from the military and to cover the scars left from the Apache attacks. Because he had lost thirty pounds, he needed to take time in New Orleans to fully recover his strength and add back those needed pounds. A help wanted sign was at the loading docks, and Thomas quickly secured the position. To save money and be able to take care of his horse, he found a part time job after hours working in a livery stable. With this income he not only could care for his stallion, but was also able to board him in the barn for free.

On a hot August afternoon when Thomas had unloaded cargo from a ship, he stood on the dock drinking a cup of cold water. He poured the next cup over his head trying to cool off from the intense heat and humidity before continuing his labor. As a ship docked, he took out his handkerchief and wiped the excess water from his face preparing to begin the task of unloading the arriving cargo.

The gangplank was lowered, and people made their way down to the dock below. Laughter and merriment filled the air as loved ones met the passengers in embraces and handshakes. As he prepared to begin the unloading, a woman on the dock caught his attention. Her long ebony hair rippled with the breeze, and her laugh sounded familiar. There was no doubt about her voice, and as Thomas admired the woman who held his heart, he noticed a tall, well-dressed handsome young man beside her.

"I can't believe we're finally home," laughed Suzanne, trying to push her hair from her eyes. "The cathedral always welcomes us to the city. It's so beautiful."

"That sounds like you didn't enjoy your travels," the man teased.

"Oh no. It was the most wonderful experience of my life. I loved every moment of it. It's just that New Orleans to me is as fascinating as Rome or Athens. Oh, yes, I did love seeing Italy and all of its glory, but it's good to be home."

The man took her arm and pushing the loose strands of hair from her face leaned down and kissed her. "How about me? Is there any love there as well?"

Suzanne ran her hand across his face. "How could there not be?"

She and Carden made their way to the awaiting carriage, and Suzanne paused to view the ship once more. When she glanced across the men working on the dock, she noticed one that seemed to be staring straight at her. There was something about the man that seemed familiar. As she stared at the man who was stripped to his waist, tanned by the sun and his long hair tied behind his head, a feeling of nostalgia gripped her

"Ready?" Carden whispered.

Suzanne turned back to the carriage and found her seat. She again looked for the man, but he had vanished, and disappointment seemed to overwhelm her. She shook her head as if to banish the thoughts and began to thank Carden for the amazing adventure.

Little Rock, Mississippi

John could not believe his journey was finally over and he would see his wife very soon. He wondered if Becca was fine and if their baby had been born. As usual, the two old hounds napping under the porch ran out to greet them with their normal yelps, wagging of tails and whimpering. Sarah and Lott rushed to the front porch because they had been listening every day for the sound of their returning family.

"Lands-a-mercy!" Sarah exclaimed. "You don't know how long we've been waiting for you. We are so excited to welcome and get to know each of you."

John and the children dismounted, and the children, all eyes, stood not knowing exactly what to say. Finally Tommy walked to Lott and Sarah and shook Lott's hand. "I'm Thomas, but you can call me Tommy." Then he pointed to the girls. "My older sister is Sarah Elizabeth, but we call her Sally. My younger sister is Mary Virginia or just Mary. Now for my brothers, the older one back there is Richmond; he's six, and Jonathan Alonzo is two, but we just call him Lonnie." As Tommy introduced each child, Sarah took them in her arms and gave them each a huge hug.

"You don't know how glad we are that you are safe and at home with us." The children began to smile and relax knowing that they were accepted.

Sarah looked closely at John then exclaimed, "Son, you have certainly lost some weight on the road, and you look like you need a good hot bath and a razor."

John leaned down and gave his mother a kiss on the cheek. "That sounds like paradise to me. Wait till you hear all we have been through these past months."

Sarah took Lonnie in her arms. "All right children, get on inside, and we'll see if we can round up something to eat. I know you're hungry."

"Can Mary and I help you in the kitchen?" Sally asked shyly.

"Sure, I need all the help I can get; that would really please me," smiled Sarah placing her arm around Sally as she put Lonnie near the steps.

"Mister Wilson, me and Richmond can take care of the horses, if that's all right with you," Tommy said.

"Let me go with you to the barn and show you where the horses will be stabled, and then you can feed, water, and brush them then head to the house for dinner."

"What about the baby?" Lott asked looking down at the little tot crawling up the steps.

Sarah chuckled. "Looks like you just volunteered for a job, my love. Let him go with you to the barn while you are showing Tommy and Richmond what to do." Lott grabbed Lonnie and threw him up into the air bringing a giggle from the little boy. Sarah placed her arms around each of the girls and headed to the house with them.

John called out anxiously to his mother. "Talking about a baby, where can I find Becca. It doesn't look like she's here."

A wide smile formed on his mother's face. "With the children moving in, she moved back with her parents. All your things are down at the Walkers."

A worried look formed on his face. "She's all right, isn't she?"

Sarah was beaming as she answered, "You best go on down there and see for yourself. You know the Lord works in strange and wondrous ways."

With dust flying, John galloped down the road to Little Rock and the Walkers. He leapt from his horse leaving it untethered and ran up the front steps and into the house. "Becca!" he shouted. "I'm home. Where are you?" Not hearing anyone, he called out again, "Where are you, Becca?"

A soft voice from the back of the house answered, "I'm back here in my bedroom."

John rushed down the hallway and into her room to see his beautiful wife resting on soft pillows under a light spread. Tears formed in her eyes, and she held out her hands for her husband. After a long embrace and kiss, she said, "I've been worried about you, but my many prayers have been answered. I have missed you so much."

Pulling a chair next to her bed, John sat studying every feature of her lovely face and then realizing how thin she was, replied, "The baby, did you lose the baby?"

Rebecca just smiled and touched his hand. "Darling, we have a beautiful baby. Go see."

Rebecca pointed to the cradle on the other side of her bed. "The little darling is right over there."

Barely able to breath, John walked gently to the cradle and looked down. A little dark haired baby lay sleeping with its fingers in its mouth. "Becca, she's so beautiful. Just like you," he softly said.

He reached to pick it up but looked at his nasty hands and quickly pulled them away. "I'll be right back," he said. "I've got to wash my hands."

In a few moments, John returned and tenderly lifting the little fellow, carried it to Becca.
Cuddling it, he smiled at his wife. "Darling, she is the most beautiful child I have ever seen."

Rebecca giggled. "I'm sorry to tell you husband, but handsome would be more fitting."

"Handsome!" John exclaimed. "You mean I have a boy!"

"Yes Husband, we have us a darling, handsome little man and dear. We waited as long as we could, but it seems that your son decided he wanted to be here to greet you when you got home."

"Becca, both of you are healthy and fine, aren't you?"

Rebecca laughed again. "Yes, John, we are perfect, especially now since you are home."

All of a sudden excitement filled John's heart and overflowed; he ran to the porch and hollered to the top of his lungs, "We have a son! World, we have a son. Thank you Lord!"

John soon returned to Rebecca and leaned down to hold her.

"You know, dear husband, some soap and water might be of good use for you. I almost didn't recognize you behind all the dirt and hair."

"I know and I'll clean up soon, but for now, just let me look at the two most important people in my life."

After dinner, Sarah gave the girls John's old room, and the boys stayed next door in the room that had belonged to Thomas and James Earl. The children settled into their rooms and tucked their few belongings away then returned to Lott's room to say goodnight. Tommy and Richmond expressed their excitement about farming and raising horses, and the girls beamed at Sarah as they realized she would be a blessing in their lives. After the family shared a Bible story and prayer, the children returned to their rooms with Lott and Sarah following to tuck them in.

That night as Sarah and Lott snuggled under the covers, Sarah whispered to her husband, "Old man, our lives are going to change, aren't they?"

Lott pulled her even closer to him. "Darling, life is just getting better and better. I've missed having children laughing, teasing and fussing around here. The Lord has truly blessed us with abundant joy."

20

Stranger in the Low Country

Consider it pure joy, my brothers, whenever you face trials of many kinds, because you know that the testing of your faith develops perseverance. Perseverance must finish its work so that you may be mature and complete not lacking anything. If any of you lacks wisdom, he should ask God, who gives generously to all.
—James 1: 2-5a NIV

Suzanne returned to her grandfather's plantation excited with the news of her travel and eager to hear of all that happened while she was away. The voyage across the Atlantic and Mediterranean was the most exciting venture she had ever experienced, and the visits to the ruins in Rome and Athens were incredible. Elaborate dinners, parties and dances lingered in her mind, and she could still feel the sway of the ship above the rolling waves and the taste of the salty breeze as it tossed her hair and freshened the air. The loving care shown by Carden was her best memory, and she knew Carden could give her a rich life of love and adventure. Still with all the grandeur she had seen, New Orleans and the Low Country held her heart.

Carden spent as much time as possible with Suzanne. He had met his match in every way. She was beautiful and bright, and the sparkle of her eyes prompted his plans for their future.

September rolled into November and with it came the harvesting of sugarcane, the busiest time of the year. With the threat of frost and a massive crop, extra laborers were employed and working hours were from daylight to dark in cutting, stripping, stacking and shipping the cane to New Orleans for processing

As Suzanne stood on the balcony outside of her second floor bedroom, she stretched her arms above her head and lavished the cool fall breeze that brushed across her body. Out in the distance she could see numerous workers as they cut and threw the cane into wagons. Occasionally singing voices floated through the wisps of wind to interrupt her thoughts. The sun tipped the horizon and flashed its rays across the countryside sparkling the morning dew. *What a beautiful morning* she thought. *God is in His heaven and there is peace on earth or at least in my life.* With energy increasing, she tossed back her head and went inside to dress, get breakfast and saddle her horse for a ride across the plantation.

When he rode across the one quarter mile bridge, he couldn't help think this two thousand acre island deep in the Low Country was nothing but long, dark green branches of sugar cane waving in the morning breeze. Its vastness swallowed the thoughts of the few acreage that was farmed at home. As he rode along, the ground began to slope upward, and far in the distance, a cluster of live oaks stood. The morning light sparkled through its foliage, and somewhere ahead a speckling of white revealed what he sought. This must be The Oaks at last.

George heard the rider approach and opened the front door. He looked to see if the visitor was Mister Baudin coming for Suzanne, but instead saw a newcomer and became apprehensive.

"Sir, is this the Bourdeau place?" the man called.

Taking a step back, George muttered, "Yes Suh, it is."

"Is Suzanne Olliver here?" he continued.

Twitching nervously about, he finally answered, "She is. What's yore name?"

"Just tell her an old friend is here to see her."

Not comfortable with the answer given, he tightened his lips, walked inside, and mumbled under his breath. "I'll tell her, but she probably won't be seeing the likes of you."

The stranger was in awe of the massive home. At glance, it appeared to have a basement plus three additional stories and a roof supported with huge Corinthian columns that wrapped around the entire house. The grounds were immaculately kept, and behind the house, he saw several large barns, and across the way, lush green fields were feeding some of the finest horses he had ever seen.

George walked to the stairway. "Miss Suzanne, there's a man outside who wants to see you, but I don't think you oughta."

"Why's that?' she called down while dressing.

"He's a rough looking fellow. Big man with long hair and beard. Kinda dirty looking. I can't figure he has no business with you. If you want, I'll fetch Sam, and we'll get out shotguns and run him off. That is if you want us to."

"Well, he must want something," Suzanne answered walking out into the hallway.

"Miss Suzanne, one thing that don't make no sense is this man is riding one of the finest thoroughbreds I've ever seen."

All was silent upstairs. "Is it solid black?" Suzanne finally asked.

"Yes'm, it shore is."

Suzanne grabbed her light jacket and quickly put on her riding shoes and swirled out the door, ran down the steps almost knocking George over. She opened the door and just stood in the entrance inspecting the man saddled in front of her.

He just smiled at her silently then finally broke the moment. "Morning," he said.

"Is that all you can say to a Southern Belle?"

"Who said you was a belle? I thought you might be the cleaning woman."

"Cleaning woman. Looking at you, I'd say you are the one needing cleaning," she laughed. "If you're any kind of a gentleman, you'd get off that horse and give me a hug, you old mountain man."

Leaping down, Thomas walked to Suzanne and picked her up off her feet and after swinging her around several times, gave her a long embrace. "You happy now?" he asked releasing her.

Looking up she answered. "I am happy, but seeing you has made me even more happy. Where have you been all these months?"

"I'm still dodging the military, and I'm on my way to California. Thought I'd drop by to check on you."

Suzanne frowned and looked into his dark eyes. "How long will you stay?"

Thomas ran his hand across his beard. "I'm leaving now. Like I said, I wanted to be sure you're all right."

Suzanne shook her head and without thinking said, "You can't leave now."

"Why not?"

Suzanne twirled her loose hair. "You just got here and need to visit a spell - maybe even a bath, and we'll get Macy to wash up your clothes, and you can see Mama and Papére and ride over the plantation and -.

"No more ands. I'll stay till morning. Then I'm riding west."

Suzanne gently reached up to push his unruly hair back and cringed at the scar across his hairline. Looking closer, she saw a scar across his left cheek, and to the corner of his right eye there was a star shaped scar that seemed to melt into his eyelid. "What happened to you?" she murmured.

Thomas looked again into her eyes. "Hard times. Least I'm still alive."

George stood shaking his head in wonder. *Where in the world did Miss Suzanne meet a man like this one?* he thought. *And to invite him inside the house was unthinkable. He might be staying,* he reasoned, *but ole George is gonna have his pistol in his pocket at all times.*

Suzanne grabbed Thomas by the arm and pulled him inside the door, "Macy, get some hot water in the washtub and see if Uncle Andre's clothes are still upstairs."

"George, if you will, take care of Mister Wilson's horse."

"Suzanne, you don't have to do all this," Thomas countered.

"Yes I do. You're special."

After Thomas had been soaking in soapy water for quite a while, Suzanne called out. "Thomas, I'm having your clothes washed, and George is cleaning your boots. You want me to cut your hair and maybe give you a shave?"

All was quiet inside. "You can cut a little off my hair and maybe trim my beard, but...but you might want to wait a while before you come in."

Suzanne could hear him chuckling and quipped, "I hadn't plan to come in until you were proper."

"I know that, but you always seem to set yourself up for a little teasing."

"We'll have some things for you in a minute. When you are dressed, call for me."

Thomas sat silently as Suzanne cut his hair. He had removed his shirt. Suzanne blushed when the locks fell upon his upper body drawing her eyes to the scar on his shoulder. "Thomas, what cut your shoulder?" she asked running her finger down the scar.

"Apache Arrow."

"What about the scar on your lower throat?"

"Apache knife."

"All right, what about this round scar on the outside of your chest? Was it an Apache too?" Thomas chuckled. "No. That there is where one of Mister Lincoln's minie' balls visited with me up at Sharpsburg, Maryland."

Suzanne's uncle's clothes were a little tight, but would do while his were drying. The slippers issued seemed feminine to him, but until his boots were cleaned, he guessed he could tolerate the outfit. He was just glad that Homer and John couldn't see him dressed like this. As he stepped out, Suzanne's eyes widened and immediately she placed her hand over her mouth.

"I look ridiculous, don't I?" Thomas stammered placing his hands on his hips in defiance.

"No. You look perfectly handsome," Suzanne gasped. "What a transformation."

"Scars and all," countered Thomas.

"Scars and all. George will definitely not recognize you," she laughed.

Later that day Mrs. Olliver returned home from a visit, and at dusk, Mister Bourdeau came in from the fields. They were reintroduced to Thomas, and they welcomed him to The Oaks. As they enjoyed supper that evening, conversation flourished and Thomas, feeling at ease, related their recent search for the Lewis children and the difficulties they faced with the Apache. Tired from a long day, Thomas asked to be excused and retired to a guest room upstairs.

The following day, Carden came to call on Suzanne, and feeling uncomfortable, Thomas asked Mister Bourdeau if he could accompany him to the fields. Compared to Carden who was well educated, articulate, ambitious and handsome, Thomas felt inferior and knew that Suzanne had found a perfect match in Mister Baudin.

Thomas had breakfast with Mister Bourdeau, and before the sun tipped the horizon, the two were riding to the fields. Mister Bourdeau first took Thomas on a tour of the worker's living quarters, and then they rode to the men who were cutting the cane. The two dismounted and wandered to the shade of a live oak and began to talk. An immediate bond formed, and Thomas was surprised at the comfort he felt with this old gentleman who seemed to speak to his heart. He was amazed when Mister Bourdeau told of his humble beginnings.

"Yes, I was about as poor as they come. Not only was I a poor man working at the docks of New Orleans, but I spent many an hour fighting, drinking and causing devilment. If it hadn't been for meeting a sweet Christian woman, I might still be that poor old soul. My life changed and with several hundred acres that my wife inherited from her father, we began our journey and what you see here is our dream."

"You've worked hard, Mister Bourdeau."

"No, Son. We worked hard. My beautiful wife carried a heavy load as well."

Thomas could feel his legs getting restless. "You mind if I go down and give the men a hand. I think this old body needs some exercise."

Mister Bourdeau smiled and gave Thomas a pat on the back. "You go on down. I ain't been feeling too chipper for the past few days. I think I'll just sit up here a spell."

Having watched the process, Thomas realized that with a slight change, the loading of the cane could be maximized. Leaving his coat draped across his saddle, he rolled up his sleeves and walked toward the men as they haphazardly threw stalks of cane up on a long wagon. Seeing Thomas with Mister Bourdeau, the workers felt he must be their new foreman. Thomas stepped up on the wagon bed and called out, "Listen up, men. Let's make a steady line and send the cane up the line to me. If we stack each stalk neatly, our productivity will increase. You understand?"

The men nodded their heads, formed a line and passed the cane forward in handfuls; the last man handed them to Thomas who stacked each stalk as neatly as possible. Three wagons were filled better and faster than the slipshod way the men had been loading.

"All right, which one of you can take over my job?"

A brawny Negro man stepped up. "I can do that, sir."

"Good," stated Thomas jumping down. "I'll take your place now and throw up to you."

Surprised that their new foreman was actually working with them and not just sitting on a horse giving orders, the men worked even harder.

In the meantime, Mister Bourdeau was totally amazed at the improvement on the field. Thomas had simply walked down, taken charge and rolled up his sleeve to labor as a hired hand. Right before dusk, Thomas, whistling as he walked, stepped on the back porch to clean up. Mister Bourdeau met him at the door to inform him that they had saved him some supper.

While Thomas enjoyed his meal, Mister Bourdeau sipped on a cup of coffee across from him. "You seemed like you enjoyed the day. You didn't even take a dinner break."

Thomas stopped his chewing and took a sip of water. "I had a grand time down there. I love to work. A lot of happiness comes with farming."

"The men seemed to listen to you. I've never thought of how I could save time and wagons in the way you introduced."

Later that night, Thomas and Mister Bourdeau sat on the back porch to relax and discuss the day's activities while Suzanne was entertaining Carden. Mister Bourdeau reached into his pocket to retrieve his pipe which he packed for an evening smoke. Blowing a ring of smoke into the air, he looked at Thomas. "You know, I can't seem to keep a foreman around here. They either up and quit, drink too much and I have to fire them, or they just can't work the men. I watched you today and the way you relate to my workers, and I just wonder if you would consider taking the foreman job for me. I'm just too old to be doing what I try to do. I'd pay you well." Another smoke circle floated upward.

All was silent for a moment, except the croaking of frogs across the bayou and the singing of cicadas. "Mister Bourdeau, I'd take pleasure in working for you, but it would be just a matter of time before someone would recognize me, and I'd be either caught, or I'd have to run. That could prove embarrassing to you folks - harboring a criminal."

"Number one, you're not a criminal, and two, in this short time, you have become like a son to me. I wish you'd think it over."

Thomas nodded his head. "I'll give it some thought, sir."

Thomas spent most of the night awake and contemplating his decision. Watching Suzanne court another man would be a torment he couldn't endure. While he was working today, he could envision her with Carden, embracing him and confiding in him, and it tore at his heart. He really enjoyed Mister Bourdeau and sincerely wanted the job he had been offered, but staying could mean capture and heartache. Thomas begin to pray about the situation and soon felt at peace with his decision.

At breakfast, Thomas told the family that he had decided to stay and help until the harvesting was completed. Each day he grew closer to the workers and continued to maximize productions, and each day he had time with Suzanne when she rode at noon to deliver dinner. Sometimes it might be as simple as ham and biscuits and other times, a full meal, but the moments they spent together under the old live oak were tender and captivating. Their conversations were meaningful and full, even though their interests and backgrounds were unique and different. On the days Suzanne did not come, Thomas knew that Carden was visiting and he tried to close his mind to thoughts about their relationship. He tried to be happy for Suzanne, but it was difficult to think of her caring for someone else even though he knew there was no place for Suzanne in a life on the run from the law.

On Sunday morning Carden came to accompany Suzanne and her family to church services. During this time, Mister Bourdeau ceased his harvesting and encouraged his workers to attend church and rest on the Sabbath with their families. Thomas chose to stay at the mansion and relax. If Carden had not come, he would have loved to have escorted Suzanne to church and give his thanks in worship of the Lord.

When the family returned from church, Frankie rode in from New Orleans for an afternoon visit. Following dinner, Judith asked him to sit with her and update her on city news and his job.

"Mother, keeping up with The Oaks investments is going quite well, but the challenges of the political arena is interesting, frustrating and to some extent, hopeless, but I really love serving in a political position."

Judith then turned to all mothers' main concern. "Tell me about your love life, Son? I guess you have every young lady in New Orleans and Baton Rouge at bay," she winked to him.

Frankie shook his head and pushed his blond hair back in frustration. "No mother. I've got only one on my mind, and she apparently doesn't want anything to do with me."

"Son, that can't be."

"It certainly is. I've written her three times, and she has yet to answer me. The time I spent with her was the most fulfilling time of my life. She is simply perfect for me," he sighed.

"You're talking about Lucretia, aren't you?"

"Yes ma'am, I am, and I think I truly love her, but what do I do?"

Judith placed her arm around her son's shoulder. "Son, if it's meant to be, it will. If you are sure you love her, keep pursuing her. Don't quit."

After lunch, Carden excused himself to attend business in New Orleans. Suzanne decided to search for Thomas. She found no sign of him in the house, so she asked George his whereabouts.

"Yes ma'am. Last time I saw him, he was down at the barn brushing his stallion."

Suzanne hurried to the barn and found him with his sleeves rolled up and shirt partially unbuttoned. She was surprised at how she was both enamored of and intrigued by him both physically and emotionally. She blushed at that realization and then decided to act on it.

Sneaking in to surprise him, she crept up to the stall where he was working and grabbing him by the shirt, said, "Gotcha!"

Thomas shook his head. "You didn't scare me. I heard you tipping up and could smell your perfume even before that. You forget, listening and reading signs has kept me alive," he stated as he continued brushing his horse down.

Leaning her arms over the top railing of the stall, Suzanne tugged at his shirt again. "You should have come to church with us today. He preached on forgiveness."

Frustrated by her interference, he turned to her. "Will you please quit pestering me? I've work to do."

"I need your attention, and that horse doesn't."

"Carden can give you all the attention you need, and this horse has saved my life many a time."

"You sound jealous to me, Mister Thomas Wilson."

Thomas laid his brush down and smiled at Suzanne. "I would have loved to have attended church today, and I truly appreciate the love, mercy, grace and forgiveness the Lord has showered on me. But, not today."

"Why not go today?"

Thomas leaned over and gave her a wink. "My dear that is entirely my business."

As Thomas was leaning near her, she imagined how it would feel to have Thomas in love with her. *Perhaps it is just wishful thinking; with Carden I already have that assurance.*

"A penny for your thoughts," Thomas's eyes twinkled as if he had read her mind.

"And that, Thomas, is entirely my business." They both began laughing and continued the banter.

Later that evening Suzanne noticed her grandfather's lamplight lit in his study, so she made him a fresh cup of coffee and knocking on the door, entered. Her grandfather laid down his spectacles and looked at his granddaughter. "What did I do to deserve this pleasure?" he queried.

"Just being you, Papére" Suzanne answered handing him the cup of coffee.

Knowing his granddaughter had something on her mind, he sat patiently and waited for her to begin. When she had not begun, he asked, "Dear, I've known you for a long time, and it's moments like this, I am sure you have something special on your mind. You might as well go on and let me know the predicament you're in"

"Is it that obvious?" Suzanne answered pulling up her chair closer to her grandfather.

"What's on your mind, dear?"

Suzanne took a deep breath and exhaling softly said, "If you were in trouble and you wanted someone you could trust, who would you choose?"

With a frown her grandfather looked carefully at his granddaughter. "Are you in trouble?

"No, not me! I'm talking about if it were you."

"Oh," he exclaimed. "Thomas would be my man. Why?"

"Why not Frankie or Carden?"

The old gent scratched his beard and thought for a moment. "Well, Frankie, although I think he's doing well, is still young and searching for his identity and is inexperienced in dealing with perplexities. I am not sure he is mature enough to make the right decision yet. Now as for Carden - he's intelligent, ambitious, and I really think he has a bright future, but he hasn't experienced conflict. How would he react when faced with possible death? I just don't know."

"And Thomas?" Suzanne asked.

"Sweetie, the man has seen more death and turmoil than most men see in a lifetime, and he's still standing and fighting. Not only that, he's totally honest and trustworthy. If my life depended on it, he would be the man that would stand with me. No, he would be the man who would stand in front of me."

"You sound as if you like the man," Suzanne added with an understanding smile on her face.

The old man squeezed his granddaughter's hand. "It's more than that, I adore the young man. He is becoming like a son to me. In one sense, God has blessed me by bringing him into my life at just the right time."

"Papére. That is my problem. I thought that the possibility of a relationship with Thomas was of the past, and that my future was with Carden, but why did God bring Thomas into my life again?"

"Sweetie, that is a question that only you and God can answer."

With the harvesting almost complete, Mister Bourdeau made plans for his fall festival to honor the workers. On Friday he would host a barbecue for the workers and their families, and Thomas would let all the men and women off at mid-afternoon to prepare for the evening activities. Mister Bourdeau had hired a string band from the parish west of them to furnish the music. Because of the bumper crop, he would reward his workers a bonus pay for their efforts and dedication. On the following night would be a ball for his friends, business associates and local politicians. Since this was an annual event, the Low Country eagerly awaited the festive celebration.

As Saturday evening arrived, horsemen and carriages of people swept in from all corners of the parish and state. George and two other workers met the guests and took care of their horses and carriages while Mister Bourdeau, Judith, Suzanne and Frankie gave a cordial welcome at the entrance of their home. Carden soon rode in dressed in a black tuxedo, white shirt and black bowtie and as usual, well groomed. Suzanne walked out to greet him, and after he offered his hand, she led him into the house.

The people first enjoyed a barbecue feast on the back lawn, then at nine o'clock, twelve members of the New Orleans prestigious string orchestra would be furnishing the music for the evening in the third floor ballroom.

That afternoon Thomas found a package in his room and upon opening it, found a new black tuxedo, white shirt and black tie with a note attached. "Thank you for all your service and dedication. You have earned this plus more. With a grateful heart, Mister Bourdeau." When he picked up the coat, he found four hundred dollars in gold coins, but he knew the sum was too large and must be returned.

When the beautiful music began to flow with the evening breezes, couples turned and floated to the soothing melodies, but Thomas was not in attendance. Several times Suzanne glanced over the crowd trying to locate him, but couldn't catch a glimpse. Carden was a grand dancer and kept her engaged the whole night, but she finally sent him to get her a cup of punch and then made her way to her grandfather. "Papére, have you seen Thomas?"

Her grandfather shook his head. "No darling, but he's probably around here somewhere."

At around ten thirty, the door to the ball room opened, and Thomas walked in. Dressed in his new tuxedo, hair neatly combed and his face clean shaven, he was definitely the most handsome man in attendance. He quickly made his way to Mister Bourdeau.

"I want to thank you for the outfit, but I can't accept the other. It's too much."

Mister Bourdeau reached his hand out to Thomas. "Son, you've earned every bit of it. You made the harvesting easier and faster, as well as worked with my men smoothly and efficiently. You did well, and you deserve it more than you can know."

Thomas thanked him, but before he could turn around, several young women had walked over to greet him hoping for a dance, but he declined the invitations and thanked them as well. Suzanne was amazed to see Thomas amidst several young women and could not believe how handsome he looked. As the young women left, Suzanne excused herself and headed his way. "Why are you so late?"

"What difference does it make? I'm not much of a dancer, so I probably shouldn't have come at all."

Suzanne raised her eyebrows. "You came in respect for Papére. He really thinks highly of you."

"And what about you?"

Before Suzanne could answer a dark complexioned woman with long flowing hair brushed up to Thomas. "I don't believe we have met," she softly said. "Perhaps you will accompany me out to the balcony for a breath of fresh air?"

Thomas looked at Suzanne and then back to the woman, "Yes ma'am, it will be my pleasure to escort you."

As he walked away, he turned to Suzanne. "It's too bad you don't share your grandfather's feelings."

As Suzanne watched, she grew angry that he had not realized how much she did care. *I guess I deserve this. How can he know the extent of my feelings when I'm not sure.*

Her grandfather chuckled as he watched his granddaughter's impasse. "Darling, he's his own man. You best make up your mind how you feel, because he plans to leave soon."

At around eleven o'clock, Carden made his farewells to Suzanne and Mister Bourdeau so he could rest before boarding the ship to South America in the morning. Suzanne had lost her escort and began to look for Thomas who was now spending time conversing with her mother.

"Are you having a good time?" she shyly asked.

Thomas winked at her. "It's been quiet an interesting evening, but I don't really care for the attention I'm getting."

Suzanne could feel jealousy beginning to show its ugly head, so instead of getting angry, she decided to seize the moment and have some fun. The orchestra had struck up a melodious waltz, and Suzanne held out her hand and challenged Thomas. "I have the perfect way for you to lose some of that attention you think you have been getting. Do you think you can manage one dance tonight?"

"I certainly can manage it, but haven't you danced enough for one night?"

"Well, there is one particular man that seems to have forgotten to notice me, and I think he owes me at least one dance."

Thomas took her in his arms and on to the dance floor. He began to waltz with her as no other man had. His rhythm seemed to be impeccable, and their bodies seemed to move as one. "I thought you said you couldn't dance?"

"Well, I was forced to go to all those dances back in school, and I guess a little of it stuck."

"Even though I may regret this complement, you are not only the best looking man here, but you are an amazing dancer."

"Did you ever think that maybe it is because I am dancing with you?" Thomas pulled Suzanne a little closer and continued to move her to the music.

When the music stopped, Suzanne knew her decision was made. "Thomas, do you think we could go for a walk. I want to talk to you."

Thomas escorted her to the balcony which surrounded the dance floor. The full moon illuminated the grounds below, and silence seemed to be the only music in the night. Suzanne shivered, so Thomas took off his coat and wrapped it around her shoulders then pulled her gently to him. "Beautiful country out here, isn't it?" Thomas whispered in her ear.

Suzanne shook her head. "Thomas, in a way, you are a stranger to me."

"Why's that?" he frowned.

"Well, you've changed a lot. You're more at ease and at peace with yourself."

Thomas pulled her closer. "Suzanne, I had an experience with the Apache that changed my life."

"Yes, they almost killed you," she countered.

"That's right, they did, but in that moment of death, I prayed to the Lord for forgiveness for my sins and for the lives I've taken, and he answered my pray. I was prepared to meet my Maker, but he saw fit to forgive me and allow the Apache to release me."

Suzanne turned and looked into his eyes. "Thomas do you remember the time last year when we were out riding and you told me that you cared more for me than just friendship?"

Thomas, surprised, cleared his throat but said nothing.

"Did you mean it? Do you love me?" she probed.

Thomas looked ardently at her. "Have you done something to alter this love?"

"No, I certainly haven't."

"Suzanne, when you love someone deeply, you don't give it up."

"Are you saying you love me? If so, why can't you just say the words?"

Thomas loosened his hold on her and looked out across the night. "Because it is too painful. You know I'm a wanted man, and it is just a matter of time until someone will recognize me, and I will probably hang. If I'm not caught, my life will always be on the run. What kind of future can I offer you?"

Tears formed in Suzanne's eyes. "I love you Thomas Wilson more than you will ever know."

Fighting back his own tears, he whispered in her ear. "If you have any sense at all, you'll forget you ever knew me and marry Carden. He's a fine young man with a bright future."

"Don't you know that you have made that impossible?" she stammered.

"Suzanne, I'm leaving in the morning, and I'm not looking back."

Suzanne looked up once more into his watering eyes. "I want you to do one more thing for me. I want you to kiss me just once."

Pulling her to him, their lips touch first tenderly, then passionately.

As the dawn brightened her room, Suzanne rose from a sleepless night, dressed quickly and hurried to the kitchen hoping to see Thomas once more. No one was there except Macy who was cleaning up morning dishes. Suzanne looked out the window searching the grounds.

Macy laid a plate she had been washing aside and said, "He's done ate, Miss Suzanne. He and yore Papére is out at the barn. Your Papére ain't too happy 'bout him leaving."

Suzanne looked toward the barn as Thomas led Champ with a bedroll tucked behind the saddle and saddlebags bulging. Since there was no question Thomas was indeed leaving, she pushed her hair back and hurried to the front porch.

As Thomas mounted up, he reached down and clasped Mister Bourdeau's hand. "I appreciate you giving me work, sir, and it has been a pleasure getting to know you."

While still clasping his hand and with tears glistening, he spoke. "The pleasure is all mine. I just wish you'd stay on. We still have about three more days of work."

"The man, Levi, who worked under me, can do the job for you," Thomas explained.

"But he's a Negro," Mister Bourdeau rebutted.

"Mister Bourdeau, practically all of your workers are Negroes. Times will be changing. He'll do just fine."

Then Thomas looked at Suzanne solemnly standing on the porch. Touching the rim of his broad brim hat, he softly said, "Suzanne."

As Thomas sat on his horse taking in one last glimpse of the woman he loved, a rider met Mister Bourdeau and handed him a note. He reached into his pocket and pulled out his spectacles then read the letter. "Thomas you need to look at this," he called.

Reining the horse in, Thomas took the note, read it then dropped it to the ground. He closed his eyes and prayed, "Why Lord? This may be more than I can carry."

Suzanne picked up the telegram and lowered her head in sorrow. *Please be informed. Sarah Wilson is ill and not expected to live. Newton Station: Mississippi.*

Suzanne reached up for Thomas's hand. "What will you do?"

"I have no choice. I have to go home."

Suzanne shook her head. "Thomas you can't go home. They'll catch you for sure and they'll hang you."

"Suzanne, my mother always told us children that she'd walk a rotten log over hell for any one of us. I guess this time it's me on that log."

Desperately Suzanne pleaded, "Thomas, she wouldn't want you to come. She's your mother; she'll understand."

"Suzanne, I have to do this for myself as well as her. I love my mother, and I want to be there even if it means that I will face those charges. Maybe it's best this way, for everyone."

Suzanne knew he was referring to her future too, but she was not willing to let go of Thomas without a fight."

"Papére, there has to be something we can do."

"Thomas, I think we need to make some plans so that you just might get there safely. Getting out may be more difficult. Get on down and let's see what we figure out.

21

A Time of Reckoning

I come to you for protection, O Lord my God. Save me from my persecutors – rescue me! If you don't, they will maul me like a lion, tearing me to pieces with no one to rescue me.
—Psalm 7: 1-2 NLT

Thomas traveled by steamboat up the Mississippi to Vicksburg under the alias of Sam Cook, then went by rail east toward Meridian. At the town of Forest, approximately thirty miles west of Little Rock, Thomas would exit the train where Mister Bourdeau would have a man and horse waiting for Sam Cook. Thomas wore a new dress suit with tie, was clean shaven with his hair shorter and neatly combed and oiled, plus he wore a pair of clear glass spectacles. If he changed his persona, this disguise could work.

The train stopped with a screech, and smoke enveloped the walkway as the train approached Forest. The depot in the small town of Forest was a shanty byre with a rickety porch, and beyond the depot was not much else. As Thomas collected his belongings and disembarked, he carefully scanned the depot then stepped to the ground. A cold north wind whipped at his face and sent smoke from the train swirling low adding to the tension he felt. He saw no soldiers posted, just an older couple and a young woman with two small children, so he stepped under the porch and anchored himself on a bench. As he began to fidget contemplating his new role and his ability to carry out the change, his fears were interrupted by a voice. "You Sam Cook?"

Thomas jumped up and walked to a man who was leading a horse. "I'm Sam," he replied.

"Here's your horse." The man handed him the reins and without saying another word, walked away. The animal was certainly not like his stallion, but Mister Bourdeau felt it would be safer to ship Champ separately. The animal would be transported to Newton Station where upon arrival, a telegram would be sent to John saying that Thomas was headed west and wanted his father to have the thoroughbred.

Thomas decided to ride cross country to the village of Union and then on home to Little Rock. Since he had hunted this area as a boy, the creeks and swamps welcomed him home and sheltered him from encounters with people who might recognize him. Due to the buffeting of the cold wind, Thomas shivered then lifted his collar, wrapped a rag around his neck and pulled on gloves. The weather was bitter cold but also a blessing because few people would venture outside. After several hours of riding, the darkness made finding his way more difficult. He was almost convinced he was lost, when he saw a light ahead and recognized Boler's Inn, a stagecoach stop west of Union where General Sherman had made an overnight headquarters on his return trip from the raid on Meridian in the war. The smoke churning from the chimney called to his aching body for rest, but he knew that he must continue his trek. Pulling out his pocket watch and holding it toward the faint glow, he saw it was now three in the morning. The wind had finally subsided, but even in the frigid air, his heart warmed because he knew he was just eight miles from home.

With a faint glow in the east and a glaze of white frost covering the ground, Thomas rode up the trail that led home. His elated heart at being home became disconsolate as he pondered his mother's illness. He was eager to see his family, but fearful of being recognized and caught and shuddered at the thoughts that sped through his mind.

As he approached the old log house, precious memories flashed before him. Taking a long deep breath, he exhaled and sat ruminating until the silence began to worry him. Here was peace, while his life was in devastating turmoil. As the silence grew, it occurred to Thomas that the hounds had not welcomed him, but when he listened closer, he could hear faint yelps of dogs pushing some critter down in the swamps near the creek. *Oh, to hunt again and have the carefree life he once knew.*

Tommy had keen ears at night and was concerned to hear a horse snort outside. He rose from his bed and slipped to the door quietly opening it. He noticed the horse first and wondered if a horse had managed to escape from the barn. When he saw a man dismounting, Tommy reached for the shotgun by the door and crept into the open hallway making sure he stayed hidden in the shadows. His pounding heart became so vociferous he could hear the beats in his ears. He raised the shotgun and stammered, "I've got you covered, mister. You better state your name and intent or you're a dead man."

Thomas recognizing Tommy's voice decided to tease his cousin. "Son, you are looking at one of the meanest roadman in the country. I'm here to steal your horses and burn this place down."

Tommy shook and started stuttering, "M...m-mister, I'm fixin to blow you away."

Thomas began to laugh. "Tommy put that thing down before you hurt yourself. It's me, Thomas."

Tommy in his nightgown continued to hold the gun on the stranger. "Mister, you're lying. I don't know how you know my name, but Thomas wouldn't be anywhere near here. Now you best go on and leave now."

The man continued to laugh and soon the chuckles awakened the memory of Thomas's voice, and Tommy finally relaxed his shotgun. "Cousin, you sure 'most got yourself blown away. What are doing here?"

Thomas walked close to Tommy. "You've become a man, I see."

Tommy flung his arms around Thomas. "You've come home," he exclaimed.

"How's Mama? She still alive?"

"Yes, she's alive, but I am glad you're here to see her."

Thomas began to untie his bedroll and saddle bags, but Tommy quickly offered, "Let me take your horse down to the barn? You go on inside."

"Can't let you do that, Tommy."

"Why not?"

"It's cold out here. You go get some warm clothes on, then you can take care of my horse."

Tommy turned once more to his cousin. "Why are you so dressed up? And them glasses look silly. You in some kind of show?"

Thomas nodded his head and chuckled to himself. "Just go do what I asked. We'll talk later."

Thomas walked quietly down the open hall, and as he opened the door, was met with thick warm air. His father was sound asleep and snoring in a rocking chair next to the fireplace, and his mother lay motionless with several pillows behind her head. She appeared pale and older than he last remembered. Dots of perspiration covered her face, and her breath was short and sporadic. As he walked quietly toward her, he noticed a pan of water and washrag, so he dipped the rag in water, squeezed it out lightly and began wiping her face. He folded the rag and laid it across her brow to cool the fever he saw in the flush of her face. Sarah opened her eyes and a slight smile formed. "I knew you'd come, Son. I've been praying for you."

224

Pulling a chair close to her, he took her hand and whispered, "I'm walking that rotten log, you know."

Sarah attempted to laugh but coughed with pain instead.

"It's okay, Mama. You need to rest now."

Sarah smiled then closed her eyes.

Thomas placed several more oak logs on the dying embers then went to the kitchen to start a fire in the oven for making fresh coffee. In a few moments, he returned with two cups and pulled a chair next to his father. Nudging his father's foot, he tried to rouse Lott. "Papa," Thomas softly called.

His father jerked his eyes open suddenly realizing he had fallen asleep. He looked at Thomas and tried to regain his senses.

"Wake up old man. You got company," Thomas chuckled softly.

Rubbing his eyes, Lott felt he was dreaming. "Son, what are you doing here?"

"Thought I'd come home for a spell."

A wide smile crossed Lott's face. "I can't believe you're here. We have missed you so much, Son, but you know it's still dangerous. You are going to need to leave as soon as possible."

"Dad, I plan to stay a while, but we'll be careful."

Sister began to rouse to prepare breakfast and take her turn caring for her mother. She could smell the coffee and knew her father had to be tired, so she wrapped herself in a quilt and headed to the kitchen. As she entered, she noticed a strange man at the table with her father and looked intently at the stranger then erupted into smiles and laughter. "My big brother is home!" she called. "Thomas! Don't you look distinguished?" She ran and grabbed him around the waist and squeezed him heartily. "Thank the Lord you're home!"

Thomas returned the hug and swung her around until her quilt flew into the air and settled on the floor. Hearing the commotion, the children across the hall ran into the room to investigate. They rushed together at Thomas to hug him but sent him tumbling to the floor with them all on top. Thomas was pressed into the cold floor by the children's weight upon him as the children chattered, laughed and welcomed him home. The room was in a state of pandemonium, but the joy on all faces made Thomas so glad to be home.

As the banter ceased, across the room a faint voice called, "You children have got to be quieter. How can an old woman get well with all that racket?" They looked over and were surprised to see Sarah leaning up on her pillows, her fever finally broken. They rushed to her side and began thanking the Lord for His healing power. During this whole festive time, baby Lonnie lay sleeping soundly in the crib that Lot and Toby had specially made for him.

A few moments later, Tommy walked in from the barn, and Lott raised his hand for silence. "All right family, you need to quieten down. I know we're all excited about Thomas being home, but we got to remember that Thomas is still in grave danger. If the Yankees catch him, it will be a most difficult situation." He cleared his throat and continued. "What we've got to do is keep his visit quiet. We tell no one. Not anybody. You hear me?"

They all nodded their heads, and some yes sirs were heard.

"Now, we'll need to have someone lingering outside all day watching for visitors. If anyone comes around, even the doctor, we've got to move quickly to get Thomas out of reach. Now Tommy, Richmond or I will be outside during the day. When someone comes, we will alert Thomas so he can get to Sister's room where he can quickly exit quietly if needed. Now, I hope all of you realize the importance of this. Thomas's life depends on our secrecy. Now, does everybody understand me?"

All agreed.

Rebecca and John bundled their son for a visit to check on his mother. John went directly to his mother's bedside to evaluate her condition. "Mother, I am so glad you are better. We have been so worried."

Rebecca took the baby close to Sarah's side. "He seems to be growing every day." She sat down on the bed letting Sarah enjoy the sight of her grandson.

"Now, who do we have here?" Thomas called out as he entered the room.

"Thomas, you came home. I was hoping you would, but I knew it was a risk." John quickly stood and gave his brother a hug. "How long you been here?"

"Just got in yesterday. Rebecca, come give me a hug and bring that beautiful baby. I hear it's a son."

Rebecca stood and gave Thomas a hug and then put James Earl in his arms. "Here's your nephew. James Earl, meet your Uncle Thomas. We've shortened the name to Jim."

"James Earl. Jim. Our oldest brother is probably smiling down from heaven about the name." James Earl, the oldest Wilson had died in the war and was certainly missed by his family, even though they knew he was with their heavenly father.

The next several weeks brought happiness to the Wilson family. The children loved having Thomas at home, and Sarah seemed to be recovering to Doc McMahan's surprise. Doctor McMahan shook his head in wonder that a woman Sarah's age could improve from a lung sickness that usually caused death. Lott, Tommy and Richmond stood their post faithfully.

Besides the doctor, only a few had visited because most knew Sarah needed her rest. As Thomas watched his mother recovering, the time for his departure was drawing close. As much as he wanted to stay, his life depended on leaving those he loved.

Later Thomas found his father at the barn. "Papa, I've got to be going. Mister Bourdeau will soon be sending Champ to you. When the horse gets here, I need to be gone. I want you to do what we dreamed. I want you to raise horses, and Champ is the best. One day, when I can get back, I want to see a lot of colts that run just like he does."

"Son, you need that horse. We are going to make it fine here. You don't worry about us. You take Champ with you when you go."

"You know, I love you, Papa, and I want Champ to stay here. I want you to make our dream come true."

Newton Station: December 8, 1868

The train from Jackson began to decelerate and halted to a standstill releasing puffs of steam. A steady flow of people came from the steps of the passenger cars to the walkway below while others stood patiently waiting to board. Down the line, a door slid open on a cattle car, and a ramp was positioned for the animals to safely exit. A large Negro man stepped inside and with reins in hand, led a beautiful, well groomed, thoroughbred down the incline. Having been in the care of the Bourdeau's for several months, Champ had never looked better. The crowds of people gathered watching the magnificent animal and wondering about the owner. An old man who had come down from the livery stable pushed his way through the crowd and carefully examined the animal, then nodded his head. "This here is Champ. Lott Wilson owns him, but his son, Thomas, is the one who rides him. Ain't no horse can outrun this amazing creature? Yes sir, he's one of a kind."

A soldier took notice of the horse and name that he had heard and sprinted to the federal headquarters as fast as he could. Waving the guard aside, he paused momentarily to catch his breath, then stopped at the door and knocked.

"Is it important?" a voice called from inside.

"Yes sir," the soldier gasped.

"Come back later, I'm busy."

"Sir, what I just found out is something you've been waiting a long time for."

"Well come on in, but it better be good."

"Sir, the Wilson horse has arrived and is at the station."

"That is interesting news. Well, we know a telegram was sent out about Mrs. Wilson's impending death, and now with the arrival of the horse, we might have a chance at catching that murderer. The second telegram said Wilson headed west, but I have a feeling he is visiting his dying mother. You go down there, see who claims the horse and let me know immediately. If it should be a big burly man, arrest him. If he resists, shoot him. You understand?"

"Yes sir. I understand."

After getting word that the stallion had arrived, Lot, along with Tommy and Richmond left before daylight to retrieve the horse from Newton Station. Lot let Tommy ride Champ home because he knew Tommy was like Thomas and had a way with horses. Tommy fell in love with the stallion and was thankful to sit astride such a masterful horse. He planned to take good care of Champ and make sure its colts were treated the same way.

The soldier knocked on Colonel Lowery's door. "You may enter," came a voice.

The private, with cap under his arm, saluted and reported, "Sir, an old man and two young boys just picked up that horse."

The colonel thought for a moment. "Well, something is definitely happening at the Wilsons. Could be we need to post a lookout at their farm."

He scratched his head in thought. "Private, tell Lieutenant Turner I want a twenty four hour surveillance of the Wilson place, and they need to take special care not to be seen. You understand me? I am a colonel now, so I expect total obedience. Understand?"

"Yes sir. Lieutenant Turner and a twenty four hour lookout," he exclaimed while saluting.

Two days passed and Lieutenant Turner reported in. "Sir, I think your man is there. A man to your description walked out on the porch and wandered down to the barn late one evening. Stayed down there a couple of hours then went back inside the house."

"Could have been his younger brother?" Lowery said, lighting his pipe.

"No sir, I am familiar with the younger man. He, his wife and baby have also been visiting. I may be wrong, but I'm pretty sure it was Thomas Wilson, sir."

Lowery went to the window overlooking main street and finally said, "Lieutenant, get a detachment of about twenty men and have them ready by three in the morning. I think it's time to pay the Wilsons a visit."

In the dark, frigid pre-dawn hours, federal soldiers quietly surrounded the Wilson place staying far enough away so the hounds could not pick up their scent. Shuffling and blowing breath on their cupped hands, the men tried to warm themselves. A slight trace of smoke floated from the Wilson's chimney, and across the countryside, a rooster welcomed the morning.

At the break of day, Colonel Lowery who made a special point to lead this arrest, rode into the open alerting his men to tighten the enclosure. As the men neared, the hounds under the porch burst out barking and growling. One hound growled reservedly as she guarded the porch, but Lot's prized coonhound bolted toward one of the soldiers and grabbed him by his britches legs. A shot rang out, a yelp and the dog lay dead below the feet of the soldier.

The sound of the gunshot caused Lot to bolt from his bed and run to the front window and push the curtains aside. He pulled on a set of socks, and throwing on his heavy woolen coat, Lot grabbed his shotgun and ran outside.

"What in tarnations are you men doing? What did you do to my dog?" Lott shouted as he stepped on the porch.

Colonel Lowery rode to the porch. "Put the gun down, old man. We're not here for you. I'm here to arrest the man who murdered my brother. I know he's in there."

Lot stood his ground, stone faced, laid the gun down on the boarded porch and stated, "Sir, this is private property. Under law, you have no right to search my place or be on my property."

That's where you're wrong, old man." Lowery smiled an evil smile. "I expect to see Mister Thomas Wilson walk right out of that house and into handcuffs."

Hearing the commotion, Sister, Sally and Mary, all sleepy eyed, wandered to the porch and stood mystified by the mass of soldiers surrounding the house. The children clung to Sister's nightgown, and moments later Tommy and Richmond joined them and edged next to Lot.

"Sir, my wife is desperately ill. We don't need this intrusion" Lott answered looking back toward his bedroom.

"Well sir, just tell him to come out and we'll be on our way." Lowery resisted the urge to send soldiers inside which could end in more death.

Richmond saw the dog in a pool of blood and rushed down the steps to the hound. One of Lowery's men kicked the dog and looked at the boy. Laughing he said, "Won't be hunting coons no more, Sonny."

Richmond walked to the soldier and kicked him with all his might. "Son, you better be careful what you do."

Lott picked up his gun and pointed it at the man and said, "You hurt my nephew, and you will be the one to pay with your life."

Lowery looked hard at his soldier. "Step back from the boy. We came for the man who shot my brother; no one else is going to get hurt. Put down your gun, Mister Wilson, and go get your son."

Lot knew he could not turn his son over to this monster, but how could Thomas get away with all these soldiers surrounding the house.

Thomas stood quietly inside knowing he should have left as he had planned and now there would probably be no escaping, but he prayed for a miracle.

Lowery tired of waiting for a response called to his sergeant, "Sergeant, take two men and torch the barn."

"Sir?" The bewildered sergeant asked.

"It's an order. Burn the barn and all the animals in it."

"But sir, is that necessary?"

"Are you planning to disobey a direct order from your commanding officer?" the colonel shouted angrily.

"No sir. Men, let's go." The sergeant motioned to the two closest soldiers.

"You can't burn the barn. We have our prized horses in there," Lot countered.

"Then I suggest your son come on out before we go in and get him, which means he will probably lose his life."

Tommy turned to Lot. "They can't hurt our animals, can they? It just ain't right to kill innocent animals. You want me to go down to the barn and protect them?"

Knowing that Lowery would do anything, even hurt his family, Thomas called out from inside, "You can stop your men. I'm coming out! I'm not armed, and my hands are up."

The colonel smiled. "No search warrant needed Mister Wilson. I've finally got the man who murdered my brother. I'll not be back here anytime soon."

Thomas walked out slowly with his hands up and to the soldier who would handcuff him. Even when the Apache were about to kill him, he had never felt such sorrow. The look in the eyes of his loved ones wrested his heart, and he hated causing them such grief. Because Thomas was moving slowly, Lowery nodded to a soldier nearby, and with the butt of his rifle, the private slammed it into Thomas's back sending him to the ground. Instinctively, Lott ran down the steps to protect his son, only to be held back by two soldiers. Two soldiers put Thomas on a horse, and Lowery led Thomas away from the house.

The family solemnly watched the detachment leave. Then Lott spoke to Tommy. "Son, go saddle me a horse. I'm going with them."

"Why are you doing that?" Tommy frowned.

"Lowery is consumed with hate, Son. I need to make sure Thomas gets to the jail alive."

"Can I go with you?" Tommy pleaded.

"No Tommy. This could be dangerous. Go bury my dog and take care of things till I get back. Lord willing, I will be back."

John was again employed by Everett Law Firm in Meridian who had asked him to continue his apprenticeship with their firm. Today as he arrived at Newton Station from Meridian, he was immediately met by people who informed him that his brother had been arrested and was being held in the jail up at Decatur. The community was upset because they knew the federal controlled government was being unfair when they planned to kill a man who had only defended himself.

John quickly got his horse from the Newton livery stable and raced the seven mile road to Decatur. As he dismounted, he was stopped by an armed guard.

"What you need, fellow?" the guard barked, raising his rifle.

"I understand you got my brother in there, and I want to see him."

The soldier shook his head. "Got orders. No one can see him."

"What officer is in charge here?" John asked.

"Captain Jacobs. His office is in the court house across the street."

John located the office and knocked on the door, and a voice inside told him to enter.

A middle aged stout man with white hair, beard shortly trimmed and reading glasses sat at a desk, so John walked to the man and extended his hand. "Sir, I'm John Wilson, and I'd like permission to see my brother Thomas who is in your jail."

The officer leaned up and took his hand. "I'm Captain Jacobs. As for seeing your brother, that's impossible. I've got orders that he's to have no visitors. Have a seat, Mister Wilson."

As John sat down, he tried to think of a way he could talk to his brother and then smiled in satisfaction when the solution presented itself. "Sir, I'm an apprenticed lawyer working with a firm in Meridian. It looks like to me that this Thomas Wilson is going to need legal representation. You know that is the American way; fair representation, or has our legal system changed here in the South?"

The captain rubbed his beard in thought. "You got something, young man. You know, I'm familiar with your family and Thomas, and this whole thing makes no sense to me. I had dealings with your brother during the Olliver killing, and personally, I was impressed by the way he handled the situation. That shooting down at Walker's Store has sure got some loopholes. I talked with the boy that was with Lieutenant Lowery the day he was killed, and what he told me sure wasn't what the official report stated. I can't figure why Washington is so interested in this case with all the killing going on down here. It seems to me someone is out for vengeance, and if that's the case, then your brother don't stand a chance."

He continued. "Now, remember I haven't spoken to you today about any of this, but you take what I've told you and run with it."

The captain dipped his pen in ink and wrote a note, then handed it to John. "Sir, you may go down and visit your brother. I mean your client. If there is any way I can help you undercover, talk with me in private."

The Newton County Jail was a ten by twenty foot brick building with a ceiling enclosed by two by twelve oak boards, and it was divided into two rooms. The outer one was for housing the guards, and the latter smaller room which was well barred, held the prisoners. A small wood burning stove sat in the guards' quarters. The jail was damp, dark and in the prisoner's section, cold. Handing the guard the note, John entered the enclosure. Thomas sat up when he saw his brother and walked to the bars. John was surprised that his face was badly bruised and his bottom lip split.

"What happened to your face, Thomas?"

"I guess I got angry, which didn't do me any good with so many soldiers near."

"Look, I plan to get you the best lawyer in Mississippi. We're going to fight this thing. The truth should be heard and upheld." John tried his best to encourage his brother because he knew Thomas needed strength to face the coming trial.

"You know the truth doesn't always win, but I sure hope you are right."

"Well, this time I plan to do everything possible to make sure it does."

The next morning John rode to Newton Station and caught the ten o'clock train east to Meridian. He hurried to the law office where he was in training and sat down with Mister Everett to discuss the situation. John relayed all he had been told about the incident and gave a list of those at the shooting.

Mister Everett adjusted his glasses and kept nodding his head as he thought to himself. Finally, he raised his head and looked straight into John's eyes. "This case isn't going to be easy. We're dealing with the Federal Government and have to play by their rules. This Washington administration is bent on pounding us to our knees. That so call official report is a hanger and with practically no witnesses except the one soldier who has seemed to disappear, I don't see how we can win."

John cleared his throat. "You're going to take the case even with all the odds stacked against winning?"

Everett broke into a wide smile. "John, I wouldn't miss it for the world. You do the research and collecting of witnesses, and I'll give them union men the fits. Those Feds don't know it, but they are sitting on a ton of dynamite, and I'm gonna light the fuse."

"But there's only one witness. Who do I collect?" frowned John.

"Character witnesses, my boy, character witnesses."

As Captain Jacobs was about to leave for dinner, the door opened and a spit and polished Colonel Lowery along with a well-dressed elderly man entered. "Going somewhere?" Lowery asked with a sly grin.

"Just to find something to eat, sir," Jacobs answered, saluting.

"You can wait on that. Captain Jacobs this is Mister Robert Townswell from Washington. He is with the Attorney General's office under the honorable Henry Stanbery."

Attorney General's office resounded through the captain's head. Astounded, he replied. "Please to meet you, sir. Is there some way I can help you?"

Townswell, a thin man with long slicked back hair and a single eye glass, took his hand. "Please to meet you, Captain. We need to talk," the man softly said with a northern accent.

Settling in front of his desk, Captain Jacobs offered each a cigar, but only Lowery accepted.

Townswell took out his notebook, carefully turned the pages then looked at

Captain Jacobs. "Listen carefully to what I say. Since this war has ended, there has been nothing but turmoil down here in these states. Government men have been beaten, some killed even including federal soldiers. The poor Negroes whom we have given our blood to free are being persecuted and denied their rights"

Townswell paused to gather his breath. "In addition, we have discovered a secret organization called the Klu Klux Klan made up of Confederate veterans who plan to do all they can to control the Negroes and take back their government. God forbid. We also understand that General Nathan Bedford Forrest is heading these outlaws, which is another big problem."

"What does that have to do with me?" Jacobs asked.

"Captain, this Wilson man murdered two federal soldiers, and we feel that he and maybe some of his comrades were in on the possible murder and disappearance of a group of men we sent to apprehend him back in East Texas. With this case, Washington wants to send a loud message to the South that we will not tolerate violence and murder. Our plan is not only to have state newspaper coverage, but we will flood the country nationally with this case. At first we thought we would have a closed hearing and trial, but we decided to open it to the public. Our thinking is that the more people who witness this trial and its outcome, the better our message of retribution will be. It will make them think twice before continuing to terrorize our country. Also, this Thomas Wilson will swing."

Jacobs hated what he was hearing and felt making a statement to the country using Thomas Wilson as a scapegoat was wrong, but he asked, "What is my part in this operation?"

Lowery blew a large circle of smoke to the ceiling. "The trial will be held in this courthouse, and you will insure that order exists at all times."

"When is the trial scheduled?" Jacobs asked concerned over his responsibility and knowing there was preparation to be made.

Townswell once again looked to his notes. "Let's see. Today is Friday. We should be ready to proceed by, let's say, by Monday."

""Monday!" the captain exclaimed. "It'll never happen, I need time."

Colonel Lowery brought his fist down hard on the table. "You heard the man. Monday!"

Somewhat irritated by Lowery's arrogance, the captain glared at the colonel. "What is your duty in this trial?"

"My job is to oversee everything but the judge and their proceedings." Lowery smiled blowing a circle of smoke toward the captain. Lowery paused and looked the captain in the eye, then his face filled with hatred. "As well as the hanging of Thomas Wilson."

22

Tipping the Scales of Justice

Rescue me, O Lord, from liars and from all deceitful people. O
deceptive tongue, what will God do to you? How will He increase your
punishment? You will be pierced with sharp arrows and burned with
glowing coals.

—Psalm 120:2-4 NLT

Newton County Courthouse, Decatur, Mississippi as it appeared in 1867.

All was quiet in the reserved room of the Newton County courthouse except
for the constant tapping of fingers atop a large desk. "Gentlemen, I'm General
Andrew Haskins, originally from Ohio," stated a large, grey haired man dressed
eloquently in military uniform. "Before the war, I was a practicing lawyer and
short term judge. For some strange reason, Washington wants me to preside over
this trial. To tell you the truth, I'd rather be going home."

A soft laughter followed and he continued, "From what I'm hearing, this
is a closed case, but I still believe in the American way - that a man is innocent
until proven guilty, and when this case is concluded, I want to walk out of here
with a clear conscience. My orders are to stretch out the proceedings for as much
publicity as possible. We are to send out a message that killing and lynching will
not be tolerated here in the South."

"Why not a citizens' jury?" asked one of the majors.

General Haskins lowered his glasses and inspected the men who had been selected. They were all majors: Joseph Hallman, Jeffrey Jackson, Timothy Babbitt and Frank Lane. "Gentlemen, we're here in Mississippi. Where in the world would we find an unprejudiced jury? Most of the men either fought for the South or supported it. You think these Southerners would convict another Southerner? That's why Washington wants a military trial, and that's why you are here."

"When will it start?" asked another major.

"Well, this is Friday. We'll begin proceedings on Monday, December eleventh, and men I do plan to celebrate Christmas at home. It's been five years since I've seen my family."

In the Meridian law office, Mister Everett took off his glasses and began rubbing the smudges with a soft handkerchief. "John, we've got our work cut out for us. Washington is sending down quite a team. I don't know much about General Haskins, but I do know the prosecuting attorney, James Parker, and his reputation precedes him. Not only are they charging Thomas with the murder of the two soldiers, but they will try to prove he's responsible for the disappearance of the men assigned to arrest him in Oklahoma."

John shook his head. "We had already left Cass County when the government men disappeared. They can't hang that on Thomas. You got to remember, Homer and I were riding with my brother. If they hang that on him, I guess we'll be involved as well."

Everett replaced his glasses and leaned back in his padded chair. "John, they'll play the devil to pin the disappearance of those men on you all. Until they find bodies, how can they convict Thomas on that charge? What we've got to do is clear Thomas of the killing of the two soldiers."

"What's our plan?"

"Well, we'll start with reputable character witnesses for Thomas, but in the end, we must prove it was self-defense."

"How's that?" interrupted John entranced by the thought.

"We've got to prove that Thomas was fired upon before he took action."

"Do you think we have a chance?"

"Well, we're going against Washington. You might say we need a prayer and a miracle."

At the Newton County military headquarters, Captain Jacobs paced the floor frustrated at the magnitude of his assignment. He was to maintain order during the trial in Decatur—an open trial that would bring every southern citizen in support of Wilson and the South. Among these would be friends and neighbors of the Wilsons plus men who fought with Wilson during the war. Many would be armed, and if it were true what he had heard about the newly organized Klan, there could be trouble. He decided every person entering the courtroom would be searched and he would post ten soldiers in the courtroom and another fifty outside to deter possible uprisings. With sentiments high about Wilson's innocence and the Federal Government's unfairness, this trial could be one disaster. *Why in the world was Washington not listening to the likelihood of Wilson's innocence?*

Because of the hammering and sawing, Thomas was unable to sleep and finally threw off his blanket and tipped up to observe the structure through a crack in the boarded window. Soldiers were busily erecting a platform, and he heard them laughing.

"Looks like they're having a good time. And my good time will come when you are hanging from that platform," Colonel Lowery sneered.

Thomas walked over and stared into his face. "You're mighty confident, ain't you, Yank?"

"You don't have a chance. Washington is here, and it's a closed case. You should have thought twice and given that horse of yours to my brother."

"Your brother was foolish for trying to steal my horse and shoot me. He should have been honest and given some respect for property. His attitude got him killed."

Angered, Colonel Lowery stormed out cursing Thomas at length.

The Wilson family realized that Thomas had put his life in danger by returning to Mississippi and were devastated by his capture. The children were traumatized by the whole affair, especially the harsh treatment he had received from the soldiers, and they were afraid to sleep across the open hall so they made pallets on Lott and Sarah's bedroom floor. The family was in constant prayer for Thomas - that God would spare his life.

On the Sunday preceding the trial, the entire family attended church with their friends and neighbors. Pastor Adams, a visiting preacher, knew the situation that was troubling not only the Wilson family but the community as well, so he focused his sermon on the power of prayer. At the close of the sermon, the congregation gathered around the Wilsons and prayed in earnest for justice.

Monday, December Eleventh

It was a cold, crisp winter morning as throngs of people began to flood into the small village of Decatur, the county site. The courthouse, a two story framed building, stood like a beacon summoning all to the demise of Thomas. Many came in covered wagons in order to spend the night near the courthouse while others traveled in buggies. Some rode in on horseback while locals simply walked. By nine o'clock it was estimated that the crowd numbered over a thousand with more still on the way. The grounds around the courthouse and village were like that of an ant hill that had been disturbed - people scurrying everywhere. Although many believed that Thomas was innocent, many just hated the Yankees and the harsh reconstruction government that was stealing their freedom and taxing them beyond limits. Soldiers nervously surrounded the courthouse with rifles in hand and bayonets attached.

Captain Jacobs stepped from the north courthouse door and was amazed by the masses of people. He shuffled down the steps to Sergeant Ripley. "Sergeant, keep the men tight, and let no one enter unless authorized. If shooting breaks out, tell the men to move immediately inside the courthouse. It'll be safer there."

"You looking for trouble, Captain?" Ripley asked while keeping his eyes on the people meandering nearby.

"Sergeant, there are at least five or six hundred men out there, and I'll bet my soul that half of them are armed and war hardened Southern veterans. If there's shooting, we're out-manned and out-gunned. We won't stand a chance, so moving inside may just save your life."

Even as cold wind thrashed his face, anxious perspiration formed on Ripley's face. "Lord forbid, Captain. Four years of facing them fellows in war was enough for me."

At ten o'clock the soldiers formed lines that led up to the courthouse doorway while Colonel Lowery stood at the entrance to admit citizens to the courtroom. Members of the press were admitted first, then authorized witnesses, followed by members of the Wilson family. After that, citizens were received as room permitted. The majority of people would have to remain outside. All were searched and weapons were confiscated. Even though most could not gain entrance, runners would relay the proceedings at intervals. Tensions were high.

At ten thirty the doors to the courthouse were closed, and soldiers were posted. Since the courtroom was located on the upper floor, soldiers were posted there as well. Looking from the window of the judge's chamber, General Haskins shook his head. "There's a lot of angry folks out there."

"You can handle it, sir," resounded Major Jackson gazing outside.

"Handle it. I've never presided over a situation like this. That crowd is dangerous, and here Washington wants blood. What about justice? Is that to prevail? I'm not even sure of courtroom procedure. I only served as a judge for four months before the military called me. Come to think of it, I've never held a military trial."

A few minutes after eleven, the general and the four majors walked from their chambers and stepped on a platform overlooking the people. With a courtroom and a bitter cold morning, the windows were covered with fog, and a rumble of people conversing filled the room. The smell of burning hickory rising from the potbellied stove mixed with that of smoked tobacco. A long table was arranged at the front for the general and his officers, and with the pound of a gavel, the room was silenced.

A side door screeched open, and Thomas, handcuffed, walked in escorted by two soldiers. Since Thomas had only been allowed to meet with his attorneys in jail, he instantly searched for his family and found them sitting on the wooden benches in the front row. Most of his family put on a positive front, but Sarah began to tear up. Only Tommy, Sally and Mary had been allowed to attend. When Thomas sat he glanced once more to the crowd. To his surprise, Suzanne and Frankie were right behind his family. Suzanne gave him a smile then nodded to him.

After gaining order, General Haskins introduced the majors serving as the jury and then introduced the prosecuting attorney, James Parker. Finally he introduced the defending attorney, Mister Sam Everett. As an assistant, John sat directly behind Everett and Thomas.

General Haskins cleared his throat. "Ladies, gentlemen, I will be serving as judge for this trial, and I will not tolerate any kind of outburst. If you become unruly, you will be escorted outside. There will be no tobacco smoking in here." A low mumble spread among the crowd.

"Now for our business. Defendant, will you please stand and state your name."

Thomas and his attorney stood. "I am Thomas Wilson, sir."

"If you will, remain standing. Mister Wilson. You are charged with the murder of two of our federal soldiers as well as involvement with the disappearance of a Mister Stevens and three army scouts who were ordered to apprehend you."

"General," interrupted Everett. There is no proof whatsoever that Mister Wilson had anything to do with the disappearance of Stevens."

The gavel came down. "Mister Everett, you are out of order, sir."

"Now, back to the cases. Mister Wilson, how do you plea?"

"Sir, I know nothing about the disappearance of Stevens and as far as the shooting—"

"Mister Wilson, just simply tell me how you plea?" muttered Haskins somewhat irritated.

Thomas looked him straight in the eye. "Sir, I am innocent of all of the charges."

The judge nodded his head. "That's all I wanted to hear, sir. You may sit down."

For all general purposes, the first day of the trial was a complete waste. The session only lasted a little over three hours and was directed toward explaining the procedure of a military trial and how it differed from a civilian one. A little background was given regarding the charges against Thomas, and at two o'clock, the general closed the hearing.

Thomas tried to step to his family as they eagerly waited, but was quickly prodded away from them. Squeezing through the crowd, Suzanne reached out to him but was pushed back by one of the soldiers. "Thomas, are you all right?" Suzanne asked.

"I'm all right." Thomas answered. Immediately he was shoved back "No visiting with anyone," muttered the soldier.

As the people were emptying the courthouse, Frankie moved to Sister who was still beside her parents. He edged up behind her and gently reached for her hand. Surprised, she quickly turned to see who it was. "Oh!" she exclaimed. "You startled me."

A smile crept across her face as she looked up at Frankie. "Thank you for coming to support my brother. It means a lot to our family to see you and Suzanne here."

"It was important for me to be here to support you," Frankie answered admiring the beautiful woman in front of him.

Sister blushed as he continued to stare.

"Have you got time to talk with me before you leave?" Frankie nervously asked.

"I'll ask mother and see when we are leaving." Sister's parents were now surrounded by friends and neighbors giving them encouragement, and she knew it would be a while before they could get free. Frankie grabbed Sister's hand and led her to a bench on the grounds that was well away from the crowds who were leaving.

He paused a minute as they settled into the bench, then asked, "Cretia, why didn't you reply to my letters?"

Sister looked away from him and began pushing her unruly hair back. "I just didn't think that I should."

"I don't understand. What would be wrong with answering my letters? Isn't it the cordial thing to do, and didn't we enjoy each other's company?"

Sister turned back to look at him for a few moments and finally said, "Yes, I did enjoy your company. Our time together was special, but—?"

"Cretia, what are you trying to say to me? Do you not want to see me again?"

"Frankie, you gave me perhaps the most special evening I have ever experienced, but I see no future in our relationship."

Frankie was silent as he thought about her words. "Cretia, that makes no sense at all. You enjoyed the evening with me, and I loved being with you. Shouldn't that mean that we need to spend more time together?"

"Frankie, your world and mine are so far apart, and there is so much ill feelings between our families."

"Cretia, you can't hold me responsible for what my father might have done. It's not fair. So are you refusing to see me again?"

A smile formed on Sister's face. "I didn't say I wouldn't see you again. I just wanted you to know we have some obstacles that have to be resolved."

Frankie shook his head and smiled. "I take that to mean that we will spend time together because I intend for us to resolve anything that might keep us apart."

"Well?" Sister answered raising her eyebrows.

"Well what?"

"Well, are you going to ask me to dine with you tonight?" she asked as she took his hand.

Frankie stood, pulled her up and planted a kiss on her forehead. "Yes, will you have dinner with me tonight and tomorrow night and the next night and every night forever."

"I think we just need to start with tonight, Frankie." Sister chuckled.

Sister got permission, and after Frankie drove Suzanne to the boarding house, he and Cretia ate an early supper at the local diner in Decatur. Frankie carried Cretia home in the rented buggy and was glad that John was still with his parents. Sister invited Frankie back to the kitchen for a cup of coffee, and after preparing steaming cups, they sat in front of the sizzling fire with John.

Frankie looked at John who sat quietly by the fire.

"John, what can you tell me about this trial? It really seems unusual in procedure."

John shook his head while throwing another piece of oak into the fire sending sparks flying. "Well, from what Mister Everett says, the government is using this trial to send a message to the South. It's really not about Thomas as much as it is to teach the South a lesson about what happens when you fight the new government. You notice all those newsmen in there today?"

Frankie took a sip of coffee then asked. "When they finally get to the case, which one will they cover first?"

"They'll take the disappearance of Stevens and the scouts first and save the shooting for last."

"John, tell me all you can about both cases?" After a lengthy description of both cases, Frankie looked at his friend. "I'll tell you what, in the morning I'm going to wire an associate over in east Texas and see what we can find out. I picked up some talk about one Cullen Baker that I understood got poisoned a few weeks back. I have a feeling we might just gain some helpful information."

A frown crossed John's face. "We met Baker in Clarksville, and he's a rough one. Didn't take much to get him shooting. You know, he rode with the Lewis's children's father during the war as a horse soldier. Thomas said that he was the one who took care of Stevens according to the bartender. Now to win the other case, we've got to prove Thomas was just defending himself. We know it's true, but proving it will be almost impossible."

The military court allowed local citizens to take the stand and testify about the character of Thomas and his family throughout Newton County. Everett knew that the court wanted to prolong the case, but he hoped that the military jury would listen carefully to each testimony. Of course in the end, character references validated nothing, and soon he would have to figure out some way to affirm his client's innocence.

On Thursday, December fourteenth, James Parker came into the judge's chambers. General Haskins buttoned up his military jacket and brushed off one of the sleeves, then looked at James Parker. "What can I do for you?"

Parker dressed in a black suit and tie answered. "Sir, today I'm going to present our case on the disappearance of Stevens."

The general frowned. "I hope you have some proof that Wilson was involved."

Parker nodded his head. "Sir, I have completely nothing at all to connect Wilson with Stevens, but in the incident that occurred in Oklahoma, I can show that he is a ruthless man capable of killing Stevens. This description of Wilson will introduce the very traits that will help convict him of the crime in Little Rock."

The general adjusted his glasses. "I hope you know what you're doing. For all we know, Stevens and his men are alive. This could all backfire on you."

Parkers laughed. "General, I know what I'm doing. Washington didn't send me down here to be beaten by a Mississippi backwoods lawyer."

Haskins looked at the man and wondered if Parker was a confident and clever trial lawyer or just a complete fool.

Striking his gavel, General Haskins called to the crowded courtroom, "Court is in session. Mister Parker proceed."

Parker walked in front of the jury, then staunchly faced the people. "Ladies and gentlemen, today we will investigate the disappearance of Mister Stevens and the army scouts. There is no question in my mind that Thomas Wilson had the motive and opportunity to kill these men."

Mister Everett quickly stood. "I object! Mister Parker is speculating. Those government men could be down in New Orleans as we speak, drinking and partying."

A roar of laughter rattled the window panes and a man in the back called out. "That's the way to tell him. Those men are probably drunk as a skeeter bug."

Haskins slammed his gavel down hard. "I'll tolerate none of this foolishness. Mister Parker would you proceed and stick to the facts. Sergeant, remove the man back there who wants to make mockery of my court."

All became quiet as the man was ushered out of the room. For the next several minutes, Parker read the report describing the entire chase of Wilson through the time Stevens and his party was escorted out of Oklahoma by the Choctaws. When finished, Parker stated, "I'll present a witness to the whole affair. Your honor, I call Private Ken Clarke to the stand."

Private Clarke, a tall and thin youngster dressed in uniform walked up, was sworn in and then took a seat.

"Private, is what I read a good description of what happen to you men?"

Nervously the young man twisted in his seat before answering. "Yes sir, it is."

"Were you at any time in fear of your life?"

"Yes sir, I was?"

"Tell us all about it?" smiled Parker looking to the press that was hastily writing.

"Well, when the Indians tied us up, I didn't know if I would live to see another day. That night some of the Choctaw drank some liquor and started shooting arrows at us, dancing around, and shouting. One of them even threw a hatchet at me. I ducked, and it stuck in the tree above my head."

Parker once again looked at the press then to the jury. "Thank you, soldier. That's all."

Haskins asked Everett, "Sir, would you like to cross examine this man?"

"Yes sir, I certainly would."

Everett approached the soldier and looked him straight in the eyes. "Did Stevens inform the Wilsons that if Thomas didn't come out, he would burn the house and kill everyone in it?"

"Yes sir, he did."

"Did any of your party get more than a scratch?"

The private looked over to Parker and softly answered, "No sir."

Did you get mistreated on your escort out of the Oklahoma territory?"

"No sir."

"Why did you give up on the mission and return to your unit here?"

"Sir, I was tired of Steven's attitude and how he was treating everyone. When he gave us a choice, I chose to leave because I knew Stevens was going to get us all killed. They all laughed at me, but I valued my life too much to continue to ride with an arrogant and reckless man like Stevens."

"So are you saying that Stevens actually threatened to burn down the house and kill everyone there, and Wilson did not even seek revenge at all? That instead, he had you escorted out of Choctaw territory to safety?"

"Yes sir, that's true."

"Do you think this is a man who would kill innocent men?"

Parker stood quickly. "Objection."

"Oh, I take it back, but it does give you something to think about, doesn't it?" Everett eyed the jury as he made the last statement.

Parker was frustrated that his information had done more to prove Thomas innocent than guilty, so he readdressed the witness.

"What did Thomas Wilson tell you before you were escorted out?"

Scratching the side of his face, the private thought for a minute. "Sir, I'm not sure which man said it, but one of them said if we decided to come after them again, our lives would be in our own hands. That's why I wanted out."

Parker looked intently into the face of each major on the jury. "Gentlemen, that was a threat to kill."

A soft mumble covered the courtroom as people realized that Thomas was in deep trouble. As the judge was about to recess for the day, Frankie handed John a telegram. After reading it, John smiled and handed the telegram to Mister Everett who studied it carefully and then stood up. "General, I have some information that will clear up this whole matter."

"Let's hear it and it better be good. Understand?" the general replied.

"Sir, this letter is from a Mister George Blackwell, a Texas Ranger working the northeast area of Texas. It states that Stevens and his men were killed by Cullen Baker and a couple of his men in a dispute in a tavern in Clarksville, Texas. The information came first hand from the tavern owner who witnessed the killing, and later Blackwell apprehended another one of the group who admitted to the shooting. That man has been hung. As of this date, the bodies have not been recovered from the swamp where they were reported buried."

The people attending went wild with shouts, screams and laughter knowing Thomas was indeed innocent of that charge.

The soldiers stepped closer with drawn muskets, and the people finally settled down. Dropping his head in thought, General Haskins finally looked at Everett. "Sir, why didn't this tavern keeper come out sooner with the information?"

Without being asked, Thomas said, "Sir, Baker is a dangerous man. If the keeper or anyone else had turned him in, it would be their life."

"Where's Baker now?" the general asked looking directly at Everett.

Frankie raise his hand and was acknowledged. "Sir, he was poisoned a week ago, and that's when word of the shooting got out. He's dead, sir."

General Haskin pounded his gavel. "Court dismissed for the day. We'll convene tomorrow morning at nine o'clock."

As the courtroom emptied, General Haskins approached Parker who was making notes of the day's activity. "Parker, as they say in the South, you took a whupping today. I only hope you have a better day tomorrow," he voiced as he left the room.

That evening, Sister decided to spend the night with Suzanne in the boarding house while Lott, Sarah and the Lewis children returned home. After supper, the children decided to make a pallet of folded quilts before the roaring fire. Most nights they were chattering, asking questions and feuding, but tonight they sat quietly watching the fire dance in the fireplace. Sarah was mending a torn shirt sleeve and knew that the children seemed worried. With all the turmoil, she knew that a good talk was in order. "Children, I think we need to discuss your long faces. This has been a real difficult time for our family. You need to always tell us when something is bothering you."

Sally, staring into the fire spoke softly, "It's the middle of December. We're just missing our parents and the joy of celebrating Christmas with them." A tear trickled down her face. "I'm sorry, Aunt Sarah. We don't mean to be ungrateful. We don't know what we'd have done without you and Uncle Lott taking us in."

Sarah realized that with their worries that they had totally forgotten about Christmas. "Children, we love you and know how difficult it is for you at this special time."

Lott had been listening and moved over to sit on the pallets with them, and Sarah joined him. Lott hugged each one and spoke, "Children, what happened to your parents was heart breaking, but God has truly blessed us by bringing you into our lives. This I promise, no matter what happens to Thomas, we will not leave the Lord out of our home. We will celebrate Christmas, and Sarah and I want you to understand that we love you as our own children. Now in about a week, we will start looking for a tree, and we will decorate the house, because Christmas in this home will be a time of joy celebrating the birth of our Savior." After a prayer of thanks, the children embraced the old couple and settled in for the night.

23

Tipping of the Scale

Therefore the LORD longs to be gracious to you, and therefore He waits on high to have compassion on you. For the LORD is a God of justice; how blessed are all those who long for Him.
—Isaiah 30:18 NASB

Frankie, unable to sleep and in sock feet, lay on his bed staring at the ceiling. The boarding house certainly lacked in many ways, but it was clean, and since the bedrooms were on the second floor, heat from below made the accommodations acceptable. He was happy that he had a chance to pursue Cretia. He knew their differences were insurmountable, but he planned to do everything possible to mend those differences. Knowing that Cretia was in a bedroom down the hall brought a flutter to his heart. One day he could imagine waking up every morning to her sweet face. As midnight approached and Frankie reached to extinguish the lantern, he heard a light tap on his door. His heart pounded thinking that it could be Cretia, but instantly realized she would never consider anything so improper. Instead he slipped out his revolver and walked silently to the door. "Who's there?"

"It's Captain Jacobs. I need to speak with you. I mean no trouble."

Frankie opened the door and studied first the man then the hallway. The captain was in civilian clothes, long overcoat and a slouch hat. "You by yourself?"

"I am," Jacobs answered calmly.

Frankie directed him inside and pointed to a chair next to the window while putting his pistol away. Jacobs leaned over, pulled the curtains shut and took a seat.

"Am I in trouble?" Frankie asked sitting on the edge of his bed.

"You got that information about the killing out in Texas rather fast."

Frankie wrinkled his brow. "Something wrong with that?"

"No, I meant it as a compliment. With your information, Wilson was cleared of the first charge quickly."

Frankie broke into a smile. "Then Captain, what in the world do you want with me at this time of night?"

The captain looked down in thought then back at Frankie. "I'm going to tell you something that could get me in a heap of trouble, and since I really don't know you, I'm hoping that I'm not making the biggest mistake of my life."

Noting the seriousness on the captain's face, Frankie sat up straight listening carefully.

"Your friend is in deep trouble. If the government has its way, the boy will swing. Now the account of the shooting that will be read tomorrow is flawed."

"What do you mean?"

"Just listen. The soldier who gave the report had one more year of military service, but after he gave his account, he was dismissed from the army the very next day. If you want to save Wilson's life, you need to find that boy and fast."

Feeling excited but overwhelmed, Frankie asked, "How can I do that?"

The captain reached into his pocket and pulled out a piece of paper. "All the information you need is here, and there's a train leaving Newton Station at six in the morning headed north. You'd be wise to take it."

Frankie looked at his pocket watch. "Sir, it's already twelve thirty in the morning. It's eight miles down to the station."

The captain picked up his hat and walked toward the door. "I gave you what you need. The rest is left up to you."

Frankie rose from his seat. "Why are you telling me this?"

"Let's just say that I believe in justice and truth."

After the captain left, Frankie shook his head and quickly began pulling on his boots. Whether the man was on the level or not didn't matter, because if what he said was true, then he would do the best he could to bring the man in.

A light rain fell the next morning almost like fog. On this cold and dreary day many spectators stayed home thinking the trial would continue for weeks. After shaking the rain from their jackets, Suzanne and Sister moved down the aisle to their seats. Sarah, Lott, and Tommy sat on the front row but Mary had stayed home with the younger children. Sister noticed that Frankie had not yet arrived. "Where is that brother of yours?"

"Who knows? He may have had to return to New Orleans on business. He sure has become responsible in the last couple of years and seems to really enjoy his political position in Louisiana."

General Haskins met Parker down the hall from the judge's chamber and handed him a telegram. "You're not going to like this, but the attorney general was not pleased with your work yesterday."

Parker unfolded the telegram, studied the comments and then scowled.

"This means nothing. After today, he will be singing my praises."

At ten o'clock, the general walked into the courtroom, and after declaring the court in session, he took a folder and removed a document. "Mister Thomas Wilson, will you stand? You are charged with murdering two federal soldiers."

"I object!" exclaimed Mister Everett. "Murder has not been proved."

There was a buzz of quiet remarks and then the courtroom silenced waiting for the judge to speak. "Mister Everett, you are definitely out of order, but I do stand corrected. Mister Thomas Wilson, you are charged with killing two federal soldiers. You may be seated."

"Now, I will be reading the report given by Private Joe Taylor. He was the only surviving member of the detail at the shooting. So states, 'When our detail approached Walker's Store, Lieutenant Lowery noticed a fine looking horse tethered outside. Stepping inside he found that the horse was owned by Thomas Wilson. Stepping back outside, the lieutenant told Wilson that he wanted to buy the horse for military purposes and would pay his price. Wilson then became irate and began cursing the lieutenant. Wilson said that no Yankee would ride his horse. The lieutenant wanting to see the horse, untethered him and was leading him around when Wilson walked up and jerked the reins out of his hands. At this point both men were angered. The lieutenant, having a cold and trying to fight off a sneeze, reached into his pocket for his handkerchief. Wilson must have thought he was going for his pistol. Wilson drew out his long knife and throwing it, stuck it right in the officer's chest. The lieutenant fired twice at Wilson before falling to the ground. One bullet grazed Wilson, and the other was high. Wilson then ran down and grabbed the pistol that had fallen from the lieutenant and shot the other soldier, Nat Bates, from his saddle. If it hadn't been for a Miss Suzanne Olliver, he would have also killed me. Miss Ollliver saved my life.'"

When the reading was completed, a subdued silence filled the courtroom. "Mister Wilson, will you please stand. How do you plea?"

Thomas had been allowed to bathe, shave, and given a change of clothes by his lawyers. He proudly got to his feet and faced the judge and jury. "General, I don't know who wrote that report, but it's the most ridiculous thing I've ever heard. Sir, I definitely plead not guilty because the report is inaccurate. I killed those men in self- defense. I-"

The general interrupted. "A simple not guilty plea will do."

"Yes sir. I am not guilty of those charges."

The crowd erupted into cheers.

The gavel came down and order was restored. The general cleared his throat. "We'll have no more of that, and if it occurs again, the courtroom will be cleared. Mister Wilson, you will have the privilege to give your account, and with God as my witness, we will have justice in my court. If you will, sir, you may take the stand. Once Thomas was seated, he gave his account of the shooting and when finished, the prosecuting attorney, James Parker approached him with a knowing smirk on his face. For a moment, he simply stood there eyeing Thomas. "Mister Wilson, were you a member of the resistance army?"

Calmly Thomas looked at him. "What kind of army is that?"

"Let me rephrase. Were you a member of the Confederate Army?"

Thomas shook his head. "Yes sir, I was."

"Did you consider yourself a good soldier?"

"Yes sir, I did my best. I followed orders."

"Let me tell you what information I have received about you. Almost from the beginning your officer, Major Tucker, noticed how fine a shot you were. While others on the line just pointed and fired at the mass of soldiers, you took careful aim. You brought your man down."

"That's right, I did. My father taught me when squirrel hunting to aim for the head. Don't mess up the meat. So my hunting experience made me an excellent shot."

Parker shook his head. "I did not ask you a question yet. Refrain from speaking until you are answering a question, then you can have your say. Now, you were so good, that they gave you a scoped Whitworth rifled musket and made you a sniper. Most of the military frowned on that type of killing. Mister Wilson, what did you Southerners do when you captured a federal sniper?"

Without hesitation, Thomas answered, "They were executed. The same way you Yankees did."

"So be it, Mister Wilson. In other words, snipers were considered murderers."

Mister Everett quickly stood up. "I object, General. Whether Yankees or Southerners, they were under orders."

"I agree, move on Mister Parker, and I hope you have a point in all this," Haskins reprimanded.

"I do, General. Mister Wilson, who were you to target?"

"I was ordered to target officers first, then flag bearers in advancing lines and then men manning cannons."

"It was also recorded that you killed a Union general on horseback from over six hundred yards out. Is that true?"

Thomas shook his head and expressionless said, "Sir, I shot a lot of people. I'm not sure of the rank of each one."

"Just how many men did you kill, Mister Wilson?"

Thomas began to perspire and with trembling hands said, "I have no idea. Maybe fifty, sixty. I was following orders."

Suzanne seeing him struggling with the demons haunting him from the battlefields, dropped her head in prayer and pleaded that God help him withstand the barrage of questioning dealing with the war.

Parker faced the crowds, then looked directly at the Wilson family a moment, then turned back to Thomas. "Mister Wilson, you were such a good soldier that you deserted your comrades in sixty three."

"Yes, but—"

"I didn't ask the question yet, Mister Wilson. My report tells me you then made your way to West Texas and the Arizona Territory and began killing Apaches. Is that true, Mister Wilson?"

Almost at breaking point, Thomas took a deep breath. "Sir, General, once again I was under orders. The Apache were killing men, women, children and burning homes and stealing livestock. The government wanted them stopped in order to protect the homesteaders."

Mister Everett stood up again. "General, what has all this got to do with this case?"

General Haskins looked hard at Parker. "Mister Parker, I hope there is a point to all of this, but frankly I agree with Mister Everett. You better connect this and wrap it up quickly, or you will cease this line of questioning."

Parker determinedly looked at the general. "Sir, if you all will consider what I have revealed, then you will see that Mister Wilson has done nothing for the last five years but kill people. You could say he is a skilled murderer, and the reason he deserted was that he became mentally deranged. Killing those men in Little Rock was normal behavior for him."

Everett shouted out. "Sir, I strongly object! Those statement are incorrect because the killings were done in war and by government order. James Parker is the deranged one."

The crowd began calling out in agreement. Some were clapping, and some were shouting unfairness. Noise came from every direction. The press were fervently writing the latest development. Tommy leaned over to Lott and asked. "Did Thomas really kill that many men?"

Lott sighed and replied, "Tommy, war is not pretty. I'll explain more about the war later, but, yes Son, he killed a lot of men. That is why he left the army, and it is why he left the Texas Rangers. He was tired of all the killing and couldn't live with the fact that he had killed husbands and sons. I hope you will never have to be in a war, Tommy."

It took the general several minutes to calm the courtroom. "This court will come to order. If this disorder occurs one more time, all spectators will be dismissed and will not be allowed to return. Now we are going to dismiss for the day, and court will not resume until Monday. Counsel be prepared to examine this witness again on Monday."

Headlines across New York, Chicago and Detroit read: Klansman will Hang – Killer is Deranged – Sniper, A Deadly Killer – Murdered Over Fifty Federal Soldiers. One newspaper headline in Philadelphia stated that Thomas Wilson was probably a member of the notorious gang operating in West Texas under Cullen Baker.

The rain had stopped overnight, a northerly wind was drying and refreshing the air, and the sun rays were filtering through the clouds. Thomas talked the posted guard into playing a game of checkers with him. The guard pulled an old barrel up to the bars and with his freedom to reach through, the game was on. At mid-morning the outside guard called, "Wilson, you got a visitor." Thomas, thinking it was one of those pesky newspaper men, called back, "He can wait. For once, I've got a good game going."

"Don't think you want to miss this one. She's a beaut."

Laying the cards down, he called back, "Send her on in then."

When the outer door opened, Thomas raised his eyebrows and quickly stood. "What are you doing coming in here? And how did you get permission to see me?"

Suzanne smiled at the guard as he stood mesmerized by her beauty. Nodding his head, the outer guard motioned to the other guard to leave the couple alone.

Suzanne studied Thomas for a moment. "Same old Thomas. Here I am and you seem upset to see me instead of thankful. When are you going to realize how much I love you and that I would do most anything to make sure you are all right."

"You shouldn't have come. I don't want you in a place like this. I don't want you to worry about me."

Pushing her long dress to the side, Suzanne settled on the chair facing Thomas and reached out to place her hands on his. "Well, it looks like you are going to have to get used to my love. Now tell me how you're doing, and yes I saw the gallows outside, so don't mention that to me."

Thomas chuckled at her feistiness, and love filled his eyes. Grasping her hands, he whispered. "Well, Suzanne, I am actually doing the best I'm able. It's pretty cold, and the food is lacking, but overall, I am okay. How about you?"

Suzanne smiled. "I guess I have prayed more in these past few days than I have my whole life. I am terrified for you and so afraid of losing you."

"Suzanne, I told you not to make plans. I knew one day I would be right where I am today, and I am at peace with the outcome. I have the Lord's forgiveness, and I have your love even if it is only for a few days. Now you have to promise me that when they hang me that you will not come. I don't want you to remember me that way."

Tears were mounting in Suzanne's eyes. "I promise you, but Thomas I plan on that not happening. I plan on a miracle. I plan on spending my life with you."

"Suzanne, that's the next thing I want you to promise. I want you to be happy, so I expect you to find someone special to marry one day. I want you to have a full and wonderful life."

"I hear what you are saying, but for right now, I don't want to hear that. I want you to fight and fight hard for the truth. You hear me. I expect and demand that."

Thomas chuckled and gripped her hands firmly. "There you go again with that spitfire determination. You are some kind of woman even if you probably need a strong man to tame that spunkiness, but to tell you the truth, that man would not be me, because I actually admire those qualities in you."

"Well, there's probably no man on earth that can change some of my so-called qualities." They both began to laugh as Thomas shook his head in agreement.

"Suzanne, how is my family holding up?"

"They are doing the best they can. It is really hard on the children. They don't understand why the government would want to harm you. The whole family has been in prayer for you."

"I know this is the worst time with Christmas in a week. It sort of spoils the holiday."

"Well, I know that they plan to celebrate Christmas. Sister was talking to your mother this morning, and she said that the children need to have a good first

Christmas with them because they are really missing their parents during this season."

Thomas chuckled. "Is Papa gonna let them bring a cedar tree in the house?"

"Yes he is, but he keeps complaining about bugs in that tree. I just don't understand that."

Thomas chuckled to himself. "I can just see him now. I'll tell you the whole story when I get out of here."

"I like that. You just said, 'When I get out of here.' That is the way you have to think. Expect a miracle, Thomas. If you can't expect a miracle for yourself, you expect one for me. I don't plan to lose you. You understand?"

"Yes ma'am. You know I would pretty much do anything for you. That is, within reason. Tell me one thing before you leave. How in the world did you get them to let you in here to see me?"

"You can thank Captain Jacobs for that."

Suzanne squeezed Thomas's hands once more and walked out of the door hoping that she had brought a little hope to the one she loved.

Monday, December Eighteenth

The morning was bright and clear, so the village was once again crawling with spectators. As Sister found her seat, she searched for Frankie, but could see no sign of him. Instead, Timothy Johnson, a close childhood friend tipped down the aisle and settled in beside Sister. "How do you do, ma'am?" he said giving her a nod.

"What are you doing here? I thought you were in Memphis gambling and chasing skirts."

Flipping a large roll of greenbacks onto her lap, he laughed. "Dear Sister, I call it gaming, and the young women up there in Memphis simply love this ole boy."

Turning to him she couldn't help but smile at the man who was always teasing her. "Bout time you got here. You know Thomas is in over his head." Slyly she clutched the roll of greenbacks and pretended to be placing them into her purse. Then watching his eyebrows rise, she flung the roll back to him. "You can take this. It's nothing but the devil's wages." Both Tim and Sister began to laugh, but quickly quieted as the courtroom was called to order and Thomas was told to take the stand.

Everett slowly looked at each member of the jury and then turned to Thomas. "My first question is why did you desert the Army of the Northern Virginia?"

Thomas shifted in his seat. "Three weeks before I deserted, my older brother, James Earl, died in the hospital in Richmond. Then after that terrible battle up in Pennsylvania, my younger brother, John, was listed as missing and presumed dead. Well, I was the one who encouraged John to enlist upon my father's disapproval, and when he was listed as killed, I kind of fell apart. Here I lost both of my brothers, and in every battle, all I could see was death, mutilation, pain and sorrow. After two years, I'd had enough. I headed for home."

"Then what?"

"Me and a couple of other deserters stopped by my folks' place, and fearing the regulators, we thought it best to head out west. Finally reaching West Texas and needing money, we befriended a man who we found out later was a Texas Ranger. He talked us into enlisted, and we began safeguarding the settlers against the ruffians and Apache."

"All right Thomas, why did you desert them?"

"At first, we just handled the outlaws and the Apaches who were raiding folks, but then one day, we were detached to a Calvary troop who said they were after hostiles. One morning when I thought we were raiding a war party, it turned out to be a village of men, women and children. At the break of dawn when the bugle was blown, we swept into the village. When I realized what was happening, that Apache women and children were being slaughtered, I knocked down a soldier who was aiming a pistol at a child's head. I knew I could not let that happen. I grabbed the child and after a two day's search was able to return him to his mother. She had survived the massacre, and I promised her that I was through with killing and was headed home. That's when I returned to Mississippi."

When Thomas finished his statement, the press with pens in hands sat amazed and slowly began writing a different story from the one yesterday.

"General, Majors, does this sound like a murderer, or is he a man to be admired, a champion dedicated to doing what is right?"

The spectators had grown amazingly quiet at the revealed character of Thomas. Even the newsmen seemed perplexed that the information given did not match the shooting incident reported.

"Now that that is clear, let's turn our attention back to the shooting," Everett stated. "In the next few minutes, I plan to show you that Thomas Wilson shot those men in self-defense. For right now, Thomas, you need to step down as I prepare to call my next witness."

Thomas returned to his seat wondering who Mister Everett would call to reveal the happenings on the day of the shooting.

"I call Miss Suzanne Olliver to the stand," Everett continued as Thomas shook his head to reveal his displeasure.

Suzanne was dressed in a black skirt and white blouse and was an amazingly stunning witness. Before being sworn in, the general spoke to her. "Miss Olliver, if all the women in the south are as beautiful as you, I can see why those boys fought so hard." Suzanne blushed, and gentle laughter was heard throughout the courtroom as the comment brought a welcome relief from the tension.

Everett cleared his throat. "Miss Olliver, were you down at Walker's Store when the shooting occurred?"

"Yes I was."

"Tell the panel what you observed."

"I was in the store talking with Mister Walker and Thomas when Lieutenant Lowery walked in and asked to see Thomas outside. At first I didn't think anything about it, but when I heard loud voices, I walked out to see what was happening. When I reached the door, I saw Thomas and the lieutenant angrily speaking to each other. Seeing me, Thomas quickly pushed me back inside and told me to stay there. No sooner than I was inside, I heard two quick shots, then a scuffle. A piece of the door splintered off and cut a gash across my neck." Suzanne instinctively reached up and placed her hand where the gash had been.

"Then I heard another shot, a louder one followed by what sounded like a pistol shot. When I went outside two soldiers were lying on the ground, and Thomas was aiming the pistol at the other soldier, a young boy. I told him that it was over and to let the boy go."

The general looked at Parker. "Do you want to cross examine this woman?"

"Not at this time, sir."

After Suzanne had taken her seat, Everett faced the panel. "Gentlemen, from what this woman said, when pushing her inside there was an immediate shot' proves that Lowery fired the first two shots. Wilson had been hit by one of those bullets and to defend himself, he threw the knife that hit Lowery. As Wilson stood there, he saw the other soldier had pulled out his carbine and began to fire at Wilson. Wilson saw the lieutenant's pistol on the ground and dove for it and turned and shot the soldier who was trying to kill him. Again in defense.

Gentlemen, if you use logic, you know this is what actually occurred down at Walker's Store and not the earlier account. As for the last soldier, you can understand why Wilson would be pointing his gun at him to kill him. You would do the same if two soldiers had been shooting at you. But Wilson did not kill the soldier when he realized the man was not planning to shoot him, that it was over and he was safe. Gentlemen, Thomas Wilson was fighting for his life, and that is called self-defense. I say to you again, it was self-defense."

Clapping and shouting erupted from the courtroom and many were on their feet standing in support. Even some of the reporters unconsciously had risen to their feet and seemed to be supporting Thomas.

After order was restored, Parker licked his lips and nodded his head to himself. "Your Honor, now I'd like to recall Miss Olliver to the stand."

Once seated, he asked, "Miss Olliver, can you tell me the exact amount of time from when you were pushed inside until you heard the first shot?"

"I'm not sure. Perhaps seconds."

Parker looked at the majors. "Gentlemen, she says she's not sure, perhaps seconds and to me that is little vague. Having been in battle, you men know that a lot can happen in a few seconds time, and you know men can do miraculous deeds when mortally wounded.

"Miss Olliver, what is your relation with the defendant?"

"I object General. I see no relevance." Everett called as he stood.

"I am going to allow this line of questioning. Answer the question, Miss Olliver."

"He is - I really care about him."

"Do you care enough to alter your story?"

"No sir. I do care for him, but all that I have said is the truth."

"Miss Olliver, I would say that your so-called care for the defendant has blinded you to the truth. Now we have all heard the report of the only man who actually saw what happened. You admit yourself that you were behind the door. I say that Wilson killed Lieutenant Lowery first and you are mistaken about the time. Is that possible?"

"No sir."

"Well I say it is. There is no reason the soldier who saw everything would write a false report. So what we have here is a woman who is trying to help the man she loves."

Parker sat down in triumph knowing that the story that had drawn everyone's sympathy had just vanished into thin air. Suzanne was distraught feeling that her testimony could have actually hurt Thomas.

The general dismissed Suzanne. "Are there any more witnesses to be called?" He paused to see if the trial was over. "Well, then we will begin closing statements. Mister Parker, you are first."

Parker began to recant every detail of the military's report. He again presented Thomas as a murderer who enjoyed killing. He reminded the jury that the report given was official and true, and that all that was said by the defendant was to save his own skin. He reminded the jury that the only witness was a woman who was obviously in love with the defendant. "General and Majors, if this comes down to a decision between the defendant's story and the official account of our military, you have no choice but to believe the official account because there would be no reason for it to be false, but Wilson's account would definitely be false because he is trying to get out of taking responsibility for his murdering ways. Gentlemen, this is an account of cold blooded murder, and the decision must be guilty."

The spectators were devastated by the statements and knew that Thomas would be hung. All that Parker said made sense. Thomas had every reason to lie, but the soldier who gave the account would have had no reason to lie.

As Everett took the stand, he knew that the case he had presented was not enough to clear Thomas. He hoped he could sway the jury with the uncertainty of the event. "General and Majors, remember that until there is a preponderance of evidence, you cannot say guilty. If this account were accurate, where is the soldier that witnessed the event? Why was he not called here as a witness to affirm what he saw? Could it be that the military has something to hide? I say that the written account is false, and the given account is the truth. You heard the testimony, and you know that Wilson spoke the truth. All of the evidence has shown that Wilson is not the type of man to kill the innocent. This shooting was in self-defense. I repeat; it was self-defense. You must not convict a man unless all evidence proves that he is guilty. You do not have the evidence you need for a conviction, and you must say a loud and unequivocal 'Not guilty.'"

Tuesday, December Nineteenth

The sky had once again become overcast and rain was on the way. The citizens of Newton County as well as the press waited impatiently for the court to resume. Slowly the morning slipped by, then mid-afternoon struggled in. At three fifteen, the doors were opened, and all knew the end was inevitable.

An unusual stillness hung over the courtroom as all feared the worst and prayed for a miracle. The panel of majors walked in and took their seats while Haskins straightening his uniform coat remained standing. "Ladies, gentlemen, members of the press, this has not been an easy case. It is basically one man's word against a soldier's written account of the shooting. These are perilous times we are in and the killing of our federal soldiers cannot be tolerated. After much deliberation—"

The door in the back of the court room banged open, and Frankie rushed down the aisle and whispered to Mister Everett. Two of the soldiers who were guarding the courtroom grabbed Frankie and escorted him to the back of the courtroom.

"What is the meaning of this?" shouted General Haskins.

Everett, wide eyed and noticeably excited, exclaimed, "General, we have the soldier who witnessed it all, and I think the court needs to hear what he has to say."

The courtroom again grew in tension and whispers were heard throughout. Parker looked back at Colonel Lowery with a scowl on his face.

"This is highly unusual, but because of the nature of this trial, I am going to permit this witness. It will allow us to get a second affirmation of the written report. There will then be no doubt that the verdict we have reached is fair. Where is this man, Mister Everett?" General Haskins asked.

"He's in the hallway, sir."

"Bring him in."

The door opened and a tall, lanky young man with unkempt hair strolled in, escorted by one of the guards. With everyone looking at him, he became self-conscious and dropped his head. He was escorted to the front and looked intensely at Thomas. After being sworn in, General Haskins turned to Parker with a frown and asked, "Why didn't you make sure this court heard this man's testimony?"

Parker cleared his throat and sniffed. "Sir, I had no idea where he was."

"It seems to me that if Mister Everett could find him, then you should have been able to do so." stormed Haskins. "A man's life is on the line, and this man is a major witness. Sir, in the back, come a little closer and tell me how you were able to find this man?"

Frankie straightened his jacket. "The military keeps excellent records. I got his name, rank and his attachment and upon his discharge, where he would reside which was Logan, Ohio. It was a little difficult to get him here, but I'm glad we made it in time."

Haskins rubbed his beard in frustration then looked sternly at Parker once more. "Sounds like this was easy enough to have been done by the military."

General Haskin turned his attention back to the young man who seemed to be nervously waiting. "So your name is Joe Taylor. Who was your commanding officer?"

Taylor pointed to Colonel Lowery. "That's the man, sir. Captain Lowery."

Colonel Lowery stood and spoke. "Sir, I can explain, I have been promoted to Colonel."

"Colonel, sit down. I will definitely hear from you later. First, I want the report of the incident read to this young man."

Major Hallman, one of the jury, took the report and slowly read it out loud. When finished, Taylor with a puzzled look, shook his head.

"What's your problem Mister Taylor?"

Taylor looked down to Thomas and then to Colonel Lowery. "Who wrote that report, sir?"

"You gave that report. What's wrong with it?"

Taylor shrugged his shoulders. "Sir, that's not the report I gave."

The general adjusted his glasses. "Then what did you report?"

"Well, we were riding through Little Rock, and the lieutenant spotted a fine horse tethered out front. He told us to hold up while he went inside. When he came out, the man down there was with him," he said pointing to Thomas.

The young man continued. "Well, the lieutenant started saying he was going to confiscate the animal for the army and that man down there said the horse wasn't for sale."

"The man you are referring to is Thomas Wilson who is sitting in the first row," stated the general.

"Yes sir, that's him."

"Continue with your report."

"Well, Lieutenant Lowery said that he didn't plan to buy it, that Mister Wilson was going to donate it to the army. I could tell the men were about to come to fist-a-cuffs when all of a sudden Mister Wilson about to sneeze, pulled out a handkerchief. I guess the lieutenant thought he was going for a gun, so he pulled out his revolver and fired two shots at Mister Wilson. Mister Wilson dropped down and pulled a knife and hurled it at the lieutenant. It struck him in the chest, and he tumbled to the ground. Seeing a fight was at hand, Nat Bates took out his carbine and shot at Wilson. The shot knocked off the pommel from lieutenant's saddle, but Wilson had managed to get behind the lieutenant's horse in time. Wilson picked up the lieutenant's gun and fired and killed Nat."

Taylor wiped the perspiration from his face before continuing. "Seeing them men fall, I knew I would be next, but a woman came out of the store and told him that it was all over and not to shoot me. Then Mister Wilson told me to go back to whoever my officer was and tell them the truth, and that is what I did, sir. That report is not what I said. Sir, I told the truth."

The courtroom was so quiet that not even a breath was heard. Haskins sat contemplating the turn of events. Finally the general turned to Parker. "What have you got to say about this?"

Parker stood up. "Sir, I was not informed about the true account."

"Then who in tarnation changed this account?" stuttered an angry general.

Parker looked at Colonel Lowery. "He was the commander in charge. Why not ask him?"

Lowery stood up and facing the inevitable, he stated, "Sir, I have always had trouble with this man, Taylor. He doesn't know what obeying orders even means and is a noted liar."

"Mister Taylor, whose signature is on this account?" The general got out the report and handed it to Taylor.

"That is my signature."

"Why did you sign it if it wasn't true?"

Taylor sat for a moment ashamed to speak, then finally found courage to say what must be said. "General, I can't read. I wasn't a good student and reading was something I just couldn't figure out. Sir, I just thought that Captain, I mean Colonel Lowery had written what I told him."

General Haskins paused for quite a while, then he looked at Colonel Lowery. "It appears to me that you, Colonel Lowery, wrote a false report and then had this man sign it knowing he couldn't read a word of it. Do you realize that we had planned to execute an innocent man based on your false report? It looks like now that you will be the one under a military trial."

Angered, Lowery stood and pointed his finger at Thomas. "That man and all the other scum of the earth Southerners killed thousands of our soldiers. And when we come down here to restore order, they still continue to kill us. If that man had given my brother the horse, this all would not have happened, and my brother would still be alive. Wilson and his like deserve death."

Lowery stormed out of the courtroom while General Haskins motioned to Captain Jacobs to arrest the colonel. The press was eagerly writing what would be an unbelievable story for the northern newspapers.

After a short deliberation with the jury, General Haskins pounded the gavel to quieten the courtroom. "Gentlemen, this is still America, and we must uphold the values upon which our nation was founded, and that means that justice must prevail. With the account that Mister Thomas Wilson and Joe Taylor gave, there is no question in my mind that Mister Wilson acted in self-defense. Now, Mister Wilson, will you please stand?"

Everett, Thomas and John stood together facing the general.

"Mister Wilson, I want to apologize for what you have endured. Sir, you have conducted yourself as a gentleman, and with that, I proclaim you innocent of the charge of murder, and you are released to your home, family and to hopefully a long life, sir."

With that, a roar shook the courthouse as people laughed, clapped and shouted knowing an innocent man was now free. Leaving the courtroom, Parker looked at General Haskins. "General, you might have to hang up your uniform. The attorney general wanted this man hung. You just defied his wishes."

General Haskins shook his head. "I hope you are wrong. I hope our attorney general wanted justice because that is what prevailed today."

24

A Rainbow from Heaven

Bless the Lord, O my soul; Who pardons all your iniquities; Who heals all your diseases; Who redeems your life from the pit; Who crowns you with loving kindness and mercy. For as high as the heavens are above the earth, so great is His mercy toward those who fear Him. As far as the east is from the west, so far has He removed our transgressions from us. Bless the Lord, O my soul!
—Psalm 103: 1, 3, 4, 11, 12, 22b NASB

The door of the court house burst open and a man screamed, "He's been acquitted!"

An old man sitting on the step of the courthouse turned his ear to him. "What's that, mister? Don't know the word."

"Sir, that means that Thomas Wilson is a free man! Hey, everybody, Wilson was found innocent!" he shouted at the top of his lungs. "Free! You hear me, free!"

Shouts, screams, cries, prayers and even gun shots rattled the entire village of Decatur. People hugged each other, and some danced in the streets rejoicing. Several of the men who had brought musical instrument with them in their wagons, pulled them out and gathered on the steps of the courthouse. Fiddles, guitars, mandolins and even one string bass formed up, and good old country blue grass music floated across the grounds. Hearing the commotion, Captain Jacobs rushed outside and then began chuckling to see the way Southerners celebrated.

"Sir, there could be trouble!" called one of his men.

"Well, maybe, but there is no way we'll be able to control this group, so we might as well go to headquarters and let these folks continue their celebration."

"Capt'n! Somebody set fire to the courthouse!" shouted a soldier pushing his way through the people.

Jacobs muttered. "What's next?" Smoke was rising from behind the courthouse, so he took a shortcut by running through the lower level of the building and bounding outside. There his eyes beheld the gallows engulfed in flames. He took a breath of relief. "Good riddance," he exclaimed. "'Bout time that thing came down."

After placing his papers into his briefcase, General Haskins walked to Everett and John as they were preparing to leave. He extended his hand. "Mister Everett, Mister Wilson and you sir, Mister Olliver, I would like to congratulate you on the way you handled this case. You know, you just beat the Attorney General's Office and the men in Washington as well."

Everett smiled. "Sir, it wasn't us. Our case was based on the truth, and we placed it in God's hand. I've always want to believe that truth will prevail, but in this case, the Lord had His hand in the victory."

The general nodded his head in agreement. "Men, this has been an eye opener, and you, Mister Olliver, if you ever want to work with me, you'll have a job. In fact, if any of you want a job, notify me. Well, I'm headed home to my family. Hope you have the best Christmas ever."

As the general began to walk away, John asked, "Sir, can you tell me why Washington placed so much interest on this one case?"

"From what I can tell, Lieutenant Lowery and his brother Colonel Lowery have a father who is a U.S. Senator in Washington representing the state of New York. He took it hard when his son was killed. They all wanted Thomas to pay for the lieutenant's death. They knew if it became a national case, then revenge would probably trump justice."

Thomas turned to his family and began giving them all hugs, and standing by his sister was Suzanne. He took her into his arms and lifted her from the ground. "I'm a free man. Looks like you are going to have to tell me a little more about those feeling of yours."

As Thomas exited the courtroom and walked to the front steps of the building, he was met with cheers and shouts. Thomas just smiled and pointed toward heaven. He then made his way through the crowd and began shaking hands and thanking all those who had stood by him.

He glanced at the heavens and saw a beautiful rainbow spreading across the sky, and his joy was complete as he realized how God had forgiven him and delivered him through the valley of the shadow of death. As his family and friends stood near, he was overwhelmed by God's mercy.

Frankie had managed to get close to Sister, so he reached over and took her hand in his. "Hello, beautiful."

"Frankie, I will never be able to thank you enough for what you did for my brother. How can I ever show you how much it meant to me?"

"Your thanks is enough, Cretia, but agreeing to spend time with me tonight sure would be an added victory, at least for me."

"You have changed so much from what I remember. You are a wonderful man, and I would be honored to celebrate with you tonight."

"Cretia, I want even more. I want you to celebrate with me every night for the rest of your life."

Lucretia realized his intent and squeezed his hand. "Frankie, I will definitely think about what you said."

Frankie took her in his arms and gave her a long hug as he whispered. "Cretia, when we are alone tonight, I surely would like to taste your sweet lips again, my love."

Sister blushed and then she smiled at the man she admired, and with a twinkle in her eyes, she teased, "I will certainly consider it."

The fire cracked and popped as a burning log fell sending a few sparks flying near Sally and Mary as they chattered and giggled on the floor by the Christmas tree and threaded popcorn that would be strung on the tree later that evening. Richmond and Lonnie were outside chasing chickens, while the rest of the young men had taken to the woods squirrel hunting. Lott, took a draw from his pipe and thought back to the dismal Christmas Eve when it was only Sarah, Sister and himself suffering the loss of James Earl who had died up in Virginia and John who had been reported as killed in battle. *But, oh how the Lord had showered them with His blessings. There was certainly no loneliness around the place now*, he laughed to himself. He now actually savored every free moment he and his wife had together although the hustle and bustle of the children were a sweet gift from God.

That evening after a supper of baked ham, scrambled eggs, grits and some of Sarah's browned biscuits, the family retired to Lott and Sarah's bedroom. The Christmas tree near the corner was neatly wrapped in strings of popcorn and colorful ribbons. Lott's four red candles, arranged on the mantle above the fireplace surrounded in short cedar branches brought color to the room. As in the past, each candle represented Lott's four children. When asked about the fourth candle, he reminded the family that James Earl was with his Heavenly Father and that was more special than being with his earthly father.

Bringing in both benches from the kitchen, the family sat circling the fireplace. Sarah then opened the family Bible and turned to the chapter of Luke, and after the reading of Christ's miraculous birth, the entire family held hands and prayed together. After closing the prayer, Lott got up and walked to the mantle and took down the four candles.

Sarah looked in confusion. "Darling, what in the world are you up to?"

"Have faith dear," he answered. "You'll see."

Returning with a sack, he began to fill the mantle with new red candles; one after another until he had carefully placed twelve candles, all now burning brightly on the mantle. When finished, the entire family looked baffled. Lott, with a wide smile stood like a sentry on duty. "How 'bout that?"

Puzzled, each family member just shook their heads. John smiled at Rebecca who was cuddling baby Jim and then back to his father. "Papa, those candles always hold some special meaning for you. You might as well go on and tell us what they mean."

"Well, you see, I used to have only four children, but with the addition of Rebecca and little Jim, that makes six. Then here comes Sally, Tommy, Virginia, Richmond and Lonnie and that folks, is eleven. The Lord has blessed Sarah and me with eleven children."

Thomas shook his head. "Papa, you put twelve candles up there. Are you and Mama expecting a little one?"

"Oh no!" Sarah immediately said. "Never!" Everyone broke into laughter at her response. "Lott, what in tarnations did you mean placing that twelfth candle up there?" Sarah whipped back.

Lott looked knowingly at Suzanne and Thomas. "Well, it sure seems to me like we may soon be getting another addition to our family."

Suzanne blushed as Thomas grabbed her hand in his and whispered, "Welcome to the family, my beautiful Louisiana belle."

Suzanne had stayed with Sister for the past few days and was amazed at the love this family shared with each other. As she sat in the old smoky log cabin instead of her lavish mansion with her every need and want met, she realized that she would trade every single luxury for the love she found in Thomas's arms and the love this family shared.

The rest of the evening, the family talked, sang Christmas carols and teased the children about whether they had been good enough for Old Saint Nicholas to appear. Before retiring, Tommy stood before the family. "Losing both of our parents has been really difficult, but, you, Thomas and John, I want to thank you for finding us. And Papa Lott and Mama Sarah, our parents would be so glad that you have come into our lives." The other children stood with Tommy, then Sally spoke, "We just want you to know how very thankful we are for each of you and for the mercy that God has shown us." The children embraced both Lott and Sarah who followed them to the bedrooms to tuck them in with prayer.

Thomas winked at Suzanne, then took both of her hands in his. "Let's you and me go get some fresh air?" Thomas took one of his mother's woolen sweaters and wrapped it around Suzanne's shoulders then they both walked to the front porch and eased down on the top step. As the full moon laced its light through the bare oak limbs that fronted the house, Suzanne remarked, "You know, you have a wonderful family. They have been so kind and good to me."

Thomas nodded his head and then pulled her close to him. "Suzanne, I need to tell you something very important." He watched as her face showed concern.

"I have not been as truthful as I should have been with you."

"What do you mean, Thomas?" Concern mounted on Suzanne's face.

"I didn't tell you how I felt, because I have nothing to give you. But Suzanne, I want you to know that I love you so very much. Words cannot express my love for you."

"Do you know how long I have waited to hear those words? Thomas, your love is all I need. I have come to realize that every advantage in the world means nothing if there is no one to share your love."

"But Suzanne, your family is among the richest in Mississippi and now Louisiana. Now you take Carden, he is educated, has a bright future, meets people well and I hate to say it, but he is a handsome man. There is no way I can ever measure up to him."

"Thomas, you are forgetting the one item that he does not have. He has my admiration, but he doesn't have my love. Sometimes it's amazing to me how you can be so wonderful yet so stupid at the same time."

"What do you mean?"

"You are a man tested by fire. Most men never experience what you have survived. You are completely honest, dependable, hardworking, handsome and best of all, Godly. How could I help but love you with all my heart?"

Taking her hand, Thomas looked longingly at her. "Are you saying that you truly love me even though I have nothing to offer you?"

Suzanne looked into his eyes. "Thomas Wilson, I have loved you the moment my horse ran your horse off the road, and that love has continued to grow."

"Well, if you feel that way, then I have another question to ask you."

"Well, I think it is certainly about time." Suzanne said.

"Would you like to spend the rest of your life with an ole fool like me?"

"The answer to your question is yes. I will marry you and love you for all eternity."

Authors Note

In this story, the Lewis children's return to Mississippi is an actual event in the author's family history. In 1867 Lott Williams, the author's great-great grandfather, heard that his son in law, Jonathan Lewis who ran a ferry on the Sulfur River in Cass County, Texas, was murdered. Five months later his wife Sarah (Sarah Ann Williams Lewis) died leaving five children. Lott and his son Joseph F. Williams (see photograph below) went to Texas to bring the children home to Mississippi. After they returned, Lott filed for guardianship even though two of the children were almost grown. The children remained with the Williams family, and one of the Lewis boys actually married the younger sister of Joseph's wife, Fanny Hayes Williams.

Below are the names of the Lewis children with their birth and death dates:

Sarah "Sally" Ann Lewis, 1852–1883

James Thomas "Tommy" Lewis, 1854–1916 (see photograph on page 273)

Mary Virginia Lewis, 1857–1925

Richmond Golden Lewis, 1862–1937

Jonathan Alonzo "Lonnie" Lewis, 1866–1932

Joseph F. Williams

Thomas Lewis and his wife, Martha Elizabeth "Bettie" Walton Lewis.

When the author's first novel *Hillcountry Warriors* was published in 1996, he received a letter from one of his high school classmate's mother who was a descendant of Thomas Lewis telling him of the story above. She also stated that she thought it would make a fine novel and hoped he would take it into consideration. Finally, after several decades, this has become a reality. In the novel, John and Thomas Wilson represent Lott and Joseph Williams. Surprisingly, after extensive research, Smith found that many of his high school classmates and friends were descendants of this Lewis family. In earnest, Smith tried to locate individual pictures of the children, but presently has only located one. The actual murder of Jonathan Lewis is still a mystery. Even though Tommy witnessed his father's murder, the author was told that he never liked to speak of it.

Readers Guide

Chapter 1

1. Lott assembled his family together to discuss plans for their future. Give at least three reasons why it is important for families to gather when there are major decisions to be made.
2. Thomas is drowning in guilt and despair. Has anyone you know ever been consumed with grief and depression? What should be your first response? What steps should you take to help?

Chapter 2

1. Thomas looks at the wooded area under the massive oaks and hickories and states "This must be God's Eden." Is there a place where these words have meaning for you? Where is the place that gives you peace from the demons of worry and fear?
2. Thomas refuses to talk to John, his parents, or Suzanne about his guilt. Is it better to discuss your guilt, grief, and fears with someone you trust or does talking make these feelings intensify?

Chapter 3

1. Lott and his family honor God but yet they are facing an impossible tax bill. If God takes care of those who love Him, why do Christians suffer and why are they persecuted? Why do bad things happen to God's children?
2. Lott tells John that he wants him to follow his dreams. Should a child place his dreams and future ahead of the needs of his family even if given permission to do so?
3. Lott knows his sister will need help. At what point does a person step in and intervene in a family problem? What should they do to help until that time?

Chapter 4

1. Lott is reluctant to share the tax problem with his family. Is it better to protect those we love by shutting them out of our problems and walking away or allow our problems to enter their lives?
2. Frank Olliver Sr. becomes inebriated at home. What should a wife do about a husband who becomes intoxicated? What roles do submission, respect, and love play?

3. Frankie's father is often unkind and demeaning toward him. Are there some things that we just shouldn't forgive? Should you forgive someone who does not admit his wrong nor seeks your forgiveness?
4. Frank interferes with Suzanne's relationship with Thomas because of past problems with the Wilson family. When should parents interfere with their children's relationships?

Chapter 5

1. How do you treat a friend you know is doing wrong? Was John the right kind of friend to Tim? What made John be committed to Tim regardless of their dissimilarities?
2. Mr. Walker had hurt his daughter when he hid the letter that had come to John for Rebecca when Rebecca was engaged to Frankie. Mr. Walker felt he was doing what was best for his daughter. What was the result of his actions?

Chapter 6

1. When John accuses Tim of cheating on the horse races, Tim replies that John and his family cheated using the mustang in the sprint race. Do you think he was right? Why or why not?
2. Suzanne's father is adamantly opposed to her relationship with Thomas. Should a daughter (or son) follow her heart or her parents?
3. Thomas took some of the earnings and gambled. Sarah admonished him. Thomas wanted to help his neighbors whom the new government were over-taxing. Are there times when it is okay to be dishonest if it will benefit others?

Chapter 7

1. Was Thomas' greatest sin killing men in war or pride in killing? Why?
2. What does the sermon about David really teach us? David broke at least three of the Ten Commandments. Which ones did he break? Is anyone beyond the mercy of God? Why or why not?

Chapter 8

1. When Thomas heard the shots and saw the cabin, he took a few moments to catch his breath and regain his composure. What are some of the methods you can use to help you face tragedy or conflict in a calm manner?

2. Even though Thomas did not respect Suzanne's father, he dreaded telling her of his death. Have you ever had to tell someone about a loved one's death? What should you do and what should you not do?
3. Because Lott felt that his brother's death was caused by Frank, Sr., he felt justice had been served when Frank Sr. died. Is it wrong to feel justice has been served when justice brings harm to someone and their family?
4. Suzanne and Thomas decide it is best to end their relationship. What are reasons good enough to terminate a relationship with someone you think you may love?

Chapter 9

1. Thomas is suffering from PTSD. Do you know someone who has Post Traumatic Stress Disorder because of battles fought? What can you do to help? What should our military do to help?
2. Thomas runs from the incident at the store because he feels that he will be convicted of murder even though he had not fired first. When is it best to run from a bad situation? Should parents encourage their children to turn themselves in when a crime is committed? What circumstances demand an opposite reaction?
3. Thomas seems to be sinking in more problems that he can emotionally handle. What do you do when you feel life has hurled more at you than you can handle? Do you give up and live in hopelessness? How can you turn the negative in your life into something positive?

Chapter 10

1. What did Frankie learn from his father that made him a better man? In what ways have you learned from the mistakes of your parents?
2. Lott invited the soldier in and was kind to him. Sister stated, "I sure find it hard to love those that want to hurt my family." Is it more difficult to forgive someone who hurts you or someone who hurts those you love?

Chapter 11

1. The man at the ferry was kind to John because he had served with the Newton County Rifles in the Civil War. How can Americans show their appreciation to servicemen who have represented us in war, even if we don't always agree with the reason for the war?
2. John felt all alone and his imagination began playing tricks on his mind. Have you ever set out on a task that you had to do completely alone? How did your imagination make it difficult?

Chapter 12

1. How would you explain the scene at the church? Does God send angels when we desperately need them? Do you believe there are ministering angels today or were they only present in Bible times?
2. Frankie was selected to replace the late state senator of Louisiana, and Frankie had a great desire to help heal their broken land. Do you think most politicians begin office desiring to make a difference? How can politicians stay true to this desire?
3. How do Frankie's thoughts "He no longer would let his father's negative and hurtful words define him as a man. Even though he would never enjoy the approval of his earthly father, he would strive to be a man who honors his Papére, his family, his state, but most importantly his Heavenly Father" describe his character?

Chapter 13

1. John faced many trials and testing on his trip to the Oklahoma Territory, but he persevered. When and in what circumstance has perseverance and testing brought you maturity?
2. John was relieved and elated to be with his Aunt Hatta. How do you feel when you see relatives you haven't seen in a long time? What do you do to let them know you love them?
3. Thomas faced an unsolvable problem when Stevens and his scouts approached his aunt's home. Have you ever faced an imminent problem with no clear solution? How did you arrive at a solution?
4. Do you feel the men tracking John are just doing their job and are not really the enemy? Is it important to know the purpose of a job and if the job is based on truth or is all work good if it is used to support a family?

Chapter 14

1. Do you believe the statement by Homer that white men are like locusts that destroy and consume everything as they advance across the land? Why would the Indians have felt this way?
2. Is the statement "The white man preaches Jesus, but lies, cheats, steals, and kills to get what he wants" historically true?
3. Do you think the Indians or the African Americans were treated more harshly? List ways each was mistreated before deciding.

Chapter 15

1. Private Clark decided to leave the group of scouts and told them despite their ridicule. Have you ever been ridiculed or accused of being fearful when you chose to stand against an issue instead of going along with the majority? How did you respond?
2. When Thomas tells John to go home because he should be with Becca, John replies he has given his word to his papa to bring his cousins home. Are there times that even when you give your word you should not keep your word?

Chapter 16

1. How do revenge and justice differ? How did Stevens' desire for vengeance cost him his life?
2. When Frankie thinks of his father, he thinks only of disappointment and emptiness, but was glad to have a grandfather who showed him love.
3. Stevens and his men were killed by Cullen Baker. Did Stevens deserve to be killed, was justice served, was this killing wrong, or was it just another evil deed because of sin? What emotions did his death bring to you? Why?

Chapter 17

1. Suzanne was excited about the possibility of travel. Have you ever traveled or lived in another country? How did that experience change your life?
2. The Lewis children left their home and wanted to begin again in the west. How would you have felt about leaving all and finding a new home in the west if you had been born after the Civil War?
3. When Thomas sees the enemy in his confused mind and tries to harm John, Homer and John decide not to tell Thomas what happened. Do you think that was the best approach?

Chapter 18

1. When you see that children are making huge mistakes, should you interfere? Should Big Dan have done more to keep the children from entering Apache land?
2. Although Thomas was fearful of death, he welcomed the end of his trials and hoped risking his life for the children would atone for his sins. What makes it easier for you to be willing to risk your life to save someone else?
3. As Thomas contemplates his death, a Bible verse is spoken softly in his heart. Has any scripture come to mind when you have gone through hardships? What are some Bible verses that would be helpful during difficult times?

4. The small boy from the Jicarilla tribe recognizes Thomas and Thomas is saved from death. Do you think God intervened by sending the Jicarilla tribe and the little boy or was it just a coincidence? How does Psalm 86:4b, 5, 15 at the beginning of this chapter apply to Thomas and God's plan for Thomas?

Chapter 19

1. The Lewis children were left and there was no one to guide them. It is important for parents to have a plan in place for the care of their children in case they should die (for example, when going on an airplane or in the face of severe sickness). What keeps parents from doing this?
2. Tommy had watched his father's murder. How do you help someone who watches his parents being murdered? How is this grief different than just seeing your parents die of disease or sickness?
3. Lott and Sarah open their homes to their nieces and nephews. Would you be willing to open your home to relatives that needed a family? Would you be willing to be a foster parent?

Chapter 20

1. Thomas and Mr. Bordeau seem to have an instant connection. Have you ever felt a deep relationship to someone who is not a relation of yours? How did that relationship affect your life?
2. What was the worker's attitude about Thomas after he had spent the day in the field working with them? What does this say about leadership?
3. Mr. Bordeau chooses Thomas as the man he would trust with his life. If you were in trouble who would you trust with your life and why?
4. Thomas decides to return home even though he knows he could be caught and hung. Would you face death to visit a loved one who was very sick?

Chapter 21

1. Captain Jacobs knows that Thomas is being treated dishonestly. When you know that something unfair is occurring do you interfere even if it could cause problems in your workplace?
2. Captain Lowery is determined that Thomas will die in recompense for the death of his brother. How does the verse at the beginning of the chapter fit Captain Lowery and Thomas?

Chapter 22

1. How is a military trial different from a normal trial? We know that the pendulum of justice swings, but does it always bring about total justice?
2. The Wilson family decides to celebrate Christmas even though Thomas is facing death. Why is it important to celebrate even when difficult circumstances abound?
3. Parker makes the statement, "General, Washington didn't send me down here to be beaten by a Mississippi backwoods lawyer." Overconfidence can become a weakness. Can you think of a time this occurred with you?

Chapter 23

1. How is Frankie a true friend to John? What qualities determine true friendship?
2. Lott tells Tommy that war is not pretty. War is very difficult for those returning from it. Post Traumatic Stress Disorder (PTSD) is defined as a mental health condition triggered by horrifying events with symptoms of flashbacks, nightmares, and severe anxiety. Those suffering also avoid talking about it, have overwhelming guilt or shame, are self-destructive, and cannot maintain close relationships. What are events other than war that could cause PTSD?
3. If you had been on the military jury after hearing the evidence given and you had no prior knowledge of events, would you have convicted Thomas? Why or why not?

Chapter 24

1. Wealth doesn't necessarily bring happiness. What does Suzanne say brings joy? What do you think gives abundance?

CPSIA information can be obtained
at www.ICGtesting.com
Printed in the USA
FFOW04n2009050318
45413584-46113FF